DISCARD

THE
CHATEAU

STEPHEN COULTER

SIMON AND SCHUSTER · NEW YORK

SBN 671-21730-5
Library of Congress Catalog Card Number: 73-20756
Designed by Edith Fowler
Manufactured in the United States of America
1   2   3   4   5   6   7   8   9   10

*I would like to acknowledge my indebtedness to Mr. E. C.
Large's great history of plant pathology,* The Advance of the
Fungi *(London: Cape, 1940), which gives an admirable account
of the controversy over the oïdium on vines in the middle of the
last century.*

S.C.

To Simone
with Love

PART ONE

1

The square by the river at Blaye on that warm evening of April 1852 was almost deserted, for word had passed around that the paddle boat that occasionally carried passengers across the river had broken down and would not be calling. Nobody had told Susannah Gautier, the young woman sitting alone on the bench by the pile of trunks and traveling baskets, and no one was likely to. The people of Blaye crossing the square in their clogs eyed her with a mixture of curiosity and mistrust. She might stay there till midnight and their caution would only grow. She was obviously a stranger, sitting under her white sunshade in her brown traveling dress, an erect, cool young person. Perhaps, they conjectured, she was a governess or a companion? Certainly not a servant. Yet her bonnet was plainly from Paris, she had no escort, and what respectable young woman would simply be sitting there alone like that for so long?

Some of the knowledgeable young blades had made up their minds already; there were labels on the trunks which said Splendide Hôtel, Paris. One fellow knew from an uncle about *that* place; and when they looked at her clear profile, her creamy skin, her thick beautiful yellow hair curled on the nape of her neck, they nodded confirmation to one another. Rumors had been going around of a new house in the Rue Sainte Catherine in Bordeaux, and if this young woman wasn't painted up as her kind usually were, that was because they were going in for a new style to catch the bourgeoisie. They would be indistinguishable from respectable women and so make it all easier in a town where husbands could always run into friends of their wives. The young men watched her eagerly. With any luck they would see the madam arrive and carry her off. For romantic reasons they expected the madam to be smoking a cheroot.

The villagers were not entirely to blame for their mistake. Nobody in this part of Blaye had seen the young woman arrive in the mail coach with her husband, Francis Gautier. The coach had hardly pulled up for a moment at La Guyenne Café on the northern outskirts of the little town when Francis had caught sight of a group of friends and called out to them.

"Oh, Sue"—he turned urgently to her—"I must talk to them. I'll tell the driver to take you on to the landing place. Wait for me, will you? It's only five minutes away, around the corner there. I'll tell him to put the trunks down."

He jumped out, spoke to the driver and hurried across to the group of young men, and they all disappeared, talking boisterously, into the café. A couple of them had glanced back over their shoulders as if Francis had spoken of her, but that was all. Perhaps it was how they put a woman in her place here.

She tucked back a loop of her hair and straightened her back. She did not need to count the strokes of the church clock that was striking. She knew she had been waiting an hour and was tired of it now. They had been traveling all day again, the third day on the interminable road from Poitiers, and she longed for a change of clothes, cool water to wash in. She dared not hope for a bath.

Young Gautier, glad to be home, had easily thrown off the fatigue of the journey, but his wife was troubled in her heart and uncertain. They had been married in Philadelphia in February, and for the two months that had passed since then she had been absorbed in all the excitements of the journey, first through the southern states to Vicksburg and New Orleans, then the crossing to Europe, crowned by the stay in Paris—much too brief. The shops, the theater, the people had enthralled her. Each day had been full and complete, she had simply forgotten there was to be an end to the journey. It seemed it could go on forever. She had been all surface, watching Francis, anxious to please him, engrossed in her love for him. They had existed together in a timeless bubble.

But then! From Paris they had started off for Bordeaux and the southwest. The train, in which Francis had insisted they travel first class, rattled them noisily at great speed through the countryside as far as Poitiers, and there, in blazing sun, it had stopped. There was no more line. Hot and tired and rather impatient at the lack of progress with railways, so modern had the two of them become, they had transferred to the mail coach with all the luggage, had gone on with slow, jolting, maddening monotony day after day, at nine kilometers an hour. And at last, amid the dust and the dappling light through the roadside trees which gave her a headache, the golden bubble had burst. At last she felt she had truly left behind her old life in Philadelphia with Aunt Maxine and Aunt Ady. It had gone—vanished. Yes . . . but what was the new life to be?

Of course she had already wondered how his family would take the marriage, but she had simply put the question aside because she had been too happy. But sitting there jolting in the coach, she had begun to see there might be serious problems and she asked herself anxiously what their reception was going to be. *Family* was a great thing here in France, she understood that. How were they going to take to a stranger, a foreigner, an American?

Gautier already reposed in her so completely that he was not very alert to her moods. In some ways he might have been married to her for ten years, so great was his trust and confidence in her. As he watched her sitting opposite him in the coach, he loved her soft-hued skin, the fine high contours of her face, the dark eyebrows contrasting with her blond hair, and she seemed to him perhaps most beautiful when she was serious, as she was now.

So when she looked at him and asked what his family was going to think, he laughed. Was she still worrying her head about that? It would be all right, she would see. She didn't know then of his need to find everything "all right."

"Then why haven't they written?"

He gave a little careless shrug. "Come out with some French right away. They'll like that." She saw it was an evasion.

She turned her head away, looking out the window, thinking suddenly, because of his words, of Miss Rosa, Aunt Maxine's grotesque old "housekeeper" who had taught her that queer and racy French. Yet the basis had proved perfectly good in Paris, and it was this in any event to which she owed her first meeting with Francis.

He had described the family. His mother, Madame Victorine Gautier, was a widow and he had two brothers: Abel-Cherubin, the elder, and James, the younger, aged nineteen. James and his mother would be living with them at the family vineyard, the Château La Guiche, in the Médoc wine country. There was also a half-brother, Jules Raynal, his mother's child by a first marriage, who lived some distance away at Libourne, and uncles on both sides with their families. They all saw one another frequently and seemed a tight-knit clan.

The mother, it seemed, was a woman of silent habits, a rather tough-minded, inaccessible person. Abel-Cherubin, aged thirty-six, a sugar refiner, lived with his wife and son in Bordeaux and consequently, Susannah had been glad to learn, took no active part in running the vineyard. James was "the poet of the family," interested only in the stage.

Francis spoke of them all with unfailing cheerfulness. He had given her no warnings about them, marked out none of their foibles. Never once, as their journey brought them closer, had he said, "Now, my dear, for heaven's sake remember this or that." He behaved as if he had never noticed their faults, and she loved him all the more for it because it was his sweet nature. But they certainly must have been surprised by the marriage. She knew she was right in her instinct that Gautier had not gone to America looking for a wife. He could hardly have gone so prepared to fall in love. He had written home frequently to his mother telling her about their meeting, his visits to Chicago and St. Louis and his return to Philadelphia, where he had stayed on as their love had deepened and he had asked her to marry him.

But what did the Gautiers think? How had they taken it? It was a mystery. He had never had an answer, never a single solitary letter. True, they had left Philadelphia the day after the wedding and had been on the move pretty much ever since. All the same, a letter ought to have caught up with them somewhere along the way. Francis had made assiduous inquiries everywhere. There was the telegraph; nothing had come and there had been nothing awaiting them in Paris, though Francis had sent on the hotel address.

Did the silence signify disapproval . . . hostility? One morning in Paris, when the hotel clerk had shaken his head at yet another inquiry for mail, Susannah had seen Francis's frown and his look of puzzlement. But he had thrown it off the next minute. She realized she didn't know him— Oh, she knew him in deep secret ways, but there was so much else she could only guess at. She knew she had adopted a sort of voluntary blindness, launching out with him on this new life, having never seen him among his own people; and sometimes it frightened her a little. Yet she loved and trusted him absolutely, and their moments together were so close and entire she thought nothing could ever override that.

And so, sitting there on the bench at Blaye, she thought she really must take her mind off it, and she straightened a fold of her dress and looked out over the open square in front of her.

Blaye was all in tones of brown and ocher, a great citadel with its bastions, old stone buildings, a few shops and rows of plane trees, a dusty, friendly-looking place, not too thriving. To her it looked immeasurably old, not merely physically but in its ways and habits. It certainly wasn't bustling. The people moved slowly, their faces were creased and weathered, the color of the brown earth. To her right, through the bushes, she could glimpse the river, a muddy brown too.

But her thoughts came back to Francis and the immediate future. This was the first hour she had been alone without him since their marriage. And this was the setting in which she would be living with him from now on, this place or something like it. How was it going to change her? For she knew in her heart that another thing was troubling her. In the past, whenever she had thought of their arrival and the meeting with the family, she had felt Francis's protection. She could turn to him, take his arm and look up at his frank, cheerful face and push the doubts back. But today the small silly fact of his going off with his men friends and leaving her had deprived her of this comfort and allowed the doubts to break through.

Why had he done that? He must know she would feel awkward alone there. It was a little break between them. She shifted on the bench, telling herself she was being ridiculous and making too much of it. They were his friends, he had known them long before he had met her. He had his life too, after all. But it was his first assertion of that sort of maleness, "the male pre-

13

rogative," as if there really ought to be any such thing between two young people newly married, and it disturbed her. It sent an involuntary little shudder through her soul. She felt she was surrendering something of him; it was almost like an intimacy being talked about. And so the first faint touch of unhappiness brushed her.

The air in the square was still with a hint of thunder. She longed for a cool drink. Presently a gust of wind came out of the stillness and, turning her head to avoid the dust it lifted, she saw Francis and three of his friends coming toward her.

Even at this distance she could see that he had been drinking. His face was flushed and he was laughing with the others in a tipsy way. She had never seen him the worse for drink before.

2

Francis Gautier was a slightly built man of twenty-eight with thick curly dark hair and a boyish eager face. He was sweetly good-natured, and his quick generous spirit showed in his hazel eyes and his vitality. He wasn't a habitual drinker, and when he drank too much it was out of sheer good will and exuberance, out of eagerness to be companionable, because he hardly cared for the drink itself. He had done his military service with three of the young men in the group, and they had wanted to hear all about his travels and about the United States.

He had been tempted to tell them he had gone to America on business, to "explore the American market." He half believed it himself, because like most people he could find compelling reasons for doing something he wanted to do. But they would have laughed at him. So he had told them the simple truth, that he had gone after his father's death because it had been something Pierre Gautier had promised himself half his life to do.

Pierre Gautier had been a fumbling pioneer, a man with an impossible vision. For nearly a century, since the loss of Canada, French trade across the Atlantic had been built on the Antilles, the sugar islands in the Caribbean. But Gautier had thought this pifflingly limited. He thought it was pathetic. It showed fatal lack of enterprise and imagination. Look at the vast filling spaces of the United States and Latin America! That was where the future of the French Atlantic trade lay.

The Englishman Richard Cobden, who declared that Amer-

15

ica would one day make England a second-class nation, was his prophet. All down the west coast of France lay a chain of magnificent seaports—Brest, Lorient, Nantes, La Rochelle, St. Nazaire, Bordeaux. And Gautier, ignoring or sweeping aside objections, talked about them capturing the trade for Europe, becoming the gateways between the Americas and the whole of the Continent, expounding his theories into the night to anybody who would listen, excitedly pulling out maps, charts, trade figures, shipping tables to prove them. And the bourgeois from Bordeaux who had drunk his wine and listened would, of course, drive away winking at one another and tapping their foreheads. They would lay their fingers alongside their noses and wink. Why should they help to bring prosperity to one rival port, let alone five?

Yet America was something in the minds of the people along the western French seaboard which it could never be for the earthbound peasants of the French interior, hidebound clods that they were, folk almost in love with their dungheaps. American ships and seamen had been in and out of Bordeaux for generations. A Louisiana accent was no more unusual on the Bordeaux waterfront than one from Bristol. And perhaps an idea of the prize that was being snatched away from them was stirring uncomfortably in French minds, for Frenchmen feared and suspected the English commercial methods, the ruthlessness of the new rising business class and the breakneck pace of English industrialization. Even in Bordeaux—where England held a special place because the whole southwest, the old province of Guyenne, had once been under the English crown—these feelings were not unknown. Yet plump Bordeaux shipping men and merchants who could talk to you about unloading at Basse-Pointe, Martinique, or the price of coffee in Guadeloupe, had rarely been beyond New York City, New Orleans or Tampico. And so, listening to his father in the chaotic study at La Guiche, Francis had determined to go at the first opportunity.

He had had no idea of finding a wife. He and Susannah had met at the home of the French consul in Philadelphia, where the consul's wife had arranged what she called a "conversazione" for him to meet some of the French-speaking members of the community, though he spoke excellent English. It had been full of earnest matrons, and he was, after a decent interval, mapping his escape when Susannah walked in.

He had had no hopes about her at first. She was well off, living with an aunt, Aunt Maxine, otherwise Mrs. Walter Abdy, in a big, rather flashy town house. Her mother was dead. Her father, "a traveling man" about whom Mrs. Abdy suggested there was something disreputable, had never appeared and rarely been spoken of. A second aunt, still more regal in manner, lived nearby. Susannah's young sister, Maisie, it appeared, was being brought up by an uncle in Vicksburg, Mississippi.

Francis felt something was amiss in this background. He couldn't put his finger on it, and since he was not given to mysteries he forgot it. He had enough instinct to see that if he probed too deep he might destroy something. Mrs. Abdy lived in style on Spruce Street, drove her own prize high-stepping pair and phaeton, had the acquaintance of all the leading citizens, at least the males. Aunt Adelaide, the second aunt, was married to John Drew Belton, a local banker whose mansion on Walnut Street was one of the centers of Philadelphia high life. John Drew Belton's snobbery, his taste for kicking the lower orders, impressed even Francis, who rarely noticed these things.

At first the aunts tried to keep him away from Susannah. He would call and a servant would say she was out or in the country. But he persisted; he was head over heels in love with her and had hardly had a chance to test her feelings. It took him two months to get on a firm footing with her, the most agonizing months of his life. Then one evening she had tremblingly told him she loved him too. To his surprise the aunts raised no objection. But only Mrs. Abdy came to the wedding.

Now, seeing her on the bench in the Blaye square, he felt a stab of tenderness and pride. She looked so pretty and tempting under the sunshade. He was muzzy with wine. He hadn't drunk so much for months, but they were good fellows. He didn't see the look of anxiety on his wife's face, but he noticed that she got up as soon as she saw him, which made him realize for the first time that she had been waiting. She wouldn't mind. Francis never attributed motives; and he wouldn't have understood if she had reproached him. He simply thought she wouldn't mind. *He* wouldn't have minded if he had had to wait.

"Sue." He took her hand as they came up. "This is Louis Barzac. My wife. Germain Foy and François Chaumet."

They shook her hand. The first two bowed; Chaumet jerked her hand up like a pump handle and kissed it. They were short

17

and thickset, two with blotchy wine-red complexions. They stood shifting their feet in a sort of common silent amusement, eying her and pulling their mustaches as if the whole thing were a joke. It was the male touch again.

"Did they tell you there's no boat?" Francis said. "It's over at Lamarque, on the other side, can't move." His speech was thick and she hated seeing his freshness blurred by the drink.

"Aren't we going to get across then?" The Château La Guiche was in the parish of Cantenac, and he had told her that if they could get across the Gironde—for the little paddle boat only ran occasionally—they would have an hour's drive on the other side. If not, they would have to spend the night at the Hôtel de France and go around through Bordeaux in the morning.

"The engineer's just arrived from Pauillac. He's picking up some gear. With luck we may be able to go over with him in his pinnace. Let's go and see."

He took her arm and they walked to the river a hundred yards away. Susannah stopped with an exclamation. It was like a flood, like the Mississippi—an immense brown stretch of water extending away to the low farther bank. Francis had simply talked about "the Gironde" and she had imagined a modest little river meandering under willows and past rustic walls. But this! The muddy brown water swirled in whirlpools close to the bank and farther out ran in heavy currents that churned up scum and carried along branches and debris. Stretches of it looked like taut Chinese silk. Elsewhere over the sandbanks it was tan-yellow. About a third of the way across a great green-covered island rose up and she could see others upstream. It must be two miles to the other side!

Below them at the jetty was a little steam pinnace painted black and red with a tall brass funnel and a busy official air. Francis went on board, came back to say it was all right and he lifted her onto the deck. Then he and the three others went off to get the trunks.

The sun had gone down and Susannah saw there was no hope of getting to the house till after dark. Ramparts of yellow clouds were piled up in the west, pushing a breeze before them. The crew moved busily about the pinnace. She waited, but Francis didn't come back and she guessed they were drinking

18

again. Never mind, she thought. She tried to close her mind to it.

At last they reappeared, noisy now and clowning comically. The others stood swaying and singing some army song while Francis climbed on board.

He looked red and foolish as he put his arm around her. "Good fellows, eh? I don't see them very often."

"Where's the luggage?"

His face changed. They had forgotten it! They all charged tipsily back to the square. The little fat engineer was impatient to go and blew his whistle; smoke poured from the funnel. Presently they came back with two men pulling a handcart with the things on it. The three called out and sang some more as the pinnace pulled away. Francis laughed a lot and stood waving and happy, and at that moment she thought what a sweet man he was. His arm was around her and she pressed close to his side, waving too.

The pinnace moved out over the river in a great curve and then swung back again, skirting the sandbanks.

All the same, she couldn't help wondering in her heart if he wouldn't be different now that he was back. People changed when they were away from home. It was like speaking a language you only knew imperfectly; you became another person in a strange way. They reached the other side.

Now the family, she said to herself.

3

She never forgot the drive through the soft spring night, Francis beside her in the fiacre, the horse trotting gently, the road winding at first through meadows, then little pine copses and then into the open between the vineyards. It was peaceful, the smell of resin was in the air, the sky clear but moonless. The lights of houses showed at intervals, some at the ends of avenues of trees. Francis dozed most of the way but woke before they arrived and sat up.

"Lord, it's a good thing I don't have to do *that* too often. You're not cross with me?" He took her hand.

She smiled. "No. Where are we?"

"Oh, it's a bit farther on. This is—wait a minute—yes, this is Montferrat's land. It runs up there to the old tower." He began to point to estates, talking excitedly, his boyishness back. "Now this is Onslow's, Coote Onslow's. You'll meet them." He looked at her. "You're all right, Sue, aren't you?"

It was a little touch of reassurance. They could not have expected any of the family to be at Blaye. The long silence had only begun to trouble him in Paris, but . . . oh, well, it did no good to worry in advance.

"Perhaps they don't expect us tonight," Susannah said.

"Look, there it is."

She looked across in the direction he was pointing, across the dark open space between them and the house. It was almost hidden by trees, but she saw the pale white shape, dreaming and ghostly against the dark massed foliage, a long elegant eighteenth-century façade of three stories and the tiny black figure of somebody passing the lights in front of it. From another age! It was much bigger, much more charged with other times and vanished hopes, than she had imagined. No round candle-snuffer tower like those she had seen in pictures of other French châteaux. It had the simple classical lines of one of the great colonial houses in the South at home, near Vicksburg.

Then the road dipped and it was hidden. Ten minutes later they turned off along the stony drive and crunched up to the porch. Two other carriages were standing farther up the drive. As they got out, a servant couple came out of the house, a small man of about fifty with a fierce gray mustache, and a young girl.

"Joseph!" Francis wrung the man's hand. The girl hung back, red-faced with pleasure, till he turned to her too. "Emilie. How are you?" A red setter was barking madly and jumping up at Francis.

Joseph said something quietly and Francis turned to Susannah. "They're all at dinner. Didn't expect us. The Chabots too. This is Joseph, my dear, and Emilie. Joseph, my wife." Joseph bowed, and then over the girl's shoulder Susannah saw a tall heavily built man in black standing in the wide entrance hall of the house watching them. The light shone on his bald head, on his plump jowly face with its clipped black side whiskers that extended down to his chin and there were carefully kept from joining.

As Francis followed her look, the man came forward. "Well!" He stopped a few feet away, dipped a forefinger into his waistcoat pocket and stood looking coolly and arrogantly from one to the other.

Francis said, "Susannah, this is my brother Abel-Cherubin. Susannah, my wife."

Abel-Cherubin stepped up stiffly, gave her the formal greeting as a member of the family, a cold little kiss on each cheek, and stepped back. "We thought you'd gone for good," he said to Francis. "Better if you had."

Francis gave an embarrassed little laugh. "We're sorry to be late. It was lucky we got here at all tonight. Did mother get my letters?" His words were an obvious attempt to keep things smooth after Abel-Cherubin's remark.

21

"Your letters!" Abel-Cherubin gave a snort. "Ask her." He stood aside for Susannah to enter.

She moved forward thinking that if the family could get their encounter over among themselves it would be easier for everyone, so she said to Francis, "I must change my dress. Could Emilie show me upstairs and get my trunk brought up?" They had had to leave most of the luggage at Lamarque to be picked up next day.

"Yes, of course." Francis gave the orders and she followed Emilie indoors. The wide hall went deep into the house, dividing it into two wings. At the end the white-painted staircase rose in a slim graceful curve. The landing was gloomy; the bare floor creaked under them as Emilie led the way along a passage papered in grimy red and opened a door. It was a big, rather low-ceilinged room with light-colored walls, a four-poster and a fireplace. The windows, now shuttered, must overlook the end of the drive, she thought. But like the landing and passage, the room was shabby and in need of attention, in need of some money spent on it. The heavy old furniture was mismatched, the upholstery sagging and worn, and the red velvet curtains had bleached in the sun. Two oval portraits of a couple hung on the wall. A door gave on to a small dressing room with a threadbare couch.

Emilie came back with a pitcher of water as Joseph and the driver brought in her trunk. She had the girl open the trunk and lay out some clothes, then dismissed her and began to get out of her dress. The water was cool and fresh. Presently she paused while drying her face and neck. She could hear angry voices below. It was Abel-Cherubin and somebody else. Then she heard Francis saying, "Damn you, it's my affair! It's in my hands." A woman tried to intervene, but they ignored her, raising their voices. A door slammed, sending an echo through the house and muffling the sounds, but she could hear the argument continuing.

Susannah stood staring in front of her, the towel lifted to her bare shoulders. What were they quarreling about? About her? She hated it, she hated the thought of going down. Had it been the wrong thing to leave Francis alone? She did not know what to do. She was horribly nervous. She wanted to keep clear, yet she couldn't stay here forever. And she ought to show she wasn't afraid to be with Francis, oughtn't she? She put the

22

towel aside and dressed. She kept listening. Once she heard the door open below, and steps sounded in the hall as if Francis were coming up; but they retreated again and a moment later the argument resumed. When she was ready she smoothed her hair on either side of the middle parting, pinned the curling ends on her neck, gave a final look in the mirror and went out. The voices were lower now but still vehement, and somebody banged his fist on the table.

As she reached the bottom of the stairs, Francis said, "I'm handling my own property!"

"I demand an answer," Abel-Cherubin said.

"Oh, go to the devil!"

Another male voice put in silkily, "I have some interesting information from my correspondent in Philadelphia."

"What?" said Francis scornfully. "Pouf! What information? What do you mean?"

"That I'll save for later."

Her heart was beating with fear. As Francis said, "Damn it, Chabot, you'll answer me!" she lifted her chin and walked into the room.

4

Four huge silver candlesticks blazed on an Empire table big enough to seat twenty. Francis was half out of his chair glaring at the thin man lolling opposite; Abel-Cherubin was perched forward, eyebrows raised. A large woman with Francis's eyes and darkish-red hair in a bun on top of her head, whom Susannah recognized as Francis's mother, faced the door. Another woman, whose round face was framed in curls, sat between Abel-Cherubin and a dark youth with a nascent mustache. Nearest her was a thickset man with red hair and the weathered face of a laboring man.

For a second or two Susannah stood there waiting for the irretrievable to be said. The thin man, focus of the scene, was obviously Léon Chabot, Francis's maternal uncle. His lawyer's face was lifted in the light, the sharp nose parallel with the sloping forehead, his lower jaw tucked in under the long judicious upper lip. His egg-shaped head had a fuzz of blond hair at the back and his neck was encased in a tall collar with white linen cravat.

Then they all caught the mother's eyes on the door and turned. There was silence as they stared.

Long afterward Susannah felt that they had looked at her at that moment as if she were a challenge to them. She knew nothing yet of their mistrust, their suspicion of outsiders, their inward-turning, their pride in their "otherness," their dark moods and their taste for isolation. She caught the cynical intelligence of Chabot's look, the sensuality in Abel-Cherubin's; she had heard their quarreling and sensed the hatreds and feuds in the house. The dark tones of the room, the black in which the mother and the men were all dressed, the shadows cast by the candles, the generally dilapidated air of the house—everything was heightened in that one quick flash of knowledge that she was going to have a fight to keep a place here and to defend her marriage.

Then Francis said, "Susannah," and left the table and led her forward. Gravely, in silence, they moved around from one to the next. She bent to the mother to receive the "family" kisses; Chabot stood and embraced her distantly; Abel-Cherubin bowed. The youth was James, the youngest son; the woman was Marthe, Chabot's wife; and the red-faced man was Jules Raynal, Francis's half-brother.

With tenderness Francis watched her go through it. He had forgotten his anger already and thought how beautiful she looked in her new iris-blue gown with the candlelight on her hair.

Places were set—Susannah next to Madame Gautier, Francis on the other side of James—and the soup tureen was brought back, Susannah's first experience of the ritual soup that began every meal. At Francis's suggestion, Raynal, who sat a little apart at the table, brought up a crusty black magnum from the cellar in a basket cradle. The men reached out and examined it, handling it carefully.

"Palmer 1841," Raynal said.

They sampled it with serious, silent nods. It was the one family gesture of celebration. She caught Francis's eye down the table and smiled as he lifted his glass to her and they drank their first toast in the house.

At first she waited for someone to start the conversation, but no one did except Francis, and his attempts elicited nothing. Gradually she understood they were not going to speak. She felt self-conscious, constrained and wretched. The meal proceeded in silence. She had merely checked the quarrel. She was aware of them observing her, of the unexpressed resentments, their critical eyes on her, the hostility toward the outsider who had penetrated their most private and armored sanctuary, the family. The only sounds were Emilie and Joseph coming and going

25

as they served the food—she glanced gratefully at their friendly faces—the small tapping of cutlery on the plates, the wine being poured. And Susannah saw that it must have taken spirit for her husband to break away from them to go to America. At last when they had finished and a good deal of rather horrible tooth-sucking was going on, Madame Gautier pushed back her chair and they rose. Susannah saw Abel-Cherubin and Chabot exchange a swift glance. Abel-Cherubin moved around to intercept Francis, but Francis shook his hand off and led her toward the door. She heard Abel-Cherubin's sibilant oath, then they went into the salon.

"What plays did you see in Paris?" James had followed them.

"Oh. We went to the Opéra Comique." Nervousness at the impending violence had brought the color into her cheeks, but she faced him. "It was amusing."

"Not to the Français?"

"No. We were only there three days."

He was obviously unimpressed. He had something of Francis's freshness but a sharp touch of his own.

"Oh, a piano," she said and went over to it, glad of a diversion.

"Do you play?" James said invitingly and opened it. The keys were broken and scarred and he ran a finger down them, producing a muffled, contorted jangle of sound. He laughed at her grimace.

Francis came up. "Will you have coffee, my dear?"

They sat with his mother while he talked happily and enthusiastically of the journey—of Paris, St. Louis, the gold of California—and Susannah listened to the other men's voices in the dining room and dreaded their coming in. Was this a pattern for the evenings she would spend here now? She felt the force of family, of blood. She felt the strength of these people in their rancor, the strange cohesion they had, even in their hatreds. His mother had once been less of a stranger, less of an outsider than she herself was. Would she, herself, in turn become that silent and watchful woman in the chair facing her? The mother sat like stone, hardly asking a question of her son, only nodding now and then, her hands clasped in her lap; yet her eyes were alert and seemingly uneasy, full of old bitterness and perhaps longing. How long was it before they accepted you, if they ever accepted you?

In a strange way Susannah felt a responsibility. She knew instinctively that her will was stronger than her husband's. There was a transparency about him which she loved. He gave everything of himself to her, there was no holding back. He was utterly clear and honest and entire. But looking at him now, she was a little afraid. And how hard it was to guess the future!

At last Francis said, "You'd better go to bed, Sue. I'll be up in a moment." Gratefully she rose and took her leave of Madame Gautier and James, then turned toward the dining room, but Francis touched her arm. "You can go up this way. I'll explain." He showed her a way out on the far side that avoided the exit through the dining room. "All right?" He smiled at her at the foot of the stairs.

"Yes."

"I'll be up."

Upstairs she undressed for the night, loosened her hair and brushed it. When she was ready, she lowered the lamp and climbed into the big high yielding feather bed. It was a solemn, even awesome, moment to her, getting into this bed for the first time, a new stage in her life. She didn't know why, but she thought of it as a family bed, the center of life and death. It was covered with a huge balloon of an eiderdown, light as light; but the night was too warm and she pushed it off.

She lay staring up at the ceiling, at the pattern of shadows, the tiny spirals made by the heat of the lamp. The deep quiet of the night surrounded her; she had the impression of space outside, wide dark open space. She wished Francis would come up. Here she was in her new life . . . here she was. What would it bring?

Abruptly out of the silence there was a loud outburst of voices below, shattering her drowsiness. She sat up staring at the door. A minute passed, then another, then there were steps, the door opened and Francis came in.

"Aren't you asleep yet?" he said offhandedly. He was subdued, preoccupied and turned away from her.

"What's the matter, Frank?" She sometimes called him Frank when they were alone together.

"Oh . . . nothing." He got unhurriedly out of his clothes,

27

poured water into the bowl and sluiced himself. He stood toweling his face and arms—and suddenly he had forgotten it, thrown it off. He came to the bed naked, his face shining, climbed in beside her, leaving the lamp burning and put his arms around her, burrowing deeper into the deep warm bed and pulling her close to him and kissing her.

"What was the matter?" she said.

"Oh, nothing to worry about."

"What were they saying about Philadelphia?"

"I don't even remember." He smiled and hugged her in happiness. "We're home! We're home!"

5

The land was poor. Clay and sand mingled with flint, limestone and gravel. Swamps of leeches spread inland from the mud flats of the river. In the parishes where wheat would grow, the yield was meager and could not support the men who labored at it. They were stubborn and superstitious people, bound by some vague and unremembered fear learned in the Middle Ages that each small plot of land, however wretched, must bear its crop of wheat or suffer the evil eye.

The Gironde area formed a rough triangle. To the west were the great sand dunes, the highest in Europe, and the Atlantic. A lake or two but hardly a stream of any consequence. To the south the empty marshes and forests of the Landes stretched to the foothills of the Pyrenees and the Spanish frontier. Here no crop would grow except a little rye and millet and none but the hardiest trees, the black oak, the tamarisk, the maritime pine. In summer the hot southern sun drew a steaming miasma over the immense gloomy solitude. In winter the country shook under the Atlantic gales. A race of short, crooked men strode the swamps on stilts, herded their sheep, carted wood, living scarcely better than the animals, speaking a tongue understood by no others, quick in their resentment of intruders. The eastern boundary was the Dordogne River, which formed at its junction with the Garonne the great river of the Gironde. Through the triangle ran only three potholed roads; apart from that nothing but dead-straight tracks through the forest.

But in sand, in stones, in three feet of gravel, the vine will grow. To the men who cultivated it, it seemed that the vine had been created for places where nothing else would flourish. And as if their character must match the soil they worked, they starved or ate something like their fill, met disaster and success with the same bitter obduracy, the same mistrust, as if even the stones would one day deny them their livelihood. A hailstorm could wipe out a year's work in half an hour, a frost kill a man's hopes overnight.

The Napoleonic wars brought ruin. Men who had 150,000 francs in wine casked in their cellars could not raise a credit of 1000 francs. Napoleon offered them loans at 4 per cent on half the wine they surrendered in bond. What could he, a Corsican, know of their suspicion? They shook their heads and refused.

In 1842 the great estates of Lafite, Latour, Margaux and Château d'Yquem rose up like feudal castles above the general sea of debt, penny-pinching, genteel poverty and outright misery around them. Even then more than half the surface of a famous place like Lafite was in copses, moorland, pasture and farm patches. Pierre Gautier had known half the vineyards in Médoc up for sale—and no takers. Men like Gautier took in five years of harvests, one after the other, till the stored hogsheads of wine scraped the roofs of their cellars, and they could neither sell it to pay their taxes nor raise a mortgage. The great Major General Palmer, the English soldier who collected together four hundred acres of choice vineyard in the 1830s, believing it would fructify and prosper, was bankrupt by 1842.

Many a debt-ridden owner of a hundred acres couldn't repair his roof. The penniless barons and tatterdemalion marquises watched their workmen hack at the stony soil with hoes. The better-off used oxen or cows, but most of these still pulled a crude plow that hardly differed in design from the wheelless Roman swing plow. Wheat grew among the vines to feed the laborers, and it was threshed by flails or the treading ox.

Cheap bread was the staple food of agricultural laborer, town worker, small tradesman and artisan alike; and every town, village and hamlet in the triangle had its deformed and scrofulous population to show that they did not even get enough of that. So journeyman, cooper and peasant clung to their plots of vine among the great domains, savoring the harsh brew they yielded because it was their own. The land was parceled out, split up and redivided under the law which shared an inheritance among all a man's children, no matter what he wished, so that they would fight for a strip which none of them could cultivate with profit but none would give up. Credit they would not have, since it involved trust and dealings with strangers.

But change had begun. The bankers of Bordeaux and Paris and London, the new-rich men of industry and trade were casting their eyes on the prime vineyards of Médoc and Sauternes and buying them up. No man who was not already solid, who did not have the virtues conferred by money, could aspire. But to those who could, a vineyard in the Médoc or Graves added something—something dynastic. It gave the grocer the touch of the nobleman, endowed the sausage maker with influence and turned the haberdasher into a person of consequence. No matter that the newcomer had no taste, that he knocked down an eighteenth-century house and put up a plaster and plush horror in its place. He could speak of his vineyard and his vintages along with the Rothschilds and the Pereires. Poverty was still a neighbor. But now fortunes were going into the land. Property! That was the cry now. Property! Yet the risks were no less. Nothing had changed fundamentally, least of all the men.

It was notorious that the Château La Guiche was badly managed. At intervals in his dreaming Pierre Gautier had had bursts of enthusiasm for the estate, but they had never lasted long enough to do much good. It covered nearly sixty-nine acres in the parish of Cantenac, the heart of Médoc, and of these, fifty-six acres were under vine. The Château produced only between thirty-five and forty tuns, that is, calculated at four Bordeaux hogsheads or barrels to a tun, between a hundred and forty and a hundred and sixty barrels a year. Ten years before old Gautier's death it had been one of the finest Médocs, for the vineyard site was exceptional. But with the vagaries of Gautier's attention, its reputation had declined, and now for the wine brokers and merchants of Bordeaux its quality was superior bourgeois— above the ordinary but below the nobility.

Pierre Gautier's property at his death had included a fine building on the Cours de l'Intendance, the main business street of Bordeaux, some houses in the town, the vineyard and two hundred francs in cash. This was to be divided among the four surviving members of the family: his widow Victorine Gautier and his three sons, Abel-Cherubin, Francis and James.

The old man had been baffled by Abel-Cherubin, half afraid of him and his mercantile soul. He wanted Francis to manage the vineyard and calculated that if he could maneuver Abel-Cherubin out of the way, an enterprise that would not be easy, his widow and James would allow Francis to take charge. With the cunning that was the contradiction of his nature he had watched until Abel-Cherubin was in financial straits, then made his move. He told Abel-Cherubin that he would assign him the major part of the Bordeaux properties, with immediate possession, in advance on his inheritance, if they could come to a settlement.

Abel-Cherubin had dipped his finger into his waistcoat pocket. He guessed what his father was up to, but he was in difficulties and did not have much leeway. He had pushed open the door of the old man's office, and father and son had sat down and haggled coldly for two days among the sea charts and shipping tables, each showing no more mercy or understanding than he would to a stranger, the old man rallying himself periodically with scorching brandy. In the end Abel-Cherubin had got more out of him than he had intended, calculated at 10 per cent of the whole. Gautier knew he had been worsted. But the vineyard was safe. Fourteen months later he was dead, and the four mourners had sat in the dark and fusty office of Monsieur Parenteau, the notary, signing the papers dividing the property among them. Abel-Cherubin had his 10 per cent in Bordeaux buildings plus 15 per cent of the vineyard. Victorine Gautier, Francis and James shared the remaining 85 per cent of the vineyard, getting 28⅓ per cent each.

James, being still a minor, could not dispose of his share until he became of age. But he was not interested in the place and had willingly turned his share over to Francis in return for the guarantee of an income and a lump sum with which to buy himself out of military service. Francis thus had a majority share and the management of the property had fallen naturally to him.

The dog barking woke Susannah next morning. Francis was gone, the bedroom was suffused with sunlight that came

32

spilling through the shutters and made two bright yellow blobs on the floor. She got out of bed, went over to the window and pushed the shutters open. The warm radiance poured over her. How strong the sun was already—it must be midmorning! In front of the house was a small grassy plantation with birches, pines, mulberry trees, even a palm tree with fanlike spiky leaves and, in the middle, a lake fringed with bushes and irises. Beyond, to the right, were the vines, rows and rows of leafy stumps rising about a foot from the ground. To the left, by the stony drive leading to the road, was a yellowish meadow with three cows grazing.

All around over the barely undulating landscape she could see other vines. A copse stood here and there, greenhouses flashed in the sun and smoke rose from many a red-roofed hut in the still morning air. Swallows were wheeling above, the air was warm and she had an impression of openness, of space, of clearness. She felt excited and happy, the whole of last night's somberness swept away.

Steps crunched below, she retreated quickly.

"Hello! Susannah, you up?" It was Francis. She threw on a robe and went back. He was standing there looking up. "What do you want for breakfast? Eggs?"

"Yes."

"All right. I'll tell them. Don't be long."

He had disappeared again when she got down. Emilie brought breakfast, and she sat alone at the vast table in the dining room feeling a little guilty and wondering if the others would appear. She was surely the last down? The whole house was quiet. *Was* there anybody in the next room? She got up and looked into the salon—it was empty. In daylight the shabbiness shocked her. Half the chairs were broken, the webbing of the carpet showed through, the great heavy pieces of furniture seemed to be stored there rather than assembled for use or comfort, as if they were an accumulation of unwanted legacies from other, vanished families. A dozen portraits with black backgrounds hung high up around the room—a feature of many a Médoc house had she known it—made it look worse.

As she finished her breakfast, Francis came into the dining room.

"I didn't hear you get up," she said.

33

"At five!" He had all his sparkle and freshness.

"Is that the usual thing?"

He laughed and kissed her, put his arm around her. "Come on. Let's look around."

Outside were flowerboxes and half a dozen pretty small trees in tubs. "Orange trees," Francis said.

"Are they?" She was excited by the novelty.

"You have to put them inside in the winter."

She looked up at the house again, half fearful of finding it a disappointment, but it was as lovely as she had glimpsed it in the dark—the columned porch rising to a classical gable, the row of third-floor windows, set back slightly, opening on to a slim balcony and, above, the gently sloping slate roof. There were more trees behind.

"I'll show you my part first, eh?" he said. "You can see the house later." They walked out to the first rows of vines. "Here you are, this is one piece. We talk about a piece of vine here, it just means a plot of vines. This is what you call cabernet sauvignon, that's the kind of grape."

"They're all bent and twisted. Are they old?"

"These vines? About forty years old."

"Sounds ancient!"

He looked at her and laughed. "Plenty of vines here are a hundred to a hundred and fifty years old and still producing."

She hung on his arm happily. "And what are they doing over there?" A man with two oxen harnessed to a plow was standing talking to another between the rows of vines.

"The one with the plow's doing the second plowing, that means he's covering the foot of the vines with earth. The other fellow is Monsieur Josserand, what you call a price maker because he quotes you a price for whatever work he does for you. He does the pruning and the dressing and a lot of other things. Lives with his wife and children in one of the cottages at the back there. You can just see the roof . . . there, see? We've got seven couples like the Josserands—six other price makers and their wives, all living here or hereabouts. They each work about seven acres. Josserand's got a special position, he's the senior of them."

"Where does it go to?"

"You mean the boundary? Down as far as there, to that lit-

34

tle dip, then across to there." He stood pointing out the boundaries of the estate. "More at the back."

She noticed now that the place was much less orderly than
she had thought at first. Some of the vines seemed to be planted
any old way. Strips of meager wheat and grass and tall reeds
grew about, there were patches of meadow, and rubbish seemed
to have been dumped on bare plots.

"Oh, here's Laverne." Under his breath he added, "Very
important fellow."

A tall man in a workman's blouse with a red leathery face
and graying hair came up and took off his beret respectfully but
unhurriedly.

"This is Monsieur Laverne, what you call the *maître de
chai*, our cellar master," Francis said. "That means he's in
charge of the winemaking. My wife."

Laverne bowed, looking at her with bright blue eyes, and
she got the impression of a slow, kindly, quiet man who would
be ruggedly independent. He inquired politely about Francis's
voyage in a way that set their relationship as a rather formal
one; no question of their calling him by his Christian name like
Emilie or Joseph. He was *Monsieur* Laverne; and she thought it
was unlike home, where he would have been John or Tom quite
naturally and with no loss of dignity. Then Francis said, "Monsieur Laverne, would you show us around?"

They followed him back behind the house into a lofty, spacious whitewashed building where great oak vats were standing
along one wall and the sharp sourish tang of wine hung in the
air. This was the *cuvier* or vatting room. That day Susannah
didn't understand much of the explanation that followed, it was
too new, too detailed. She listened patiently while Monsieur Laverne explained how the grapes were brought in, scraped from
the stalks on this rack here, put into the treading press and trampled here, the juice carried away into these vats and left until
fermentation was over and then poured into the barrels—which,
it seemed, was far from the final stage of the process.

One whitewashed outbuilding led into the next. It was cool
inside. Buckets and glass instruments stood in odd corners with
rakes and curious half-barrels. The sunlight on the stone walls
outside, seen from the cool semi-darkness, looked a blaze. Now
and then Monsieur Laverne would say something to Francis

about "chaptalization" or degrees of alcohol and the two of them would nod sagely. She paused, watching one of Laverne's men lighting a wick on a length of wire.

"He's sulphuring," Francis said. "That wick is a piece of sulphur and now he's going to put it into the barrel, see? It cleans the barrel of impurities before it receives the wine."

"I see."

Laverne took leave of them, and Francis said to Susannah, "Now come down here." He lit a candle on a barrelhead and then led the way down a flight of steps. "Careful of the steps. Can you see?"

"Yes, I'm all right." At the bottom under a blackened arch she could see an iron grille and a dark space beyond.

"This is the private cellar." Francis unlocked the grille, swung the door open and led her in, holding up the candle. It was cool and faintly odorous and dark. Great cobwebs festooned the bottles in the candlelight, sooty webs as thick as moss clung to the iron bins fixed from floor to ceiling where the bottles lay. Dimly she made out further arches and ramifications of the cellar beyond. He took a slip of wood from one bin, blew the dust off and peered at it to read the name. "Haut-Brion 1848."

"Is that something special?"

"*Is* it? Good Lord, it's one of the greatest. With time it may be the greatest ever."

She pulled a mock-solemn face and he kissed her.

"But they're not level, your old bottle racks. Look."

"No, that's how they have to be. You have to keep the bottles tipped down a little toward the cork end. The wine has to be in contact with the cork, otherwise, if there's a space between the wine and the cork, the wine spoils, gets corked."

"Has it all been here long?"

"Most of it. Anyway, you can't touch it for a year after it's bottled, because it's going through what you call bottle sickness. You have to let it get over the shock of being exposed to the air when it's transferred from the cask to the bottle. Takes six months to a year."

"Hm. I'm learning." Her eyes were bright in the candlelight. She kept close to him as they walked down the narrow passages. His voice sounded close and flat. He stopped by an old stone bottle rack.

36

"We're under the house here. My father had his own cellar down here somewhere. There's supposed to have been a secret chapel down here too. See, vaulted roof." He held the candle up and she saw that the roof was higher.

"Was there?"

"Nobody's ever found it," he said.

They wandered on through the cellar maze and at last came back to the iron grille again. Francis locked it behind them and led her up by a different stairway. They came out into a big empty room with tall windows shuttered from outside. At the far end he swung open double doors on to a cool dim interior where barrels were laid out in long straight rows.

"There, that's the *chai*, the main cellar. It's called a cellar even though it's above ground, and this is where the wine finally matures in the cask. That's last year's there, sold already." He glanced around and, catching his expression, she thought he looked slightly uncomfortable. "It's late. Should be delivered in Bordeaux already."

"Is it a good year?"

"Yes, not outstanding but good."

She stood looking out over the ordered rows of barrels, the product of such skill and patience. It was rather beautiful. She didn't know why—perhaps because, in its imperfect, even commonplace way, it was an expression of love. She would have laughed at the idea six months before, but now it was different and to her surprise she was touched and got her first feeling of pride. "Yes, it's splendid," she said.

Outside, a carriage and two saddle horses were in the drive, and when they got around to the front of the house four people were standing talking to Madame Gautier by the porch.

"Oh, it's Coote Onslow," Francis said. They checked their pace slightly while he identified the visitors in a low voice. "He's the fellow with the beard, our English neighbor. And that's Constance Canning with him, Lady Canning. English too. The Cannings have a place down the road. The old man is Monsieur Parenteau, the family notary. The other man I don't know."

Onslow called out boisterously, "Hello! So the traveler's back. And how were the great United States?"

"Wonderful."

Smiling, he led Susannah forward. The introductions were made. Lady Canning, a woman of striking dark beauty with blue eyes, about thirty, in a long full English riding skirt, said, "How do you do?" in a quiet way. Onslow, whose beard was parted in the middle and brushed up either way, was big, bald and jovial-looking. His round red face shone, his voice was loud.

"From Philadelphia? Begad, know it well. Was there myself five years ago. Charming place. You know the Piggots? Schuyler Piggot? Married Charlie Adams's daughter. Very old friend of mine. And Tom and Martha Lamont? Yes, yes." He didn't seem to want an answer; he beamed at Susannah. "Well, we're delighted to have somebody from Philly here." It was slightly patronizing.

Monsieur Parenteau, the notary, was a little old man in a rusty black coat and high collar, a figure out of another age. A dewdrop hung from his great hawk nose, his jaw jutted out with piratical ferocity and his redingote had obviously been cut for the season of 1789. He made a low bow.

"Allow me to present Mr. John Lovell, of London." He indicated the other man at his side. "I took the liberty of asking Mr. Lovell to accompany me. We have business together farther on at Pauillac when I have concluded here."

Lovell bowed. Onslow broke in to explain that he and Lady Canning had been riding past and had caught sight of Monsieur Parenteau turning in in the carriage. Onslow had an appointment to make with the notary, so they had followed him in to arrange it.

"That's all right then, Parenteau?" Onslow said. "Wednesday at three."

They all stood talking together for a few moments, Onslow doing most of it. Susannah was happy to hear English again. Lovell, who was smartly dressed in a well-cut three-quarter coat, buff waistcoat and white linen cravat, didn't say much. He had a longish face, the slightly forward set of the mouth faintly outlined on each side; his deep-set intelligent eyes met Susannah's briefly. As she was wondering about him, Onslow asked, "Are you in business here, Mr. Lovell?"

"I'm just beginning," Lovell said noncommittally with a smile.

Constance Canning said to Susannah, "You must come and see us. We are just down the road."

"I should like to."

"Do you ride?"

"Yes," Susannah said. "Though I haven't a horse yet." Lady Canning didn't pursue it, perhaps her words had been simply formal politeness. Susannah caught something reserved about her; she didn't look at all the partner for the boisterous Onslow.

"Well, we only stopped for a moment," Onslow said. "Come along, Constance. Forgive us, Gautier, we must be getting back. We'll expect to see you and your wife." He helped Lady Canning mount; the others watched them start down the drive, then moved back to the house.

"If you would care to wait indoors," Madame Gautier said to Lovell.

"Thank you."

"Oh, Mother," Francis said. "I've been showing Susannah around a bit. Will you take her around the house when you've got time?"

"Very well."

He had caught sight of Abel-Cherubin and Chabot approaching from the direction of the vines with James and Raynal in tow. He waited till his mother, Susannah and Lovell had gone in, then turned as the others came up. Abel-Cherubin and Chabot were looking ready for war.

6

Francis knew what was coming and wasn't looking forward to it. Abel-Cherubin and Chabot had stayed overnight "to have things out." They disposed themselves around the large, rather gloomy paneled office still hung with old Gautier's maps and charts and were soon arguing.

Francis was a man with a happy temperament. He could push disagreeable feelings out of the way, just as he often managed to forget the things that caused them; and when he couldn't forget them he disguised them, so that they became tractable and inoffensive. He rarely thought ill of people, he wasn't resentful and for the most part didn't notice when people were negligent, so he was always amazed if others took some piece of forgetfulness of his for willful neglect or deceit. It would never have occurred to him. He was sparkling and eager and full of vigor but not very inward-searching, and his sudden flares of anger, which were rare, usually came because people made a fuss about things that weren't worth making a fuss about. Why must they see things so gloomily?

Monsieur Parenteau sat enthroned at the big Louis-Philippe desk because he and his chief clerk had been keeping the accounts in Francis's absence. Abel-Cherubin had found this an unsatisfactory arrangement and now complained about it at length. He spoke of Francis's irresponsibility, "gallivanting about the United States." He produced his own figures and complained that bills and receipts were missing from Monsieur Parenteau's accounts; moreover, several matters in the general running of the property had been mishandled. Francis explained that he had been away longer than expected, that he had written and told them he had met Susannah and when they were returning. If there had been queries, why hadn't they written to him?

Old Monsieur Parenteau, who had known them all from birth, sniffed his dewdrop and during their argumentation went slowly back and forth through the two sets of accounts.

At last Abel-Cherubin said to Francis, "I'm told you sold the whole of the 1851 before you went."

"Yes, I did," Francis said, tapping with his foot.

"Might I ask who to?"

"As a matter of fact, I sold it to Simcoe Baynes."

"So you admit it, damn you. A slap in the face! An insult to the whole family!"

"He offered me a fair price."

"Fair price! You knew I would sell to the devil before I'd sell to that scoundrel."

"But what's the point of getting him against us? Heavens, why don't you forget that old business?"

Simcoe Baynes, senior partner in Baynes and Sheehan, wine merchants, was a powerful member of the Bordeaux Chamber of Commerce. He and Abel-Cherubin detested each other. Two years before, they had fought out a court dispute over a factory and warehouse site on the Quai de Bacalan, fronting the Gironde. Abel-Cherubin was in occupation as tenant, but Baynes had managed to buy the property from under him and had obtained an eviction order against him. When Abel-Cherubin had failed to comply to the letter, Baynes had had Abel-Cherubin's property seized and it had cost Abel-Cherubin eleven months of effort and a good deal of money to clear the legal entanglements that Baynes threw around him. Later Baynes had systematically blocked Abel-Cherubin's applications to the Chamber of Commerce for permission to extend loading rails from his refinery to the quay, and this had worsened the bad feeling between them. In any event, a dispute involving money was not a thing to forget, ever.

"You realize you will not be able to go through with it?" Abel-Cherubin said. "The sale is pledged to Jacobsen."

"No, no. Jacobsen's contract hasn't been renewed since father's death."

Monsieur Parenteau, appealed to, confirmed that no new

formal document had yet been signed. On the other hand, a certain usage had grown up that Jacobsen was entitled to regard as established and might put forward as supporting a claim at law.

"He's as good as had our word," Abel-Cherubin said.

"You can't get out of it," said Chabot.

"The signature was a mere formality," Abel-Cherubin continued. "Jacobsen has had the wine for the last five years, he expects to get this, and he will! He is certainly getting my share and I've told him so."

Francis said patiently, "We've always sold the production as a whole. It's the only reasonable way to do business. You know how bad it is to try to market it in dribs and drabs. The merchants play you off against each other and you get the worst price in the end. It's bad enough as it is. Anyway, it's all sold to Baynes."

"Then where is the money? Where is your famous fair price?"

"As you see, I've put in a credit to the estate."

"In other words you've spent it?" Chabot put in. He was sitting back with his head in the air, looking critical, and an onlooker might have asked what he was doing there at all since he had no stake in the vineyard. But he was one of the family, and family, even in its most distant reaches, had moral claims that were sacred.

Francis gestured to the accounts on the desk. "There are those payments to come. I have to collect them."

It was true he had taken more money to the United States than he needed, expecting to bring back a fair portion of it. But he hadn't calculated on falling in love. In Philadelphia he had been openhanded. Mrs. Abdy and Aunt Adelaide kept households where money was obviously not spared, and he had to keep up, to arrange little parties and attentions. After a while hints had been dropped, not by Susannah but by Miss Rosa and other intimates, that he ought discreetly to make a present now and then to Mrs. Abdy and Aunt Adelaide if he wanted their support in his courtship; and it would be tactless not to be generous, since they were used to rather handsome things. The advice was offered in a spirit of helpfulness. He had complied; the ladies had been gracious enough to accept. As things had progressed and he had become accepted in their circle, the aunts had set up delightful entertainments as opportunities for him to meet their many friends, and he found himself paying for most of these festivities. How could he appear mean in such circumstances? Mrs. Abdy—Aunt Maxine as she asked him to call her now—had arranged the wedding reception on a lavish scale. And then—he had not told Susannah—because she was suffering a temporary shortage of funds, Aunt Maxine had asked him to foot the bill; she would have her bankers send the money on. On the way home they had spent what remained in the Paris shops—for when would Susannah get the chance to go again?

"You discounted the contract note, did you not?" Abel-Cherubin asked. "You raised the money on Baynes's signature?"

"Well, I had to. I was in a hurry to catch the sailing."

"You raised the money *at six per cent discount?*" Abel-Cherubin's voice had a ring of horror.

"Yes, I think it was six."

"You *think!*"

A shocked sound came from Chabot. Abel-Cherubin's jowls quivered. Any discount at all was bad enough—but not to be sure of the rate! How was it possible—his own brother? It made him look ridiculous. Chabot would talk about it in that cynical way of his, it would get around Bordeaux, to his club. "Gautier's young brother, you know, can't remember how much discount he accepted," and they would eye him as if he were an accomplice. It was preposterous!

"Baynes's broker was ready to take the wine," Francis said. "We might have got a worse price later." A trace of his fresh young smile still lingered, as if he wanted to reassure them that everything would be all right.

Abel-Cherubin pulled a paper out of his pocket and threw it angrily on the desk in front of Monsieur Parenteau. "There's your contract note. Look at it! Do you call that a fair price?" It was a copy, but before Francis could answer, Abel-Cherubin snatched it up again and read out, "A hundred and ninety francs a cask."

"What!"

Monsieur Parenteau gave a sniff and pulled out a big red handkerchief.

"The price of any clogmaker's vinegar!" Abel-Cherubin said.

"Well, they weren't offering more," Francis said.

43

"Have you seen today's price? Three hundred francs! I'm damned if I see why we should pay for your fiddle-faddling around in America." He flung the contract note down again.

Francis sighed. "I went for everybody's benefit, you know. It was, if you like, an investment. I went to see the market, that's why I went to St. Louis. It's never been developed properly. It's not been studied." He was all enthusiasm again at once. "Do give me a chance to tell you about it. For instance, I heard some very hard things about the wine being sent there, all sorts of mistakes are being made and—"

"And you propose to remedy them, perhaps," Abel-Cherubin cut in.

"Ha!" said Chabot.

"You will have to see Baynes and tell him he can't have the wine. Jacobsen is getting it."

"But I can't do that," Francis said, looking worried.

"And I expect six months' interest at three per cent to be paid in for the use you have had of the money. Kindly make a note of that, Monsieur Parenteau."

Francis began to lose patience. "The property here has to be managed by one person. I have the signature, I hold the general power of attorney and I have got to do things as I see best."

"You break your word to an important merchant—"

"Oh, come, I did not!"

"You sell the wine for nothing, you fritter away the money—"

"Nothing of the sort!" Now their voices were raised.

"And you cannot account for it. And we are to sit by and say nothing? We'll see about that!"

Francis sat struggling with his irritation, struggling with his bafflement. It was a painful moment. He always muddled along with the bookkeeping, the daybook, the ledger, the tax register and so on. He detested it, for figures bored him and he had never acquired the patience they demanded. Sometimes he did not have a clear idea where the money had gone, but he was never very distressed, because he knew it would come out all right. Usually when he had paid James his money and given Abel-Cherubin and his mother their shares, he seemed to be out of pocket himself. He told himself it was probably just an impression and that if he took the trouble to go into things he would find he had taken more than his due. Anyway, he didn't much mind, there were always other exciting things claiming his attention.

But now he remembered. "Oh, wait a minute. We've forgotten, on that last account, Abel-Cherubin, that you owe your share of the new vats. And those plows from Masson, I don't think you paid for them."

"Experimental plows! A sheer waste of money!"

"But they are the latest thing. If we can only get used to them, I'm sure they'll give results."

Chabot said sharply, "Raynal?"

Raynal, who had sat wordless so far, shifted uneasily. His thick hands were folded peasantlike in his lap. He kept a small vineyard of his own at Libourne and his word therefore carried special weight. He shook his head. "They can't use them. They are no good."

"There you are."

"But they're new. If they'd really persevere—"

"Let us"—Monsieur Parenteau tapped with his snuffbox till they were silent—"let us settle the accounts." He took his pen, Abel-Cherubin picked up his papers with a sigh and they went through them again. The conclusion was inescapable. Even when Francis had paid in what he owed and they had set off other income against debts, the finances were in a poor way. They had six or seven months' running costs to meet, including the pay of the price makers and the men who did the heavier work, before they could expect funds from the sale of the next harvest. Monsieur Parenteau looked from one to the other with his little quick eyes. It would be pointless to call for a new subscription of funds; Abel-Cherubin was much too stingy, Madame Gautier would refuse and Francis . . .

"Oh, heavens." Francis forced a smile. "It's surely not as bad as it seems. Really, you know, I've only just got back. Let me get things in hand."

Chabot looked sardonic.

"I shall expect a financial settlement for my share in fifteen days," Abel-Cherubin said. "And we cannot, of course, contemplate losing the difference between a hundred ninety francs and three hundred francs a cask, so you will have to tell Baynes without delay."

"But how can I?"

"One moment." Chabot held up a hand. His sharp eyes were on Francis. "Monsieur Parenteau has a further matter to raise. A very serious matter."

They turned expectantly to Monsieur Parenteau, but Abel-Cherubin spoke first. "What is the situation with your wife?"

"My wife?" Francis frowned.

"Yes, your marriage situation?"

"Please!" Monsieur Parenteau rapped on the desk, silencing Abel-Cherubin. He turned to Francis. "My dear young sir, as you know, your father's great wish was to preserve the property intact—he wished to make it indivisible and keep it in the family. He wrote his will with that in mind. And upon each of you, as you remember, he laid a solemn injunction—to separate your property from your spouse's when you married by means of a marriage settlement. You, my dear young sir, have recently married, and quite naturally your brothers wish to be sure that you have carried out this obligation."

Francis stared at Monsieur Parenteau. The long recital of the will that November day in the notary's ancient office came back to him, how they had all sat around, the stove red-hot, the windows shut, a gale outside, old Parenteau's voice droning on through the repetitions and the legal formulas while he had thought of his father raking a hand through his mop of gray hair, his hazel eyes—still so young!—bright with enthusiasm as he expounded some new scheme, some new chance to seize . . . But if there had been any special injunction among it all, he had utterly forgotten it. Had he been expected to make a marriage settlement? He certainly hadn't realized that. He felt guilty and a little ashamed.

Chabot was saying, "You understand, don't you? You, Abel-Cherubin and James are each under an obligation to separate your property from your wife's by means of a marriage settlement, so that it shall not pass to the wife or other persons outside the family."

Francis nodded, racking his brains to remember.

"Then where is your settlement? We shall have to see that it is in the proper form."

"I haven't got one," Francis said. "Susannah and I were married under the ordinary law."

46

In the silence that followed, the others stared at Francis. Abel-Cherubin had paled. Confronted with the horror of an outsider having a claim on the family money, they were all for a moment speechless.

"You have no marriage settlement?" Something approaching emotion trembled in Abel-Cherubin's voice.

"No."

"Where . . . where were you married?"

"In Philadelphia, in the State of Pennsylvania. I don't know what the inheritance law is there, but I imagine I can leave my property to whom I like."

"So that your wife can claim your estate in the event of your death?" Chabot said.

"I should think so."

"But . . . but . . ."

"Then you must execute a marriage settlement here. You must separate your property from hers," Abel-Cherubin said.

Monsieur Parenteau gave a loud sniff. "That would not be possible. And it would not prevent the lady, or the lady's family, claiming entitlement under American law."

"But the property is in France."

"They were married in the United States."

In the fresh silence this remark produced they glimpsed terrible legal complications, attachments, injunctions, affidavits, lawyers' fees, court battles. And they shuddered. A breach of this sort in the family ramparts was a thing to be dreaded. A wife who claimed a share was bad enough. A foreign wife was worse. But the idea of a foreign wife's family laying hands on the patrimony—it was beyond thinking of.

Abel-Cherubin recovered himself first. In a sepulchral voice he said, "Dear Father's will laid the obligation upon us in the gravest, the most solemn terms."

"It was not specific about a foreign marriage," Monsieur Parenteau said. "That event was not foreseen."

"But the wife must understand that any claim by her or her family would immediately be contested and embroiled in law," Abel-Cherubin said.

"Hm." Monsieur Parenteau looked over his glasses. "That would be inevitable."

"She must sign a renunciation. Yes, yes, that's it! She must renounce her rights. That's the only solution."

"Must?" Chabot laid his head back, looking along his nose. "And if the lady prefers to have . . . expectations, a propertied husband?"

"You mean, if she won't renounce? If she won't sign any-thing?" Abel-Cherubin's face was waxy.

"The lady's family is well known in Philadelphia," Chabot said. "It has wide connections, I believe." There was a trace of a smile on his lips, but Francis did not notice it.

They went on arguing over his head.

"It could be argued," Chabot said, "that the marriage with-out a settlement is a breach of the family agreement to keep the property intact. Could be argued, you know."

Abel-Cherubin shot a glance at Chabot. His eyebrows lifted, he dropped his gaze, his forefinger sought his waistcoat pocket.

Old Parenteau saw it and knew that a calculation was be-ing made.

Then Abel-Cherubin said, "Yes, of course. If Francis will not respect dear Father's will, then, yes, it absolves the rest of us. We could not be held to keep our shares in."

Francis looked at him in dismay. If Abel-Cherubin sold out, which was what he meant, James would be greatly tempted to do the same when he was of age. And their mother? It was hard to tell what she might do, but the prospect of liquid cash would be almost too unbearably enticing. And unless he could at that point raise the money and buy their shares, he would be left with only his portion of the estate. He would be a smallholder. He would never be able to keep the house up, he would not be able to get a decent living out of what remained to him of the vineyard. How many times, because of the inheritance laws which subdivided the land, had they not all seen it happen? A vineyard or a piece of land or simply a house would be left to a man's family numbering perhaps ten or a dozen people. Each would have to have his share by law. When it was not possible to divide the property, such as a house, among them, then they must all agree to sell it, all agree on the asking price, all agree on any offer made for it. Getting such agreement was often the labor of years, and since any one beneficiary or his heir could block the whole machine, the property often simply decayed in the interval. A family feud could make the whole thing a night-mare. Where the legacy could be divided up, each beneficiary

48

took his part and did with it as he wished, so that a property which was viable as a whole might be hopelessly carved up.

Francis watched Abel-Cherubin folding his accounts, his white hands pressing and smoothing the sheets lovingly and neatly.

"It is to be hoped that the lady will see reason and sign a renunciation of claim," Abel-Cherubin said.

"I will talk to Oursel about it," Chabot said. "He will know. He has been handling Mornac's dispute. Very clever."

"A renunciation duly registered in Philadelphia may be the thing," Abel-Cherubin said.

They stood up. Abel-Cherubin looked at Francis. "We shall want to hear what you intend to do. Baynes's man is coming here the day after tomorrow, I understand. It will give you a chance to tell him and settle that point right away."

7

Susannah stood at her mirror the next afternoon trying on the things she had bought in Paris. She was humming happily to herself. The trunks they had left at Lamarque after crossing the river had arrived and, helped by Emilie, she had been unpacking them with little bursts of excitement and rediscovery for the last hour. The room was in complete disorder—clothes, hats, shoes, hoops for the new crinolines that were coming in, packing paper, open trunks and baskets lying everywhere.

She turned at the mirror, looking with joy at the dress she had put on now, not a crinoline this time but a beautiful slim thing in finest muslin with deep embroidery on the blouse and a line of lacing down the front of the skirt. It was in the palest shade of lavender and she would wear it with her muslin belt in a darker shade and a row of pearls. Her arms showed to the shoulders through the short sleeves. Was it too daring for her? It was really meant for a younger girl, but it suited her and she loved it so much she had taken it.

The shutters were half closed against the heat, but even in the filtered half-light the room was warm. Francis had been gone all day. He had left early for Bordeaux on business with Madame Gautier, who wanted to visit an old aunt at Blanquefort on the way. He would pick her up on his way back in the evening.

Since the meeting with his brothers and Monsieur Parenteau he had been rather silent and abstracted, as he always was when he had something on his mind; and she knew instinctively that he was not going to tell her what it was. For all his emotional transparency, his openness, he did conceal some things from her. Men were like that, even Francis, and she was beginning to see he had a certain impermeability to outside influence.

She had asked him tactfully after the meeting if everything was all right and he had said cheerfully, "Oh, yes, yes," smiled, put his arm around her and kissed her and asked her if she had been over the house. In two minutes she thought no more about it than he did.

At the mirror she tried a cameo brooch on the dress, but it wasn't quite right. She considered it from another angle. No, it wouldn't do. "Emilie, give me that white coat on the chair." Perhaps it would be more discreet; it would be lovely with her bonnet with the little roses, and she would carry the dark sunshade. She looked over her shoulder; the girl had left the room again. Curious. The girl had been behaving a little strangely all afternoon and had already disappeared twice without explanation.

Well . . . She crossed the room between the trunks and packing, picked up the coat and returned to the mirror, and as she stood judging the effect she heard the girl come in behind her. A moment later there came a sniffle. She turned around. Emilie, with lowered head, was struggling with tears.

"What on earth's the matter?"

"It's Augustine, ma'am. Cook had to go for Dr. Cavan. The doctor's here now."

"Doctor?" She was startled. "What's the matter with her?"

Sniff-sniff. "She's poorly, ma'am."

"Why didn't you tell me?"

Augustine, the second housemaid, was a girl of nineteen, a pretty thing with dark hair but rather short and very countrified. The cook, Octavie, was Joseph's wife, a plump woman in her mid-thirties. Susannah had seen both of them at work since morning and there had been no mention of illness, certainly not of calling in a doctor. Nor had Madame Gautier warned her of anything before leaving with Francis.

"Where is she?"

"In her room, ma'am. We didn't want to trouble you."

Susannah picked up her skirts and went quickly downstairs with the girl to the back of the house where the servants lived. As they reached the kitchen, a strongly built old man with tousled hair, a ruddy face and salt-and-pepper beard came in from the corridor.

"This is the doctor, ma'am," Emilie said, still sniffing.

"Madame." Dr. Cavan bowed stiffly in an old man's way. He was tall and strong-looking but somehow not quite steady and had the rawness and watery eyes of old age.

"Oh, Dr. Cavan, how do you do? I'm Francis Gautier's wife. What is the matter with the girl? I've only just been told."

"She will have to stay in bed a day or so."

Susannah stared at him, but he rather irritatedly ignored her look.

"Please, I must see her."

He hesitated, then turned back. They went on through the warren of rooms and cubicles which Susannah had inspected with Madame Gautier the day before—pantry, silver room, china closet, storeroom, lamp room, scullery, dairy, dry and wet larders, laundry rooms and the long ugly tiled passage to the servants' bedrooms. It was all dingy, dark, in need of scouring and air and paint. The passages and bedrooms were sordid; and the girl's room when they reached it was tiny, stiflingly hot and smelly. They stood back to let out the cook carrying a bowl of water and an armful of bloody towels. The girl, white and still, looked at them from the bed with frightened eyes.

Susannah bent over her. "Poor child, what's happened to you?"

The girl's mouth trembled and she began to cry, her face contorting itself ridiculously. Susannah stood there feeling rather foolish, then caught the doctor's old red-rimmed eye and followed him out.

In the kitchen she placed a chair for him, but he drew himself up sharply, testily, and declined. The weeping white-faced girl, the towels and the odor of the room had already told her what had happened.

"It was a hemorrhage?"

Dr. Cavan tugged impatiently at his beard and nodded. "She was two months gone with the child." He waved a hand. "She'll be over it in forty-eight hours. Light food, no meat. She should not do heavy work for a day or two. It's just as well, or she'd have had to put the child out to wet-nurse and pay for it out of nothing—or abandon it." He began to fuss and fiddle with the things in his bag to contain his impatience. "There's no help for them," he said. Yet he did not seem unsympathetic to the girl, Susannah thought.

"They didn't want you to tell me, I suppose?" she said.

He gave her a sharp look. "No. Especially not Madame Gautier."

She understood; they had been hoping to keep the thing secret but had become frightened and called in the doctor and he had insisted on someone in the house being informed.

"I see."

"She is lucky Madame Gautier is absent," he said. It was a sort of grudging unspoken invitation, as much as to say he thought the thing deplorable but there was no point in making trouble for the girl if it could be avoided.

After a moment, Susannah said, "Yes, she is."

He nodded, apparently satisfied, and took his leave. When he had gone, Susannah put Emilie and the cook to airing the room and cleaning it and putting fresh linen on the bed. She told the girl not to worry and took in some camomile tea to soothe her. But back in her own room she plumped down in thought on the bed among the unpacked things. Strange it was. She thought of the girl's fear, of the strange secrecy of the servants' lives here. Miss Hattie, her own childhood nurse, even Miss Rosa, would have confided, would have trusted. Miss Rosa knew the deepest secrets of Aunt Maxine's life and Aunt Maxine of hers. The workpeople's reserve with Francis and Madame Gautier, with anybody "above" them, was tinged with something strange to her. She had seen Negroes at home bolder and more open, on closer terms with their masters. But here it was different; here the people were less spontaneous. There was a watchfulness. It wasn't the awe of their "betters" that she had heard of in the English. No pulling the forelock here. No, it was something else—a holding off, a mistrust, the will to stay apart, to belong to another world and not to cross over. The workman wore his blouse or his smock in that spirit to nourish the independence of his soul, his separateness from the bourgeois in his tall hat and redingote. Because they were proudly, impossibly independent people, she saw that. Deeply and desperately they

53

needed to be their own individual selves, to choose their own paths, not to be told by others. This was the old order of Europe. She would miss the great melting together of the United States, a more open life, it seemed to her at that moment.

All the same, she must try to make the relationships in the house a little better. She wondered who the girl had gone with, but she did not know enough about them yet even to guess. She wished Francis were back. She trembled when she thought of how much depended on him.

But then she stood up, impatient with herself, and turned to the trunk by the bed half-filled with things she hadn't seen for a month.

8

The carriage arrived back at eight o'clock and she ran out to meet it. They helped Madame Gautier out and Francis put his arm around Susannah and whispered in her ear, "I've got a present for you."

"Oh, what is it?" Her eyes glowed with pleasure.

"In a minute." He looked happy and squeezed her waist and she thought he must have had a successful day. "What have *you* been doing?"

"Oh, the trunks have come, so I've been parading in front of the mirror all afternoon. The room's in a terrible mess. What have you brought me?" She hung on his arm, looking up at him, impatient and radiant.

In the hall he brought out a small package and watched while she unwrapped it. It was a butterfly pendant in colored enamel on a slim gold chain, a beautiful thing. Holding it in her palm, Susannah exclaimed with joy, "It's just what I need for my dress. Oh, darling, how clever of you." She threw her arms around him and kissed him. She put the pendant on instantly, went to the mirror and studied the effect. It was perfect. She knew it had cost a bit of money, and they had arrived home with hardly any funds, so he must have got some in Bordeaux. She wanted to ask him, but it was difficult to discuss money matters with a man. Perhaps she would wait for another moment, when they were in bed tonight. But the pendant was lovely.

Monsieur Josserand, the price maker, appeared from outside, wanting Francis.

"You must come and see this now," he said. "It can't wait." He was a stumpy, gnarled creature with a pitted dark face and woolly brown hair under his broad-brimmed straw hat, an energetic and touchy man and a good worker in the vines when he wanted to be; but like the other price makers who did the pruning and cared for the vines, he had been allowed to become much too independent and spent more time on his own crops and animals than he did on the vineyard. He supervised the four men who did the plowing and heavy work and bossed it over the other price makers. He and his wife and their two sons lived in a cottage at the back of the house with a little garden, part of his price for the work he did, where they grew a few vegetables. In addition, like his counterparts, Josserand grew wheat on plots of land among the vines and kept a cow and chickens. Every task he and his wife did—pruning, picking up the prunings, carrying them out of the rows, fixing the supports, attaching the vines and so on—was priced down to the last centimeter and the last centime of money, to be bargained and haggled over; and when he had done this work, he was free to do as he wished. All the price makers had the same arrangement—it was customary throughout the wine country—but because of his ascendancy over the rest of them, Josserand was particularly important to the vineyard.

"What is it?" Francis asked.

"I'm not saying till you have seen it."

Susannah watched them turn away, then she ran up to Francis's side, took his hand and went with them. They walked out to the vines and down the paths to the farthest rows where the ground dipped. Josserand stumped on a pace or two ahead, leading the way. At the fourth row from the end he turned in between the vines. The vines were planted at intervals of three feet four inches. Each vine was in a Y shape in the low Médoc style and each of the two arms of the Y were supported, like the stock or stem, by narrow uprights stuck in the ground and tied by osier to long horizontal wooden laths which ran along the top of the uprights for the whole length of the row. The vines thus grew in espalier.

In the middle of the row, Josserand squatted down handling the leaves of a vine. "Look at this."

Faint whitish powdery marks were visible on the leaves

and the young shoots. Some leaves were covered with it, more showing on the top than on the underside.

They moved along to the next vine. Here the powdery marks had turned to gray and small black dots showed on the leaves. Some leaves were faintly brown. Josserand picked one and held it up to the light and they peered at it. On the white patches the green showed through less clearly than on other parts of the leaf.

"What is it?" Francis said.

"I don't know. A sickness. They are calling it the oïdium."

"Oïdium?"

"I hear tell they have seen it in the Languedoc. They have got it at Bourg and Bec d'Ambès."

Francis rubbed his finger on the white powder and smelled it. "Greasy. Smells of mold."

Josserand nodded. They walked along the row, Susannah following. Every vine had the grayish-white powdery marks; some in the rows beyond were also affected, others free. They stood looking out over the vines.

"Is it only just here, this spot?" Francis asked.

"None on the far side yet. But it is spreading. There was one patch there, now it's reached here."

"Oh, I don't think it's anything," Francis said.

"I heard it's a weakness in the soil. The soil is exhausted. Monsieur Guyot, who is a knowledgeable man, says so."

"Well, the buds aren't falling off. I think you'll find it will go."

Josserand looked at him closely, screwing his eyes up. "You won't say I've not shown you." He obviously was not as optimistic as Francis and grumbled to himself in a low voice as they went back toward the house.

Susannah looked anxiously up at Francis. "Is it really serious?"

"I wouldn't think so. Oh, wait a minute, I almost forgot. You are invited to the Préfet's, Madame Gautier, with your husband. A reception. The day after tomorrow."

"At the Préfet's?" She was impressed. The Préfet was the chief official of the department.

"They sent the invitation while we were away. I ran into Philippe Lambert, he's in the Préfet's office, and he said 'Oh, you're back. We got a message to say you weren't expected. Please come, I'll write you out another card.' " He didn't seem at all put out about the message that had been given. "It'll be an occasion. You'll meet everybody there, all the bigwigs."

Abruptly she was in a state over what she was going to wear, her mind selecting this, rejecting that. "Oh, Francis, I simply haven't any gloves. I must get a new pair. The ones I bought in Paris won't do. Will you take me to Bordeaux tomorrow? There are sure to be some there. I simply must go."

So next day Susannah got her first sight of Bordeaux. They were up on the green hills of La Bastide—for they had crossed the river to allow Francis to make a business call at Carbon-Blanc—and she was staring out of the window at the crescent of the river and the city below with the great sweep of honey-colored stone buildings along the waterfront, the belfry, a slim spire reaching up here and there and, in the foreground, the masts and spars of a hundred ships in the river, all with their flags out. A sight!

"I never thought . . . It's lovely!"

Down the steep hillside the chaise dashed, across the long stone bridge, and they were surrounded by the rumble of drays over the cobblestones and the rattle of chains, the cries of tally clerks, draymen, wagoners, deckhands, the hammering of coopers and the heavy cracking, crunching sound of hogsheads of wine being moved. A city of history if ever there was one—yes, and a city of wine.

Wine! The whole place smelled of it. You couldn't get away from it. The mingling smell of sawdust and horse dung only made the smell of wine stronger. All around, driving in, they had rolled past vineyard after vineyard. And now in the streets, along the waterfront, in the dingy offices, in the ware-houses, in the excise and city toll sheds, the cellars and the tav-erns, everybody seemed to be talking wine, buying wine, drink-ing it, arguing over it. Everywhere you turned you saw more barrels, more bottles, more walls painted over with signs for So-and-so's cellars—Vins du Premier Choix! Médoc! Sauternes! Graves! Pomerol! Red winy faces glowed. Stoop-backed brokers rinsed their mouths with Cerons or Côtes de Bourg, spat out and named a price. Noses trained to the finesse of bloodhounds' dipped into glasses and came up with a château name, a vintage. Tasters passed their tongues around their palates and picked out a wine from the north and one from the south of the same hillside. Men who had served six years' apprenticeship to become coopers fashioned barrels with the care of artists. Goblets of Sauternes gleamed like liquid gold in the dim recesses of lawyers' offices where a will was being read, a marriage contract haggled over, a sale being sealed, since life and death themselves were bound up with wine and mothers here gave a restless infant a crust of bread dipped in wine to quiet it. Nor did any duke possess a finer cellar than those of the Bordeaux municipal brothels, for hadn't the great Dr. Dupin-Lamotte's guide, under the heading of "health establishments," awarded them three stars and a note, "Worth a detour"?

Susannah loved it all. Long after she had bought her gloves, she led Francis from shop to shop, just for the fun, talking away in high spirits, wanting to see everything. In the streets she kept stopping at the gingerbread stalls or watching the jugglers and the acrobats; and she couldn't refuse any of them a coin, with the result that ragged boys gathered around staring at her and Francis had to drag her away.

Since they had come by chaise, Susannah wanted to go back by steamer.

"Too late to get one all the way," Francis said.

"Well let's try partway."

This entailed a long dusty walk back along the quayside. At the ticket office Francis found they could get a steamer to Macau in an hour's time; they would have to hire a chaise on from there. They stood in the din and dust, tired now and rather aimless, then Susannah said, "Let's wait over there," and pointed across to the café on the quayside opposite.

"All right," said Francis, ready for anything now.

Inside, the café was bustling, steamy and noisy, full of men who seemed to have nothing else to do but sit drinking and talking at the top of their voices.

"What did you say the time was?" she said, glad to sit down. She was tired of walking but happy.

"Ten minutes to three, if you please, and we've had no lunch. I'm starving. If you hadn't wanted to traipse all over town we could have been on the way now." He wasn't at all bad-tempered really and had enjoyed their excursion as much as she had, had loved her pleasure in it, had walked beside her with huge pride, looking at her, swelling when she took his arm, noticing how people looked at her, the women as well as the men, just as the men at the other tables kept looking at her now.

She was tucking her hair into her bonnet, wishing she could ease her feet in her lace-up boots. "Then order something. We've got time. Look, there's the waiter now. I don't want anything to eat, but I want some wine."

"Yes, monsieur?" The waiter bowed, his eye on Susannah.

Francis ordered a mutton chop and vegetables for himself.

"I want some of that white wine," she said, "the one we saw that fat man drinking in the wine merchant's. It looked so good."

"Sauternes?"

"Yes, Sauternes."

"A nice Sauternes, monsieur?" the waiter said.

Francis consulted the list and chose one and when the waiter had gone he said, "What a way to talk for a winegrower's wife! Do you think you go by what wine looks like, madame?"

"Well, that fat man seemed to know. He had a face like a bunch of grapes!" She laughed.

"If you want your face to get like that, you'll start tippling."

"Don't worry, I'm going to start immediately."

The waiter came with the wine, a dusty bottle full of golden promise. Susannah watched him draw the cork with care, pull it halfway, then flip down a lever on his corkscrew and ease it out by leverage the rest of the way, a long cork nearly as long as her forefinger. The waiter sniffed it quickly in a funny way, with a little quick gesture, and poured the wine for Francis's approval. Francis tasted it, nodded, and the man half filled Susannah's glass. She lifted the glass. The soft, delicate, rather sweet taste was delightful. She took another swallow.

"Look out—that's wine! You've had nothing to eat."

"It's lovely. What is it?"

"You wanted Sauternes. It's an 1846." He turned the bottle toward her and sat back playing the expert a bit. "A good year, better for whites than reds. They had a lot of hail and drought that year and some of the wines are a bit hard, but generally they're excellent."

She pealed with laughter at his unusual pomposity, then to mollify him said, "Whereabouts is it, Sauternes?"

"Sauternes? About twenty miles south of here, where the great whites come from."

"Well, can't we grow some of this?"

He grinned affectionately. "No. Médoc, where we are, is red. Sauternes and most of the Graves are whites."

"You mean we've got black grapes?"

"Doesn't make any difference. You can get white wine from black grapes—you only have to take the skin off. Champagne's made from black grapes, for instance, but we're a red district."

"A clever one, aren't you?"

"Look here—"

"Well, *I* think it's delicious," she said and took another drink.

"I can see what's going to become of you. You're going to take to drink."

"I'll go to ruin my own way, sir."

By the time Francis had eaten his lunch she wanted to giggle. Her fatigue had lifted, she felt carefree, on tiptoe. She loved Bordeaux, she loved Francis, the steamy café and the red-faced noisy men. She loved everybody. Finally he said, "Do you realize you haven't stopped talking for fifteen minutes? The trouble with you, my girl, is you're tipsy."

"I know it," she said happily. "I love it."

He burst out laughing, looking at her with bright loving amusement, and took her hand, thinking how exciting the slight flush in her cheeks made her look with that fair coloring, bringing out the depth of her beautiful skin, making her eyes liquid and shiny. He wanted to make love to her now, at once. He imagined her yielding, and he leaned over and kissed her ear and whispered, "You're so pretty, my love."

"You're tipsy too."

He jolted upright. "Wait a minute! Do you hear that? That's the steamer hooting. Come on, we've got to run." They scrambled up.

"Oh, my gloves!" She turned back for the package.

"And let me tell you, you've got to walk out on a gang-plank to get on board!"

61

9

The great salons at the Prefecture made a fine sight with the chandeliers ablaze on the gilded paneling, the necks and shoulders of the women shining in the tall mirrors, the glint of jewelry and bright uniforms here and there among the men. The reception was in full swing.

"My dear, this is young Gautier's new wife, our new neighbor," Coote Onslow said as he approached. "She's from Philadelphia, and as you see, she is charming."

"How do you do?" Sarah Onslow smiled. "Coote told me about you. Are you settled yet?"

"Don't let my wife—"

"I'm just beginning," Susannah said.

"—don't let my wife lead you astray on household affairs," Onslow insisted, leaning forward. "Keeps the most expensive table in the county." He gave a sort of polite laugh, lifting his chin, and his wife tapped him with her fan in mock reproof. She was a blond fair-skinned woman of thirty-five or so, still pretty. Her face, broad under the eyes, tapered to a small chin, like some quick animal's. Her fixed smile was amiable, kind, well-meaning, but her quick eyes said something else.

"You must come and see us," she said.

"We should love to."

More smiles and bows as they passed on. Susannah exchanged a glance with Francis, and he bent toward her. "You're the best-looking woman here." She winked at him.

They moved among the guests. The handsome old rooms were crowded, yet the trained eye could discern the fine gradations of the social hierarchy. The groups of wine merchants, known as chartrons, were distinguishable by something indefinably grandiose that was missing with the mere merchants in grains and colonial products, who were much below them on the social scale. If there was a distinctiveness among the chartrons, it was in their genial Irish faces, which lacked a little of the general solemnity, Susannah thought. The old aristocracy, Orléanist to a man, were noticeable by their dry reserve. And the rest, who belonged to none of these groups—the shipping men, the landed proprietors big and small, the doctors and lawyers—had a touch of respectful deference which marked them out as those with the farthest yet to climb.

Yet they all really looked and thought much the same, since the cast of their minds was much the same. Save for the aristocracy, which did not count, they were all members of the middle class, the great bourgeoisie. And they all felt quite obviously that after the struggle up from the primeval slime, history and human development, mankind itself, had reached its apogee in the triumph of their kind. It was the perfect blossoming of human existence.

All the women, save for a few aged dames, wore crinolines, so distances were kept as they maneuvered like ships of the line. The men were in redingotes of heavy black cloth, white pleated shirts, white gloves and high collars wound with white cravats. And across every male waistcoat hung the heavy gold watch chain, the mark of consequence. It all looked rich, solid and heavy. Everybody was a person of substance, you could see that. Everybody knew the value of money, it would be ludicrous to doubt it. Money, the religion of property, the consciousness of their *moral* superiority were in their flesh, in their souls. When they wanted to praise a man they said he was a model of vigilant circumspection. They said he kept his accounts with order and regularity.

They were clever, shrewd, disabused, opportunist, intelligent, reactionary, enormously wary. Above all wary. They had hard heads and tight fists. They had been clever enough not only to keep their property during the Revolution of 1848 but to keep control of the city in their hands. In the full tide of revolution

—only four years ago, after all!—they had continued to run their City Council, their banks and their counting houses and sit in the Chamber of Commerce, their stronghold, where the real power lay. They had been frightened; but they had known how to conceal their fright. They had handled the red emissary from Paris brilliantly and made him quite ineffective. And when the Revolution was over, they had carried on as if such an episode were a mere ripple against the eternal verities. For nowhere had men resisted change so strongly as these.

The reigning families were the wine merchants, the chartrons, known as such from the district to the north of the city, once the site of a Chartreux monastery, where they lived in dynastic splendor. The elegant crescent of the Pavé des Chartrons was the smartest street in Bordeaux. The chartrons were Protestants and mainly foreigners—Irish, Germans, English, Danes, Dutchmen. The French among them were also Protestants, families who had crossed from the Cévennes district to be among others of their minority; and with these, in the Quartier des Chartrons, lived the rich Portuguese and Spanish Jews. So the money and the commercial power of Bordeaux were largely in the hands of foreigners, or men who were French for business purposes, and of all these the kings were the Irish.

Susannah was thrilled and happy, because it was her first big social occasion in France. As they walked about and stopped to talk to guests Francis knew, she studied the women's clothes and found them elegant. She studied the men and found them interesting. The women were watchful, obviously competent; they knew their roles to perfection, they would defend their caste ferociously. But they were mere foils to the men. It was a male-dominated society.

With her blond coloring, Susannah stood out strikingly among all the brunettes present. Matrons, having asked who she was and been told, said, "An American? With money? I didn't think young Gautier had the brains."

Abel-Cherubin and his wife were seen to bow rather distantly, the Chabots yet more distantly, and people said, "Hm, that doesn't seem to fit."

"I heard it was a surprise. None of them knew of it till he'd married her."

"Young Gautier, my dear, will never manage."

"I'm told she's an orphan."

"Well, she's pretty, you can't deny it."

Susannah had caught sight of Lady Canning with a big brown-skinned man leaning on an ebony cane. "Who's that with Lady Canning?"

Francis followed her look. "Oh, that's Byam, her husband. Haven't you met him yet? Sir Byam Canning, baronet. Father was English, mother a colored Creole." She looked with interest at Canning, who was now greeting another guest. "The fellow speaking to them now is Jacques de Mornac, the Count de Mornac."

Susannah had noticed Mornac looking at her earlier rather obviously, and she studied him now—a tall man about forty with powerful shoulders and a small head, dashingly good-looking and arrogant with his clipped black upturned mustache and a rapierlike face. He was speaking with vehemence to Canning, and she caught a touch of coarseness about him.

"I'll introduce you in a minute," Francis said, obviously a bit reluctant. "Oh, Tom, how are you?" It was a tall well-built man of about thirty-five, unmistakably English. "Susannah, this is Tom Mowbray, another of our English friends. My wife."

"Madame." Mowbray bent over and kissed her hand. He had a trim dark beard, gray eyes, an intelligent, handsome, slightly malicious face.

"Tom's a great sportsman," Francis said. "He can tell you all about dogs and birds and rabbits and so on."

"I sold him Lad, your setter, in fact," Mowbray said. "Dog's ruined now, alas."

They stood talking, and Susannah explained that she had only just arrived and knew very few people so far. Presently she saw that Francis had drifted away and was busily engaged in conversation with a group of men guests.

"So, dear lady, you are making your first acquaintance with Bordeaux," Mowbray said in his English way. "Well, here before you, you see the finest efflorescence of the merchant class, the aristocracy of money. A splendid sight, eh? All penetrated with their own social importance. All happy in the certainty that only the bourgeoisie have brains. Sooner offend the Bishop than cross the President of the Chamber of Commerce— that would mean real damnation."

She glanced at him with surprised amusement; but there was not the faintest smile on his lips.

"See the three distinguished gentlemen on our right—Mr. John Laffan Jennings, the tall one, Mr. Michael Scully with the red hair, and Mr. Abraham Curran—all Irish and all monarchs of the wine trade. And they all intermarry. Jennings daughter marries Scully son, Curran daughter marries Jennings son, and so on. Mr. John Laffan Jennings, they will tell you, owns eight cellars each holding four hundred casks, plus twelve other *vaulted* cellars each containing a hundred and twenty-five casks, and two *further* cellars each holding three hundred and fifty casks, a total of fifty-four hundred casks or twenty-one thousand six hundred barrels. Three of his cellars are devoted to bottles, the number of which amounts at times to *seven hundred thousand*." He made a solemn face and she laughed.

"We have some fine old French families in Bordeaux, as you can tell by the names," he went on. "We have the Johnstons, the Bethmanns, the Lawtons, the Eschenauers, the Baours, the Browns; and among the newly distinguished ones the Brandenburgs, the Bartons, the Schroders, the Schillers, the Gadens and the Klipschs. The portly pair over there are two more—Mr. Ignaz Hagenbach, known as Baron Hagenbach, and Mr. Gustave Boehmer. Never was a community more gracefully endowed, wouldn't you say?"

"They'd be all right, I take it, if they rode to hounds?" she said with a smile.

"What?" He shot her a quick startled look, gave a little laugh and changed the subject. He lowered his voice and said, "Bald gentleman on the far side with waxed mustache. Secret police. Name of Aynard."

Later on Francis got into an argument with two merchants named Bernsdorf and O'Kane.

"I tell you, I heard the same complaint pretty well everywhere, from New York to New Orleans. They'd bring out a bottle labeled Margaux or Lafite and they'd say, 'Taste that,' and it'd be the poorest stuff you can imagine. It's a mistake to do these things."

Testily O'Kane said, "These Americans are all the same. They want Bordeaux wines but they won't pay the price."

"And they insist on having them sent over with high-flown names like Margaux and so on," Bernsdorf put in.

"But it's damaging the trade. We're going to lose the market if it goes on," said Francis.

"Come, come, sir! They're not going to deprive themselves of the finest wines in the world."

"But they're not *getting* the finest, that's the point. One day they're just going to slap the same tax on everything labeled Margaux as if it were real Margaux, then we'll be caught."

"Nonsense. It's an old established custom to send ordinary Bordeaux to America labeled Margaux or Saint Julien."

"Well, they're pretty independent people in California—"
Their laughter stopped him.

Susannah, who had heard none of this, was speaking to Lady Canning about the difficulty of changing banknotes in Bordeaux, where shops would only take gold.

"Yes." Lady Canning nodded and extended her hand to a man who had come up. He bowed and touched her hand with his lips. "Do you know John Blood?" she said to Susannah. "Madame Francis Gautier."

He had a lean blue-chinned face, black hair and dark eyes with little creases in the eyelids. A touch of the highwayman, she thought. Mowbray had pointed him out to her earlier, calling him an "Irish rakehell but a gentleman," an estimate which other guests did not seem entirely to share, for Susannah had noticed the discreet turning of backs that marked his passage through the room. He looked a man of sardonic temperament, as if it amused him to scandalize them and observe the horrified looks of the bourgeois. But from what Mowbray had said, there was little they could do to keep him out, for he had powerful friends in Paris, including Morny, ex-Minister of the Interior, who had arranged Louis-Napoleon's coup d'état.

"How do you do?"

"Madame Gautier is American," Lady Canning said. "From Boston."

"Philadelphia," Susannah corrected.

"I have only a slight acquaintance with your husband, madame, but I am persuaded all at once he has devilish uncommon qualities," Blood said.

Susannah smiled, hoping she wasn't going to blush.

"Tell me about California," Blood said. "That's the place

to make for, eh? Not Bordeaux."

"Perhaps not for a woman, sir," she said, standing up straight.

"Ah? Yet I can't see a woman of spirit aspiring to . . . what you see around you."

"You'd have these gentlemen firing pistols into the ceiling then?" she asked with a smile.

"Damn it, I would!" He laughed appreciatively and looked at her with new pleasure.

All at once the voices in Francis's group got rather loud. As Susannah turned to her husband, she heard Bernsdorf say angrily, "You can leave the defense of the Bordeaux wine trade to us, sir!" She thought Francis looked a little flushed as he disengaged from the group and joined her.

"What was *that* all about?" she asked quietly.

"Oh, nothing. Just arguing about the wine trade." He smiled and squeezed her arm.

"Francis!" a voice exclaimed from behind them.

They turned, and Susannah saw the look of pleasure on his face. The woman was small and dark with an olive skin and brilliant dark eyes. Francis introduced her as Madame de Monteiro. She obviously knew she had to mute her effects or she would be too sumptuous. Her dress was plain and her only jewelry was a diamond necklace. And as they sat together by the window, Susannah felt little stabs of jealousy.

Madame de Monteiro carefully tried to keep the conversation among the three of them, but her attention was emphatically on Francis. Her dark brilliant eyes kept darting quickly to Susannah as if to say, What do you think of me? Don't you see how your husband laughs? You can't match this clever talk.

They had obviously been close in the past, though Francis had never spoken of her. Once or twice Madame de Monteiro made amused little compressions of her mouth as if she were suppressing a desire to smile. They made an attractive sarcastic little fold at the corner of her lips. She had a knowingness about her. Francis responded to her in his frank eager way, and Susannah could sense the other, secret current of communication that ran between them. She felt that Madame de Monteiro stimulated and amused him. The talk between the two of them was going quickly back and forth now and by contrast she felt

68

slow and dull. Was she too dull for him? Wouldn't he have been better off with a woman who kept him up to things like this one?

"Damned good-looking woman," Blood said to Mowbray on the other side of the room.

"Who's that?"

"La Monteiro."

"Oh . . . Hm . . . I hear she's being kept by Regis Gautier now."

"That puppy."

"And speculating in property."

"Yes, she'll do well at it," Blood said. "She's got her . . . connections. Manages her fat husband like a servant. She's a clever little creature."

"The devil, too."

"What do you want, a parson's wife?"

"Never found a woman I'd give an hour's company of Nellie my setter bitch for," Mowbray said.

Blood laughed. "All the same, she'd give a man a fast ride, La Monteiro."

Susannah saw John Lovell approaching. She had noticed him earlier and he had bowed.

"Oh, Mr. Lovell, how are you?" Susannah said. Madame de Monteiro had just left them, they had risen and, seeing Lovell, she couldn't help speaking to him. It was to counterbalance Madame de Monteiro. It was jealousy, if you like, and childish, but she couldn't hold back. She smiled at Lovell. She wanted to talk at all costs; she wanted to get rid of the effect of the other woman.

"Did you conclude your business at Pauillac satisfactorily the other day?"

"At . . . ? Oh, that. Yes, thank you. I was simply seeing someone. It wasn't of any great consequence."

"I thought you might be staying there."

"At Pauillac? No. I have my business here in Bordeaux, at least for the time being."

Her eyes were shining, the color had risen in her face, the outline of her lips was perfect. He thought she was a lovely creature—that pure, quiet beauty, a sort of aura of purity and youth. The day at her house, seeing her arrive on Francis's arm, he had had a shock and had felt it again as soon as he had seen her tonight; and he had watched her across the crowded room, the line of her neck and shoulders, her cheek, the movement of her eyes.

"I'm still a newcomer," he said. "I've only arrived lately."

"I hope you may decide to stay, sir."

"I believe you have only recently arrived yourself, madame?"

"Yes. I hardly know anything about Bordeaux yet. I trust we may have the pleasure of your calling on us."

"Thank you, I should like to."

The guests were crowding into two rooms where the buffet had been set out. She felt Francis touch her arm and took her leave of Lovell. They moved into the other room and stood at a corner of one of the long tables. He whispered gently to her, "You shouldn't have spoken to Mr. Lovell like that."

"What?" She stared at him.

"You can't address a man first."

She wanted to say, What about Madame de Monteiro just now? But she checked herself. Didn't it give Madame de Monteiro a special status that she *could* speak to a man first? Then she was not a respectable woman? "It was perfectly natural, I—"

"Never mind," he said. "Don't talk of it now." And in the next breath: "You're a success. They like you. Mustn't spoil it." He smiled at her and she thought, of course it was important in this provincial town that *they* should like her; but something made her say, for a joke, "Perhaps they're sorry for me?"

He started as if he had been stung and for a second, before he saw she was joking, his face became blank, horribly and frighteningly blank. Then his shoulders relaxed and he smiled again and said, "Oh!"

Quickly she put her hand on his arm, ashamed of herself. Yet the utter blankness of that look continued to haunt her. She told herself he hadn't meant to reproach her. And she was being ridiculous. Of course he had had love affairs in the past! But with that sort of woman?

She hung on his arm, wanted to reassure him of her love, to make up to him for her silent silly thoughts. Another couple they already knew were at the buffet in the same corner,

70

Georges Gaveau, a school friend of Francis's, now a Bordeaux shipping agent, and his wife, whom they had run into in Paris. Susannah wanted to talk, to show Francis she was happy.

"But I haven't been anywhere yet," she said to Jenny Gaveau. "Francis is going to take me around. I want to see the dunes and the forest. And we're going to the theater next week, aren't we?"

"If you'd like to," he said, and she saw that all trace of the frightening shadow had gone. She chattered away. Francis thought he had never seen her so spirited and lovely. All the men's eyes were on her, you couldn't help noticing. He caught sight of Abel-Cherubin along the table, and for an instant the thought of the marriage settlement went through his mind and the demand that she renounce her rights. But he dismissed it.

It was quite late when she said, "We ought to go. It's a long drive."

"Yes."

They took their leave and went out into the warm spring night to find Joseph with the carriage. As they rode back home, the little difference was forgotten. They were happy. She nestled in his arms and felt at peace.

A lamp left alight downstairs threw its yellow radiance on the drive of the house. Everything was still. The open night lay around them. The rim of the new moon was reflected in the little reed-fringed lake. The trees stood massive and unstirring in the night air.

Francis for some reason was hungry and went through to the kitchen to find something to eat before he came to bed, but Susannah went straight upstairs and undressed.

It had been a great success, she thought happily. She had looked her best and she had been a credit to Francis, which was the important thing. She had met a lot of new people, among whom she must make friends, so that even though they lived out here in the country, they would have a regular social life. She had a great part to play in helping Francis in this way. And now, in the intimacy of this room, the image of Madame de Monteiro faded, seemed to become unreal. The room was too closely theirs for Madame de Monteiro to enter it for an instant.

She sat brushing her hair. She thought of John Lovell, then

71

of Sarah Onslow and her strange, rather feline face and the touch of anxiety with which Coote Onslow had watched his wife. Now *there*—

A sound at the door. She had told Emilie to go to bed, that she would do her hair herself. "Yes? Come in."

She turned. It was Madame Gautier, almost spectral in her strangeness. Susannah got a fearful shock and almost cried out. Madame Gautier carried a lamp and was wearing a gray peignoir, her hair half loose, a detail which had some foolish power to frighten Susannah, as if it were a sign of madness or the unknown.

"Oh, Mother," she said with an effort. "Is something the matter?"

Madame Gautier's face was like stone. The robe made her bulky, her neck hung thick and veined and the touch of red in her hair was coppery now.

"Is everything . . . I hope we didn't wake you up."

Silently Madame Gautier put the lamp down. "Why did you conceal the truth from me about Augustine?"

Susannah felt a sickening compression of her heart and stood up facing her mother-in-law. "The girl was ill. I . . . I didn't want to trouble you."

"You called the doctor. You conspired with the other servants not to inform me."

"Oh, but I didn't, Mother. It was nothing like that. I . . . I . . ." She was in confusion, not knowing how Madame Gautier had found out. Possibly Emilie and the girl herself had said she had called the doctor, implying that she had known about it earlier than she had. "I hardly know the servants," she said. "How could I conspire with them?"

"Yet you agreed with them to conceal it?"

"Hardly agreed—"

"You fetched the doctor behind my back, when I was out of the house."

"But I did *not* fetch him. He was already here."

"Don't lie."

"Mother, I—"

"Don't lie! Why did you conceal it?"

"The girl was upset. I didn't want to upset her any more."

"You have been in my house five days. You are trying to undermine my authority already."

"Of course not."

"I will not have secrets in my own house! And it is my house! Do you understand?" The mouth with its bluish lips opened in protest, outrage. The voice that had always been so toneless and defeated was vibrant now, and in the frayed gray drabness of the robe she seemed full of some old dark reproach, something that had once been aching and yearning but long since turned to vinegar in her soul.

Susannah was twisting her fingers in dismay. Quietly she said, "Yes, Mother."

"Who is the man, since you are so intimate with my servants?"

"How could I know?"

The mother made a scornful sound. "The girl will go tomorrow."

Susannah lifted her head to speak but checked herself. Madame Gautier picked up the lamp. "Keep your place! . . . If you have a place here."

Susannah, gazing at the floor, heard her go. She turned away, her thoughts in confusion, her pulse hammering, her cheeks hot with humiliation. Why had such a thing to happen? She pressed her hands to her burning face. Why, why had it to happen? She was full of dismay and uncertainty. Everything seemed suddenly to tremble in her new uncertainty. She felt separate and alone, everything was insecure. And she couldn't let them turn that girl out. She could not. She didn't know what she would do, but she couldn't let them do that. She was in such confusion she did not know what to do.

She thought she heard Francis in the hall below, and as quickly as she could she dimmed the lamp, climbed into bed and lay there with eyes shut trying to stop herself trembling, to stop her thoughts.

"Did you call down a little while ago?" he asked, still munching, when he came in ten minutes later.

She didn't answer, pretending to be asleep.

10

In the morning Susannah dressed nervously and went to the mirror to do her hair. Francis had been up and out early, and though she had been awake she had let him go. She had awakened first, with her mind instantly full of last night's scene, as if she had been dreaming it. For a moment she did think it was a dream she had struggled out of. Then she knew it wasn't and she was upset, nervous, horribly depressed. She longed to tell Francis, to explain and ask him to smooth it out, but he was sleeping. And then when he woke he got quickly out of bed and dressed and she said nothing. The moment was not right. It made her think that she was already a little older in her marriage because, before, any moment had been the right one.

When she heard him outside, his steps crunching away on the gravel of the drive, she got out of bed and began dressing without pushing the shutters open. She dreaded the encounter with Madame Gautier. They would both be moving about the house together. And what could she do about the girl? She didn't know.

She buttoned her bodice, smoothed her collar and pushed the shutters open to let the sun stream in. When she had finished her hair she went downstairs. James, breakfasting alone, looked up from a newspaper and she bent to give him the good-morning kiss on his cheek and offer her own cheek for his. There was a great deal of this family good-night, good-morning, good-bye and hello kissing. They couldn't separate for a few hours without it and she had already learned to adopt it, meaningless as it was.

James put a piece of bread in his mouth and said, munching, "I was speaking to a fellow yesterday who said the rich don't much care about owning land in the United States." He was always talking to her about America in a rather condescending way, asking questions but managing to talk down to her.

"Well, I don't know about that," she said. "There's not a land-owning class as you have in France and England, if that's what you mean." And then as soon as she had spoken she wondered if he was getting at something else.

"Not even the important people, they don't care for it?"

"The important people? We don't have the same ideas about the importance of people. Society isn't the same."

"Oh, but this fellow was saying there are the 'best sets' in New York and Boston and Newport and so on. Very swell and snobbish."

"Yes, there are. You do have them on the Atlantic coast, but . . . well, they're more the European idea. You don't get them in the West, and that's the American idea.",

"Ha!" he said. It was always condescending, his talk.

Emilie brought her coffee and she ate breakfast hoping Madame Gautier wouldn't appear. James read his paper, a theater journal, for a few moments, then sat watching her critically, watching her table manners, of which, it seemed, he never tired, and because they differed from his own he found odd, even a little comic. And she . . . she didn't like the great bowls in which they drank their morning coffee and had Emilie give her hers a quarter full.

Then James began talking of going to Paris. She listened, half her mind on the servant girl and what she was going to do. But at last she couldn't hold back any more, she had to brace herself and go about her tasks in the household. She got up and went through to the kitchen with trembling heart.

Octavie, the cook, was feeding stale crusts to her tame crow, which was lolloping about on the windowsill, sawing its head up and down. The cook talked to the bird as if it were human, and when she laughed in a certain artificial way the crow lifted its beak in the air and made a grotesque laughing sound too. The cook pealed with delight. It cheered Susannah up. Yes, said Octavie, the girl was still in her room, rather poorly but better on the whole.

Susannah had decided she was going to ask Madame Josserand to put the girl up until she was well, and by that time she would have thought out the next step. She went in to Augustine, who was in bed, and told her not to worry. "I'll make arrangements for you."

Ten minutes later Madame Gautier came into the kitchen.

"Oh, good morning, Mother," Susannah said, nervously wiping her hands on her apron and going over for the good-morning kiss. Madame Gautier made a little movement with her head, indicating she did not want it. Susannah halted, abashed, and turned away. Nothing more was said.

For the next hour Susannah was busy in and out of the kitchen. Madame Gautier came and went and Susannah felt her watching, listening to what she said to the servants. Her uncertainty returned. Tension and stress were in the air like electricity; she felt something was going to explode. She finished what she was doing, then went quietly out through the hall into the open. She was oppressed and wretched and helpless.

The dog Lad came running up and licked her hand. Then she saw Francis coming toward her. She felt such relief! She ran up to him and put her arms around him. "Darling." He was so fresh and open-looking and she loved him so much. She said, "I . . . I want to talk to you."

"Eh?" He gave her a quick little sidelong look.

"I must talk to you."

Arms around each other, they strolled slowly down the drive toward the vatting room and the other buildings, the dog frisking around them. Susannah told him all that had happened, carefully explained the whole thing. He listened, eyes on the ground, simply nodding occasionally. They halted in the open space in front of the outbuildings. As she talked, explained how unhappy she was, he was reaching out and snatching playfully at the dog, amusing it. The dog darted in, bounded away again as soon as he grabbed for it, then dashed back, jumped up and bounded away again. All at once it stopped, sat down and started giving little shakes of its head.

"You must talk to her, Frank, and tell her I did *not* know about the doctor, that of course I wasn't intriguing with the servants against her. I don't know what to do, I—"

He had bent down and turned the dog's ear inside out. He studied it. "Do you know, I think he's got a canker in his ear," he said.

76

She stared down at him. He had hardly been listening. Was the dog more important? The *dog?* No. It wasn't that. She saw it wasn't that. She saw that he had used the dog as a pretext not to face the problem. He didn't want to see it. Conflict between her and his mother was an unpleasant fact; he would not face it.

He was squatting down, intently studying the dog's ears. She wanted to plead with him but suddenly, blackly, saw it would be no good. Under her breath she said, "It's all right. It doesn't matter. I don't want to bother you," and turned away. She half expected him to call out, come after her, but he didn't. He went on, with bent head, examining the dog. Still she couldn't believe it and every step she took she expected to hear him coming up behind, overtaking her. But no, he didn't.

Susannah walked back along the front of the house, but instead of going inside she crossed to the little garden opposite the entrance and, following the path among the trees, reached the bench by the waterside. She felt sundered from him. It was her first revelation of failure in him. She had appealed to him and he had turned away. She felt terribly oppressed and alone, alone, alone. It was their first separation. A true severance. He was suddenly a stranger.

Everything seemed to weigh on her, the family, the remoteness from anyone she knew, the house with its shabbiness, dirt, its great size, the oppressed lives of the servants. There was something stifling about it. And she realized that if anything worse happened it would be the same thing. She would be alone, she would have to face it on her own. She saw this as a revelation. And yet women here had no position, so if she were alone she would be nowhere. If her husband did not support her, stand up for her and take her side, she would be nothing. She would be lost.

A woman alone counted for nothing. She had seen enough, had sensed enough to understand that women here were utterly subordinate to the men. Inside marriage or out of it they were dependent on the men. The woman could do nothing without the man, did not have half the freedom here she had in the United States. Francis had even chided her for speaking to Mr. Lovell first at the Préfet's. The men simply would not make much of a woman, they refused to. Unless she were disreputable. *Then* there was a special knowing, smirking ceremoniousness about it. But otherwise women were below them. The man thought of himself as superior to the woman in all serious things, and if by chance he discussed such things with her, he condescended. Look how James spoke to her! An American would consider her opinion as good as his.

And she felt instinctively that the whole balance of married life was different here. In America the woman held a position, here she must always defer to the husband. The husband simply took it for granted that his pleasure and convenience prevailed. His wife trailed after him, she was his consort, she lived in his shadow. And he expected her to do things that no American husband would suffer his wife to do.

How did Susannah know these things? She had been in Europe so short a time. But she had taken in hints here and there, had watched without knowing it, and she sensed them in her woman's way.

Oh, she saw that the women here would get their way sometimes by cajolery, flattery, taking advantage of the man. But to build marriage on the basis of cunning? On reserve? Inner silence? Dissimulation? To keep one's own counsel and watch for a chance to circumvent the other's wishes secretly? She hated the idea. Hated it. It would destroy something intimate between them. There would be no deep sincerity. Calculation with someone you loved? It was horrible. Perhaps she would come to it in the end, but if she did she would be someone different then, utterly changed. As it was, perhaps she was naïve. Some people would say it was weakness to be too open and straightforward. If "cleverness" was managing other people, manipulating them, well, then, she would be foolish. Marriage for her was giving everything of herself openly and completely, and she had thought Francis held back nothing from her. But now she knew that had been an illusion. He did hold back, out of weakness. There was a secret self in him she had not touched.

So she was wretched. She despised Francis's weakness. She was terribly disappointed in him. That was almost the worst, the disappointment. It meant she must confront things alone, she must rely on herself.

She sat there quite still, a neat pretty figure on the bench, her face still flushed with emotion. The shadow of the trees stretched out over the still water. Insects hummed in the air.

And then she came around. Her natural resilience returned. She loved Francis and he loved her, she was secure in his love, *that* she was sure of. She was making too much of a passing difficulty. Families here were more closed, more self-protective than at home. It was an older order of society, and she would simply have to be patient until they got used to her and she to them. All the same, she was wounded and knew she was alone and must fight for herself. It went deep into her heart that Francis had abandoned her. She was trying to arm herself.

She rose and went back into the house. Emilie avoided her eye.

"What's the matter?" Susannah asked her.

"Nothing, ma'am."

There obviously was. "What is it? Is . . . is Augustine all right?"

"She's gone, ma'am," the girl said.

"Gone?"

"Madame Gautier gave orders. She's to send for her box later."

So she had been sent away, packed off! Anger and shame rose up in Susannah. "Where has she gone, do you know?"

Emilie hesitated, looking at the floor as though afraid to say, then said quietly, "She'll be with old Madame Bechu a bit. I don't know after."

"Where's that?"

"On the road to the village."

Susannah went through to the girl's room. Anger seemed to fill her body; she became short of breath for a moment, she was so angry. She felt herself stifling. The door of the room was open. The girl's box had been dragged out from under the bed and stood, still open with its few poor things in it, in the middle of the room. Susannah stared at it, angry and ashamed. Then she went back and told Emilie to get Joseph or one of the men to hitch the horse to the yellow gig and put Augustine's box in it. Emilie looked rather scared but obeyed.

Susannah hurried upstairs to her room. She was ashamed she had not been more effective, that she had not stood up for the girl. And she saw that if she accepted this, it would set a pattern. Perhaps that was what Madame Gautier wanted, to force her into the same defeats and humiliations she had gone through herself. Wanted that without knowing she wanted it. Why shouldn't the intruder suffer as she had?

Susannah shuddered within herself. She did not want an

open quarrel with the mother. But she must be herself. And she would see to the girl.

She changed into a plain brown dress and put her bonnet on. At the door she turned back. Money. She had a few gold louis left; she put them into her purse and went down.

Madame Gautier was in the entrance hall. "Why have you sent for Joseph?"

"I have an errand to do," Susannah said.

"Joseph takes his orders from me or my son. I can't have him obeying whims."

Susannah faced her squarely, lifting her head, feeling nervous but determined not to give way. "I don't want to quarrel, Mother, but you shan't stop me. I am taking the girl's box to her."

"The box remains here!"

Susannah walked past her, her pulse hammering. The drive was empty—no horse and gig. She felt a great plunge of despair, then at the corner of the house she saw Joseph standing about unhappily. She hurried to him. The yellow gig was there ready, out of sight, with the box in it, but he had not dared to bring it around.

Joseph made a movement as if to stop her, but Susannah quickly jumped in. "Madame, it's not—"

"Never mind, Joseph, don't you come. It'll only get you into trouble." She took the reins. "Tell me how to get to Madame Bechu's."

He told her, looking miserable, and she started the horse just as Madame Gautier appeared. Horse and gig were past her in a flash. Susannah's heart leapt with joy, the earlier wretchedness thrown off, but she was trembling. And poor old Joseph would catch it. She didn't think about Francis.

The horse was awkward, did not like the gig, and she had all she could do to keep him from veering to the left and running them into the ditch. She pulled him back but he kept straining over. Fortunately the road was empty, and presently Susannah saw the cottage Joseph had described. She pulled up, tied the horse to the gatepost and went across. The woman, old and gray-haired with blue-knuckled hands, had seen her from the window and stood at the open door.

"Madame Bechu? I'm Susannah Gautier, from La Guiche. I believe Augustine's here, isn't she?"

"Come in, ma'am."

"I've got her box with me. Can we bring it in?"

They went to the gig and carried the box inside. The cottage was a one-room hovel, with earth floor, lopsided table and two beds, but fairly clean. Augustine was lying, still dressed, on a bed in the corner, looking washed out and weak but no longer tearful. She had "awful pains," she said.

Old Madame Bechu stood by wringing her hands. "I can't keep her after tonight, ma'am. My son is coming and we've only got this one room."

"I see." Susannah looked around. "Isn't there an outbuilding or somewhere he can sleep?"

Madame Bechu shook her head. "Like as not he'll come in drunk too, ma'am. 'Tis no place to have the lass about."

Susannah was caught now. She had taken on the girl and she had to see it through. What could she do? She thought of the Onslows but realized they would never do, the explanation would be too awkward. The Gaveaus? Perhaps, but too far. And then she thought of the doctor, Dr. Cavan. Impatient and short-tempered as he had been, he had also been sorry for the girl. Yes, that was it. She must find the doctor and ask him now.

Madame Bechu directed her to the doctor's house. Susannah climbed into the gig and drove into the village. It was a big rambling house on a corner with a yard and a coach house, rather old-fashioned, and even she could see how much it needed repair. An elderly servant woman showed her in.

The doctor sat plucking irritatedly at his beard as he listened to her. He tut-tutted, jiggled his foot. "Do you know how many bastards we get every year in this parish, young woman? Two fifths of all the children born. Two fifths! And what do the mothers do with them, eh? Leave them in the street! Abandon them! A public charge. A charge on charity—if they live. The girl was fortunate."

He ranted on, vexed, bad-tempered. Susannah pleaded with him to take the girl in, at least temporarily.

He had no room, the old man said. "I have my son and his family coming here—his wife, their two children. I have my housekeeper, my young valet. I am seventy years old, young woman, and I still have to do my doctoring. I have to get out on my rounds every day."

But in the end he agreed, as she had believed he would.

81

Madame Sicard, the housekeeper who had let Susannah in, would give the girl a room in her part of the house. It would be a bare room, but it would be shelter. Yes, yes, he would send to Madame Bechu's to tell her and to get the box.

Susannah thanked him and started on the drive back. She was dreading the consequences of the scene earlier, but she didn't mind now that the girl was to be looked after.

The horse, heading for home, was going too fast and kept pulling over to the left again. Susannah tried to keep him in a reasonably straight line, but the right-hand shaft seemed to irritate him in some way and he pulled away from it. Whenever she brought him back to that side, he veered wildly off again.

The gig was spanking along. It shook and bumped with the awkward movement of the horse and the bad road. All her attention was taken up by the powerful brown flanks of the horse, his neck curving under the pull of the reins in her hands, his frothing mouth, his blind willfulness. They crashed into potholes, slewed across the road, swung back. She gripped the reins with her own fierce willfulness. They were rushing now, as if the horse felt he was gaining, his will gaining, outdoing hers. She braced herself and strained as hard as she could with the right-hand rein, bending backward. The horse's head came around further, the open frothing mouth was angry, the ears laid back. There was hatred and anger in the curve of the frothing mouth, the sweating arch of the neck.

Gradually she gained on the horse. Her will gained gradually. He kept up his furious pace, but the tension between her and the horse seemed to slacken in some subtle way. She could almost feel the still-angry submission flow back to her through the reins she held. She gripped them, triumphing.

A cart appeared around the bend in the road ahead, moving slowly. They rushed toward it; the cart horse seemed to catch the anger of the gig's horse and tossed his head. Suddenly the gig pitched into a pothole and Susannah flung a hand out to keep her balance. The horse, feeling the brief yielding of the bit, veered as if he were going to crash into the cart. Susannah saw the two men on the cart suddenly jump up. With all her strength she wrenched the horse back to the right of the narrow road, and with a lurch the gig tipped over into the ditch.

11

Twenty minutes after Susannah had driven away from La Guiche, a smart green and black landau with gleaming brass lanterns turned into the drive. Inside were Simcoe Baynes and Jamet, his broker. Francis, who had been submitting to his mother's rage, the insane, screaming, incoherent storm that tore periodically out of the still center of the woman, saw them arrive and went along the drive toward them. From the kitchen came his mother's voice railing at Joseph, rising and wailing in her fury.

He walked quickly to put himself out of earshot. He didn't know why Baynes should have come himself and he was apprehensive about it, thinking of the interview he had escaped so far because Jamet had put off his visit. It was unusual for the merchant to come at this time of year. In the normal course of things the merchant paid his visit with his broker during late autumn or winter, when he tasted and compared the wines on offer and decided which to buy. But after that, keeping an eye on the purchase was the broker's job, and he alone came around to inspect it during the weeks while the casks were being topped up before delivery. Moreover, Simcoe Baynes, head of Baynes and Sheehan, the third or fourth most powerful firm in Bordeaux, was a patrician. It was going to be much more difficult to get out of the sale with Baynes himself. Francis wondered uncomfortably if Abel-Cherubin had been letting hints drop in Bordeaux and Baynes had come out to investigate.

"How de do. How de do." Baynes nodded, not giving his

hand. He was a short, fat, round-faced man of forty-five or so with resentful protuberant gray eyes. His head was thrust forward and his lips were compressed. He was wearing a black coat in the latest loose style, a tall stovepipe hat to give him height, and his waistcoat buttons were set with small garnets, matched by a larger pair as cufflinks. He strutted.

Jamet, obviously overcome at being with Baynes in person, shook Francis's hand and said quietly, "Mr. Baynes would like to look around."

Baynes, staring out toward the vines, lifted his cane in an imperious gloved hand and said, "Where's your boundary here?" He might have been a buyer who has condescended to look over an unpromising property.

Francis led them forward and pointed out the boundaries, explaining there was more at the back. He hoped Baynes would not go into the vines and see the spreading oïdium. But Baynes wanted to go indoors.

"Let's see the place." He took charge and strutted through the vatting room and cellars, poking around everywhere, looking resentful and disapproving. He rapped casks with his cane, kept finding fault, and the cowed Jamet agreed with him.

"What's this?" He indicated some piled casks.

"That's some 1850 I'm keeping."

"Ha! You're likely to keep it for a while yet."

The 1850 was a bad year but Monsieur Laverne was nursing it and hoping it would improve with age. Francis, who wished Laverne was there, could not satisfy Baynes. Baynes contested whatever he said and took an age verifying that Jamet had marked all the barrels that were due to come to him. He made Jamet take another sample, although he already had one, scoffed at Francis, pooh-poohed him, lorded it over the whole proceeding.

Baynes was indeed conferring a favor by being there at all. The chartrons, the masters of the Bordeaux wine industry, would have no interference. They laid down the law to the vine growers, and no mere owner of a vineyard, even the greatest, could stand up to them. The merchants were the real producers of claret wines. They mixed the wines they bought at will, sugared them, acidulated them as they thought fit. They dosed Médoc wines with Queyries, produced "improved" Bordeaux by mixing it with cheap wines brought in from the Roussillon 240 miles away and sticking high-sounding labels on it. They loaded casks of claret as ship's ballast and sent them to Cochin China and back or had them rocked about in the Atlantic breakers off the Gironde coast. They controlled the quality, they rigged the market, they settled the price. They bought up the harvests of a man's vineyard for years ahead, sent their inquisitors among his vines and into his cellars, dictated to him. And if the brokers, who had every reason to keep the merchants sweet, classified the grower's wine as inferior, the merchants would let him wait as long as they pleased. They could make him or ruin him. For without them, he could not sell. On the bottle was the name of the merchant and the merchant's only. That was how the customer knew what wine to buy—by the name of the merchant. In the main it was what he went by. So-and so's Médoc, So-and-so's Sauternes, and so on. And so, without the merchant and his parasite middleman, the broker, the vineyard owners were helpless.

At last, back in the vatting room, Baynes halted, and Francis saw the moment had come. Baynes planted his cane in front of himself, slapped both hands on top and stood with feet spread wide. "Well, why haven't I had delivery yet?"

"I've been away. I was in the United States and I've only just got back."

"No reason. I should have had it by last month at latest. You're lucky I've been having work done in my cellars, so it suited me to wait."

Francis shifted uneasily, but it had to come. "Mr. Baynes, I . . . I should have told you earlier, but the wine is more or less . . . well, promised to Jacobsen."

"Eh?" Baynes's moist gray eyes fixed him.

"You see, Mr. Jacobsen's had our wine for some years. I'd overlooked that. It really belongs to him. My father had an understanding with him."

"You signed a contract note with me, didn't you?" Baynes said.

"Yes, but—"

"Yet the wine belongs to Jacobsen?"

"It was an oversight, as I say. Really, I'm sorry to go back on the agreement. I'll repay the money."

Baynes looked at him, then began to snigger. His lower lip sagged, showing his long bottom teeth. "Eh, my manikin, you'll

85

repay the money, eh? You have to go back on your word, eh? You listen to me. You have that wine, every last cask of it, in my cellar by tomorrow or I'll know why."

"Surely we can come to some understanding," Francis said.

Baynes's voice rose. "Understanding! You sign a contract of sale with me, you fulfill it to the letter—that's the only understanding I'm interested in. You may think yourself lucky you've sold your damned wine. And I'll have you remember you've sold this year's to me too, at the same price. So don't go trying to pass that off to Jacobsen."

Francis was white. "I don't think we said at the same price."

"At the same price!"

"It really can't be done, you know, Mr. Baynes. I—"

"Can't be done, eh? And who do you think you are of a sudden? You think you can make a bargain today and break it tomorrow to suit your fancy?"

Jamet was looking on, shaken.

"I was in a hurry to catch the sailing to the States. There was a mistake about the price—it was too low."

Jamet put in a murmur of protest, but it was drowned by Baynes's bellow. "Confound your impudence, sir! And what do you think you're selling here? Lafite? Château Margaux? You're lucky to get the price I'm paying."

"I wasn't—"

"The second contract note—you have a copy there, Jamet? —specifies the same price. And that's what it'll be." Jamet fumbled out the note, nodded confirmation and held it out, but Baynes waved it aside.

"What's more, I hear you're spreading tales about the bad wines shipped to the United States," he said to Francis. "I give you fair warning, young man, I am lodging a complaint about this talk with the Chamber of Commerce. Do you hear?"

Francis felt horribly shaken. It was dangerous to antagonize a man like Baynes. That had not been his idea at all. Scenes of this sort upset his whole balance, confronted him with unpleasantness he must somehow skirt around, block out. He tried to think of some conciliatory formula, but Baynes was stalking away. Francis went after him, but Baynes spun around.

"Thank you, I'll see myself off the premises. And if your casks are not in my cellar by six o'clock tomorrow evening, you'll answer for it." He turned and went, followed by the whippetlike Jamet.

Francis stood there in consternation. It had been worse than he had foreseen. Now he had offended Jacobsen and made an enemy of Baynes, the worst of both worlds. He walked slowly down the vatting room, gazing at the floor, struggling with his feelings, trying to find some bright aspect, something to lighten the reality. He went over it again. After all, nothing was final. It was still only April. Between now and the autumn, Baynes's temper would have cooled. Of course, Abel-Cherubin and the others did not know he had pledged this year's wine too. Thank heavens he had not discounted that note as well. After all, that was something to be thankful for. It would be all right. He couldn't help feeling it would be. And the price might not be so bad, one could never tell. It would all settle itself in some way, no doubt. He straightened up, feeling better already. There was always a cheerful side.

A movement behind the end vat caught his eye and a young man in boots and smartly cut riding costume stepped out. It was Regis Gautier, his cousin on his father's side.

"Hello, Regis. I didn't know you were here. How are you?"

Regis Gautier stood glowering at him. He had a dark, handsome saturnine face with a certain puffiness in the cheeks and a look of self-indulgence; but this was partly counterbalanced by his fine dark eyes and black eyebrows, and his hair was receding in a way that showed his head to advantage. He carried himself with the assurance of a man about town. Now his lips were compressed and he was shaking slightly.

"I overheard every word of that," he said with a tremble in his voice.

Francis looked at him in surprise. "Did you?"

"So you've sold *this* year's harvest to Baynes too, in advance?"

"Yes. I have."

"I'll be damned!" Regis Gautier glared as if he were about to explode. He took a step back, looking Francis up and down, slapped his boot hard with his riding crop. He slapped it again and again, glaring at Francis. Then abruptly he stalked past him out of the door.

Francis turned and watched him go. Now Abel-Cherubin would be told at once.

12

_____

The gig with Susannah in it tipped into the ditch and over-turned. A tangle of blackberry bushes partly broke the impact, but Susannah was thrown out, arms stretched wildly before her, and fell on her side. In the shock she fainted momentarily and when the two carters ran up she lay unmoving. Then she came to herself and stirred, the great hooked thorns on the branches clutching and tearing at her. Pain shot through her arm and made her stop moving. The two men, a rough red-faced pair, didn't seem to feel the brambles as they crashed through to her and with many precautions and reassurances gently released her. They lifted the brambles away from her, detaching them as gently as two women with a child, and carried her carefully between them to the roadside.

She had lost her bonnet, her dress was ripped and her hands and face were bleeding from many scratches, but it was her right arm that hurt most. She unbuttoned the cuff and turned the sleeve up a little. She felt very shaky. A bump had come up on her forehead too. She began to think she was going to faint again. The men made her lie down on the grass verge, but after a moment she sat up again; and when one of them brought back a half-bottle of brandy from the cart, she only consented to touch it with her lips. She saw that the tangle of branches had saved her.

She was glad to sit there quietly, dabbing at her scratches and nursing her arm while they released the trembling and fearful horse, then righted the gig and examined it. One wheel was askew and it could not be used. So they hitched the horse to the back of the cart, lifted Susannah into it and took her home.

On the way she recovered somewhat, and by the time they reached the house she was talking to the two men, two vineyard workers from Cantenac. Her arm below the elbow was swollen and hurting. As they came up to the gate of La Guiche, a man rode out on a black mare. She recognized Regis Gautier, whom she had met at the Préfet's reception, but he affected not to see her and cantered away down the road looking puffy and irritable. She thought, Well, never mind *that* just now.

She made the men put her down outside the gate. "I'm perfectly all right now. Thank you. Thank you for your help."

They looked at each other, looked back at her doubtfully, and the elder man said, "We'd better fetch somebody, ma'am. You're in no state to be by yourself."

"No, no. I can get to the house. I'm all right. Turn the horse into the meadow there." She fumbled out her purse, but they would take nothing for the trouble; and when they had turned the horse loose they stood watching her.

Susannah started down the drive feeling anything but steady. Her legs were horribly shaky and she felt they might give way at any moment. Her head swam and she had to stop for a moment. She seemed to be getting the reaction to the crash now. The drive was empty, but beyond the far end of the house she saw Francis talking with Monsieur Laverne by the vatting room. She was thankful that their backs were turned, and as she watched they walked away out of sight. She went on some more, reached the stone bench and sank down on it. She felt awful. Her face felt bloodless, there was a clammy sweat on her forehead and she was on the verge of vomiting. She drooped on the bench, the ground swayed, the wave of cold nausea rose and she vaguely heard the two carters pounding toward her down the drive as faintness enveloped her.

A glass knocking against her teeth was the first thing she felt when she came to herself. She was lying on her bed, still dressed, and somebody beside her—Emilie—was holding a tumbler of water to her lips.

"Don't . . . my arm . . ." She lifted her other hand, the

girl moved away a little, then Susannah sipped the water. The girl's startled face hung over her. Susannah lay recovering. They had carried her upstairs. . . . In a moment she stirred and sat up awkwardly, but when the girl moved to support her she fended her off, afraid for her arm. "Give me a pillow."

Presently she felt steadier. "Don't make such a fuss, Emilie. Go and get some hot water and some arnica and then help me get undressed."

But the girl had hardly reached the door when steps drummed along the corridor outside and Francis burst into the room in a great state. "Susannah! What on earth have you been doing?"

"It's all right, it's nothing— Oh, careful! My arm."

He bent over her, clasping her shoulders, staring at her with his scared, wild, anxious face close to hers. He smoothed her hair. "Are you all right? Are you? You've hurt your forehead."

"It's only my arm."

"Scratches all over . . . your dress . . . Good Lord! What've you done to your arm? Where?"

"Don't touch it. It hurts."

"Just here?"

"Yes. Those men were awfully good. I hope you gave them something."

"Yes." He was looking at her arm, now slightly blue under the swelling. "Can you move your fingers?"

"Yes." She did so.

"I don't know . . ."

As soon as Emilie came back he said, "Tell Joseph to fetch Dr. Cavan at once." He took the bowl from the girl, bathed Susannah's forehead and the scratches; he was gentle. Then he helped her out of her clothes and into bed.

Yet all the time something was lurking, something else was on his mind. She saw his wretchedness, saw his misery. He was trying to wait before he spoke of it, but in the end he couldn't wait. It pushed itself forward. She lay in the bed and he walked unhappily up and down the room; his mood had changed.

"Why did you do such a thing?"

"*I* do it?"

90

"Mother's told me all about it. The last time Tom went out with the gig he had an accident. He hates the gig. Why couldn't you ask?"

"How could I ask?"

"Joseph knew. He should have stopped you."

"He tried to, as a matter of fact, but I wouldn't listen. Don't blame Joseph."

"But why not listen? Why take things into your own hands?" he said.

"There was nothing to listen to."

"And what a moment to choose. I'm in a fearful rush. Baynes was here kicking up a row and wants his wine."

"There was no reason to turn the girl out of the house like that. And less reason still to keep her box from her."

He looked at her with a pained, worried, patient expression, as if he were dealing with a child who didn't understand. "You could have left that to somebody else. It was all arranged for. She would have had the box."

"It was kept back out of spite, as punishment."

"Nothing of the sort."

She looked at him. Did he really believe that had not been the reason, or was he turning away from the fact? "Why, then?" she asked quietly.

"If you had just left things as they were."

"You mean I'm simply to do as I'm told?"

"Come, come." He shook his head unhappily, as if to say she was being unreasonable. "But why interfere? Why not leave things to people who know what to do?"

"I'd told the girl I'd make arrangements for her. I felt some responsibility."

A patient sigh. "Nobody's trying to deprive you of your responsibility, Susannah."

"But . . ." It was denying the obvious! When it suited, you simply denied the obvious. She looked at him strangely.

They argued on in a constrained way, both of them wretched but both unyielding, then they heard a carriage below —Dr. Cavan. He sent Francis out of the room while he examined Susannah. He was dry and sat at the bedside feeling her arm very gently. "You've broken it, broken the radius." Her wrist was sprained too; the scratches and bruises were nothing

91

and otherwise she was unhurt. She felt she was going to faint again while he was setting the arm and putting it into plaster and this seemed rather ridiculous, since he was deft and didn't hurt her. When it was all done, he let Francis in again and told him she should rest for a day or two but there was nothing to worry about.

Francis saw him off, came up again and said in a harassed way, "Now I've simply got to get on. I've got to get a hundred and fifty barrels loaded and into Bordeaux by tomorrow." He moved briskly across the room, snatched a coat from the wardrobe and hurried out. Outside she heard his hurrying steps on the drive, his voice calling to Laverne. Implied reproach.

She lay back in the bed. So the result of it all had been to make her look unreasonable, impulsive and interfering. And there had been no concession of rights to her. Francis had spoken softly and looked patient. Yet she felt separated from him. It was strange and painful, the feeling of separation. She had imagined that, faced with the obvious—the obvious after all!—he would admit it, yield to it. But he wouldn't, and that made him strange to her. And it was hard to accept strangeness in him. It didn't make her doubt she loved him, but it made her tremble because it changed their love in some mysterious fashion.

She was no longer so lost in him. She no longer abandoned herself to him entirely, was no longer merged and lost in him. But being lost in him had given her strength. She had forgotten the gray shapes that had pursued her before, the sudden moments of panic when she would feel that existence was going to crush her, when she was overpowered by the grayness of life. How strange that he had never had these feelings of fear and grayness! But no! He was always bright and cheerful. He was eager and bright and active and happy. Every discomfort could be kept at bay by assuming the best.

One day in Paris a pickpocket had stolen his wallet. It had only contained a small sum; but though it had been obvious to her, it had taken the entire day and part of the next to convince him that he had not simply mislaid it, that it would not turn up. So bright! So happy! It was odd that you shouldn't be naturally happy—that's what he proclaimed. There must be something wrong with you if you weren't. And so she felt all the more wretched at having broken his bright confidence and made him miserable.

Her arm was awkward and in the night it throbbed painfully and burned as if the plaster were too tight. She lay half awake, half dozing, sometimes thinking Francis was there. It was late when she did hear him come in. The lamp was low. He turned it down further, went silently through to the dressing room next door and shut the door after him. In a little while she heard him drop his boots, then the spring of the old sofa squeaked as he lay down on it. She decided he was spending the night there so as not to disturb her in the bed; but she was unhappy and lay staring at the shadows. At last she dropped off to sleep.

At daylight he woke her again moving about next door, then he came through and tiptoed out of the room. A moment later the dog barked outside. She heard him hush it and heard his steps retreating.

The pain in her arm was duller, yet she did not think she could go back to sleep. Somehow she didn't want to try and felt perversely uncaring. For once she felt aimless, as if her life had momentarily lost direction. She was listless. She reached out to the chair beside her and looked at her little gold watch with the ring of forget-me-nots enameled on the dial, the one her father had given her, telling her with his drunken charm that he had won it at cards, then, seeing her disappointment, saying that he had really bought it for her. She peered at it in the half-light, ten minutes past five.

The lamp was still burning. She lay there a moment longer, then got out of bed and went across to the shutters and looked through a crack, seeing nothing but the familiar surroundings quite still in the cold early morning light, a cloudy day.

She sank down wearily on the bed again. She knew her husband loved her with the fullness of his heart; she was sure of that. But their love had begun to change.

13

Francis paced nervously up and down on the Quai des Chartrons that afternoon waiting for the rest of Baynes's wine to arrive. Half had come and they were moving it across the quay from the lighter in which it had come down the river into Baynes's cellars. From where he was he could see the entrance courtyard a few yards up the Rue Bareyre and the great arched doorway to the reception bay under the painted sign *Baynes & Sheehan* where the loaded drays were maneuvering and men in their leather aprons manhandling the casks. But the rest of the consignment in the second lighter had not turned up.

Francis made his way through the heavy traffic to the casks and bales of merchandise at the water's edge. Plenty of craft moving on the river, but he couldn't make out the lighter. He didn't understand it. Occasionally the excise men stopped a barge carrying wine to verify its papers, but it was rare.

The evening before, they had turned out the laborers and three price makers at La Guiche and moved the 150 barrels of wine into the lighters on the river. Heavy work it had been, they had kept at it late and he had been up again at five o'clock. The lighters had not in fact left until nearly eight. Still, that had been time enough; it was under two hours downriver to Bordeaux.

But then when they had left, he had not been able to throw off his discomfort, a lingering sort of wretchedness within him. It had made him restless, it was so unusual. He didn't know what to do with himself. He didn't want to go back into the house, so he had hung about the vatting room feeling terribly uncomfortable. Finally he resolved it by telling himself he had better be there, better be present when the wine was delivered, and he had saddled the horse and ridden to Bordeaux. Anything was better than indecision with him, he knew that. Not to know which course to choose always made him wretched, and he would sooner risk doing the wrong thing than prolong the uncertainty.

At Baynes's he had found one of the two lighters had just arrived but not the other. Laverne, who had come down with the first, said they had seen the second steer to the bank about an hour after they had started out but hadn't thought anything of it particularly. But now it was three o'clock, and unless the rest of the wine appeared soon they were in for trouble.

Francis peered past the unloading ships, trying to see the missing lighter. He was tired, had hardly slept, and at the back of his anxiety were the nagging thoughts about Susannah. The scene with his mother over the gig, then the accident and the argument with Susannah had all upset him. He was discovering that Susannah had difficult moods and humors—and he had expected her to be more pliant. Getting her to settle into her new life was proving more troublesome than he had foreseen. He hadn't foreseen it at all. How could he have done so? These were possibilities one simply took no heed of unless one were like Abel-Cherubin. Yet he hadn't expected her to be so willful. And then his mother's resistance to her depressed him. He sighed. He could understand his mother. She had never asked him why he had married a foreigner, but he had read the reproach in her look.

Yet . . . that wasn't all. He adored Susannah, he loved her with passion, yet now he was beginning to be baffled by her. He was beginning to see that she was escaping him. He had said to himself that he didn't want to make her slavishly obey him, didn't want to dominate her as Abel-Cherubin did his wife—but secretly, though he didn't know it, this was what he did want. He had expected it to happen of itself, had expected her to conform to his wishes naturally. And so in his present state he was baffled by her and disconcerted.

Hitherto their wills had mingled as intimately as their

95

feelings—how amazed by it they had both been! They had hardly recognized their individual separateness, hadn't tried to, hadn't wanted to, as though together they had been half numb with love and happiness, each living in the other. But now they were slowly beginning to revive, to move apart again, to recover their own bodies and minds, recognizing them almost as altered selves. They were beginning to exist individually.

Francis sensed that she had begun to exist outside of him and it was loss to him. It was the escape of some intimate essence of her that should somehow be permanently his, because he was the male. This was the sense in which she was most *his* and the escape made him uncomfortable. He didn't know why it was. He thought it was his passing dissatisfaction over the accident, but the deeper reason was her escape from him. Perhaps he had expected them to go on for a long time in their first exalted state, engrossed with each other. Why not? People did. He loved her passionately, and one's own love wasn't like any other's. But now, when he saw the change coming about in this other way, he was disturbed in his heart.

A church clock struck the quarter hour. He turned back uneasily toward Baynes's. Baynes's cellar master, Koechlin, had already rejected three casks and he continued testing the wine, having his men examine every cask as it came in. It was his perfect right, indeed his duty. A big man, the cellar master, especially for a firm like Baynes and Sheehan, an artist, a bosser, up to every trick of the trade, a high-court judge for sagacity, with a nose, a palate, a horse dealer's eye that could tell the size of a barrel to an inch, and he was cocksure enough to turn away three hundred casks with a wave of the hand.

Before Francis had crossed Baynes's courtyard he could hear Koechlin's voice. Inside the cellar, among the casks, it was cool and dim. Koechlin was bawling, "Clear those pieces away from there. Get them out of my cellar." He was a big bald man, head and shoulders above the others, with mutton-chop whiskers and one arm shorter than the other, an Alsatian from Bischwiller. The aproned men moved quickly to do his bidding. A weedy uniformed man from the Revenue Office was yawning nearby at his desk, one of Koechlin's foremen was pouring wine into a conical glass on the counter, and beyond in their cubicle sat two clerks hunched like vultures at their ledgers and daybooks, which had to be posted with every movement of a piece of wine. Koechlin bent for a moment over his little tally clerk, taken up with some documentary problem.

Francis stood by the door. He was glad to have Laverne as a buffer to Koechlin; but something was wrong with Laverne; he had been hanging about as if he had something on his mind. Francis didn't know what it was and this wasn't the moment to inquire.

The foreman at the counter had filled the glass. Beside it stood a second glass of wine from the sample Jamet had taken at the time of the sale and which the wine now being delivered must match in every way. Koechlin straightened up, still talking to the tally clerk, then turned and picked up the two glasses. He held the glasses up to the light, side by side, and squinted at them, comparing the color and the clarity, for wine that was cloudy had to be treated quickly in the cask if it were not to deteriorate. He took his time. All the men watched him.

Slowly Koechlin's mouth tightened. He put the glasses down and with a gesture of irritation waved the freshly poured glass aside. "Where's Laverne?" he called out. "Fetch me Laverne!" Then he caught sight of Francis by the door. "Monsieur Gautier. Monsieur Gautier, how much longer have I got to waste my time on this? I've a good mind to throw the whole lot out. Six pieces not racked—look at it. You think I've got nothing better to do than amuse myself fining down your wine as soon as it's in?"

"It's been racked. It was all right when it left."

"Then maybe you'd better take it back, my good sir, and do your work on it."

One of the clerks was at Koechlin's elbow and in an adenoidal voice said, "Mr. Baydes wants you."

Koechlin glared at Francis, then turned and in a deliberate fashion crossed to the office cubicle, where he adjusted his voice and warbled down the speaking tube, "Yes, Mr. Baynes?"

Francis slipped out. On the quay he saw Laverne coming toward him. "They're here now." Laverne jerked his head toward the river. "Just coming up."

"The other lighter? I told you they would be." Francis felt enormously relieved.

"One of the men is ashore. Says they broke down, had

trouble with the rudder. That's the story. I don't know. The fellow's half drunk."

"Well, they're here. That's the main thing. Koechlin says the wine isn't clear, claims it hasn't been racked. He's turned down six pieces so far."

"It's been properly racked, sir, and we know it. He's trying to make trouble." The blue eyes dropped, then looked up again and Francis caught the worried look once more. "There's something I have to tell you. I was half hoping you wouldn't be here and I'd handle it myself but, well . . . seeing the mood they're in, you'd better know before it's too late."

"Yes, yes, but it can wait for the moment," Francis said, turning for the river. "I'd like to get the unloading started."

"It's soon said, sir, and I think you'd better hear it now."

Francis paused.

"You'll find Monsieur Abel's share isn't here. It's twenty-three pieces and I've had to replace them with the 1850."

Francis stared at him. "They're not . . . ? But it's all sold. We can't replace it now, especially with the 1850. Who told you to do such a thing?"

"As for replacing them, I did it myself. The other was Monsieur Abel. He came to me the day after you got back. You remember the day Monsieur Chabot and Monsieur Parenteau were at the house, and Monsieur Raynal?"

"Yes. Well?"

"He said I was not to send his share to Baynes. Said he'd told you he had sold his to Jacobsen as usual."

"But why didn't you tell me?"

"Well, sir, knowing Mr. Baynes, I could see trouble. I thought the best way was to pay no mind to what Monsieur Abel said. I'd have taken it on myself, say I'd forgotten, and I dare say it would have been all right. When it's done it's done. Still, I thought I'd keep out of the way while you were with Monsieur Baynes yesterday. But Monsieur Regis found me, you see."

"Yes, he was there while I was with Baynes."

"He said Monsieur Abel didn't want any mistake about his share. I was to have it put off at Jacobsen's place on the way down river or . . . or I'd answer for it."

"But you should have asked me!"

98

"Aye, I was going to. But your lady had had the accident. Cast your mind back, sir. The people were in a state, the doctor was coming. I could see you were upset. It was bad enough. I judged it wasn't the moment to make it worse. So I had twenty-three pieces of the 1850 loaded. After all, they're better than nothing."

"So that's what that damned lighter's been doing all this time, unloading at Jacobsen's?"

"Yes. I'm sorry, sir." He was miserable and contrite. Francis looked at him in dismay. He had forgotten all about Abel-Cherubin's demand, had not for a moment thought he meant it seriously. Half the time people said things they didn't mean. "But they'll never accept the 1850. Never!"

Laverne said awkwardly, "I can try to say something. Pass it off as my mistake. We might gain a little time to turn around in."

For a second Francis was tempted—but no, it wouldn't do. "No. No. I'll . . ." He stood considering, aware of Laverne's embarrassment. "You'd better get them unloading."

"I'll see to it." Laverne escaped with obvious relief.

Oh, Lord! Francis did not know what to do. Koechlin would not accept the pieces of 1850 for a moment. It was a bad year, the wine had no maturity and prices were very low; the quality did not nearly come up to the 1851. No chance at all, of course, of slipping it in unnoticed. Nobody could get twenty-three pieces of inferior wine past Koechlin, even when he was dead drunk. They wouldn't even get a solitary piece past the foreman because, for one thing, it wouldn't have Jamet's mark on it; for in accordance with practice, Jamet had put his mark on all 150 pieces the day he had bought them.

Francis walked slowly down the quayside among the wagons and piles of cargo, coils of rope and barrels. What was he to do? The discomfort of the problem pressed on him and he sought for a way out. All that old quarrel with Baynes, so stupid. Why were people so difficult? Such a waste of time. And what were twenty-three barrels of wine from La Guiche? Nothing, nothing at all. Any merchant would carry you for that amount, charge you interest on the money, no doubt, and watch that he made his usual percentage, maybe a bit more. But Lord, it was nothing, twenty-three barrels. Baynes, of course—it gave Baynes a chance to get at a Gautier, either him or Abel-Cherubin. If Baynes wanted to be narrow-minded, that was his affair. As for it having been a mistake to go to Baynes in the first place, well, he probably wouldn't have got to the States and found Susannah otherwise. Besides, what was the good of going back over things? It was all water under the bridge now.

Yet if he didn't deliver the wine, he couldn't believe Baynes would take him to court. Not for twenty-three barrels. Surely not. Still, he didn't want to be prosecuted for default just now. But surely it wouldn't come to that. No.

He tapped his foot in the discomfort of uncertainty, in the secret knowledge that he had failed to reassure himself. He let his attention drift to a ship off the quay loading wine, a German ship. It was too far to make out the name. A man on the bowsprit was working on the gammoning and a few passengers stood on deck looking shoreward and pointing. On the quayside men were shifting the heavy casks of wine to the loading barges.

Francis became absorbed in the scene, as if he had nothing better to think about, yet he really took in nothing. He was aware of time passing. Aware of it pressing in on him. He grew more tense but still did not move. He began to feel the little prickle of sweat on the crown of his head that he felt at moments of extreme discomfort. He stood waiting, staring stupidly at the ship, at the workmen. After all, what need was there to rush back?

He walked along the quay, passing the canvas storage tents, pausing to watch some activity now and then. He'd go back presently. And they would just have to accept the 1850, that was the solution. After all, they'd just have to. Pity, but there it was. If he hadn't got the missing pieces they couldn't have them, could they? He'd just tell them so. They would have to accept what he had. Exactly. If not . . . Well, if not, they would have to deduct the missing wine and he would have to pay Baynes the money back.

He began to feel the problem was not quite so formidable, was solving itself. Problems, after all, could be shaped. He felt the return of his optimism. It would be all right. All this fuss about twenty-three barrels!

A three-master, the *John Stepley* from Boston, much bigger

than the usual 250-ton Bordeaux ship, was maneuvering in the river. A shout through a megaphone came over, the anchor chain rattled out. The small boats swarmed around. Francis watched a moment and then, as he turned away to walk back, he came face to face with Simcoe Baynes.

Baynes stopped, looked him up and down. "So here we are. Stretching our fancy legs instead of attending to our business."

"Good afternoon, Mr. Baynes." Francis was horribly shaken by the unexpectedness of the encounter.

"Our business has already been thoroughly attended to, hasn't it, eh?"

"I was just going along to your cellars now."

"Oh, you were, were you? You've been hanging about there already by all accounts. But you choose the right moment to disappear, eh?"

"I'm sorry it wasn't delivered all together. We had a bit of a delay."

"Well, you can get along there now and you'll find the law's on your back."

Francis went white. "Mr. Baynes, I wanted to explain we were a bit short on the whole delivery—"

"A bit short, were ye, my fancy young cock. And what sort of a fool do you take me for?"

"Really, if you'll let me—"

"What do you mean by trying to hoodwink me?"

"If you'll let me explain. There were twenty-three casks short, so I—"

"Explain? Explain it? You know what that's called, young man? Fraud! That's what it is, an outright attempt at fraud. Trying to pass off inferior goods for goods already contracted for is fraud in this country, and you'll see if you can explain that away to the law."

"Mr. Baynes, I know as well as you that the 1850 is only nine degrees. I didn't mean to pass it off as anything else."

Baynes waved it aside. "Aye, and you're in deeper water than that. There's a contract note that you discounted with my name on it going around this town with a promise to pay on delivery of the goods. Do you think I'm having my good name treated like dirt by a whippersnapper like you?"

"There's no call to be offensive," Francis said.

"Offensive! Why, by God, sir, I'll see you dancing before I'm finished with you! You'll be dancing a four-handed jig all on your own!"

Baynes's face was congested, his eyes full of hate, but he was steady, not a tremor about him. "And if you set foot in my cellars again, I'll have you thrown out by the scruff of your neck."

A voice behind Francis said, "Good day, Monsieur Gautier," and Francis turned and saw John Lovell. Lovell was smartly dressed in fawn coat and waistcoat and carried a cane.

"Oh . . . good day," Francis said in confusion.

Lovell bowed coolly to Baynes. "John Lovell, at your service, sir."

"How de do," Baynes said. "I'm talking to this man and ye can wait till I've done." He waved a contemptuous hand at Lovell.

"If this gentleman is in some difficulty, perhaps I can help," Lovell answered coolly.

"I'll thank ye to mind your business and keep your nose out of mine."

Baynes made to move aside, expecting Francis to follow, but Lovell said sharply, "Just a moment!" and Baynes spun around at his tone.

"I couldn't help overhearing. Certain terms were used which I'd find hard to let pass."

"Eh?" Baynes bristled. "So you would, would you?"

"I would, sir!"

"And who are you, sir, to pick up another man's quarrel for him?"

"Please!" Francis intervened angrily. To Baynes he said, "Mr. Lovell is an acquaintance of mine. We needn't make a public brawl of this."

"I gathered Mr. Baynes thinks he has suffered a loss on some wine you have delivered," Lovell said. "I was going to offer to make it up to him."

Baynes snorted. "And why should I give a tinker's cuss about your offers?"

"Because you're a man of business. I happen to owe Monsieur Gautier something, and if he will allow me I'll settle it in this way."

Francis saw Lovell had said this to spare his feelings in front of Baynes, for, of course, Lovell owed him nothing.

"And I'll even add a little extra by way of courtesy," Lovell said, "if we can agree that business between gentlemen demands the minimum of courtesy."

Baynes looked at Lovell with narrowed eyes. He studied the steady eyes on his. Slowly his expression changed and his choler seemed to subside, but he was strung taut. "Eh, and you're somebody then, I'll grant you, my young buck. There's few men in this town would step between Simcoe Baynes and another man in a quarrel, I'll give ye that. Aye, and you're a fine-feathered bird, too, eh? Oh, no offense, no offense, I'm sure. But I'd be a bigger fool than I was to begin with to say ye nay if there's any sound reason to believe you can do what you say."

"Here's my card, sir. I'm a newcomer to Bordeaux. I have just taken over an old Bordeaux firm. You may know it." Lovell pointed across to a tall-windowed stone building on the quay-side with a ground-floor office. There was a side entrance to the cellars and a painted sign in blue: *Collard & Sons. Wine Merchants. Established 1760.*

"And what might you have taken over there, the funeral department?" Baynes sneered.

"I'm the new owner, Mr. Baynes. As you'll learn."

"Oh, so we'll learn it, shall we?"

"For our present business, the wine Monsieur Gautier owes you will be replaced from my stock with a better vintage. If that's agreeable to you, Monsieur Gautier?"

"I'm greatly obliged to you, sir," Francis said. He was genuinely astonished. Somehow he had not connected Lovell with the wine trade, though now he couldn't imagine why not. Collard and Sons, once one of the great wine houses of Bordeaux, had long been moribund, owned by an aged Demoiselle Collard and left in charge of a staff who were all too old to carry on. Now he noticed the group of workmen standing among the wine casks on the quay who seemed to be waiting for Lovell to finish his conversation and come back to give them orders.

"And who's to judge if it's a better vintage?" Baynes said.

"Your own cellar master."

Baynes stood there; he took a long look at Lovell and at last he said, "Very well. I'll accept your offer."

"If you'd care to step across now, Mr. Baynes, you may assure yourself I am able to keep my word," Lovell said.

"Thank ye. I've no time now. I'll take your word and you'll do well to keep it, let me tell you that."

"Then one moment." Lovell turned to the group of workmen and called out, "Mr. Thornton, please."

A stocky man with an English look hurried over. "Yes, Mr. Lovell?"

"Mr. Baynes, this is Andrew Thornton, my cellar master. Mr. Baynes of Baynes and Sheehan."

"How do, sir."

"Mr. Thornton, I want you to go to Mr. Baynes's cellar at once. See the cellar master, Mr.—?"

"Mr. Koechlin. I know him, sir," Thornton said with a glance at Baynes.

"See Mr. Koechlin and tell him with Mr. Baynes's compliments that he is to give you a note of how many pieces of wine he has declined to accept from Monsieur Gautier today."

"There'll be thirty and more," Baynes put in.

"About thirty pieces or so. And he may come to our cellar tomorrow morning and you will replace them with a superior Médoc which he may taste on the spot. Are we agreed, Mr. Baynes?"

"Aye. It'll suit me."

Thornton looked from one to the other, then nodded and went off toward Baynes's cellars.

"I have your word that any legal proceedings you were thinking of will be dropped?" Lovell asked Baynes.

"As soon as I have the wine."

"Then I'll have your hand on that now, sir, with me and with Monsieur Gautier," Lovell said.

Baynes gave him his hand, then shook Francis's. He stood looking steadily at Lovell, his mouth tightened to a crack and turned down at the corners, and he looked hard and mean. Slowly and deliberately he said, "And you, Mr. Lovell, you're a bigger fool than you look. Good day to you, sir." And he stalked away.

Francis, who had felt rather foolishly out of it, stared at the retreating figure as Lovell beside him began to chuckle softly.

14

Lovell wouldn't hear a word spoken that evening about his generous gesture. He laughed and said he had wanted to see Baynes on his hind legs. " 'Begin as you intend to continue' is my motto," he said. "Baynes is one of my future competitors."

"Oh, they all hang together here, the merchants. Like a club."

"Then I'm going to be odd man out."

Perhaps Lovell was a bit of an odd man out by nature, Francis thought later. At all events, Lovell was at pains to make sure Francis's pride shouldn't suffer from his intervention in the quarrel. "He played a dirty trick on Collard's way back, and I wanted to let him know the firm's alive again, so I'll ask your forbearance, sir."

"Well, you got me out of a hole." Francis liked his frankness.

They had gone to an old-style waterfront restaurant, with sawdust on the floor and a good atmosphere, the Louis d'Or. Each had eaten a dozen oysters and then lamb chops, and not until a Brie was served, with Beychevelle in their glasses, did Lovell begin to talk much. Then he told Francis about himself.

Eighteen months before, in November 1850, he had been a shipping agent in Calcutta, he said. His widowed father, dead for six years, had left him a prosperous business, and Lovell had carried it on, not much liking it but used to the life. He had a comfortable house in the Alipore district, six servants to wait on him and the attentions of several young ladies of the resident

English colony, in particular the Misses Scrope, daughters of the local puisne judge. For at age twenty-seven and without attachments, he was an eligible party. In answer to Francis's questions he said he had known India all his life, had been to school there and only visited England for holidays. But it wasn't until later, he confessed to Francis, that he had found that these facts of his life had given him a special invisible coloring, a special status, that he was English without being English.

At all events, at breakfast in Alipore one Monday after the mail packet had arrived, he had been surprised to find a letter beside his plate from a firm of London solicitors named Gearing and Gearing. It said that if he were indeed Mr. John Lovell, son of Ambrose Lovell, born in Colchester, Essex, on 11 May 1824, et cetera, he was the beneficiary under the last will and testament of one Elizabeth Collard, lately deceased in the arrondissement of Libourne, Gironde, France, and they would be glad of an early communication from him. Mademoiselle Collard, in other words, had left him a legacy.

To Lovell, Mademoiselle Collard was but the dimmest of memories and until that moment he had entirely forgotten her existence. She was his grandmother's sister—his great-aunt—whom he had seen only once as a child and remembered as a small frail creature, already old, who wore white and used a lorgnon to look at you. He duly wrote, and the solicitors replied that the legacy was eight thousand pounds in cash and securities, and "other property," unspecified, on which they would require his instructions.

"Well, you know," Lovell said to Francis, "that letter came just at a moment when I was feeling an itch for a change. I wanted to strike out somewhere fresh. I'd had enough of Calcutta, I'd really had enough of India. It wasn't home. England was always home, though I'd hardly been there. And so I up and sold the whole damned lot—the business, house and all—and in two months I'd cleared out of India for good."

He laughed. Francis refilled their glasses.

Well, in London it had appeared that Mademoiselle Collard had been dead for a year, Gearing and Gearing had been trying to trace Lovell, the only surviving member of the family, ever since. And the "other property," it turned out, was of all things a wine merchant's business in Bordeaux. What the devil was he to do with a wine business? Gearings in London hadn't even been to see it. All they knew was that Mademoiselle Collard hadn't occupied herself with it for years and had left it in the hands of one or two trusted but ancient employees; and the whole thing, they gathered, was now very run down, not to say derelict. They advised Lovell to put it in the hands of a competent French law firm and get rid of it for what he could.

"Well"—Lovell gave his wry grin—"there I was in London. I was home. Both my parents had been English. I'd been born in Essex but I might have been a Eurasian. All the Eurasians in India firmly talked about England as 'home,' though they'd never been there and weren't ever likely to go. In London I saw I was hopelessly out of touch with English life. And, you know, it's something that in an odd way the English don't like. They just don't like it. They even resent it in a fellow countryman. So they exclude you. Silently and unobtrusively they just exclude you. You're not one of them. I don't think they even know they're doing it. It's a sort of tribal instinct. I hadn't been to school in England or lived there, so I was like a 'bloody foreigner.' To them I wasn't a real person. I wasn't really English, so I wasn't real. Nobody un-English is; he's merely of a lesser breed.

"In London you could see the places, the preferences, the opportunities going to men who were in the swim. You could watch the sons of the governing class with their minds circumscribed by a code they had learned largely at school confidently taking the places assigned to them by right of birth—just like members of an exclusive club. I knew I'd have to grind myself pretty small to adapt to that, and I didn't think I could do it. Besides, I was connected with trade, and I wasn't therefore what they call 'out of the top drawer.' I didn't think I'd be able to accommodate to a lifetime among the great all-pervading English preoccupation with caste. I'd seen enough of that in Calcutta. For the men who rule England, I'm one of the untouchables!"

Lovell laughed again and drank his wine. Francis looked at him with sympathy. Lovell's Anglo-Saxon sort of frankness was attractive; you'd never hear a Frenchman speaking like that, certainly not a Bordelais.

So, Lovell said, he had sat in front of the blazing coal fire in his London hotel and thought about Mademoiselle Collard's legacy and had finally got the idea into his head that he might as well go and look at it. He had unfolded a map of France— green! Of course it was only the coloring of a map, yet it had seemed symbolic. It had looked like a fresh green lawn, lovely. Why not? In India he had acted as sub-agent for a firm in Pondicherry, the little French enclave south of Madras, dealing with the French correspondence and making an occasional trip down the coast to the port. After all, his mother, who had taught him the language, had been half French, whence the Collard connection. So Bordeaux it was.

"That was five months ago. You should have seen the place! Mademoiselle Collard had been dead for a year and a half by then, and the place was shut up. I let myself in and walked around. I'd never as much as seen a wine merchant's before. There were cobwebs like wool everywhere and mice and rats. Can you imagine those buildings and cellars with the vats and all the bins of bottles and the casks, the underground cellars— three miles of them—all stocked with wine I haven't even looked at yet? There was an office full of old files and correspondence and account books going way back into last century, and upstairs were the old Collard apartments, with those ceilings twenty feet high and wooden shutters that fold inside the window embrasures and parquet floors from before the Revolution and so forth. It's all there—I'm only beginning yet."

Francis chuckled. "You must be enjoying yourself. But do you mean it's been left unattended?"

"No. I found out that the old cellar staff have been coming in to look after the casks in stock. Devoted people. Well, I'd already told the lawyers to sell it. Then . . . I don't know. I wasn't happy. I stayed on in Bordeaux. I used to go there and walk around, maybe pick out a bottle and open it. I'd look at those fine old oak vats, two of them stamped 1760. I'd push open a creaking door and see a rack of beautiful black hand-blown magnums. I'd go through the ledger, the entries in that curly old script, like engraving: 'His Royal Highness the Prince of Westphalia four dozen Lafite 1795. . . . His Grace the Duke of Buccleuch six dozen ditto.' Such a pity, all this going, I'd think. Such a terrible pity. And gradually it became a sort of challenge. The place seemed to say to me that if I couldn't bring it back to life, restore it to what it once was, then . . . well, I was no good. I wouldn't be worthy of the Collards."

They each took a drink of wine. "Try some of that fourme," Francis said, indicating the cheese. "Comes from Ambert, in Auvergne. Very good with red wine."

They helped themselves.

"And then a strange thing happened," Lovell went on. "One night, it was January, I was alone there. I'd been roaming around below, then I went upstairs to the old apartments. It was late, I'd got an oil lamp and I sat down asking myself once again what the devil to do. All at once I heard something overhead, somebody was on the roof. It wasn't a bird, I could tell that. It was a person. I could hear him quickly scramble over the roof, pause as if listening, then go on.

"I picked up the lamp, ran up the stairs. The heavy door at the top was locked and bolted, impossible to open. I listened and could hear him out there, breathing heavily, muttering a few indistinct words, then the sound of him scrambling away.

"I rushed down, managed to find the keys, had an almighty struggle with the lock and bolts. I pulled the door open. It was black night outside, pouring with rain. The roof sloped gently enough and I guessed I could clamber over it at a pinch, but I didn't want to get soaked, so I didn't try. I looked around but couldn't see anything, so I went in again and slammed the door behind me. The slam of the door boomed through the empty house and seemed to echo way down in the cellars.

"Well, Monsieur Gautier, there I stood at the top of the stairs and it was just as if I had woken up, like a sleepwalker—the same shock, I imagine—and at the same moment I remembered something about old Mademoiselle Collard and the day my mother had taken me to visit her.

"I was nine years old; we had left my father in India and come to England and Europe for a visit. In Paris we met Mademoiselle Collard, and she told us how they had all lived through the Terror in Bordeaux, her parents, she herself, her four sisters and two brothers. She was just twenty-one—my grandmother was the youngest, aged eleven—and she told us how Jean, their brother, aged seventeen, had saved the family time and time again, bribing the revolutionaries, taking them all the family silver 'for the brave sansculottes.'

"One night at midnight three citizens had come with an

order for their arrest. They were all to go next day before the military tribunal, and everybody knew that was one step before the guillotine. The family assembled in tears. Jean vainly tried to move the men to pity, pointing out the lateness of the hour, the rain falling heavily, the age of his father. They wouldn't listen. In the end, all else failing, he persuaded them to share the family supper before they set out. And then, plying them with drink, the finest bottles he could find, he managed to get the leader to accept a large sum in paper money. The man took his companions aside and shared the money with them. And at last Jean induced them to let the family spend the night in the house.

"The men sealed the doors and posted twelve guards on the house, saying they would return at eight next morning. And then Jean climbed out over the roof, across the adjoining buildings, and ran through the black and streaming night to a house on the outskirts of the town and roused out a section leader of the sansculottes whom he had bribed a month before. Threatening and arguing by turn, he induced the man to intervene, and before morning the order for the family's arrest was canceled and the guards removed.

"Until that moment, I had completely forgotten the story. I'd hardly remembered Mademoiselle Collard. Because, of course, it was the same house. Time is not a continuum . . . and I had just heard Jean clambering over the roof. I had seen the black night and the streaming rain. I went downstairs and decided I was going to keep the place and try to set Collard and Sons on its feet again. And when I opened the front door to leave that night, the quayside was dry as a bone. There had been no rain at all."

"Good Lord!" Francis stared at him. "How extraordinary."

Lovell calmly cut a piece of cheese and ate it.

"Have you heard anything since?"

Lovell shook his head. "But they must have been watching and sending me luck, because next day, in walks Andrew Thornton and asks if he can have the place of cellar master if I'm going to get Collard's going again."

"That's the fellow who was out there with us this afternoon?"

"Yes."

110

"I thought he spoke very good French, by the way, for an Englishman."

Lovell laughed. "He's as French as you are."

"What! With that name and those whiskers? I'd have laid twenty francs he was English."

"So would I. He used to be cellar master for Palmer. He'd been working for six years for Lord Beltram, trying to grow vines in a hothouse near Brighton and got fed up with it. But he's a first-class man and I'm lucky to have him. We're gradually getting the house into shape. I have everything to learn, but I'm beginning."

They poured out the rest of the wine. Francis said, "I've got to get back to La Guiche tonight," and pulled his watch from his pocket. "I ought to be going."

"You'll forgive me for talking too much."

"I'm mighty pleased to have your acquaintance, Mr. Lovell, and I'm much obliged to you."

"Glad to have been of service to you, sir."

The clock below wheezed and struck one as Francis went quietly up the stairs at La Guiche. A light was showing under the bedroom door; he opened it and found both lamps turned up full and Susannah propped up in bed. She lowered her book.

"Are you still awake? The doctor told you you had to rest."

"I wanted to wait for you."

He shut the door behind him, aware of uncertainty hovering between them, vaguely threatening.

"Come and give me a kiss," she said.

He went over, bent down, and she put her good arm around his neck. He kissed her and in a moment his heart was full of love again for her, he had forgotten his bafflement over her. She was as clear to him as in their early days.

"I was worried about you," she said.

"No need." He looked down into her blue eyes.

"I'm sorry to have given you this trouble," she said. "I wanted to wait up for you and tell you I love you."

"Dear Susannah, I love you too." They kissed again. "Are you really all right?" he said.

"Yes, perfectly. How did you get on?"

"I had an extraordinary adventure. It was very lucky." He

111

stood up, began to take his clothes off. "That fellow Lovell—you remember, John Lovell?—told me the queerest story."

He told her with a sort of eager boyishness about the collision with Baynes, how Lovell had come to the rescue and all the rest. At the end she said, "But how strange."

"Isn't it?"

"Is he living there now? In that house?"

"Yes. He's a good man." Telling the story, he had interrupted his undressing and now he stood up, took the rest of his clothes off and pulled on his nightshirt.

"Well, now *I've* got some news for you," she said. "I've been lucky too."

"You mean you've waited all this time to tell me?"

"I've got a horse!"

"A what?"

"A horse. Constance Canning sent him over. It's a present. Byam gave him to her, but she says he's too much for her, too big. You should see him. What a horse! A great big red animal, beautiful. Well, not exactly beautiful, but *I* think he is."

"But you're not going to try to ride now? With that arm?"

"Of course not. But I am as soon as I'm better. You should see him. He's over seventeen hands. I'm going to call him Red."

His expression had changed. "Really . . . I don't know whether we ought to accept it like that."

"Oh, come on! I've already accepted him. He's mine."

"I mean, how are we going to return it?"

"We don't have to return it. Don't be so—" She was going to protest about his being bourgeois, but his face was serious and she checked herself. "There'll be opportunities if you want to."

He looked at her and felt a great surge of love for her, she looked so pretty sitting in bed in the lamplight. "Do you think I could sleep here tonight? I won't disturb you."

"Of course."

He took the pillows away from behind her, settled her, put the lamps out and climbed carefully into bed, careful not to jog her. He turned away, keeping over to his side. But her bad arm was on the other side and she moved in the bed close to him, her face against his shoulder. He felt her against him. He turned around and kissed her and she whispered to him.

He was gentle with her, fearful of her arm, but she wanted

him so much and he ached with tenderness for her. She lay against him afterward and the other mood seemed remote to him, as if it had concerned other people, not them. He felt his love for her was almost too much to contain and clenched his fist so as not to turn around again and hug her, he was afraid of hurting her.

She lay quietly beside him. Somewhere in the dark outside a dog began to bark, a thick, heavy, throaty barking, frightening, a big animal. After a minute she said, "What's that?" under her breath, as if she were afraid. What was a dog doing roaming out so late at night? The dog stopped, then barked again, heavily, in its throat. She pressed against her husband. "It gives me the creeps," she said.

"It's that story of Lovell's that has got into your head. Go to sleep."

15

One June morning about three weeks after the accident with the gig, Susannah was in the salon looking at the dark portraits hanging around the room and wishing she could move them out when she heard raised voices and went outside to see what it was. Josserand, the price maker, was in the drive dealing roughly with an old man who had come in from the road. The man had momentarily put down a big black bundle, but now he swung it on his back again and turned wearily away. He didn't move fast enough, for Josserand let fly a kick. His boot caught the sagging bundle. The old man turned quickly and his eyes blazed under his craggy eyebrows.

Susannah called out, "What's the matter?" and went out.

Josserand looked around, saw her and waved his hand in dismissive contempt. " 'Tis the Jew here again, that's all. I told him to get off."

Susannah went forward. "What does he want?"

"Ah, he comes peddling his bits of fancy earrings. He'll steal anything he can lay hands on."

"Well, there's nothing to steal out here. Do leave him alone."

Josserand's eyebrows went up. "Eh, ma'am, if that's the way of it, you can do as you please." He took three paces then swung around. "Let him come near my cottage, that's all, and he'll get my stick across his back." He went off muttering.

The old man shuffled forward, back bent, dipping his head

in a sort of bow and glancing up at her sideways, and she saw his fierce eye was jovial now, the old haggard face warm and humorous. She wanted to laugh.

"Madame . . . Madame . . ." It was a high tinny voice. He was small and bent and dark-skinned like a Spaniard or a Portuguese. His long dusty black coat trailed on the ground. He wore a wreck of an old hat from which his ringlets escaped. A pink gap-toothed mouth grinned behind a straggly beard. He was just an old peddler with his quick eyes, but there was a hidden spring in him, coiled and strong, fierce and secret, behind the composed patience.

"What have you got there?" she asked, eager to see what was in his bundle. She supposed she shouldn't be, for Josserand's insolence probably meant Madame Gautier had given orders to keep him out, but she didn't mind.

"Beautiful things, my young lady, beautiful things." He was already undoing the bundle and she squatted down with him, excited as a child, watching him unwrap the things and take out more bundles and boxes. Gradually he revealed his treasures—trinkets, silk, haberdashery, pins, silver things— there always seemed to be one more promising little bundle, one more secret thing to find.

"Beautiful lace. Here, look at the quality, look at the fineness. Take it, take it in your hand, young lady."

"Oh, that's pretty," she said, picking out a little necklace of tiny coral-colored seeds, the one thing he hadn't drawn attention to.

"From Algeria," he said. She let it run through her fingers, light and smooth.

"Look at this, young lady." He brought out another necklace of blue beads with strangely patterned white segments.

"What is it?"

"Very old, very old. From Africa. It is glass, first from Venice. Yes, Venice. Long ago Venice was a great city, the glass beads they take to Africa, for trade, for ivory. Maybe Marco Polo! And one day somebody steals the secret. Or maybe he finds a beautiful wife in Africa—yes, a beautiful black wife—so he stays to make his beads for her, who knows?" He laughed. "Here, Marco Polo's beads. For you they are cheap."

But he didn't press her. She watched him with fascination.

"You play the piano, young lady?" His long thin hands were unwrapping the last box; he took out some sheets of music, ragged and cruelly folded. "Old German music, clavichord, pianoforte. See, here is a date, Dresden 1740. It is beautiful. I am selling cheap."

"Our piano's broken, so I couldn't play them," she said. "I'll just take this little seed necklace and the ribbons here. How much is that?"

"This and this? Very cheap. Four francs."

"Three," she said. "Yes?"

He lifted his shoulders, smiling. "Take it."

She went indoors, fetched the money and paid him. He had almost finished wrapping the things up again; he looked up at her and said gently, as if he had not liked to ask before, "The young lady has hurt her arm?"

"Oh, it's nearly better now. Soon be out of this old plaster."

He nodded. "Something you want to sell, young lady? Old brooch, old piece of silver? I give you a good price."

"I don't think so."

"I give you Marco Polo's necklace too," and she saw he had it in his hand.

She laughed. "Not just now."

"It is yours just the same," he said. "Take it, young lady." When she hesitated, he put it in her hand as if it were worth nothing.

"Thank you." She loved it. "What's your name?"

His old eyes flashed at her. He seemed surprised, as if nobody had ever asked his name. His look searched her face. "Jacob." He nodded, affirming it: "Jacob." His eyes were bright and humorous, then he swung his bundle on his back and gave his little bow and she watched him go off down the drive. Somehow the encounter made her happy, and all morning she was fingering the necklace, wanting to show Francis, but he was away in Bordeaux.

It was a fine day, with clouds sailing slowly in from the west. The bed of sweet williams was showing dark reds and whites among the golden puffs of African marigolds, and a great burst of campanulas spread their pale blue against the house. At midday she took a couple of carrots from the kitchen and went to the paddock to see Red. The horse came trotting over as soon

116

as he saw her. He was a big lean, raw, gangling horse, steep in the shoulder, with clean hard limbs and a rusty coat. It wasn't a refined head but full of wild character with prominent eyes and nostrils. Susannah loved him. She had spent an hour or more with him every day, establishing their relationship, feeding him, holding him while Joseph rubbed him down, and now she was on a fair footing with him. But he was temperamental and on some days wouldn't have anything to do with her.

"Hello, my Red, my beautiful Red, my lovely russet, my sorrel." She called him all the reddy-brown names she could think of. "My cherry, my claret, my foxy, my gingernob, my rusty, my puce, my mad-mad-madder." The horse nuzzled her for the second carrot, then tossed his head and went off. She had been anxious about him all the time her arm had been mending, he wasn't getting enough exercise and she longed to ride him, but Dr. Cavan had insisted on waiting another week before taking the plaster off her arm.

Most of her household tasks she managed quite well, including the sewing and darning. She made a pound cake flavored with orange juice, and cookies and strawberry and lemon jellies, for Abel-Cherubin's wife was to pay them a call. But the final days seemed to go slower than ever. She was impatient and Francis was away from the house for one reason or another. At last, on the appointed morning, Joseph drove her over to Dr. Cavan's. Dr. Cavan removed the cast, examined the arm and pronounced all was well. Her arm felt light and easy without the cast.

"Then I can ride?" she said.

"Ride? A horse?" He looked at her in his usual testy way. "Have you had any experience?"

"Yes, I can ride a horse."

"Then . . ." He shrugged, as if to say, Why ask me? "Don't go jumping. We don't want another fracture. Though I don't suppose you'll take any notice."

She didn't reply. His irritability came from some deep disappointment in his life that had nothing to do with her and she didn't mind; besides, he was a good doctor. He escorted her to the door, and Joseph, seeing her without the plaster, nodded and smiled with satisfaction.

How the old carriage rattled on the way back! But she was

alive with happiness. She loved the road with the vineyards all around, the clumps of trees here and there marking a house, the oxen, with sacking over their eyes to protect them from the flies, working so patiently. At intervals they would pass two or three men standing together conferring, looking down at the vines, for the white powdery blight persisted. They would look up as she passed and, recognizing the carriage, raise their hands.

And today she felt confident in her life. She felt freer and stronger. She couldn't think of herself without Francis, didn't want to, but she felt stronger, as if she were regaining something, regaining it changed and strengthened. She and Francis had a wonderful closeness in their love. Never for a moment did she feel he kept anything of himself back from her. Only when others appeared was their harmony threatened. But she had reclaimed something of her essential self that had been temporarily submerged. She was beginning to feel her own blossoming, her own opening out. It was almost a physical sensation, a thing of her body as well as her mind, and she was full of joy and vitality in it.

This afternoon Abel-Cherubin's wife, Louise, was paying her call at La Guiche. The visit had had to be prepared for rather carefully, even Susannah's cake-making. Once before, a week after the gig accident, Abel-Cherubin and his wife had called on Madame Gautier, and Susannah had sensed the other woman's sympathy. They had only talked together a short while, for Louise had been nervously on the watch against Abel-Cherubin's disapproval. But at the end she had whispered to Susannah, "We must have a talk," and Susannah had nodded encouragement.

She was a small woman, rather older than Abel-Cherubin, with dull hair, prominent cheeks and sparse high-arching eyebrows over bony sockets. She had been a Mademoiselle Ducasse, one of the Barsac Ducasses, and had brought Abel-Cherubin a handsome dowry. But now she was obviously dominated and frightened by him.

Announcing her visit, she had committed an indiscretion. She would, her note said, come "for tea." She obviously believed that as an American Susannah would have the English habit of taking afternoon tea and was trying to be agreeable. But Madame Gautier at once suspected Louise's loyalty and announced she had an urgent mission of charity in the village which her conscience would not allow her to ignore. She was not, however, going to abdicate and made it clear to Susannah that she would preside over the opening cups, to demonstrate her position as mistress of the house, and then retire.

Susannah wanted to ask the Onslows and Constance Canning, to make a summer tea party of it outdoors and for this reason had baked her cakes and cookies and made the jellies.

But no, it wouldn't do. Madame Gautier said they would use the salon and she would ask Madame Raynal, that was all. Susannah sighed. She longed to breach the reserve in which the people lived here; strangers were only asked to the house on special occasions when everything crackled with formality. Casual dropping by was unknown. But she saw she would have to be patient.

So, promptly at half past three Abel-Cherubin's smart red and black carriage driven by Achille, the colored coachman from Martinique, turned into the drive at La Guiche. Louise stepped out in pale gray, frilled and flounced, with gray gloves, gray bonnet, a black ribbon around her throat and a blue sun shade, an effect half dismal, half comic, so that Susannah's sympathy went to her at once.

"My dear." Louise greeted Madame Gautier with cautious affection. Her anxious look seemed to ask if she had made herself dim enough. She turned to accept Susannah's kiss.

"Susannah, so nice of you to ask me for tea."

"It's nice of you to come."

"Oh, your arm! It's better?"

"I had the plaster off this morning."

"I *am* glad."

They went indoors. Madame Gautier announced that Madame Raynal would not be coming, and at her ring Emilie brought the tray in. Dutifully Susannah poured the tea from the great ivory-handled silver teapot which hadn't been used for twenty years; it had a little strainer hanging from the spout to catch the tea leaves and it was perched on a tall slim-legged silver stand which had to be very carefully managed.

"Have one of my cookies," Susannah said, offering them. "They're what we used to have at home."

"Thank you, dear."

Quietly Susannah sat in her chair watching the two while

they talked, Madame Gautier's rocklike face and neck, her bright hard eyes, the reddish hair, the smile which could suddenly illuminate her face and show how handsome she had once been. And then the dowdy, rather comic little wife of Abel-Cherubin, all anxiety to please, all quick anxious gestures and glances, knowing she could never please anybody enough to change her status in the family, yet with a hidden dash of spirit behind her timidity. She had been bent into conformity, thought Susannah, but she hadn't been quite flattened. No, not flattened completely, and her light brown eyes were perky still.

All at once Madame Gautier said, "I think you must call on the curé, Susannah. He is complaining of not seeing you. It is embarrassing for all of us."

"I will, Mother," Susannah said.

"Particularly embarrassing for me. He is bound to ask me again this afternoon."

Susannah said sweetly, "Another cup, Louise?" and smiled at the guest.

Louise glanced anxiously at Madame Gautier, then said, "Thank you, dear."

"You say you will call and you don't," Madame Gautier said, hands clasped in her lap.

Susannah finished pouring, handed the cup. "I'll call on him, but it isn't a one-sided matter."

"What do you mean, not one-sided?"

"I have to be ready."

"I should think one ought to be ready at any time."

"I have to want to go, or I should be insincere, and he wouldn't want that, I imagine."

Madame Gautier gave an impatient little shrug and pursed her lips. Susannah was surprised that her mother-in-law should bring up the subject now, but she supposed the purpose was to say something intimidating in front of Louise.

"It is bad enough that you have married outside the church," Madame Gautier said.

"Please, Mother. We've been through this."

"It is disgraceful the way young people neglect the church."

Susannah wanted to say that neither she nor Francis had minded, that Francis had married her in spite of her being a Methodist. "There's no quarrel between Francis and me about it," she said, looking down at her hands and feeling increasingly nervous.

"It is incumbent on you to take the first steps toward the church here. For Francis's sake if for nobody else's."

"I'm not thrusting my religion down anybody else's throat, so I don't see it matters."

"Matters! The curé is always wanting to know when he can expect to see you. If you have any respect for me, if you have any respect for Francis, you will see him and take instruction."

"Surely that's a thing that ought to be left to me," she said quietly. Susannah was attached to her own church, Francis had never pressed her to turn Catholic, but Madame Gautier had referred to conversion once before.

"You say yourself it is not a one-sided matter. There are others to think of."

Susannah sighed. "Very well, I will see him, Mother." She was determined not to argue any further. "Would you like some more tea?"

"I shall tell him you will see him on Sunday," Madame Gautier said, ignoring the question about the tea.

Louise was now suitably shaken. Susannah said to her, "And how's Toby?" Toby was Louise's little brown and white pug dog.

Louise clasped her cup, stirring the spoon around and around as she summoned courage to open her mouth again. She looked at Susannah; her fingers trembled a little. She looked down at her cup and up at Susannah again. "He . . . he's had a cough."

"I must leave shortly and I wish to have a private talk with Louise first," Madame Gautier put in dryly.

Susannah looked up, meeting the adamantine eyes. She was . . . she was expected to withdraw. "Oh, yes. Very well." Madame Gautier had deliberately prepared the little snub. She felt the color rising in her cheeks. She pushed back her chair and rose, forcing a smile to reassure Louise, and went out, her hand brushing her skirt.

Outside, the trees were rustling and great white clouds were sailing across the sky. She walked slowly across the drive to the garden, biting her lip with humiliation. It was so stupidly unnecessary! Over and over she repeated, So unnecessary. Was she to be cowed and browbeaten like Louise? Was that their wish? To beat her down to cringing anxiety? And why? Was it jealousy? Was it hatred of the woman who had taken a more intimate place in her son's life than she could occupy? Why was it? Tears of rage and humiliation came into her eyes. And the talk about the church had been the same thing. She was filled with humiliation. Instruction! She would *not* be converted. She would *not* take instruction. Why was it? Jealousy? But surely jealousy ought to be wearing itself out now. Surely jealousy didn't last that far into age. Surely not. No, no. It was horrible.

Suddenly the bright mood of the morning was gone. A hood seemed to drop over her. She felt stifled. Everything was black, cursed, airless here. She brushed the tears away from her eyes. It was old—an old airless place in which she would choke to death. They wanted to stifle her.

In her agitation she couldn't stay still. She felt she would choke. She snatched up her trowel, left lying beside one of the flowerbeds, and squatted down, her back to the house, digging into the earth, digging hard, angrily, blindly. Little sprays of earth and stones flew up from the trowel. She turned, still squatting, digging the iron trowel into the flowerbed pointlessly, heedlessly. Then all at once she saw she had cut a fuchsia plant in two. She dropped the trowel, stood up and turned away. But then, ashamed at herself, she went back and picked up the poor plant. She squatted down and made a fresh hole for it.

"Eh, ma'am, let it be. You'll dirty yourself." She looked up and saw Jean, the garden boy. "I'll do it. They need weeding."

"Jean. I . . . I was clumsy."

He stood there talking to her about the flowers, pointing out new things, while she calmed down. He was a nice young fellow, scarcely sixteen, with a strong brown body and curly brown hair, the son of one of the price makers. She left him and walked along to the paddock and called Red. The horse ambled over unhurriedly and she stood stroking and patting him, speaking to him to soothe herself, calming her nerves with the smooth neck and shoulders. His nostrils quivered and he blew down them.

"Shall we go out tomorrow, when it's fresh? In the morning, eh? Do you want to gallop, Red? We'll go to the sea one day.

Go and gallop along the shore in the sea. Have you ever seen the sea?"

Abruptly the horse broke free and went away. It was as if he had caught her mood.

And still she wasn't calmed down. She was trembling and angry and indignant and afraid too. Uncertainty always overcame her when things like this happened. Everything became uncertain, the basis of her life was shaken. Then she saw Emilie, her hair and skirts blowing, coming from the house, where Joseph had the carriage ready. She waited rather tensely for the girl to come up.

"Madame Gautier says she is just leaving," Emilie said, clutching her hair and looking at her with curiosity.

"Very well."

The girl turned back reluctantly. Susannah let her go, then followed to the house and saw Madame Gautier standing in the hall with a light coat and bonnet on. Susannah walked straight up and made to go in.

"I shall tell the curé you will call on Sunday," Madame Gautier said, looking at her firmly.

Susannah trembled in her heart. She pulled up. "No. I shall go when I'm ready. And as a courtesy, nothing more," she said and stood facing the other woman, determined not to move on. Madame Gautier glared at her. Her lips opened, quivering a little with anger, then she clamped her mouth shut and swept past to the carriage.

Susannah didn't look around. She went into the house, hearing the carriage door slam behind her, then the wheels crunching on the drive as it moved away. She was still shaky, unsure of herself, but glad she had stood her ground.

In the salon Louise was standing timidly by the tea table, not knowing what to do. Susannah managed a smile. Poor Louise.

"Oh, Louise . . ." She hardly knew what to say. "Come and . . . come and look at my flowers. Shall we? It's so nice outside."

The other woman seemed glad, and they walked out together, out in front of the house, examined the orange trees, then crossed over to the flowerbeds, where Jean was still at work. The wind blew Susannah's hair.

"You must let me send you some stocks," Louise said.

"Yes, would you? I'd love some."

"And some mignonette. Oh, look at those canna. What a lovely color."

"I find it difficult for flowers here. It's the poor soil."

"Yes, but you must try irises. They do well. There used to be a big alley of them at the back of the house, but I haven't seen them for a long time."

The trees gave them shelter from the wind and it was pleasant there in the afternoon sun. "Do take off your bonnet, Louise."

"Oh, do you think so?"

"Yes, do."

Louise glanced around, then took it off. They sat down. A duck with a group of ducklings paddled by on the lake, finding things among the reeds at the edge and making bubbling sounds. Susannah told about the old Jew and the necklaces, then about Red and the Cannings. Then she was constrained and quiet, her spirits drooping after the rush of anger. She was content to do nothing, to put forth no effort. She was trying to find herself again.

An hour went by and they had spoken of nothing but trivial things. Gradually Susannah forgot her own grievances, and felt Louise reaching out to her, felt her loneliness and her need for sympathy. She tried to draw her out, but she couldn't. Susannah felt sorry for her being browbeaten, sorry that she shouldn't make more of herself. Her hair could be brightened, done more attractively. Her skin was good, her eyes were pretty. Yet there was that bright perkiness, a sort of sparrowlike indomitability beneath the surface, as if she were longing for encouragement she dared not ask for.

Susannah noticed she had stopped the nervous movements of her hands, the anxious intertwining of her fingers. Something was going on inside her, but she couldn't get it out. At last she said, "You won't say anything about it, will you? You won't give me away?"

"Anything about what?"

"Well, my dear, there's been a dreadful quarrel between Francis and my husband."

"Quarrel? What about?"

"About the wine. About its going to Mr. Baynes again this

year. My husband is so angry. I do hope . . ." Her eyes sought Susannah's anxiously.

"I didn't know."

"Francis is going to make up the price. But Abel-Cherubin says it won't do. I'm sure I don't know. I do hope, my dear . . . I hope it won't stop us being friends." A quick dart of her bright eyes, a reaching out, so tentative.

"No, of course not." Then, on impulse, Susannah said, "Was that what Madame Gautier didn't want me to hear, about that?"

"Oh, no."

"Was it anything to do with me?"

Louise got red and rather agitated. "My dear . . . please don't ask me. I can't say."

"I know it may be embarrassing, but the way she did it, so flagrantly, makes me want to find out. I was humiliated."

Louise took a quick breath and looked as if she were going to come out with the whole thing, but at the last minute she checked herself. "I know . . . but she's a kind person really."

"Did she tell you not to tell me?"

"Yes, I wasn't to tell you."

"Then it was about me?"

"Yes, dear."

"What then?" There was a pause. "What am I not to know?"

Susannah felt her anger returning, the flush mounting to her cheeks; but Louise's timidity had got the better of her, she would not speak, and Susannah took her hand and said, "Never mind, Louise. Don't worry. Never mind."

"You won't give me away, dear, will you?"

"Of course I won't."

"Promise."

"I promise." Even now she thought Louise might tell her, but she was wrong. She felt consumed by curiosity; it was unbearable to her not to know.

But now Louise seemed to think that Madame Gautier might return unexpectedly and find her sitting there confiding in Susannah, and she wouldn't settle down. She fidgeted, couldn't settle. At last they got up and strolled through the trees for fifteen minutes, then Louise said she must go.

"I said I would only come for an hour. I have to call at my sister's. And Toby gets so angry if I'm away too long."

They went back to the house and Achille brought the carriage around. They kissed goodbye. "Thank you, my dear, it was lovely," Louise said, and her look said, We're allies. Susannah waved as the carriage turned out of the gate, then she went thoughtfully indoors.

Upstairs in her room she stood looking out over the vines at the view she loved. Her flash of hate had passed and she was quieter. Now she didn't blame Madame Gautier so harshly. Oh, she knew Madame Gautier wasn't unkind in her heart, could be sweet and loving—she had seen it with Francis. But she could not accept her son's wife, that was the trouble. Her attachment to Francis was too strong. It was as if Susannah were the interloper between her and her son.

And yet she strained, under that silent exterior, not to show it. Sometimes in the evening when they sat in the salon and Francis was beside his mother, close to her, holding her hand, Susannah could feel Madame Gautier straining not to be demonstrative with him, could feel the silent despair that she must soon relinquish him to her rival, his wife. It was the blood tie. How to overcome that? Susannah couldn't get closer to Francis than she was, yet there were still these other reaches of the heart where she could not touch him, that belonged to his mother, the family. He had an allegiance to his mother. When it came to choosing, his loyalty was to his mother, not to her. Yet this existed alongside his love for her. She had tried to explain to him that she didn't want to be possessive but that it hurt her. He had listened patiently, but she had seen that it meant nothing to him and this severed a strand between them. He had a stronger loyalty to his family than to her.

And it frightened her, revived her feeling of isolation. But she couldn't give in to it. Even to make peace, no. She could not give in because she felt she would be losing herself, she would be bowing to the blind force of family. It was as if *family* were separating her from him and rejecting her. She couldn't escape this sense of family here. The blood tie was the strongest thing in the world to these people. And sometimes she felt it was overpowering, would override all else, supplant love and trust and tenderness and all other feeling. And at these times family seemed to her like some dark impersonal force against which she must defend herself. Strange! And all this flowed into and inter-mingled with her love for Francis, her growing love for La Guiche and the country.

The early morning mist had dispersed and the sun was fil-tering through the trees by the river. The leaves fluttered and dappled the ground and the mossy trunks.

Susannah cantered the horse on a tight rein, letting him go a little, then restraining him, keeping him patient but feel-ing the excitement in him, the longing to gallop. Only the side-saddle, which she detested, was holding her back. She had al-ways ridden astride, only once ever tried sidesaddle. Yet when Joseph had led the horse up already saddled with the thing, she had let herself accept it. Constance Canning rode sidesaddle, and she supposed it was the convention here.

It was not yet six o'clock. The air was fresh and a hint of rain was coming into the sky. Bringing the horse out, she had had a job with him; he wouldn't walk, and with the sidesaddle hindering her, she found it the devil to manage the hindquarters as she was used to. Still, he was higher in the withers than in the hips, like an American saddle horse, so she didn't have the feeling of riding downhill. And she could tell she had his confi-dence.

She branched off the road, looking for the path Joseph had told her about, then saw it, a long empty path with a soft black surface by the river. Good! Come on then, let's go, my beauty. She eased the reins, the horse moved eagerly forward. She gave him an encouraging dig and he surged into a gallop. And then, oh, Susannah was lost between exhilaration and the business of keeping her balance, between the rushing path and the ridicu-lous feeling of having no grip on the horse.

He was magnificent! All his awkwardness in the trot was gone, his big ungainly body moved with the smoothness of a perfect machine. She laughed, she wanted to whoop. She would never be able to resist a jump if one offered. It was glorious! She felt rapturous with excitement, with the power of control-ling the great plunging muscled machine of the horse. Glori-ous! She gripped the saddle with her knee for all she was worth. Her bonnet flew off and hung by the ribbon around her neck;

her hair came half loose. They thundered down the long path.

Ahead was something. She saw a narrowing, something unclear—an inlet of mud? She steered him left. It looked like a dip or a ditch with mud at one end. He was going hard. A drop on the other side? She couldn't see. And then she did. Over the dip she could see a deep-looking runnel and fifteen feet of mud right across the path. She judged it, shortened his stride. "Red, Red, Red, let's get *ov-er!*" He raised his forehand and sailed over, landed like a prince, and without a check in their pace they were pounding away on the other side. She shouted for joy.

She galloped him hard for another mile, marked a point ahead where the path was wider, led around with the rein and turned him sharply, pivoting the forehand around the hindquarters. Without a pause, he was off again back down the path. Racing! They cleared the mud again, and on the other side she pulled him up on his haunches. His sides bellowed under her with his hard breathing; she could feel the throb of his pleasure. She recovered her hat, then leaned forward and patted his neck and stroked and talked to him. "Sweetheart, my lovely."

That day, going back, she took a long way around. Constance Canning came out as she trotted into the Cannings' forecourt.

"Heavens, you mudlark! You're covered with it."

16

In the afternoon, when the hot sun lay over the house and the vines, a laziness, a deep tranquillity came on La Guiche. Susannah loved these hours. There was a bloom of beauty on everything. Sounds came clear from far off, the cellar and the vatting room were cool and blue and time seemed to go with infinite slowness and sweetness. The summer that year, after the brilliant spring, was often rainy, but the air was warm and Susannah would sit by the lake or in the quiet house, doing needlework or crocheting or reading about making cheese or pickling beef in *The Sunday Magazine*. She had a native American pride in her domestic science and meant to keep it up. This afternoon Francis had gone to Bordeaux again to consult somebody about the disease of the vines. It was spreading and worsening and everybody was worried about the harvest.

Susannah had brought out the household accounts and was sitting with them and the bills spread out on the big table of the dining room. She had to be careful how she scrutinized the accounts, but this afternoon Madame Gautier was in the village and it seemed a good opportunity. She sat with bent head, pencil in hand, making an occasional note. A shadow crossing the window made her look up. She hastily swept up the accounts, stuffed them into a drawer and dashed into the hall, where she collided with John Blood.

"Oh! It's you."

"Madame." He smiled and bowed, kissed her hand. "I trust I'm not intruding?"

"No, I . . . Pray come in."

"My horse has slipped a shoe. I hoped I might beg assistance."

"Of course, Mr. Blood. Let's see. Where is he? In fact I don't know whether Joseph's here."

"You're very kind."

She sent Emilie to find him, and Joseph appeared saying he didn't have to go to the village for Madame Gautier until six, and he led the horse away to attend to it.

"Will you take some refreshment, Mr. Blood? A brandy and water?"

"Thank you, ma'am. I'm happy to see your arm is mended." His face under the black hair seemed leaner, his chin darker, his smile showed his white teeth—a sharp-focused handsome face.

"Yes, it's all right now." She told Emilie to bring cold water and led the way into the salon.

Susannah couldn't help liking Blood. She didn't mind about his reputation. He was a man of spirit, a man of heart, and she could be natural with him. They had met on two occasions since the Préfet's reception, once at a rather dull soirée in Bordeaux, which he had enlivened, then at a performance at the Grand Theater. Susannah found him witty and a bit scandalous, sometimes the raw adventurer, the next minute mordant, cynical, the accomplished man of the salon. But natural, absolutely natural and himself. The current fashion suited him to perfection, the longish high-buttoned coat with wide lapels and tall collars. She was curious about his past, for somehow he was not commensurate with this provincial city. He was really a type of political gallant, strong-willed and energetic, made for risk and high stakes and intrigue in the midst of fashionable society, like his friend Morny. But above all she was aware of his strength, his maleness. And a sort of quick current ran between them which gave their meetings a touch of subdued electricity.

This afternoon, while they waited and he drank his brandy and water, he entertained her with a recital of an evening at John Laffan Jennings's and did one or two caricatures of the chartrons which made her laugh. At last she looked around. Joseph was outside with the horse.

"But I haven't told you," she said, suddenly remembering. "I've got a horse."

"You have?"

"You must see him. Joseph, hitch Mr. Blood's horse and go and fetch Red."

Joseph came back leading Red with some trouble. The horse's ears were pricked up and he was moving about in lively fashion. Blood was adjusting the saddle girth of his mount and as Joseph came up with the horse he straightened up.

"What! It's my beauty. Jewel! *Jewil!*" The horse reared, whinnying. Susannah laughed with astonishment and delight. The horse trotted to Blood and nuzzled him, nearly knocking him over, and Blood laughed and put his cheek against him and stroked and fondled him and kept saying, "It's my beauty, my beauty." Then he walked around inspecting him and stroked him again.

"But how on earth do you know him?" Susannah said.

"Jewel? He belonged to me, my dear. I lost him to young Mezieres in a wager six months ago. Didn't I, my beauty? Ah, that was a bad deal, a bad, bad deal. How did *you* come by him, may I ask?"

"Byam Canning bought him for his wife, but she couldn't handle him and gave him to me."

"Aye, he's a touchy devil, eh Jewel? You have to say it with a bit of the Irish—Jewil!"

"Well, I've called him Red, and Red he is. And I'm not going to part with him," she said.

"I'm happy he's in such good hands. He'll lead you a dance. The devil never had a woman on him yet."

"You wouldn't like to wager on *that*, Mr. Blood?"

"Eh?" His dark eyes regarded her quizzically. He smiled slowly and gave a little nod of the head. "Why, whatever you wish, ma'am."

She faced him, smiling back, her lips pressed together to suppress her mirth. "It really wouldn't be fair to take your money, sir."

"It wouldn't, eh?" He laughed, showing his white teeth, but his look challenged her.

"Joseph, saddle him up. Not the sidesaddle," she said and turned toward the house.

"By God, you mean it," Blood said behind her.

She ran up the stairs like a child. She was excited, her heart racing, full of the electric response to him. She unbuttoned her dress, pulled open drawer after drawer in haste, rumpling the contents, pulling them out, not finding her riding things. She was about to call Emilie, then came across them. She discarded her dress, put on a blouse, then her riding breeches. Where were her riding boots? She hunted for them, found them at last, tucked the breeches into them, then put on the long skirt. Her hair was half loose. She stood at the glass impatiently arranging it and pinning it back, then about to run down, she halted, the doorknob in her hand. Stop. Wait a moment. Stop.

Something pulled her up, some instinct she was half afraid of. Wait. Wait a moment. She saw herself for a second from outside and turned away from the door. She could feel the flush in her face. She must compose herself, must stay back a moment longer. He would see . . . She caught her underlip in her teeth, walked back with head bent into the room. She felt a little foolish, but also half frightened of something—of her instincts. It was not only him, it was herself too. But she was filled with a strange sweetness and longing and fullness of her heart and at the same time touched by something frightening. She trembled a little and she still felt the tug of impatience to go down to him. At last she went to the glass and looked at herself. Yes, she was all right now. She stood smoothing her hair, waiting a moment longer. She thought of him waiting for her below. Then she took her skirt in her hand and as calmly as she could went down.

Joseph was holding the saddled horse. Blood smiled as she came out. Susannah went straight to the horse, hitched her skirt over her wrist, took the reins from Joseph. Blood stepped forward to offer his hand. The horse seemed to know her seat was going to be different and as she came up began to move his hindquarters around. "Red!" she said in a sharp voice, quickly put her foot into the stirrup and sprang up—Blood had to duck back—and her other leg was over the horse's back.

"*Jewil!*" Blood called out laughingly. The horse reared. She was hardly seated, but she hung on, laughing too. Now, astride, she could grip him, and the moment he dropped she swung him around, gave him a dig with her heels, and he dashed off down the drive. At the gate she swung him sharply around on his haunches and pulled him up. He obeyed perfectly. She took him back, made him walk, canter, prance about,

trotted him around for a moment or two, then held him still—
dead still—and dismounted.

"Oh, stylish, ma'am!" Blood came up smiling and applaud-
ing. "You've confounded me absolutely. I'd have sworn there
wasn't a woman who'd sit him. I was forgetting the other side
of the water."

She laughed with pleasure.

"Next time we'll have a race," he said.

"It'll be a pleasure, Mr. Blood."

The weather broke in three days of storms and continuous
rain. Everything ran with water. Streams ran through the vines.
A leak in the roof of the house dripped down the stairs and they
had to put basins out. On the third evening Susannah and
Francis were in the bedroom before going to bed; the rain had
almost stopped now. Susannah was brushing her hair and Francis was wandering about rather restlessly in his stockinged feet.
All at once he said, "Sue, I wish you wouldn't see John Blood
again for a while." He sounded embarrassed, trying to get
through an unpleasant business as lightly as he could.

"What?" Brush in mid-air, she turned in surprise. "Why
not?"

"Well, it makes talk, that's all."

"Talk?"

"You were with him alone here the other day. It was noticed." His face had colored; he looked embarrassed and horribly unhappy. It was obviously a subject he would have preferred
to avoid but hadn't been able to.

"Alone? He came to ask if we could attend to his horse. I
told Joseph to—"

"I know, I know that. But Chabot saw you joking and
laughing with him in the salon, alone."

"Chabot? I didn't see him."

"Evidently not. He says you were both sitting on the sofa
and it looked rather intimate. Then he says you were laughing
and flirting with the chap outside. It's so awkward, Sue." Francis walked miserably around the room. He hated it.

"But what nonsense! We were talking. I—" Now she remembered seeing the gray mare tethered by the vatting room

133

and thinking it was some visitor to Laverne; it must have been Chabot's.

"That's what I tried to tell him. He said to me, 'Do you let your young wife receive male visitors alone? We all know that man's a scoundrel.' "

"And naturally he told Mother? And probably Abel-Cherubin?"

"Yes. Of course." He turned, his eyes resentful now. Of course the family must know. Now at the mention of the family his defenses had sprung up.

Susannah stood up, faced him. "I surely don't have to justify myself, do I? Nothing in the least improper happened. Whatever you may know about John Blood, all I know is that he has behaved like a gentleman with me. And I have behaved toward him exactly as I would toward any other gentleman. Nothing more."

"Yes, but this isn't America."

"Frank!" She was shocked.

"A woman has to behave differently."

"You got that from your mother, didn't you?"

He rocked his head unhappily. "You apparently made an exhibition of yourself."

"Exhibition? I rode my horse."

"John Blood gave you that horse, didn't he?"

"What?" She stood still, stock still, her eyes fixed on him. It was as if a pall had come over her heart. It was like a blow. A great distance separated them. At last she said quietly, "Constance Canning gave him to me, as I told you. Do you think I'd lie to you?"

"It was Blood's horse, I'm told."

"It may have been, but Constance gave him to me. You can ask her."

He looked miserable. "I don't want to discuss it any more. You know my wishes, Sue, and that's an end of it."

They climbed silently into bed and lay rigid in the dark with backs turned. She could sense his wretchedness. He had been put up to it; it was so unlike him to find fault. He would never have thought of that himself. Madame Gautier had put it into his head. She wanted to reassure him, but somehow she couldn't. She knew he had only worked himself up to it with great difficulty, probably under Madame Gautier's goading.

He fell asleep first; she lay listening to his breathing. Presently she got up and went quietly downstairs. A great splash of moonlight lay in the hall. She pulled open the front door and sat down on the bench by the clock, her knees drawn up to her chin, staring outside. Why must it be so? She felt he was being torn away from her by the other force she could not ward off. It wasn't him. He wasn't willfully hurtful, but he was influenced by the other force. She sat staring out at the blocks of shadow and the moonlit shapes outside. Everything glistened faintly after the rain. The house was silent. It calmed her to sit there in the quiet and the ghostly light. Gradually she felt easier, gradually her spirit felt soothed; she shut the door and went back upstairs. The moonlight shone through the cracks in the shutters onto the floor of the bedroom. Her dismay had subsided, her hostility toward Madame Gautier was gone too. She stood looking at her husband from the foot of the bed in the dimness. Tomorrow he would have chased it from his mind. Tomorrow he would be his usual sweet self; everything would be all right. Tomorrow it would all be done with. He never harbored any resentments. She went to him and kissed his cheek. He didn't move, peacefully asleep.

Every other day now Francis was away consulting neighbors, driving to Bordeaux to see this specialist or that. The mysterious new disease, the oïdium, had spread all over. Everyone knew it had appeared in Provence, the Rhone Valley and Languedoc. Burgundy and Champagne were free, and outbreaks in the Bordelais area had hitherto been limited. But now it was everywhere and La Guiche was ravaged.

The disease showed itself everywhere in the same way. First a thin dull grayish-white powder, greasy to the touch, appeared on all the green parts of the vine, shoots, leaves and the grapes themselves. Under this powder then appeared small spots, which quickly multiplied and grew into irregular yellow-brown stains. In extreme cases, these joined together and deepened in color until the whole vine looked as if it had been stunted and blackened by fire. Where the disease was less severe, the stains remained like separate dirty brown finger marks. There were no holes, no scars, simply the marks, the finger marks. Young leaves withered, dried and dropped off; older leaves became brittle and the vine weakened. Blighted grapes looked at first as if they had been lightly dusted with flour. Then the blackish-brown marks showed through. Some grapes wrinkled, dried up and fell off the bunch. Others on the same bunch were unharmed. Yet others continued to swell in size but grew thick skins and finally split open. And everywhere was the smell of mold, of decay—the smell of death.

The powder and the brown marks were obviously the symptoms of the disease. But what was the disease itself? What was the cause?

"It's the soil. The soil's exhausted. What can you expect?" Josserand waved his hand toward the vines. "Year after year you want the same soil to give you the same crop. A piece of vine grows for fifty years, seventy years, starts to die—and what do you replace it with? More vines. It's been the same for centuries here. But everybody knows the same soil won't give you the same wheat, the same oats every year. It stands to reason."

"Yes but Rabaud over at Moulis planted a piece three years ago on new ground, never been used before, and it's as bad as the rest," Francis said.

Josserand shrugged, unconvinced. "That's what they tell you. You cut down a wood and you can't plant more of the same trees right away on the same spot, can you? Why should it be different with vines? And with this land—look at it, stones, gravel. You'd do better to plant *en joualles*."

"You mean grow crops between the vines?" It was done in some parts of the Bordeaux region but not in Médoc.

"That I do! Leave a bit here, a bit down yonder. Tear up the rest. Plant a good piece of wheat or oats or tobacco. Oh, you'll have to bring in manure, loads of manure, and it won't give much of a crop, I'll grant you that. It's poor land. But it'd be better than this."

But Francis suspected that Josserand only wanted more space for his own crops, for the disease was taking his livelihood away. So he ignored this advice.

Everybody had an explanation for the disease. Coote Onslow's estate manager, Bailly, a deliberate, slow-moving man, said it was an excess of vigor in the vines brought on by too much manure. "Too much of this guano from South America. Too rich. Far too rich." Fortunately he had an "old secret" against the disease. This, he confided to Francis, was to scratch the diseased shoots with a pruning hook and make a number of shallow incisions in them. Francis told Josserand to do this in one section at La Guiche.

The Marquis de Montferrat, next door, shook his head. He had seen the disaster coming. Far from being too vigorous, the vines had been progressively weakening for years and now they were "morbidly predisposed."

"But why?" Francis wanted to know.

"It's in the plant's structure," said the Marquis obscurely.

Raynal, who had consulted the biggest vineyard owners around Libourne, said the disease was caused by a mite. The mite had not been definitely identified, but they had isolated several suspects.

"But none of the young shoots close to the ground are diseased," Francis said.

"Well . . . that's the habit of the mite. It prefers the upper shoots."

Foissac, an old family friend in Bordeaux, said it was caused by a freak of the weather. "There's something they call static electricity in the air. I'm told the Academy of Science in Paris is investigating."

Some people put it down to the railways, which were disturbing the atmospheric balance with their smoke. Some said it came from the marsh mist, which had been poisoned by vapors from the earth. The zodiac was brought in, so were the conjunction of the stars and fatal permutations of the figures 1852. But the mysteries remained.

If the disease was in the soil, why weren't the vine roots affected? Why didn't the vines die off completely? If it was a mite, why did the mite attack only green grapes, never grapes that had ripened and turned color? If it was manure, why should unmanured vines get the disease? If it was excess vigor or morbid weakness, why should vines of all ages be diseased? And why should all the vines be attacked at once?

The one certain thing about the new disease was that it came from England. An Englishman named Tucker, it appeared, had first noticed the disease on the vines in his hothouse at Margate on the coast of England in 1845. Hence it had received its scientific name, *Oïdium tuckeri*. From England it had spread to France, and now every month there were reports

137

of it from somewhere new—Belgium, Spain, Italy, Greece, Syria, Hungary, Switzerland, Algeria.

But how to eradicate it? Difficult if you didn't know what it was. Nevertheless, for every dozen explanations of the disease, there were as many "remedies."

Francis tramped about the vineyard with Josserand and the workpeople trying first one thing then another. Bailly's method of scratching the diseased shoots had produced no visible result.

"Two people in Bordeaux told me that watery plaster is good," Francis said to Josserand.

"I've heard the same."

"You'll have to try it."

The men hoisted sacks of plaster and water casks into the carts and went around dousing the vines with the mixture and carefully plastering the shoots. It was dreadfully laborious. A storm broke in the middle of it and wiped out their work and they had to begin over again. The vineyard looked wretched and bedraggled, the plaster-daubed vines pitiful. And ten days later they were as bad as ever.

Correspondents wrote to the Bordeaux papers offering "proven remedies." One in *Le Courrier de la Gironde* who had scalded the foot of his vines with boiling water reported excellent results. *L'Indicateur* advocated spraying the vines with a solution of potash. *La Guienne* claimed a 50 per cent cure with arsenous oxide. Francis tried all three. None worked. Every week somebody came forward with an "unfailing remedy" which on investigation proved useless. Meanwhile, the grapes rotted and the smell of decay drifted over the Gironde.

One afternoon in the last week of July, Regis Gautier came out to La Guiche with Abel-Cherubin. Susannah was by the lake and saw them drive up together and get out. She was about to go over when Francis came along from the vatting room and greeted them. They stood talking for a moment, then disappeared together into the house. When she went in they were closeted in Francis's office. Much later she came out of the kitchen to see if they were going to stay for dinner and found they had gone. Francis offered no explanation.

17

For a young man as aspiring as Regis Gautier, the salon of
Baron Ignaz Hagenbach was an imposing sight. The Baron
himself, a bulky bearded man, was stationed beside a marble
bust of Plato and looked august. As head of the second oldest
dynasty of chartrons after Mr. John Laffan Jennings, he had
special eminence, and this was reflected in the gravity of his
demeanor.

Near him was seated Madame Hagenbach. She was a tall,
imperious, long-throated woman who refused to wear the crinoline, restricting herself to plain black. Tonight the vast promon-
tory of her bosom supported the famous Hagenbach pearls in
addition to a gold locket. Farther off, the object of Regis Gautier's special attention, Mademoiselle Aurelie Hagenbach, was
attended by Mawdistly Baynes, son of Simcoe Baynes, and Richard O'Shea, the younger son of another old chartron family.

Mademoiselle Aurelie, just twenty-one, with pale hair, pale
eyes and pale skin, had her mother's long throat and incipient
signs of her father's girth, a striking bottlelike combination. But
she was the last of the four Hagenbach daughters and Regis
was determined to marry her. She was the entrance to high
Bordeaux society for which he longed and to which he believed
he had, by his gifts and his good looks, a right to belong. At the
moment he was irritated by Mawdistly Baynes's persistence in
monopolizing Aurelie; Baynes had buttonholed her before dinner and nobody else had got near. Mawdistly! Regis didn't un-

derstand how she could endure the creature with his gangling body, his yellow hair and his stoop.

Across the room the elder Baynes was standing with the Count de Mornac, Armand Fouquet the banker, and several other distinguished guests. The whole scene had an effect of massiveness. Among the males there seemed no intermediary state between the very fat and the very lean, and among the women between the dull and the extremely shrewd. They had only just come in from dinner, so they were still weightily in movement about the room. An ornament or two shook under their tread, for their digestive systems were dealing with brioche de foie gras, oxtail soup, lobster à la Newburg, stuffed lamb, sorbet with raspberry brandy, roast guinea fowl, salad, assorted cheeses, charlotte à la Parisienne, ananas voilé, mignardises and fruit.

Dinner had been full of passionate talk. They had talked of trade, the stock exchange, food and property. One guest, a stranger, Madame Jubelin, had brought up the Salon of Fine Arts in Paris, but after an abrupt silence, broken only by the sound of mastication, the moment had safely passed.

"Monsieur?" A lackey with a silver tray of brandy and liqueurs bowed to Regis. Regis shook his head. Two other footmen in livery were passing around. When you were a chartron you showed off your domestic staff. Hagenbach employed three footmen, three chambermaids, a music teacher, cook, kitchen-maid, two porters, a groom and a coachman and complained that his wife couldn't get a good pastry cook.

The windows of the room were open to the warm summer night air. On all sides large knowledgeable noses were being bent into snifters. Regis turned to admire a statuette representing the Spirit of Commerce shown with sword and buckler guarding Civilization. In spite of his seeming ease, he was still in awe at being in such an elegant household. Yet how shaky his status here was! He had only been invited as one of Mademoiselle Aurelie's attendants. Shine as he might as a rising young dealer in colonial products, an enterprising young underwriter, an ornament to any salon and a man, moreover, who was not so bigoted a Catholic, not so narrow a doctrinarian that he would not turn Protestant or Lutheran if need be—with all this he knew he was only there on sufferance. Once Mademoiselle

Aurelie had been married off, he would have no footing in the household. And there wasn't another chartron's daughter in sight to whom he might aspire. It was now or never.

Regis felt a terrible desire to become one of these elect souls. It was an embittering thing not to have been born one, a man of his ability, or born at least with fortune enough to claim easy admission to their circle. As it was, he had some money but not nearly enough. His club cost money and, of course, as a man of the town he had to gamble. His clothes cost money. He was obliged to be seen, at the races, at the Grand Theater, at the season's balls. He naturally had to have a mistress and La Monteiro was damned expensive. He had to speculate on the Bourse. He had to do all these things to fill his male role.

Outside this, to make his way in the world, he had to rely on his brilliance, his charm, the attractions of his person. But he knew that the one essential intermediary to a good Bordeaux marriage was *the notary*. What he needed, what he yearned for, was *property*. Ah, if only he owned a nice piece of property! Something he could offer Baron Hagenbach as a suitable setting for Mademoiselle Aurelie, something that would, through the marriage settlement, pass into the Hagenbach orbit. Then— then the doors would open to him!

He had dreamed of coming into La Guiche by a chain of circumstances. But that fool Francis had not only married and complicated everything but now was actively offending chartrons like Jacobsen, a man whose son was married to Melanie, the second Hagenbach daughter. The Pavé des Chartrons did not easily forget such a slight. These men had long memories. It was agonizing to have one's carefully nurtured chances shaken by one's own cousin.

And Baynes— Oh, damn all Bayneses, Regis thought. Across the room, Mawdistly Baynes was obviously being flirtatious. Regis caught the flicker of a smile on Mademoiselle Aurelie's face at something Mawdistly had said. He flashed a glance at Baron Hagenbach. The father was watching the couple fondly. Regis felt himself coloring. The edge of his high collar was sawing into his neck. Taking care not to touch it, he shot his cuffs and walked resolutely toward Mademoiselle Aurelie and the two men. At that moment, however, the young lady caught a summoning look from her mother. She disengaged herself and went, all submission, to the Baroness. Regis took up a position to intercept her when she was free.

He cast his eye around again. In a quiet corner on the far side of the room he could see Léon Chabot, his uncle, seated with Jean Faget de la Saigne, the shipowner, and Hippolyte Balu, a local merchant and vineyard proprietor. Regis watched them discreetly but with interest. He could almost see them change their subject of conversation as soon as anyone approached! To all appearances they were chatting about insurance or the price of indigo. But Regis had an idea that they were discussing something else—their partnership in the triangular trade. In other words, a little unobtrusive slaving. For Sophie de Monteiro had picked up a hint, and Regis in these last few weeks had acquired the conviction that it was true. They were involved in the slave trade.

The government in Paris had abolished slavery in 1848 during the short-lived Second Republic—not with Bordeaux approval. The Bordeaux merchants had snorted; it was asking for trouble. A sensible man was bound to mistrust any innovation, and this abolition business was a typical piece of revolutionary folly that wiser councils would have at least deferred. The Bordeaux merchants had been active slavers; not so numerous as the men in Nantes, maybe, but more tenacious. And so when the trade was officially stopped, some quietly carried on.

It was, as Regis knew, a risky game. The English navy was on the watch and so was the French, in principle. But paradoxically, he had observed, this race of cautious men in Bordeaux had a taste for taking high risks now and then with their money. In the long wars between France and England, from the Revolution down to the end of the Napoleonic Empire, they had thumbed their noses at His Majesty and sent out ships to run the English blockade. And then they had fitted out privateers and raided the English trade in the Atlantic. Regis sighed enviously —for what business that had been! Privateering out of Bordeaux had become enormously lucrative—400 to 600 per cent profit on a single venture! They alone, the Bordeaux merchants, had captured up to seven hundred English ships a year. Why, the most distinguished families of the city had founded their fortunes on privateering.

Across the room another group of guests moved toward the

secluded corner. Chabot and his friends were already on their feet and dispersing. Mademoiselle Aurelie was taking a fond and prolonged leave of her mother, inspiring looks of huge sympathy from the lady guests. Poised for interception, Regis saw that Chabot had gone up to Simcoe Baynes and was talking to him. It irritated Regis. He had noticed earlier that Chabot seemed to have changed his views about Baynes. He watched his uncle's foxy face, the sloping forehead. Chabot was at his most sycophantic, obviously sucking up to Baynes.

But his attention was instantly torn away. Just as Mawdistly Baynes appeared from the left, Mademoiselle Aurelie at last detached herself from her mother. Regis put on his most charming smile and advanced quickly toward her.

18

Every day now during the long summer Susannah itched to do
something about the house. La Guiche was vast, and whole
sections of it were shut up, unused. The upper floors were bare
boards and a maze of rooms she had not explored. Once or twice
downstairs she had followed some passage or gone along a landing and opened a door to look in on the dim shapes of old furniture in the shuttered gloom and smell the dusty staleness. Some
doors were locked and Emilie couldn't find the keys on the great
kitchen keyboard. And Madame Gautier's watchful presence
was always there—as if there were ghosts she did not want disturbed. Susannah saw she would have to do things gradually.

One evening Francis announced that his mother was going
away for a week. Her aunt in Blanquefort was unwell. Susannah
saw Madame Gautier off next morning, and when she had gone
opened two rooms at the head of the stairs.

The heavy shutters, unopened for an age, screeched and
showered her with flakes of old paint and dust. The bright sunlight streamed in on a great cobwebbed mirror, a few chairs, a
disemboweled sofa, a dressing table and oddments—all like
corpses in the sudden glare. Dust everywhere. The paneling was
an ugly brown, the ceiling encrusted with bulbous Louis-Philippe loops and floral decorations in plaster. A great disappointment really. But the southward view from the windows over
the vines and the surrounding country was lovely. She stood
there looking out, then she looked around the room again. No,

she'd changed her mind. It would be all right. Once the rooms were cleaned they would be a welcome escape after the lugubrious salon below.

Then as she stood considering, something came back to her. James had shown her a book one day with illustrations of some of the fine old houses in Bordeaux. The rooms had had just this sort of look, these tall doors, this woodwork. Could there be eighteenth-century paneling under that ugly paint? Surely the ceiling had been plastered over too.

She ran down, found the book, turned the pages excitedly. Yes, she was confident of it. The first thing was to get the rooms into a usable state and have Madame Gautier accept the idea. She put Emilie and one of the village women who came in to help to sweeping and cleaning. She had Jean the garden boy take all the old bits of furniture out into the open to dust them and see if they could still be used and then bring in an extra thing or two from downstairs.

Francis appeared in the middle of all this. He came up slapping his boot with a willow switch. "What on earth are you doing?"

"Cleaning, dear."

"Does Mother know?"

Susannah leaned forward, dirty hands behind her back, and kissed him on the cheek. "Outdoors is your job. Let me look after the house."

"You know Mother hates things changed about."

She didn't reply and he said no more but walked away, his mind obviously on something else. Susannah watched him thoughtfully for a minute, then went back upstairs.

The heavy brocade curtains, embroidered with birds and arabesques in gold and colored thread, really looked too far gone. Emilie climbed up and unhooked them, setting them both coughing with the dust. The curtains were beautiful but almost fell to pieces in Susannah's hands; they would never stand up to a wash. This created a problem. So in the afternoon she sat down and went carefully over her housekeeping budget. In the end she decided that with a saving here and there and by adding the rest of her own money she could buy new curtains in some plain material. At dinner she told Francis she was going shopping in Bordeaux next day and he made no objection. And so at seven o'clock next morning Susannah started off with Joseph in the carriage.

It was a gray day, but she didn't mind. She was happy, her thoughts busy with how she would rearrange the new rooms and how she would bring Madame Gautier around to agreeing.

Bordeaux was noisy. Herds of oxen and cows being driven through the streets from the cattle market were mixed up with dashing cabriolets and drays loaded with barrels of wine and the water vendors with their carts. First of all she tried a shop on the Cours de l'Intendance, the main street. They had some lovely fabrics but all too expensive. She walked from counter to counter, fingering the material enviously; but it was no good. She tried another shop on the other side of the street; it was the same there. Then she thought of a large rather old-fashioned store in the Rue Sainte Catherine that would surely be cheaper and told Joseph to take her there.

The Rue Sainte Catherine was a narrow cobbled street lurching downhill between shops and crooked old houses. It was busy with traffic. Joseph put her down at the store and she went in. It was a big rambling place making a brave attempt to keep up with the smarter shops with "latest novelties" from Paris in the way of haberdashery, bonnets, lace, furnishings, Chinese furs, linen, corsetry, ribbons, bed ticking and so on. *Suppliers to the Nobility and Gentry*, said a sign in English.

The young male clerk was very polite and spread out bolt after bolt of material on the counter before Susannah. She examined them all, asked for others. But when she liked something it was too dear, and the cheaper ones . . . Well, if she put up something that didn't look right, Madame Gautier might seize on it and make a fuss and defeat her whole purpose. She stood hesitating, looking at the materials once more. She seemed to have miscalculated about prices.

The clerk moved away to attend to another customer and Susannah noticed a man at her elbow. He said something to her and she glanced at him. He was a stranger, a large well-dressed man about forty with stovepipe hat, mustache and beard, a bourgeois. He was gazing at her intently and now standing quite close. For an instant she thought he was making an inquiry, then realized it was something quite different. She was horribly embarrassed. Now she remembered catching a glimpse of him following her in as she entered the shop. She tried to catch the clerk's attention, but he was occupied.

She felt her face reddening. She moved away. The shop was busy with customers; she paused at another counter, looking at the display of haberdashery. The man was close beside her again, speaking in a low voice. Without glancing at him, she said, "Go away!" and turned across the shop. As she did so, she saw that the floorwalker, an Italian-looking man with curly hair, was glaring. He had seen her speak.

Susannah walked briskly into another part of the shop and up the stairs to the floor above. She didn't look back to see if he had followed. There were displays of children's things, traveling clothes, patent portmanteaus, cash belts. She wandered along the counters, glanced around. No sign of the man. She breathed relief. After a while she went down to the other counter again and finally settled on a pretty fabric in leafy russet. It was expensive and the present she had wanted to get for her sister Maisie in Vicksburg would have to wait till next month. The clerk handed over the parcel. Then as she made her way with it among the other customers, the man was suddenly in front of her. He smiled in a horrible way.

"Now you've finished, we can spend an hour or two together, eh?"

"Go away!"

"Don't be foolish, my dear. You're charming. I have money."

She tried to brush past, but he turned and walked with her, close alongside, his head bent toward her. She caught the floorwalker's outraged stare—as if *she* had encouraged the man. The shop had darkened, it was more like dusk than noon. She reached the street door. The man was beside her all the time, speaking, saying obscene things. She saw the sky outside black with storm clouds. Five or six people were sheltering in the doorway, and as she stepped out among them, searching the street for Joseph, the rain swept down. The shelterers stepped back, pressing her back with them. The man was against her. Susannah pushed forward through the people, but he followed, pretending to laugh, pretending they were together.

She could not see Joseph among the carts and vehicles crowding the street in the downpour. The rain splashed her.

She craned, searching the street, which was all little V's of rain and crashing vehicles and cursing drivers. She *had* to find Joseph. She felt the man's hand touch her waist, she grasped her skirt with one hand and ran out into the flooding rain. She only wanted to get away from him. She felt the rain soaking her dress. Never mind, never mind!

She couldn't cross in the traffic and had to hover at the curb. He had kept up with her. An opening appeared, she started over. He tried to take her arm. Encumbered with the parcel, she turned angrily and said, "Leave me alone!" She flung him off, and then as he crowded up again, blocking her view, a hand from behind swung him around. Over his shoulder she had time to see John Blood's angry face. There was a gristly crack, the man's head shot back, his hat flew off and he went sprawling on his back on the cobbles.

Susannah stood hunched in the downpour, not knowing what to do. Blood said, "Here, my dear, jump in." A fiacre was standing in the road with the door hanging open. Quickly Blood stepped forward, handed her into the cab. The man was lying in the roadway, a trickle of blood running from his mouth, his false teeth hanging loose. Somebody shouted over the thudding rain. Blood picked up his own hat, spoke to the driver and jumped in beside her. As he slammed the door, the cab turned down a side street.

"Lord!" Her bonnet and clothes were wet through. She put the sodden package on the floor, took off the bonnet and shook her hair out.

"Are you all right?" he said.

"Yes. I was . . . I was frightened. I'm all right now. Lord, I'm so wet."

"I saw you from the cab. He accosted you?"

"Yes, horrible creature, in the store. He was pestering me in the store. I couldn't shake him off. Then he followed me outside. Horrible."

"You'd better take this cab back home, if you've done your shopping."

"I can't. I have to go back there. Joseph is waiting with the carriage."

"I'll go and find him. Are you alone?"

"Yes. I'm so *wet*. I just came to do a little shopping."

They sat in the cab while the rain thudded on the roof. It was the first time they had been alone since he had come to La Guiche with the lame horse, and she had an idea that in some way he had guessed there had been trouble with Francis about that. She was terribly uncertain of herself, far more aware of him even than at La Guiche, aware of his nearness to her, of their privacy in the cab. A strength came from him to her, in a way that was different from anyone else. There was a fusing between them that needed no words. His eyes were dark and steady and strong, watching her. She knew she was giving away her feelings and she hardly dared look at him. The pulse was beating in her throat and she had a feeling of breathlessness. She felt ashamed and betrayed by these feelings for him, which must have been growing in her silently and secretly, and at the same time she felt a wild, trembling secret joy.

He said, "You're soaking wet. You can't drive home like that." He rapped for the driver, put his head out and gave an order. The cab broke into a clip.

"What did you tell him?" She said.

"My house is ten minutes away. I'll have my housekeeper dry your things."

"No, really, I can't do that."

"Nonsense, you'll get pneumonia. There's Mrs. Curran, my housekeeper, and a house full of servants. They do nothing all day."

They were moving quickly. The glass of the cab windows was steamed over and she couldn't see where they were going. Her clothes clung to her uncomfortably. The few minutes in the downpour had been enough for a soaking, and she imagined she might easily be in a fever if she did drive all the way back to La Guiche in them. There was something feverish in her now. She knew she was compromising herself. She felt she had given away feelings that had been hidden in herself, that he knew something secret in her—that was how it felt. And she felt terribly vulnerable with him. Yet she believed in him, she believed absolutely in his honor. Without turning her head, she could see his lean long-chinned profile cut against the other window of the cab.

The cab wheels ran off the road onto a different surface and they pulled up. She wiped her hand across the steamy glass.

They were under the porte-cochere of a mansion, and a gray-haired footman in black was coming out. Gravely he opened the cab door, helped her down.

"Tell Mrs. Curran to come," Blood said. "And take the parcel there."

"Yes, monsieur."

Blood showed her in. The entrance was imposing, black and white marble floor, great grayish-green tapestries, a glass chandelier. A monumental staircase rose to regions above. Blood took off his hat and swished the rain off as he led her in. Through tall doors they entered a spacious paneled salon with gilded mirrors, Savonnerie carpets and period furniture formally set out.

"How grand!" she looked around admiringly. "Is this all yours?"

"Not on your life. Belongs to a friend of mine. Pray be seated."

"I daren't—too wet."

"Tush, they'll dry the chair." He threw his hat aside and banged his coat with his hand.

"You're as wet as I am. I'm dripping."

He laughed and turned as a short plump woman in a plain dress appeared at the door. "Mrs. Curran, the lady's clothes, as you see, have got soaked in the rain. Will you please have them dried at once so that she may continue her journey. A hot iron on them, perhaps?"

The woman's eyes went to Susannah. "Certainly, sir." With a smile she said to Susannah, "If you'll come this way, ma'am."

Susannah hesitated, moved forward, then looked at Blood. "I . . . I must find Joseph." Their eyes met and her look said that she trusted him, trusted his honor.

"Of course. I'll have you driven back."

Susannah followed the woman out and up the staircase. At the end of a gallery at the top the woman opened a door and stood back for her to go in. It was a suite of rooms. The first, a small salon, was in the same eighteenth-century style as the salon below and overlooked a little garden. Mrs. Curran fetched a peignoir. Susannah took her wet clothes off, and the woman gathered them up to carry away.

"We'll have them dry for you in no time at all, ma'am."

"Thank you."

Susannah wrapped the peignoir around her, tucked her hands under her armpits and went exploring. There were three rooms in all, the salon, a bedroom in peacock blue and a tiny dressing room. The salon had a little alcove with a canopy covered in pale blue silk, a cylinder-front desk in marquetry and small gilded stools with petit-point seats. She walked around inspecting. One or two framed drawings of ladies in costume were on the walls.

It was madness to have come here. Madness. Somehow she had not believed she would. It had been a sort of shaky, mad pretense, and yet all the while she was accomplishing it. Every moment she had told herself, Stop! And yet the second afterward she was a little nearer. And *he* had seemed unbelieving in a way, unbelieving she would come. She thought of Joseph waiting. What if somebody had seen her, seen the whole thing? What if a servant here talked? How word spread! "Chabot saw you joking and laughing with him." It would confirm everything. Madness! And to have made herself so vulnerable. It was a sort of half-voluntary madness that she couldn't help with him, the same trembling feeling she had had at La Guiche when she had run upstairs to change—desire and resistance in herself that made her weak and breathless. And now it was a sort of surrender of herself, wasn't it? Wasn't it? *Yes*, it was. She shuddered. She paced up and down, nervous at her own thoughts, her own folly.

Then, trying to turn her mind away, she went next door. The bedroom was pretty with its blue walls; the little dressing room was all Chinese, with wallpaper showing a Chinese mountain scene, and a beautiful black and gold lacquer screen. The place had intense privacy. She went back into the salon and looked down at the deserted garden below set out with boxwoods and clipped hedges, gravel paths and rigidly aligned flower borders. It looked so . . . so strangely empty. Was it her nervousness, her imagination? In some way the light seemed different there.

A little rosewood spinet stood open beside the window with some music propped up on it. She sat down and began to play. She had the feeling that the sounds did not carry beyond the room. It was months and months since she had played. The music made its beautiful formal patterns. She played several of the pieces, then a Schubert song she had learned at home, then another.

A knock on the door startled her. She hesitated, then called out, "Come in." It was Mrs. Curran with her clothes over her arm. In spite of herself her heart gave a plunge of relief.

"May I come in, ma'am? Here 'tis, all dry. You'll not catch cold in them now."

"Thank you," Susannah said.

"I'm having the material in the parcel dried, ma'am. It's almost ready."

Susannah dressed and stood at the mirror arranging her hair and wondering about Blood in this house . . . Mrs. Curran, the servants. He appeared to have no pressing occupation and seemed to be living alone, yet he obviously wasn't attached here, didn't belong. When she had finished she gave a final look in the mirror and went downstairs. The hall was empty. Blood was sitting in the salon reading a paper with his feet up on a chair and a drink close at hand. He jumped up as she came in; he had changed his black coat for a gray one.

"I trust everything was satisfactory?"

"Yes, perfectly. It's a beautiful house. Those rooms upstairs are charming."

"Mrs. Curran says your parcel is dry and freshly wrapped. She has put it in the carriage. Will you take a little refreshment before you go?"

"No, thank you. You . . . you've been most kind, sir."

"You'll forgive me if I don't accompany you back. It wouldn't be the best thing for you to be seen too publicly in my company."

He broke off and took a step or two toward the window, then turned around again with his sardonic smile. "In fairness, I should . . . I should warn you off, you know. I feel some guilt at your being here at all. It is my fault. But perhaps my general disrepute has been conveyed to you?"

She looked at him. "Yes, but no reason given."

"Well, it would be painful to me to think I was abusing your ignorance. Apart from anything else, the English would have a price on my head here if they could; and in these cases they see that a man's reputation doesn't flourish."

"What for?"

"Oh, nothing that need alarm you. Certain . . . certain incidents in Ireland. Fortunately, I have good friends here."

He came up to her. His dark eyes looked into hers, into her soul. "Susannah—forgive me if I call you Susannah—I think of you . . . and want to say a hundred gentle things to you."

She felt weak before him, as if his strength dominated her. She stood facing him. His touch made her tremble as he took her hand, then he lifted her face gently and kissed her on the lips. She felt her lips trembling on his. She felt too vulnerable, yet in the confusion of her emotions her heart went out to him. Then he moved back. "Let me show you to the carriage. It will take you back."

The carriage was waiting. He handed her in and the footman shut the door. He stood there looking at her till the carriage moved off, and she sat back as the rain came down on the roof again, drumming with the drumming of her heart.

Madame Gautier returned to La Guiche two days early, before Susannah had the new rooms ready. When the message came for Joseph to go and fetch her, Susannah had a moment of panic; she had not prepared her explanation yet. The moment the carriage arrived, she went out and helped Madame Gautier down. Madame Gautier looked subdued. As they went into the hall, Susannah said rather nervously, "I wanted to give you a surprise. I've been arranging two of the rooms upstairs. I . . . I haven't quite finished, but they're going to look very well."

Madame Gautier's eyes turned on her. "Who told you to do that?" The look was strained, accusing.

"It was my own idea. I . . . I'm sure you'll like them." To her surprise, Madame Gautier said nothing more but went straight up to her room. Susannah waited in dread for the expected scene to break, for this initial silence usually presaged a storm. However, Madame Gautier sent down to say she had caught a chill at Blanquefort and had taken to her bed. Susannah went up, but Madame Gautier refused to let her attend to her and Susannah could only rather helplessly send up broth and jellies by Emilie. She felt frustrated and guilty. It was as if Madame Gautier's strained, accusing eyes had seen her with

John Blood, seen her in the house, could read her heart, *knew* and accused her.

For two or three nights she sat up late sewing. Her heart was timid, as if she must be quiet because of this secret, and when she went upstairs she crept into bed trying not to disturb Francis in his sleep; but nearly always he stirred, sensing her there, and put his arm around her. She was shaken and ashamed. She thought how much she had changed since the early days when she had hated the thought of concealing anything from Francis. Not so long ago! But she didn't love him less.

19

September or early October was the harvesttime, but this year
there were fearful problems. Mold everywhere! The vineyard
looked blasted. The blight seemed to be rotting everything.
More and more of the grapes as they swelled were splitting
open, and soon there would be nothing left to save. Everybody
had long faces. They must get in what grapes they could at the
first opportunity. But the weather wouldn't let them. There
were gray blustery skies and frequent rain. To harvest grapes in
rain was a despairing thing to do because the rain inevitably
got into the wine and made it watery. Normally you waited
until even the dew had dispersed before cutting grapes and you
broke off as soon as a shower came on. Every day Francis looked
at the barometer, but it got no better.

Then problems cropped up with the workers. As usual
workpeople had flocked into the country for the harvest, some
from Saintonge, the cognac country to the north and east, some
from the Landes, some from the Basque country and the Pyrenees, whom the local people called "mountain folk." They
were poor, rough-looking families, dark-eyed women and children with them, who came to the Médoc each year to be employed with the local people. But this year families who had
been coming regularly to La Guiche had deserted and gone
elsewhere, and Francis seemed to be having trouble over re-
placements. Susannah would come to the kitchen and find him
and Josserand haggling with a group of the men over the pay.

For every separate task was calculated—cutting the grapes, emptying the baskets and carrying them to the cart, loading the cart, treading the press, carrying the wine to the vats, draining the stalks, topping up the vats, emptying the vats, scalding the barrels, pouring water on the marc, cooking the meals, helping the cook, baking the bread. Every single thing had its price, every movement. There had to be a fiddler to play the fiddle while the winemaking was going on. Why? Tradition. The women and children who did the cutting, a backbreaking job, got half a man's pay; but, of course, there was a boss male called the commandant who did little else but go around shouting and hurrying them up. And he had to have a special bonus.

Francis came to Susannah one morning and said she would have to supervise the organization of meals and the lodging for the vintagers. The people themselves would do the work, but she would have to see to the general arrangements.

"When are they coming?"

"Tomorrow."

"Heavens! Are we beginning tomorrow then?"

"Sue, I keep telling you I don't know! It depends on the weather." Even he was on edge.

She immediately had a great deal to do—preparing tables and benches, supervising the cooking arrangements, seeing to the supply of food, setting up the sleeping quarters in the biggest outbuilding, for the vintagers "lived in" during the harvest. Madame Josserand helped. Apparently the vintagers were used to nothing better than straw to sleep on and were left to sleep as they pleased. A cow, an ox and eight sheep had to be ordered from the butcher, the crockery and cutlery got out and quantities of oil, salt, candles, flour, fat, lard, beans and so forth bought. When Susannah suggested more vegetables, Madame Josserand said no. Above all no potatoes. No local person would touch potatoes. "They give you the epilepsy, didn't you know that?" Octavie the cook had said to her once.

Laverne and the inside men were busy preparing the vats and casks, washing them out, rinsing them with brandy, washing down the cellars. Others were getting the carts ready.

Francis obviously hated all the paperwork this entailed, for everything had to be entered down in the books.

"Can't I help with that?" she said.

"No. You keep to your side." He never gave her an opportunity to see the books.

But instead of clearing, the weather worsened. Now it rained steadily most of the day. The workpeople lounged about, drinking, joking in their patois, drifting off to the village. The outbuilding where they had their meals was messy with the congealed remnants of meals left about. At last Francis and Josserand decided there was nothing for it, they would have to begin, and one morning they all covered themselves as best they could and trooped out.

Susannah wrapped herself in an old cloak and hood, put on clogs and went out to watch. It was her first grape harvest and she wanted to see it. The sky was leaden. The fine penetrating rain had obviously set in for the day. The mud was slippery at the ends of the rows of vines. There seemed something futile about them gathering grapes in such weather. Some of the children were not more than eight or nine years old, yet they were quick and knew what to do. The commandant, a man named Thomas, organized the cutters and carriers according to the usual method. The women and children, armed with pruning scissors and baskets, went down the rows cutting the good grapes, rejecting rotten or unripe ones. When they had a full basket they carried it to a man at the end of the row who emptied it into a tub. Two of these emptiers served every eight rows. When the tub was full the emptier hoisted it on the back of another man, a carrier, whose back was protected by a thick straw mat, and he carried it to the nearest ox-drawn cart. Two bigger tubs stood on the cart and the grapes were tipped into these for transport to the vatting room. Every dozen rows of vines had an inspector who went around hurrying the cutters on, for it was important to get the grapes in quickly.

The rain fell dismally. And such quantities of diseased grapes everywhere! Indoors in the vatting room it was better. The fiddler, an old man with thick white hair who had no more talent for playing the fiddle than Job, was scraping away. Susannah heard the cart with the grapes stop outside at one of the big windowlike openings. In the cart the men hauled up the heavy tub of grapes on an arm with rope and pulley, swung it in through the opening and tipped it over onto the treading press immediately beneath. The treading press, standing about two feet from the vatting-room floor, was like a great square stone sink, some nine feet square, with raised sides about sixteen inches high and a hole in the front for the wine to run out into a half-tub called a *gargouille*. A wire sieve lay over the treading press and the grapes fell onto this. The men took wooden rakes and raked the grapes back and forth over this sieve, stepping forward occasionally to throw out a bad bunch.

Gradually, under the raking, the grapes dropped through into the press, leaving only the stalks on the sieve. This was what they called *égrappage*, removing the stalks. They lifted the sieve off and carried it to another press to drain. Then three men with their trousers tucked up to their knees kicked off their clogs, climbed inside the press and trod around and around on the grapes. They moved in a circle, one after the other, while the old fiddler's scrapes became more vigorous, a shade more rhythmic, but no more musical. The dark juice ran out into the *gargouille*.

Laverne was supervising. Susannah stood by the door looking on. When the *gargouille* was nearly full, they slid an empty one into its place and poured the juice into a tall bucket that had a rod through the top to carry it by. Two men picked this up, climbed the ladders set against the side of the first of the great oak vats standing against the opposite wall, and tipped the juice into the vat. Finally they raked up the skins from the bottom of the treading press and put them into the vat too. That was one cartload and they stood about waiting for the next to come from outside. The vat would be filled to within fifteen inches of the top, then left to ferment, which it did eight to eighteen hours later, bubbling and hissing. When the wine was clear and cool in about ten days' time, it would be drawn off into casks.

Laverne came over and stood with Susannah. She had been thinking how clumsy it was to have the men carry those buckets up the ladders to tip them into the vat. And why not have the men in the press wear clogs? More efficient, surely? She asked Laverne.

"I dare say it does look clumsy but there are good reasons," he said. "When we carry the juice like that it gets aerated just at the right moment and improves the wine. And if they wore clogs, they'd crush the pips, and pips are acid. You'd spoil the wine. The bare foot's just right, just flexible enough, and these men are not big fellows, so they don't crush the grapes too much. All these little things make a difference."

He smiled, trying to be amiable, but she could see he wasn't happy.

"It isn't going to be a good year, is it?"

He shrugged. "We mustn't despair."

"You mean it's the rain and the blight?"

"Yes. And . . . well, we're being too rushed, too. By rights we should be harvesting two or three times, taking the ripe grapes first, then carefully getting the rest in separately. But how can you, in this weather, and with the mold and everything. As it is, they'll all be going in together, good and bad, ripe and less ripe. And we're having to warm up some of the must."

"You mean the juice, warm up the juice?"

He nodded. "Some of it. We have to do that with this weather, otherwise the wine will become what you call ropy."

Later, when she came back to watch again, Laverne wasn't there. The men seemed slacker. She noticed they weren't so careful about getting all the stalks off the grapes, and they tipped a whole lot with stalks directly into the press, so plenty of stalks got into the vat. Laverne had made them wait a bit while the rain drained off the grapes that were freshly brought in, but they weren't doing that either now. She knew each vat had to be filled the same day so as not to disturb the process of fermentation. If you spread it over two days or more you would be pouring fresh juice onto juice already fermenting and would damage the wine. So it must be haste that made them careless, she concluded.

Raynal had come over for the day, and he reported that the oïdium was worse at Libourne. At lunch Susannah said to him, "Does it make any difference if the stalks go into the vat?"

"Makes the wine harder. Bound to. There's tartaric acid and tannin in stalks. And they'd make it watery in this weather. Some people say it preserves the wine longer and gives it a better aroma, but we all take the stalks off here."

"Everybody?"

"Yes, everybody in the Bordelais."

So perhaps it didn't matter all that much? Still, she couldn't help feeling that things were wrong. They needed a firmer hand here.

At the end of the day the drizzle was falling with the same gray monotony. The people trudged in, chilled and sodden. Susannah had collected a pile of old clothes together, and when she saw that they had stopped work and were coming in she put on her cloak and hood and called to Emilie. They each picked up an armful of the clothes and carried them out through the kitchen. Francis was just outside the kitchen door, coming in wet through. He looked up.

"Where are you taking all that?"

"The children must be soaked."

He looked at her as if she were a child herself. "My dear, let them alone. They're all right."

"But they've been out in this all day."

"They're used to it. They'll come to no harm. They see to themselves."

"These things are only old rags."

"They don't want them, Sue. I assure you, they won't use them. It's pointless. Now take them back, go on."

She turned back slowly and reluctantly. She was puzzled. She told Emilie to put the clothes away in Augustine's old room. It was so unlike him. He seemed out of sorts during supper and didn't say much, and she felt sorry to see him miserable, poor darling. He was tired, working long hours from daybreak on. After supper, however, he sat playing piquet with his mother, and Susannah slipped out.

And he seemed to be quite right. The workpeople were capering noisily around their dining room clapping their hands and jigging and laughing, having somehow recruited a second fiddler and a concertina player. Half of them were tipsy; they were obviously determined to make the best of it and didn't need any cheering up.

Susannah stood just outside the door, not showing herself. She looked at the women, mostly small dark creatures, several passably good-looking, none of them beauties, one or two quite elderly. They had been out for twelve hours in the rain, at work that would wear down many men; they had come in, seen to the children and helped with the meal and the table. They would be up at dawn tomorrow, and here they were, full of liveliness and gaiety, yet never losing their dignity. They pealed at the simple jokes of the men. They raised shouts of laughter with their repartee. They were simple people. So unheroic but moving in their courage. A woman was paid like a child—fifty-five centimes for a child, fifty-five centimes for his mother—for a day's work. Shameful really. Shameful. Why did they bear it? Because they could do nothing else, that was why. They accepted it. Yet their men had a respect for them, a respect for their physical toughness, for their endurance, their cheerfulness, that men of the better class often lacked. There was a bond of suffering between the worker and his woman. That was it, she thought. Nothing binds like pain. She thought she was going to bring them those old clothes all the same, whatever Francis said. Her heart felt warmed by the women. She loved them.

But something about the harvesting went on worrying her and nagging at her. She wandered about watching them. Whenever she went into the vatting room she thought of what Laverne had said about mixing the grapes in the vats. At last she couldn't help it and spoke to Francis about it.

"Who have you been talking to?" he said.

"Monsieur Laverne."

"Well, of course if you can afford the extra work, the extra people, you can be more careful. They do it at Margaux and Lafite and the other big places. They can afford to. You take only your best vines first, bring the grapes in, go over them carefully again, make your first wine from them. Then you take your next best vines, sort the grapes over, vat them separately. Maybe you even do it a third time. Make two or three separate operations of getting your grapes in and have separate pressings. And of course you never top up your number one casks with your number two or number three. But the whole thing costs the earth."

So it was partly money too.

A few days after this, when the harvest and the vatting were nearly over, she said to him one evening before they went to bed, "I need some money. Madame Josserand says they have to have more oil, flour and beans. And the grocer and the butcher have both been asking me to pay."

"Well, they'll have to wait."

"We haven't given them anything on those big orders, you know."

"It's all right. They'll wait."

"I have to get the food, at all events."

"Oh, Sue, don't pester. I haven't got it. There's enough going in wages." Suddenly he relented and kissed her. "They'll make do, you'll see. It'll be all right."

She persuaded the butcher and grocer to extend their credit. Fortunately the harvesting and vatting were nearly done. She knew they hadn't had much money when they had first arrived from the States and since then Francis had paid out substantial sums. Where had they come from? He kept the account books locked up in the office and she knew he would evade answering if she asked him.

Francis wanted a child. So did Susannah. He wanted it really as an extension of her. He imagined her suckling it, he saw all the mysterious womanness multiplied in her by the child, that sort of ripe woman's knowingness, mystery. But *she* —she wouldn't sit there like a domestic hen, waiting around the house in the hope that a child was beginning inside her. She didn't want to *breed* in that deliberate hennish way. Time enough when she would have to take care, but till then she was too full of vitality and energy. She had too much appetite for life. So every fine morning after the harvest she went out with Red and roamed all over the country.

To begin with Francis went with her; but his Tom was no match for her mad horse, he was left miles behind, and after a couple of outings he gave up. Then she went once or twice with Constance Canning. However, Constance wouldn't get up in the early morning, the hour Susannah liked best, and so she began to go alone.

And, of course, it made a stir. A respectable woman did not go out riding alone here. Simply did not. Not even two miles to the village. It made it worse that she rode astride instead of sidesaddle. Francis wouldn't have minded all that much himself, though he didn't like her riding astride. But the family were shocked. An American! Madame Gautier made a great fuss and asked him if he wasn't shocked at that, what *would* he be shocked at? Francis listened unhappily. He must stop it, his mother said. Susannah must have more sense of decorum. It was indecent—and she had even been out on Sunday! Abel-Cherubin was disgusted and thought the whole thing sheer vulgarity. American vulgarity! The curé, it seemed, was scandalized.

Susannah left off for a couple of days, then resumed. She tried to get back before the household was up and about, but of course Madame Gautier found out. Francis sighed and tried good-humoredly to chivvy Susannah out of it. She kissed him on the cheek and said, "Then get yourself a proper mount and come out with me. Listen, I found a place by the river the other day with five jumps in a row."

"You'll have to stop it."

"Oh, come on. I don't go every day and it'll soon be too cold." And she went on riding.

He loved to see her come back with the flush in her cheeks, that rose-blush on her creamy skin. But the thing unsettled him all the same. One morning when Coote Onslow dropped in to pass the time of day and Francis was sitting with him on the stone bench outside the house, Onslow said, "And how's your charming wife?"

"Very well, thanks. I don't think she's in at the moment. She's out riding."

"Ha! Dashing gal, that."

Onslow was beaming and twinkling in his jovial, rather condescending way. He sat brushing his beard with the back of his hand, half one way, half the other. He twinkled, and the little creases puckered at the corners of his eyes. But there was something in his tone, something in the "Ha!" that struck Francis and chilled him. Onslow wasn't very bright, but like all the English he had an acutely developed social sense, and Francis had a vague, uncomfortable feeling that Susannah's riding had been discussed critically by Onslow and his friends. He told himself he was imagining things. Onslow was a good fellow. But the next minute Onslow said, "You ever go with her?"

"Oh, I have been, once or twice."

The twinkling merry eyes were watching Francis and the suggestion of something odd was there. Francis smiled back, not knowing what to say. He didn't want to make it worse. There had been such sharp curiosity in Onslow's tone.

"Well, I must push on," Onslow said finally and got up.

When he had gone, Francis walked down the drive, head bent, staring at the ground. *Had* it been anything? He felt foolish and slightly uncomfortable. Gossip about her? Gossip? Had Onslow been saying that Susannah did as she liked without his approval? Then he thought it was all ridiculous. Imagination!

He had let his mother's censure influence him. Onslow was a good jolly fellow; the Onslows and Cannings all loved Susannah. They had never spoken a word against her. It was all imagination, quite ridiculous. He threw it off.

Susannah loved the morning rides, exulted in the freedom, in the galloping horse. With the harvest over, the weather had turned and now they had days of slanting October sun, of the balmy warmth and clear air that made the Bordelais autumn so beautiful. She rode the forest paths in the scent of the pine trees and the wild flowers and waist-high ferns turning from green to bronze and bronze to ocher. A few of the earthwalled huts in the villages had pots of tawny little chrysanthemums. Soft pine needles covered the ground. The forest was hung all over with little round red fruit called *arbouses*, which you could break off and eat. Cups of golden resin were attached to the trunks of the pines where the bark had been cut away, and she passed the gaunt smoky-faced forest people walking silently among the trees with their bark knives on pole handles or with bundles of wood on their backs. They stared at her. Everybody stared. In the villages the women stopped what they were doing and stared. Sometimes, when she had gone by, she heard the young men's laughter, but it was the novelty they were laughing at, the stranger. It wasn't nastiness, she felt. Oh, now and then they called after her, but it was nothing.

Sometimes she stopped at a house to ask the way or beg a drink of water. She wanted to talk to them, to make friends. They looked at her with the mistrust of isolated country folk. They frowned with incomprehension before she spoke, persuaded in advance that they weren't going to understand her. And they stared after her when she went on. One or two responded brightly in their loud country voices, and when this happened she was overjoyed. Once she took shelter from a downpour under a market awning and the men all became silent and awkward. That day, as she cantered home past the vineyards, somebody shouted at her in an abusive tone. She turned and saw a man in a top hat brandishing a cane. Something familiar about him struck her, but he was too far off and she rode on.

She always had a joyful canter home. One thing about the horse did annoy her—he loved to rub himself against mossy trees or mossy stone walls, and once or twice, moving unexpectedly, nearly jammed her leg. So she had to carry a whip, but only for that. She was always gentle with him; she loved him and always fed him and gave him a hard rubdown herself. His sheer glistening orange-red coat was her special joy.

One day, a mile past the end of the black-earth path by the river, she came out to a place she didn't know. A few peasants' huts with little gardens behind their palings huddled close under a copse of gaunt dark pines. Beyond, she saw a pair of high rusty iron gates and an avenue of cedars. She rode up to the gates. They were open. It was too tempting; she could not resist it and turned in.

It was the park of an estate. The avenue had once been magnificent but was now littered with bits of bark and branches. And at the end she pulled up and sat gazing at a ruin, the crazy wreck of an old house. It lurched like a ship on the rocks, its back broken, a bit of roof tilting this way, a bit that, the chimneys crumbled and sprouting bushes and half the windows boarded up. The cobbled forecourt was grassy; lichen yellowed the stone balustrade of the steps. Obviously it had once been a fine place. Above the door was a coat of arms, a falcon carrying a broken chain in its talons. And she had a pang. What if La Guiche should go like this!

To one side of the forecourt was an old cistern full of water, and as she walked the horse toward it a voice behind her said, "Good morning, madame."

She pulled up with a start, swung in the saddle. It was a little man with a bald-fronted head, wearing an old pepper-and-salt coat and brown neckcloth. He was smiling amiably and bowing. A door of the house stood open.

"Oh, I beg your pardon. I didn't know there was anyone. I thought the house was . . . was empty. My horse is after a drink."

"Of course. That water there is not good. You will find a fresh trough under the arch." He showed the opening at the other end of the courtyard.

"Thank you." Rather confused, she turned the horse around. Heavens! if she had known. At the arch she had to dismount as the trough stood just on the other side. An overgrown path led toward the back of the house. She saw broken stone urns and, beyond, the glint of a greenhouse. How strange! Who was he?

He was standing at the door when she went back and he bowed and smiled again.

"Forgive me for intruding upon you, sir."

"On the contrary, you are most welcome. My visitors are too few." He had a funny childish shyness about him. He held his head down as he smiled timidly. "Pray call when you wish. The trough is always there."

"Thank you."

The little adventure delighted her. And after that she used to see him on the road. It was as if she had not noticed him before. And *he* didn't stare. He always smilingly doffed his hat and bowed, greeting her with formality and grace. She was curious about him and asked Francis who he could be.

"Oh, that's the Marquis de Talabu, a real original. Lives there all alone. A bit crazy, but harmless."

"I think he's delightful."

Next time she rode up the avenue he came out and greeted her with his shy smile.

"My horse found the way," she said.

"That is my good fortune, madame." He bowed formally. "Jean de Talabu. Your servant."

"How do you do. My name is Susannah Gautier. My husband and I are living near Cantenac. We have a vineyard there."

"Yes . . . yes." He nodded. "You are English, madame?"

"American."

"Ah, American . . . American." They were standing at the open door. He regarded her shyly. "Would you allow me . . . One moment." He turned back into the house and went out by a door on the far side of the room covered with a faded brownish-green brocade curtain.

Susannah peeped in. It was a small room that looked as if it had been improvised out of a much larger space, full of faded overstuffed Louis-Philippe furniture, piled with books, the desk and table awash with papers and writings. Charts of plants with Latin inscriptions hung on the walls; an old anatomical skeleton stood in one corner under a stuffed owl. There was an astrolabe, a celestial globe, bottles of specimens. A lumpy-looking ottoman with a shawl on it filled one corner, probably his bed; and she wondered if this was the only habitable corner of the house.

The door curtain swayed and he came back carrying a single white rose on a long stem. He presented it to her with a bow. "My respects, madame. I have passed happy times in the United States."

"Oh, thank you. It's lovely." The petals were touched with crimson, and long-stemmed white roses, she knew, were rare.

"Thank you for your visit."

When she called again he asked her inside and made her a cup of tea. He was charming, and she stayed for half an hour while he talked of Louisiana, where he had visited as a young man.

But when she told Francis he stared. "Do you mean to say you went there again?"

"Yes. Why not?"

"But it's impropriety, Sue. You can't do such a thing—a married woman calling uninvited, alone like that!"

"Oh, come on. Really!"

"I mean it—absolute impropriety."

"He's a perfectly sweet old man."

Francis said no more, but he wasn't at ease about it, she saw that. And she didn't know how to put him at ease, a failure on her part. She wondered if she would ever overcome *that* failure, because he saw these things in a different light. He had all the inhibitions of this old place, so complex, so interwoven. It was the cautious Old World. So narrow! The old code was all around them, the carefulness, deference, the heavy men, the hard-eyed women seeing that you didn't step out of line. But she wasn't going to knuckle down. To be young and careful— awful! Better to be reckless, as long as she was real, generous, genuine. Madame Gautier would rather have her a bundle of attitudes—attentive to this, careful of that, deferring to the other. Hollow! Dead! And of course bowing to the male in all things.

Well, she wasn't going to be an attitude. She had to be real or nothing. Besides, she did have the faculty of making friends. And she was learning to use her Americanism—its freshness and openness, its otherness—to get around the old social barriers, to break down people's reticence. People would accept things in her as an American that they wouldn't in one of their own.

Later in the week Francis said to her, "Listen, Susannah,

I'd like to have some people to dinner, some important people. Mother says she'll be content to leave the whole thing to you."

She looked at him, wondering what that meant, and he seemed to see her doubt because he put his arm around her and kissed her. "I'm sure you'll do it beautifully."

"Who do you want to ask?"

"Well, the Sous-Préfet and his wife. The Canon, I think, too."

"I see." Very important people.

"The Fouquets. He's the banker, you remember; we spoke to him briefly at the Préfet's. I'd *like* to get Tadouneau if we can. He's on the Municipal Council and very influential. And the Rector of the University."

"Will you give me a list?"

"Yes. We'll have to ask Abel-Cherubin and Louise. And John Lovell, I thought."

"All right." She felt a little nervous at the prospect. It would have to be done with considerable formality, for there were rules they all clung to.

In the end it took her four days to get the list out of him. She walked around the dining room with it, trying to see the seating. Fortunately they had some printed invitation cards. Francis had brought them home from Bordeaux one day soon after their arrival, proud of the inscription *Monsieur and Madame Francis Gautier*. She got these out, wrote in the names and sent them off. "Monsieur and Madame Francis Gautier request the pleasure of So-and-so's company at dinner . . ." For the Sous-Préfet, the Canon and the Rector it had to be "request the honor" of their company, and Francis had to get special cards for these.

It was as well that their finances had improved. Francis had paid the bills and given her some money, and when she asked him about it he said, "We're selling the new vintage. The broker's been by." She had caught sight of Jamet going into the cellar the day before and she decided he must have paid over something to Francis; for, though the wine was of poor quality, the oïdium had reduced the harvest so greatly everywhere that the merchants were glad to get what they could.

That morning she came back from an errand in the village and found Abel-Cherubin and Regis in the house. They were staying for luncheon. They all sat down, and conversation proceeded on the usual lines about the family, business and Bordeaux affairs. Then halfway through, when Emilie had left the room, Abel-Cherubin said to Madame Gautier, "By the way, have you heard this thing about Blood?"

"What?" Madame Gautier looked up across the table with her face set.

"This latest thing?"

"What, you mean the Comberford affair?" Regis said.

"Yes. You've heard of it, of course."

"Heard of it! You can't get away from it. My club's full of it."

Susannah kept her eyes on her plate. Abel-Cherubin addressed his mother. "Comberford's got that estate at Mérignac. What's it called? La Tour Noire. He and his wife were at Aubernon's, a soirée. You know the wife? Charming, very gracious and pretty. Blood was there too. Well, halfway through, it appears there was an incident. Nobody knows exactly what happened; there are two or three versions. At all events, Comberford said Blood had insulted his wife. Blood called him a liar and asked the wife to bear him out. Comberford forbade her to speak. Rather natural, I'd say. Whereupon Blood called him a poltroon and struck him."

"In the middle of the salon. In front of everybody," Regis said.

"Somebody or other wanted to choose seconds right away, but Comberford pooh-poohed it. Said Blood was beneath him. Comberford's a peer of the realm, after all. Said he couldn't fight a common Irish guttersnipe."

"Bog-Irish scab, I heard he called him," Regis said.

"Scandalous," said Madame Gautier.

"Wait a minute." Abel-Cherubin swallowed hastily. " 'Tisn't finished yet. The next night—that was, ah, last Thursday—three hooligans rode up to La Tour Noire. They all had pistols and were obviously looking for Comberford. Luckily the Comberfords were away in Bordeaux, at their town house. So the hooligans forced their way in. They tied up the caretakers, locked up the rest of the staff. Then they proceeded to shoot up Comberford's cellar. The whole place, the casks all holed, the floor running with wine."

169

A gasp from Madame Gautier.

"They broke into his private cellar, they carried out the best pieces, they stuck them up on a wall and they amused themselves for half an hour taking pot shots at them."

"Magnums of Lafite 1815, jeroboams of Haut-Brion 1848, all shattered."

"Imperials of Yquem 1834!"

"Then they galloped off whooping like Indians."

"I hear somebody recognized Blood as one of them."

"Have they arrested him?" Madame Gautier asked.

"Not yet, not yet."

"Mind you," said Regis, "Comberford's a puffed-up creature."

"On the contrary! On the contrary, a very sound man. A lot of good sense. Very sound in business. Whereas the other's a . . . a . . . a vile blackguard, a scoundrel."

A pause.

"I hear he's wanted by the English police too," Abel-Cherubin said.

"Blood? What for?"

"Oh, regular villainy. It appears he—"

Susannah pushed back her chair, got to her feet, reached for the sauce boat and, as they all looked up at her in silence, carried it out of the room. She was bursting with anger. Did they expect her to sit there while they trampled on her? That was what it had meant. Abel-Cherubin had waited till she was at the table to bring all this up, a crude attack on her: Look who your wife associates with. She felt they had been prising into her soul, as if they knew about her and Blood. Mauling her. She was trembling with rage. In the kitchen she hardly knew why she was there. She saw nothing. Emilie gazed at her in surprise and took the sauce boat from her hands.

"It needs warming," Susannah said mechanically and turned away. Probably she had made it worse by getting up, but she had felt so angry. Boiling! Perhaps that had been all they needed. Gossip about the scuffle in the Rue Sainte Catherine? No, no, there couldn't be. Too long ago now. She was not being realistic. Yet it had all been said with a purpose. She stood staring unseeingly at the calendar on the wall, still angry. Then the surge of emotion passed, and she told herself it had just been malicious digging at her. She went back. As she entered, Abel-Cherubin and Regis were arguing about the oïdium. They did not look at her.

"Emilie is bringing the sauce," she said as offhandedly as she could. Francis nodded absently, absorbed in what the other two were saying. She sat down. Across the table Madame Gautier's eyes rested on her, then looked away. But Susannah had seen the suspicion in them.

20

Early on the last Tuesday of October Susannah took the horse out and headed in a gentle canter through the vineyards. The air was almost like summer, the sun a smoky orange, and a trace of early mist still lingered. There was hardly a soul about. The vineyards were deserted now that most of the vines had been pruned and the outdoor work done till spring. Peace lay everywhere, peace and stillness.

Which direction should she take this morning? She longed to go to the sea, to gallop on the beach, but it was too far. So after going west for a while, she turned to the north and headed toward Soussans. As they passed a roadside copse the horse gave a nervous little quiver and shied. She held him in, changed the whip to her other hand and leaned over stroking him, calming him. She glanced around, puzzled, trying to see what had startled him, then saw the little specks of light coming through the undergrowth of the copse, flickering like sparks about to attack his feet. "It's all right, Red. All right." She dropped to a trot; they were soon past it and he was calm again.

Oh, the glorious morning! She wanted to sing. High overhead a flight of wild ducks headed west, their V-formation straggling, bunching up and breaking like a wind-blown ribbon and then re-forming. Now she belonged to this place and it belonged to her. And the horse, strangely, had given her so much of this belonging. The forest paths were dear to her, would always be part of her now: the gaunt trunks of the pines that marched so swiftly by, the great yellow sweeps of broom, the briar, the emptiness of long straight wagon paths through the trees with the deep verges of wild flowers and ferns. How beautiful it was. She loved it all.

Now, ahead, she could see somebody running toward her on the empty road. It was a boy, running zigzag on the road then onto the verge, doubling back and around again, playing with a dog. The dog was almost as big as the boy, a big brown creature, and the boy was making it run around him. He looked about ten years old, a sturdy workman's child.

Susannah kept the horse on a tight rein moving toward them. The boy didn't seem to have seen them. He was darting this way and that, overexciting the dog, she thought, because it kept barking frantically and jumping at him, then running circles around him and jumping up again. Now and then the boy flung out an arm as if to push it off. The dog's bark was deep and throaty.

Jogging forward, Susannah kept her eyes on them. The boy snatched up a stick, but it was dead wood and snapped off against the dog as it charged in. And, oddly, the dog did not pick it up. Susannah moved nearer, frowning. The boy-dog game seemed to be getting out of control; the dog was snarling. All at once something told her it was not a game. Her heart gave a sickening lurch, then she was near enough to see that the boy was breathless, not laughing but gasping, half sobbing. The dog was worrying him and he was trying to get away. As she realized this, the boy darted across the verge and ran into the vineyard bordering the road. The dog bounded after him.

Susannah dug her heels into Red and surged forward. She saw the boy frantically trying to escape. The dog was attacking him now. With a bound Susannah was into the vines and charged the dog. She bent in the saddle and lashed at it with her whip. The dog cowered, jerked its head up, snapped at her, twisted away and leapt for the boy again. Susannah swung this way and that, beating at the furious dog, which always doubled away and went for the boy.

It was an area of young vines, widely spaced and fixed to little stakes—no laths—and she was vaguely aware that the horse was knocking the stakes down and trampling the vines; but it was the dog, the maddened dog that she couldn't chase off. As soon as she was on it, it doubled back and was after the boy again. She charged around, bent in the saddle, lashed it. It leapt away. She chased it in a circle, a figure of eight, shouting to the boy to run; but he was too out of breath to move fast enough. The dog turned again and jumped, snapping at her leg. She wrenched the horse aside and the dog was running at the boy again.

Someone was shouting. Someone was running up shouting. She saw a tall big-shouldered man running up waving a cane. He had a black coat and top hat. The voice—it was the man who had shouted abusively at her that day, and now, in a flash, she recognized him, the Count de Mornac. Her attention was on the dog, and before she could close the distance Mornac was upon the boy—the nearest target—striking out furiously at him with his cane. The boy tried to duck away. Mornac hit him over head and shoulders.

"Stop it! Stop it!" Susannah shouted. Suddenly she screamed at him in a white fury, heeled the horse and rushed at them. The boy had broken away; Mornac was after him. She saw Mornac's red face, the raised cane about to hit the boy again, his sudden look as he saw her charging down. He sprang back and struck her twice with fierce quickness, fore- and back-hand, before she could wheel. The cuts stung her shoulder and breast. She wheeled. The boy had stumbled; Mornac was hitting him in a sort of insanity of anger, gasping and spluttering.

Susannah charged forward, brought the horse up hard on his haunches and lashed out at Mornac with her whip. Arm raised, he swung around. Her whip caught him again across the neck. He struck her, then staggered back flinching as she hit him again and again, across the face and head, in blind, black hate, rode him down, knocked him over, lashing at him as he went down. Sharply she turned the horse, trampling him.

She could hardly see with rage. Somehow she pulled herself up and regained a little control over herself. She felt the horse trembling under her. She was breathless and shaking violently. The boy was a few yards away, one hand to his head. Something moved to the left—the dog! She had forgotten it. It had held off during the melee but was still there, nosing in again.

"Here. Come here, quickly," she called to the boy. "Quick!" Her own shaky voice sounded unreal to her. Red was shifting about sideways uneasily, wanting to bolt from fear. She had difficulty in controlling him. The boy was facing the dog watchfully. He threw a look at her, judging the distance, then ran for her. Halfway there he half tripped up, snatched something from the ground at his feet—Mornac's cane. Gripping it, he swung around defensively against the dog. Red shied away in fright.

"Quick!" Susannah said again, bringing the horse around.

The boy ran up, glancing over his shoulder for the dog. Unwilling to let him go, the dog was padding slowly forward, neck outstretched, hair erect, lips back, snarling.

"Put your foot here. Now." She reached down and helped him up behind her. She looked around. Mornac was lying on the ground, all muddied, head hanging, trying to get to his knees. The ground all around was churned up. As she wheeled the horse and cantered out of the vineyard, the frustrated dog bounded up and ran barking and slavering furiously alongside. At the road she struck at it with the whip, and, in animal fashion, it suddenly abandoned them and ran off.

"Are you all right?" she asked in the same distant strange voice, and the boy answered yes. She couldn't tell whether he was hurt or not, but he didn't seem to be. But after that she could not speak. She was trembling violently. She didn't know where they were going. All she knew was that she turned north, the direction the child had come from. Her mind was in utter confusion. She could think of nothing, she was simply emotion —horror at the whole thing, at the sort of inevitability it had had, at its swiftness. As if nothing could have held it back, nothing. The same images kept coming to her—Mornac's red face, his attitude lifting the cane, hitting the child. Consciousness seemed to work merely in these images. She could not think. She did not see the road, she did not feel the horse, she didn't know where they were going, or care. She was terribly shaken.

How far did they go? She felt the boy tugging her coat. What? He was pointing to a side track. She took it automatically. How far? She didn't know. Presently she pulled up and turned around to him. "Are you hurt?" A place on the side of his head above one eye was cut and bruised. She could see a little blood in his hair, and the edge of his ear on the same side was torn and bleeding. But he simply shrugged at her question.

He was a plump round-faced child, nice-looking with warm brown eyes that regarded her gravely. No tears, no complaints. His clothes were poor, and now for the first time she saw he had lost a shoe.

"Where do you live?" she said.

Silently he motioned her to continue on the track. She could feel the nervousness in the horse still, his nervous trembling, and she bent forward and stroked his neck, urging him on, gradually coming to herself now, coming to consciousness. Flashes of the scene kept coming back to her and making her hot. She was horribly shaky. She felt a sort of disbelief, as if the thing had happened at one remove from her, to someone else, or in a dream. Yet of course she knew it had been real.

They rode through a hamlet. An old man with a spade looked up and watched them pass. Then at the edge of the place the boy tugged her arm, and when she stopped, he slid off the horse. A huddle of three tumbledown huts stood in a hollow with bits of an old cart outside, broken wheels and rusty stoves among the nettles. A few hens scratched in the dirt. Two of the huts looked shut, but the door of the third was open and a woman came out as the boy limped over in his one shoe.

Susannah dismounted and went across. The woman had a dark southern-looking face, like one of the harvesttime mountain folk. She was obviously the mother and saw something was wrong at once; but she had the same calm self-containment as the child. She took his shoulder as he came up, bending quickly to look at the bad place on his head and to speak to him; then she straightened up as Susannah came toward her.

"Is he your son?"

"Yes." She held the boy against her protectively.

"He's had an accident. I do hope he's not hurt. He was . . . he was trying to get away from a dog and went into the vines. The owner chased him and hit him with a stick. I . . . he seems all right, but I think you should look at him."

The boy said something to his mother in a foreign tongue and indicated his head and his back. The mother nodded, looked up again at Susannah. "Thank you," she said.

"If you need me, my name's Gautier and I live at the Château La Guiche near Cantenac. Gautier. Anybody will tell you."

The woman's dark eyes were on Susannah, just like her

son's. She nodded silently. All at once the boy held out Mornac's cane, which he had carried off. Susannah took it mechanically, then the woman led the boy back to the hut.

For a moment Susannah stood there gazing after them, then the door of the hut was shut from the inside. For the first time she felt the soreness of her shoulder and breast where Mornac had hit her. She mounted the horse and rode slowly back.

She was in a strange state, her body was vibrant, taut with a sort of fiery energy, as if the excited frothy blood were rushing through her. But her mind would not work. She couldn't fix her thoughts, couldn't concentrate. Everything was flux. She felt stunned, she took no account of anything, saw nothing. Halfway home she suddenly found a cane in her hand. A cane? She stared at it incomprehendingly—a silver knob with a crest. Oh . . . Mornac's. Yes. She flung it from her into a clump of bushes. She noticed nothing on the ride back.

Francis was not in the house when she got home. She told Joseph to take special care of Red and soothe him. She went indoors, changed her clothes, bathed her bruises. Octavie, the cook, was wanting her already. There were all the preparations to make for the dinner tonight. She went downstairs. Quietness had come on her now, a stillness. The horror remained, but she had recovered herself and she felt strong and confident in what she had done. She was all right now.

She was busy all morning, in and out of the kitchen, the dining room and the salon. Just after noon Francis appeared. She said, "Francis, I have something to tell you."

"Hm?"

"Will you come upstairs?"

"Upstairs? What for?" He looked up in surprise.

"I would rather tell you there."

They went up. He shut the door of the room after them, sensing something serious now. She was by the window and turned around and told him. He stared at her, appalled.

"And you left him there—Mornac? You left him lying there?"

"I did."

"Sue!"

"I'd do it again."

He stared at her, his face white.

21

The candlelight shone over the table, on the white cloth, on the glasses of wine and the cutlery, on the small porcelain figures that Susannah had arranged as a centerpiece. Joseph and Emilie were serving. The hum of conversation rose gently. The dinner was in mid-course.

Seated between the Rector and John Lovell, Susannah looked around at the faces. They all knew. And they all seemed to be *waiting*. It was as if the doors were going to swing open and Mornac stalk in at any moment. Mornac covered with mud. They sat in an intense awareness, awkward, nervous, a little embarrassed—in a kind of horrified enjoyment.

She had dreaded the dinner, but she was glad they had gone through with it. Francis had wanted to cancel everything, to go to Bordeaux and send messages by the telegraph.

"But Frank, it's impossible. It'll make it look as if I'm to blame. It'll— Why should we run away?"

"It'll look so brazen."

Brazen? "Why should it? The dinner was all arranged beforehand."

"Yes, but we weren't reckoning on this. We've every right to put it off."

"I'm the one involved, and if I can face it you can."

"No, as head of the household, I'm the one chiefly concerned. It's a question of decency."

"Decency? We *have* to go on with it. I only ask you one thing. Don't tell your mother or Abel-Cherubin until afterwards. It's going to be difficult enough as it is."

"It's going to be horrible." He shook his head unhappily but in the end agreed.

But by late afternoon it was clear that the incident had gone around the country like a flash of lightning. At four o'clock a messenger from the prefecture had arrived in a cocked hat and uniform with a letter from the Sous-Préfet. The Sous-Préfet presented his excuses to Madame Francis Gautier, but he was prevented by unexpected official duties from being present at dinner. An hour later the Canon's little thin red-nosed curé, Father Pindray, had brought word that the Canon was "indisposed." Susannah had let Francis dress miserably in silence in the bedroom and used the dressing room herself so that he should not see the marks where Mornac had hit her. She had not told him about that.

And then tonight, with everybody else assembled, they had waited for the Baron and Baroness de Causse and daughter, waited until it was obvious they were not coming either, hadn't even sent excuses, whereupon Susannah had hastily rearranged the table and they had all come in.

She studied those at the table now. Madame Fouquet, tall and regal, in plain mauve with jet bead necklace, alert, capable, eyes like knives, watching everything, never missing a thing. She was next to Tadouneau, a man of sixty or so with a small bony face and straight gray hair falling across his forehead. Francis was between the Rector's wife and Madame Tadouneau, a bony creature like her husband. Then came a fat man named Barbot, the Mayor's brother-in-law, and then Abel Cherubin's wife. On the other side, Abel-Cherubin sat between Madame Barbot, a toothy plump pullet, and Madame Gautier, who had Fouquet on her left.

They were all shocked—and fascinated. And they were all aloof and watching. Not John Lovell. He was quiet and she felt his sympathy, and she had found herself unexpectedly liking the fat Barbots. But the rest, the Tadouneaus, the Fouquets, the Rector—they were ice. *They* were not committing themselves to sympathy with her. Oh, not at all. It was the other way around. Behind the formality they were hostile; they hated her. She was "the American creature." Their attitude said that their presence did not commit them at all. They had come to see how she behaved after such a scandal. She was on exhibition. Gossip for the Bordeaux salons tomorrow!

"My dear, I was actually there last night, in the house. Yes! She's . . ." A woman in such a scene after all. Degrading! What could you expect of an American? Fouquet, that hard-eyed supercilious face across the table, was a bit like Mornac. Susannah had been passing behind the screen in the hall when the Fouquets had arrived, and in the brief pause after they had given Emilie their coats she had caught Fouquet's furious whisper to his wife: "Dragging me here to this! Damn you!" And the wife had answered, "Don't be ridiculous. If you're not interested, *I* am." She had the money in that family, it seemed.

And the vehement Tadouneau had been thrusting out his neck, striking attitudes, giving his glare all evening. A leading member of the Municipal Council, Francis said, a man of great influence. What did Francis want with such people? Why was it suddenly so important for him to entertain them? *Were* they necessary to him in business? She did not know.

Across from her now Tadouneau leaned forward and began a conversation about politics with Barbot. Joseph came in with more wine and she noticed that for some reason he had discarded his white gloves. When he reached her, Susannah whispered to him and turned back to the Rector.

"Such what, Rector?" He had been talking rapidly, nervously ever since they sat down and now was holding forth about the commercial hazards of being a wine broker like his son-in-law.

"I said, such risks for so little profit."

"Well, I don't see we need brokers at all," Susannah said. "Or wine merchants, if it comes to that."

"Ha! What do you say to that, Mr. Lovell?" But Lovell was talking to Madame Barbot on his other side and didn't hear. "People have to buy their wine somewhere."

"If it's only *buying* wine, that's easy. They can buy from us. But the brokers and the merchants want to run the whole trade."

"They are the people who know best, madame." He sounded peevish.

"Yes, the tricks of the trade. How to bilk the producers. The producers have got to learn to do without brokers *or* merchants."

"You won't get any sympathy for those opinions in Bordeaux, madame."

"I dare say, but it's got to come. It's our only hope."

"And how are you to do that, madame?"

"Sell the wine ourselves. Sell direct to the customers."

"Come, come."

Somebody across the table made a derisive sound, but she took no notice.

"Do you realize the complexity of our wine trade, madame?" the Rector said. "Its . . . its vastness? Why, more than half the wines we produce are sold abroad. How would you manage that, you producers?"

"Very well, I imagine."

He made a quick impatient movement. "But each country in Europe has its own tastes, its own market." He sounded very bad-tempered now. "The Dutch want this, the English want that, the Germans something else. How could you deal with that, the diversity? Why, the makeup of claret for England alone is very difficult. Takes great skill. Claret, as they call it, is a special product. And it has to be left to the merchant, the expert, to produce it."

"And why can't they have pure Bordeaux wine?"

"Pure Bordeaux?" More impatient weaving about. "Why, my dear lady, because they won't drink it! That's why."

"Because they never get it!"

"They won't drink pure Bordeaux wine in the United States or in England. It isn't claret. Pure Bordeaux wine doesn't get them drunk fast enough. They want more body, something stronger. More alcohol. So the merchant has to add Beni Carlos from Spain, Hermitage, brandy. It's what you call 'working' the wine."

"Yes, and it's passed off as genuine Bordeaux."

The Rector drummed the table, openly irritated.

"I'm told you can hardly find a bottle of genuine Bordeaux in its natural state in London or New York. It's all artificial, all adulterated stuff," Susannah said.

A snort came from Tadouneau.

"And that's fraud," she added. "All the self-admiration and pious talk about purity and protection, but passing one article off for another is fraud, isn't it?"

Tadouneau clicked his tongue. "Really!"

"Oh, come, sir, everybody knows of sophisticated wines. And since Bordeaux is such a large supplier, there's probably more doctoring, shall we say, here than elsewhere."

Tadouneau's chin quivered. "Accusations of that sort, madame, are . . . are deplorable. Really, I must say, the worst sort of . . ." He gave a contemptuous flick of his hand, turned his head to Barbot and said under his breath, "Damned vulgarity."

Susannah smiled at him. "I'm not the only one who says so, as you must know. Why not have an energetic inquiry into it? It's a good subject. Perhaps by the Municipal Council—quite impartial, of course."

"In the American style, I take it?"

"American style?" She smiled sweetly again, eyebrows up. "What's wrong with that?"

"Little about it I can admire, madame," Tadouneau said.

"What you admire, sir, would probably be repugnant to Americans."

A little gasp, a little flutter of expostulation went up, and then there was a general flurry of talk as if to cover up the awkwardness. Across the table Fouquet caught Tadouneau's eye. Tadouneau turned his mouth down.

"Ah . . ." Abel-Cherubin said; but whatever he had to say he did not complete.

The moment passed. Susannah felt she had rather let herself go. But the condescension! The dismissive scorn! She was inwardly boiling. And now she wanted to provoke them. She wanted to match them. She was *not* going to be defensive! They wanted her to be inoffensive, submissive, to accept their scornful words about America. She sat half listening to the conversation around her, Madame Barbot talking about a country house for sale, Madame Fouquet telling about her upholsterer—predictable women merely filling in the gaps between the important male talk. Oh, yes, all the gods were male here all right. She thought how much condescension was in the lives of people like Tadouneau, how important condescension and contempt were to the bourgeois conscience. And she felt that the terrible scene with Mornac had had a liberating effect on her. Why was it? Why should violence liberate her? Liberate her from what? She couldn't answer. Yet she felt she was stronger. She remembered the exultant excitement of her body immediately afterward, the thrilling rush of her blood. Was it because she had been afraid? She *had* been afraid of Mornac. A powerful man striking out in blind fury was a frightening thing. Was this the attraction of fear?

Joseph came in with the next course, Emilie with a second dish. It was foie gras with port jelly. Susannah had helped prepare it under the cook's directions with much care and she thought it was lovely. She only wished it had been for other people. Listening to Barbot, who was talking about Algeria, she watched Joseph and Emilie serving, each tending half of the table. With the foie gras she had chosen a Haut-Brion.

And she had been all through the form of things so carefully too—how they expected things done here in the European manner, with white gloves for Joseph, white apron for Emilie, the white tablecloth, a glass for each separate wine, the biggest for water, medium size for red, the smallest for white wine. There was the careful seating order—a commander of the Legion of Honor before an officer of the Legion and so forth— which it would be offensive to get wrong. She must go in first, with the guest of honor, sit down first, begin to eat first, or, according to the rules, the others couldn't eat a mouthful. Joseph must present the dishes on the *left*, beginning with the lady on the host's right, then the one on his left. But he must serve the wine on the *right*, careful to hold the bottle by the body, not the neck. The dishes must be passed around twice, except the soup, salad, cheese and fruit, and so on. She knew she was awkward. How could she be one of those steely-eyed hostesses who missed nothing, all quick responses and clever talk. Of course she couldn't, she hadn't the experience. And she could see their critical eyes watching for mistakes.

Beside her the Rector began a long discourse about local Bronze Age archeological sites. She listened, trying to watch the table too. Francis was having a difficult time with Madame Tadouneau, who had largely ignored him throughout the meal and shown more interest in what Fouquet or her husband was saying. It angered Susannah that he should put himself in a position of inferiority with such a woman, for of course the Tadouneaus thought of him as miles beneath them.

Presently she noticed there was a conversation going on between Fouquet and the Rector's wife. Fouquet was leaning close to her and masking his lips with his hand. Twice he glanced obliquely in her direction and Susannah thought she caught the word "police."

Quickly, Abel-Cherubin, who was nearer, leaned forward to hear what Barbot was saying, and he turned with nervous obsequiousness toward Fouquet to enlist his approbation. "Quite right, eh? Wouldn't you agree, Fouquet?" It was so obvious. Susannah hated it. Fouquet's forefinger flicked his mustache, two quick little flicks. He sat back looking evenly at Abel-Cherubin and did not respond. Abel-Cherubin's jowly face was flushed with emotion, as if *he* had overheard that word too.

Susannah turned to Lovell. "I've been meaning to ask you all evening, Mr. Lovell, have you seen any more ghosts?"

He smiled. "Not yet. I'm hoping to."

"At any rate they seem benign."

"Oh, partners in the firm." They laughed. "I was talking to the old cellar master the other day. He's a dear old man of ninety who still comes around sometimes and he swears there's one about."

"The son, perhaps, the one you heard?"

"Who knows?"

"How strange that story of yours was. Francis told me." She felt *he* was on her side.

She had chosen a Château Climens, a white wine from Barsac, to go with the soufflé à l'orange. As it went around, Tadouneau signaled crudely to Joseph to refill his glass. Susannah had seen him do it several times before. He was rather drunk now. The Rector smacked his lips over the Climens and began to talk about the comedy at the Grand Theater which was such a success.

But Susannah saw that none of them were disarmed. They were on Mornac's side. Mornac was much too powerful in Bordeaux society for it to be otherwise. Anything else would be disloyalty to their class. She shuddered. They didn't give a damn for her hospitality. They had withheld themselves, the Tadouneaus and the Fouquets, they had not given a particle of themselves. They could not. It was not in their bourgeois nature. With them, like gave to like, under a duly notarized deed, and even then there were reservations.

Tadouneau's face was red, he was speaking dogmatically to Madame Fouquet, the lock of hair had fallen lower over his forehead. Francis had found a loose thread in the embroidery of the tablecloth and was nervously twisting it. The conversation was rather desultory now.

Susannah glanced around. Time for her to get up. Well, it was over! She felt enormously relieved to have got through it all! She prepared to push back her chair and rise.

And then, quite clearly, above the murmur she heard Tadouneau say to Madame Fouquet, "I believe they have the habit in England—ride over a man's crops and be damned to him."

"No hunt and hounds in this case."

"No! Just rode over. Perhaps it's the same in America. Barbarians."

Silence. Everybody had heard.

"What, in America?" Susannah said pleasantly, leaning forward in her chair.

"You can ride over somebody's crops and be damned to him."

"No. That's certainly not permitted."

"Nor here either," Tadouneau growled, twirling his glass stem. "Some people seem to think it is."

"Do you mean me, sir?" Susannah said.

Tadouneau sat hunched up, staring at her. He contented himself with twirling the glass but his mouth turned down.

"I think you do, so perhaps you know the facts," Susannah said.

"Oh, come, come," Abel-Cherubin said in an agony of embarrassment, but Susannah took no notice.

"Do you know the facts?" she repeated.

There was silence at the table except for the sound of Francis's nervously tapping foot. Tadouneau, taken by surprise, had evidently expected her to let it pass; but now, goaded, he said, "I know nothing more than is common knowledge, madame. The Count de Mornac is a friend of mine, and I know his new vines were trampled down and when he tried to stop it, he was brutally attacked."

"On the contrary, Monsieur de Mornac did the attacking."

"We need not discuss it here, madame," Tadouneau said.

"But you were discussing it, sir, were you not?"

John Lovell made to speak, but she stopped him. "You made an imputation, sir," she said to Tadouneau. "Unless you can substantiate it, you are a slanderer, are you not?"

"Susannah! Susannah!" Francis was half out of his chair.

"Imputation?" Tadouneau said. "A gentleman has been gravely injured and the facts, as you call them, will be thrashed out by the authorities."

"And so it is not your business, sir."

"I make no mystery, madame. I have declared my interest already. I am a friend of Jacques de Mornac's."

"Then what are you doing here?"

"I came at your invitation and your husband's. You have perhaps forgotten?"

"You, sir, have obviously forgotten your obligations as a guest."

"I considered it too late to excuse myself when I heard of the incident. However, since you question my presence, madame, I will now withdraw." He got to his feet.

"Then you are a coward, sir!" Susannah said.

"What!"

"And a blackguard."

"Madame, I—" Tadouneau's face was blotchy and he was shaking.

"You accuse me without stating the facts, and then you want to run away. You are contemptible, sir. And now, since I have no . . . no hog keeper to take you out, monsieur, you may find the door."

"Susannah!" Francis was coming around the table.

"God!"

Tadouneau walked stiffly to the door, paused on the threshold, then went out followed by his wife. The guests were all on their feet watching him go. Susannah was trembling in a cold rage. She saw the Fouquets' pale icy faces. But of course they had loved it. This was what they—*she*, at any rate—had been hoping for. What they had come for! Well, she was satisfied. Madame Gautier had slipped out. Joseph, who had heard the altercation, had opened the double doors. Lovell gave Susannah his arm. As they went into the salon, the Fouquets came up to her. Fouquet bowed. "You will excuse us, madame. In the circumstances . . ."

Susannah inclined her head. The Rector and his wife were hovering. "I think, madame, if you will allow us, we have a long drive."

"Of course, Rector."

It was agonizing. Abel-Cherubin, his face crimson, was standing in a corner. They heard Tadouneau's carriage drive off. The Barbots stayed for a few moments, for decency's sake, but declined the cognac that Joseph brought around, then they left too. John Lovell was the last. Susannah went with him into the hall.

"If you need me, you have only to ask," he said.

"Thank you."

"You were quite right." His eyes rested on hers, he kissed her hand and walked out to his carriage.

Back in the salon Abel-Cherubin's heavy form was sprawled in an armchair. He had a large glass of cognac in one hand. Francis was standing by the fireplace. Abel-Cherubin turned his tormented eyes on Susannah as she entered, struggled heavily to his feet and faced her with a gasp. "Well!"

But the end of it was tears. She ran upstairs crying, unable to check herself. Francis hurried after her. She sat on the bed, hands to her face, tears streaming in shame and anger and wretchedness. He sat beside her, put his arm around her. "Don't cry, Sue. Don't cry. You were fine. It's all right."

But all the care, the longing to do it successfully for him, to bring him credit—all gone in this ghastly evening. She was no good to him; she couldn't do things as he wanted; she didn't understand these people. She wept bitterly; she couldn't stop. He sat with his arm around her, but she couldn't stop. It was all spoiled for him and she had spoiled it.

Then she got hold of herself. She didn't stop crying but gradually she took hold of herself. Why shame? Why should she be ashamed? She didn't aspire to be like those women—dry, watchful, ungiving, with looks on their faces so hard and grasping—she had to be herself. It was another test of her, all this. If she bowed down now, if she tried to conform, if she kneeled to their way, she *would* become one of them. Gradually her habits of mind would change, her feelings would shrivel up. She would start to look like them—dry, calculating, watchful. Oh, yes, she would be capable, but dead really, soulless, shutting out life. And she would not do that. She would struggle against that.

Eventually the tears stopped. She blew her nose, and Francis hugged her and kissed her and said she had done things beautifully. In bed she clung close to him. She was glad she had cried—otherwise she would already have begun to get like them.

But, of course, the fact remained . . .

22

The faint woodsmoke smell of autumn hung in the air next morning. Susannah was up and about early. She wasn't going to let the thing hang over her. Life had to go on. She felt the need to react physically, so after breakfast she put on her gardening gloves, called Jean and went to the back of the house to plant bulbs. Louise had brought her fifty irises and two dozen tulips and crocuses. Perhaps it was a little late for the irises, but the earth along the old path where irises had grown before was black and loamy—it had obviously been brought in from elsewhere—and she thought they would do well.

The two of them worked together planting the lovely smooth bulbs and they had almost finished when Emilie appeared from indoors. "Monsieur Jaubert and two gentlemen for you, madame."

She looked up at the girl. "Tell Monsieur Laverne."

"The gentlemen asked for you, madame."

"Jaubert?" She frowned; her eyes roamed speculatively. "Very well, I'll come in."

She got up, stripped off the gloves, brushed the dust from her dress and went in, wondering what this was. They were in the hall. She saw instantly what it was and in spite of herself her heart gave a plunge. One was a tall erect thin-legged man in dark blue uniform and cocked hat with the short Louis-Napoleon beard and waxed mustache that was the great official vogue now. He bowed elegantly, heels together, obviously proud of himself in the short waist-length tunic with the V of brass buttons.

"Madame Francis Gautier? Jaubert, principal officer of gendarmerie. This is Officer Rossi and Monsieur Dufaud, the Count de Mornac's bailiff."

"Messieurs." She nodded to them coldly. Dufaud was a broad thick man with protruding eyes and a blotchy outdoor face wearing a long-skirted jacket and gaiters. The other officer, obviously a subordinate, was carrying a leather case.

"Is there somewhere, madame, where we might be private?" Jaubert asked, looking around.

"What is the purpose of your visit?"

"We have questions to ask you, madame."

She looked from one to the other, doing her best to seem self-assured though she was horribly nervous. Francis was away. Then, seeing Emilie crossing at the end of the hall towards the stairs, she said to the men, "Just a moment," and called to the girl. She went to meet her and said quietly, "Tell Joseph to fetch Dr. Cavan, quickly."

She went back to the men. "Come this way, if you please," she said and led them into the salon. She shut the door and went across to them. Jaubert, now jauntily nursing his hat under his arm, was looking around in typical police fashion as if the furniture and interior were his business. He obviously expected to be invited to sit down, but Susannah did not oblige him.

"What is your business, please?" she said.

"We have come, madame, on the complaint of the Count Jacques Lasteyrie de Mornac. I am obliged to ask you certain questions. On twenty-six October, that is yesterday, at six fifteen in the morning, being mounted on horseback, you entered the Count de Mornac's vineyard at a place called—"

"La Tour Lissac," put in Rossi, the subordinate, and she saw now that he had a document spread out on his leather case.

"La Tour Lissac and proceeded to ride around in a wild fashion, trampling down the young vines planted there. Your entry on the property was unauthorized. When the Count de Mornac appeared and remonstrated with you, calling attention to the damage you were inflicting, you not only failed to desist but struck him with—"

" 'Savagely and repeatedly,' " Rossi read out.

"Struck him savagely and repeatedly with a whip, occasioning him severe injury, and caused your horse to throw him to the ground. While he lay helpless, you thereupon rode your horse over him several times, attempting to inflict yet more serious harm, and only by chance alone did he escape a fatal outcome. You then rode away. You do not dispute these facts?"

"Is this what Monsieur de Mornac has told you?" Susannah asked. She could see an official stamp at the top of the document Rossi had read from. It was a ruled sheet filled with careful handwriting in black ink, obviously the police report based on Mornac's deposition. "Can I see that?"

She moved over, but Rossi instantly held it flat against his chest and said sharply, "An official document, madame. An *official* document!"

"Be so good as to answer my question," Jaubert said. "Do you or do you not confirm the facts as I have stated them?"

"Confirm them? Of course I don't."

"You seem very upset, madame," Jaubert said.

How crude they could be! "Is that something you want to put in your report, monsieur? 'On being told she looked upset, witness denied it.' "

Jaubert coughed. "I must ask for your cooperation, madame. This is a serious matter."

"Serious? The account you have just given me is ridiculous."

"You do not deny making an unauthorized entry into the vineyard?"

"No."

"You do not deny making an unprovoked assault on Monsieur de Mornac's person?"

"I certainly do."

"You assaulted Monsieur de Mornac?"

"I'm not going to answer you for the moment."

"You do not deny striking Monsieur de Mornac?"

"What is the charge against me?"

"Monsieur de Mornac has filed charges of unauthorized entry, willful damage to crops and assault on his person, occasioning severe bodily harm. When I have made my report, the matter will be referred to the Public Prosecutor for action. That is all I can tell you, madame."

"I see."

"In your own interest I advise you to answer the questions fully."

"Allow me to judge my own interest, sir."

Jaubert put one hand in the small of his back and struck a Napoleonic pose. "As you will, madame, but I shall be obliged to ask you to accompany me if we cannot promptly complete matters here."

"Are you threatening me, sir?"

"I am stating the position, madame."

"You are threatening to arrest me?"

"I shall be obliged to ask you to accompany me."

"And you have a warrant for my arrest?"

"That would not be necessary, madame."

"On the contrary, I think it would be. And I think you are trying to intimidate me." She glanced at Rossi. "I want that exchange written into your report please."

Jaubert rocked on his heels. "I have come for a signed statement of the circumstances and I do not think it would be to your advantage to be obstructive."

"I shall decide what is to my advantage, sir. I have someone coming here whom I wish to wait for before answering you. I will then make a statement which you will find puts the matter in another light."

Jaubert bowed. "We might save time, madame, if I took details of your civil status, full name, date and place of birth, and so on." Susannah gave them and Rossi wrote them down. Then they waited about awkwardly. Rossi began to whistle. Jaubert and Dufaud the bailiff drifted off to one side and stood conversing in whispers. Dufaud shot her a hot glance from time to time. Susannah felt terribly nervous and prayed that Madame Gautier wouldn't come in. Jaubert pulled a watch out and looked at it. At last there was the sound of carriage wheels outside and a moment later Emilie knocked on the door and ushered in Dr. Cavan.

Cavan's quick glance took in the scene at once—the gendarmes' uniforms, Susannah standing anxiously apart on the other side of the room. Susannah went quickly to him. "Thank you for coming, Doctor."

He bobbed over her hand and stood hunched up, his angry old eyes flicking quickly from one to the other. Susannah led him forward, but no introductions were necessary. They all knew him, of course, and he knew them.

"Doctor." They exchanged polite nods.

"These gentlemen have come to ask me questions about an incident yesterday with the Count de Mornac. You have heard about it?" Cavan nodded. "I have asked you to come because Monsieur de Mornac is claiming that I assaulted him. In fact, he assaulted me. And not only me but a child I was trying to save from a dog."

"If we may have your statement in sequence, madame," Jaubert said.

"Very well."

Susannah told them. She described the scene—the dog, the harassed child, Mornac's furious attack and how she had hit him and ridden him down. Rossi, who was writing it down, couldn't keep up and she had to pause and repeat things, but finally it was done.

"And who was the boy? What was his name?" Jaubert said.

"I don't know."

"Where was it you took him?"

"I don't know where it was. A small village a mile or two away, I think, but I can't remember."

"You took him there, yet you don't know where it was?" Jaubert said. "You are well acquainted with the neighborhood, I think, madame?"

"Yes. I was very upset, that was why I didn't notice."

"And you didn't ask him?"

"No."

"And whose dog was it?"

"I don't know that either."

Jaubert gave a twist to the wirelike end of his mustache. "In fact, the boy was playing with the dog, chasing it, was he not? And you were encouraging him, weren't you, madame?"

"No. Nothing of the sort." She looked at him with sudden realization. "Is that what Monsieur de Mornac is saying?"

Jaubert's mouth tightened. "I am not at liberty to disclose what is in his deposition, madame."

"Then it is, and it is quite untrue. The child was gasping for breath."

"You did not realize he was laughing, madame?"

"What? Laughing?" She stared in amazement at Jaubert's sudden complacency. "Oh, no, no. It wasn't that. No. He could hardly keep out of the dog's way."

"And the boy is the only evidence to support your version, madame?"

"By no means. That is why I have asked Dr. Cavan to come here." Deliberately Susannah unbuttoned the sleeves of her dress, then the front. Jaubert's expression became startled; the bailiff reddened. "Dr. Cavan, I want you to see what Monsieur de Mornac did with his cane." Susannah stood straight in front of them. The dress was unbuttoned. She pulled one arm out of the sleeve, then the other, holding the dress around her at the waist.

Jaubert coughed. "Please, madame, there is no need—"

"I think there is," she said, unfastening the bodice underneath. She freed it and pulled it down from her shoulders, showing her bare shoulders and her bosom. Cavan clicked his tongue and approached. The other two were shifting their feet with embarrassment. Rossi had looked up from his writing.

Mornac's cane had left two red stripes across her shoulders and the upper part of her breast on the right. A third, a lighter mark, began on her upper arm and extended to her neck. The marks were clear on her fair skin. She turned around. Cavan examined them, pressed the collarbone here and there with his fingers, made her turn around. Gently he felt her breast, clicked his tongue again.

She turned to Jaubert. "I must ask you to take note of these injuries, sir, in Dr. Cavan's presence, so that there shall be no dispute about them. Monsieur de Mornac hit me first—these are the marks he made—and when I hit back, I was defending the child and myself from his—I don't know what to call it— his madness, sheer mad fury."

Jaubert bridled. They were outraged, they were offended. Their dignity was offended. The uniform and their function were put upon; even the bailiff was puffy. Their attitude said they were not here to see indecent displays of a woman's body. She had taken them by surprise, taken advantage of them.

"That will not be necessary, madame," Jaubert said stiffly.

"I shall refuse to sign anything unless it is put in."

"And *I* will take steps." Dr. Cavan looked hard at Jaubert.

Jaubert said uncomfortably, "Very well." Then Susannah saw his eyes go past her and he gave a distant little nod. She caught her breath and looked around, hastily covering herself. Abel-Cherubin was inside the door. For a moment he remained stock still, mouth open, gazing at the scene, then he wordlessly retreated. Susannah adjusted her clothes, pulled the dress back on and buttoned it up again. She could see they were all furious, particularly Jaubert, but she didn't care.

Rossi finished writing and handed her the report. Susannah read it through, crossed out two sentences, inserted a phrase here and there. Then she signed it. But before Jaubert could take it, Dr. Cavan pushed Susannah aside and picked it up. He took the pen from her, wrote in a deposition of his own about the marks made by Mornac's cane and signed it with a flourish. Then he threw the pen down and straightened up.

Jaubert was furious. He stepped forward, took the document and bowed to Susannah. "Madame."

"You may tell Monsieur de Mornac that if he proceeds with the charges I shall make countercharges. And I shall do my utmost to see him publicly shamed for attacking a woman and a child. Good day to you, gentlemen."

They filed out. She turned to Cavan. "Thank you for coming."

He was tut-tutting. "You must be careful. You must let me look at that again. Is the breast sore?"

"Not as bad as it was."

"I will send you some ointment. Ah, this is a bad business, a bad business. Mornac is a powerful man. Vicious."

As they moved toward the door Francis came hurrying into the room. He pulled up. "Oh, sorry. Dr. Cavan, how are you?"

"It's all right. We've finished," Susannah said.

"My dear Susannah, what is happening? Who were those men?"

23

An hour later the family were gathered in the salon. Abel-Cherubin, who had stayed at La Guiche overnight, had, unknown to Francis or Susannah, summoned the conclave the day before. They sat in a half-circle watching Susannah—Madame Gautier and Raynal, both very still; Chabot with chin lifted, looking along his nose; Abel-Cherubin bolt upright and florid; Regis with head lowered, looking up from under his brows; Monsieur Parenteau like a bedraggled old eagle; and Francis fidgety, trying to make the best of it. A tableau, she thought. All posing for a family portrait. The pale sunlight coming into the room made them look as heavy as iron in their heavy black broadcloth, their high collars, their neckcloths, their gold watch chains, their side whiskers. All solid and sanctimonious as they eyed her censoriously where she sat, a little apart, like someone on trial. The massive furniture and all those black portraits on the walls added to the ponderousness. She thought of that first day she had arrived and seen them all at the table and realized what she had to face.

"You realize you have put us all in a very serious position," Abel-Cherubin began.

"I don't see how it affects you, Abel-Cherubin," Susannah said.

"You don't *see?*"

"A scandal like this? We must all suffer!"

"It's all over Bordeaux," Regis said.

"And the gendarmes here now!" said Madame Gautier.

"Why didn't you tell someone?"

"Why call in Dr. Cavan? Why an outsider?"

"Frankly we cannot understand your attitude."

"But he's my doctor," she said. "Why shouldn't I have him here?"

"In preference to someone of the *family?*"

"I wanted him here professionally," she said.

"And you . . . you disrobed in front of those men?" Abel-Cherubin said with horror.

"You came into the room. You saw," Susannah said calmly.

"Madame!"

"I was showing them the marks of Mornac's cane."

"Sue! You didn't tell me."

They bristled, outraged, except Francis. They stared at her in horror.

"Is this . . . is this the way you conduct yourself?" Madame Gautier said. "This . . . this shameless . . ."

"A grave mistake."

"You realize that such conduct can only arouse prejudice against you?"

"You have already created a disgraceful reputation for yourself," Madame Gautier said. "This indecent riding about the country."

"It'll be the talk of Bordeaux."

"As if it weren't bad enough already."

"Anything you might have to say for yourself will be gravely compromised now."

"How could you think of such a thing, madame?"

"In front of *gendarmes!*"

"Like any . . . like any common—"

"Oh, for heaven's sake stop it!" Francis said at last. "Susannah was doing what she thought best. It will pass over. There's no call to get worked up about it."

"What! This is a matter that concerns us all."

She turned away, sickened, and they conferred among themselves. Then Parenteau said, "I think we should know the exact circumstances of the incident."

Abel-Cherubin nodded with a pained look. "Let us hear the exact circumstances, if you please."

So she went through it all again, actually feeling more

nervous than when she had told the gendarmes. It was as if it were a confession of guilt. They made her feel so unsure of herself. Somehow they always had the power to make her feel guilty. She was apart, she was not one of them. She was the foreigner, she didn't belong; and the not belonging had something to do with her guilt. They would never say outright it was *because* she was a foreigner, but the feeling was in their souls all the same. That was what they meant when they said, "Frankly, we do not understand you." They were so locked in the old narrowness that they hated anything outside. Oh, they all knew the penalty for stepping outside convention. And they shuddered at it. It was not going to happen to *them*. Careful not to make a mistake! They were ready to condemn with the rest—instantly. But now it *had* happened to them by association. So they were outraged. And they wanted to bend her to their way even now. They wanted to use this crisis to overcome her will. They saw it unconsciously as their advantage. She was guilty and now she must yield. But Susannah was not going to yield. She was not ready to give way. It was the struggle of wills again.

"And what did the gendarmes want?" Abel-Cherubin asked.

"They wanted my account. I told them what I've just told you."

"Did they saw what charges Monsieur de Mornac has made, madame?" Parenteau asked.

"Apparently he claims I made an unprovoked attack on him."

"An unprovoked attack?"

"Yes. It's ridiculous."

"Assault and battery?" Chabot cocked an eye at Parenteau.

"Articles 319-320, Penal Code."

"A misdemeanor. Carries a prison term."

"They say he's out for blood."

They all shuddered and looked at one another and then across at Susannah accusingly.

And suddenly anger flared up in her. "Good Lord, anybody would think I'm a criminal! I've done nothing that's not perfectly defensible. Anybody else with a grain of sense, a grain of feeling, would have done the same. If I hadn't been there, God knows what that . . . that maniac would have done to the child!"

"Does that justify your attacking him? Does that justify your making a display of yourself?"

"Yes! Yes, it does! Justify? What about me? I simply won't sit here and be called a criminal and . . . and a prostitute. I won't have it!"

"Really!"

"Such language!"

She was on her feet, her skirts swinging, making for the door, but Francis jumped up and caught her arm. "Sue, please, don't make it worse."

"Worse? I'm not going to be pilloried. I'm not going to be accused. I won't have it."

"Do come and sit down. We all want to help."

Abel-Cherubin said, "You seem to forget *us*, madame. Unfortunately we are in it too. *Unfortunately*."

"Then stay *out* of it! Let me deal with it alone."

"Haven't you done enough harm already on your own?"

Furious, she turned on all of them sitting there. "And what have I done? Stopped a man beating a child. A crime! What should I have done? Gone by? Ridden on? Watched the child being bitten by the dog and just ridden on? Say it's not my affair? That would have been the *wise* thing to do, would it? The *careful* thing to do? And when Mornac rushes up and slashes at the child, I should turn my back and ride off? Not my affair. His grounds, his rights. And if I'm hurt, never mind! Why, why . . . It's horrible. It's disgusting!"

They stared at her.

"You happen to have chosen a very dangerous opponent, madame," Chabot said.

She screamed at him, beside herself, "And do you think I care? Do you want me to crawl to him because he's dangerous? Do you think I calculated whether he was dangerous or not when he could have killed the child? You're all hateful. Hateful! Leave me alone." She burst into tears and ran from the room.

"Sue." Francis was after her.

"Go away! Go away!" She shook him off and ran outside. She hurried across toward the lake. She didn't want to hear them, to be near them. She didn't want Francis or anybody. But before she could reach the garden, Francis caught up to her.

"Sue, come back. It doesn't help."

"No. No. I will not. They want to crow; they want to point the finger. They hate me."

"Don't be silly. Of course they don't. How can you say such things? Nobody hates you."

"They do, they hate me!"

"They want to help. Do come back now. Come on. I'm trying to persuade Chabot to act for you. We've got to have legal advice. It's a very serious matter. Now come back."

She sniffled her tears. "I won't have Chabot. I wouldn't dream of having him. He'd be delighted to see me in trouble."

"Oh, Sue, do be sensible." He stood with his arm around her. Her tears always moved him terribly, yet he was dismayed by her stubbornness.

"No!"

"We have to discuss it."

In the end she borrowed his handkerchief, blew her nose, let him lead her back. The others sat there with their tight-lipped faces, all condemning her. She could hardly bear to look at them.

"What was the boy's name, madame?" Monsieur Parenteau asked.

"I don't know."

"You don't know?"

"*I don't know!*" She could hardly control herself.

"What can you expect?" Chabot shrugged. "Greatly weakens her case."

"What is the next step?" Abel-Cherubin said. "The Prosecutor?"

"Yes," Chabot said. "It goes to the Prosecutor. He will appoint an examining magistrate to go into the case, examine the evidence, settle the indictment and hand it on to the court. Takes a little while."

"Who is the Prosecutor now?"

"Madier de Laberat."

"Oh, yes."

"We shall need good legal advice," Francis said, looking at Chabot. "Would you be able to—"

"Not me." Chabot raised a hand, shaking his head. "Be unwise for me to advise you in any way. Do you more harm than good. Besides, I have too many clients close to Mornac. Most unwise. Don't you agree, Parenteau?"

Parenteau's head wobbled on his scrawny neck. It might have been a yes, it might have been a no.

Francis looked dismayed. "I see. Can you suggest somebody —a good lawyer?"

"Maisonneuve?" Abel-Cherubin asked.

Chabot shook his head vigorously, popping his eyeballs at Abel-Cherubin in a hard glare. "Wouldn't touch it!"

"Well, Allier?"

"Tadouneau's brother-in-law," Chabot said and sniffed.

Regis said, "Is it any good trying to approach Madier? He's in my club a lot."

Chabot made a little hissing sound between his pursed lips. "Difficult, difficult. Couldn't do it directly. Have to be done through somebody well placed."

"That's just it—who?" Abel-Cherubin said.

"And if Madier weren't sympathetic, it would only make it worse."

"On the whole the prosecution people don't like being interfered with," Chabot said. "Unless one gets somebody high up."

"Which is out of the question."

"Quite out of the question in this case."

They sat there savoring it.

"I can ask Maître Carmontel if he will take the case," Parenteau said.

"Carmontel?" Abel-Cherubin frowned. "I don't think I know him."

"Oh, pouf. Carmontel. Yes . . . well, he might take it, if it's put to him in the right way. Yes . . . Carmontel, why not?" Chabot shrugged, turning the corners of his mouth down as much as to say Maître Carmontel wasn't much of a lawyer but what could they expect for such a case?

Susannah stood up. She would not sit there listening to it any longer. "I'll arrange for my own lawyer with Francis," she said. Then she walked out. So much for family support. So much for their sympathy.

She didn't think Mornac would go on with it. He would

have the police drop the case, since he must realize he would be shown up if it went further. They would hear no more. She was confident. Yet, well . . . Francis wasn't sure; for once his optimism failed. He wanted to believe it, but he looked unhappy. "You don't know people like Mornac."

What she was more immediately concerned with was the family reaction. "What's wrong with me? Why don't they like me?"

"But they do. Don't be silly. They do. You imagine things." Of course he didn't want to face it.

"It's because I'm American, isn't it?"

"No, no. All that's your imagination."

"I won't bow to their gods, so they reject me."

"Well, that's not because you *are* something, is it?"

"Yes. I fall short. They make me feel that. They make me feel guilty. But how can I be like them? You can only become French if you're a workman. Otherwise it's not possible. You can't become French. You can become American, yes. That's something wider, it's accessible. You embrace more. Even middle-aged people can become American. You can't stifle in America—too big and dangerous. But to turn yourself into a French bourgeois, narrow yourself, curb yourself, curb your life, constrict and constrain? Terribly hard for an American."

"Society's more complex here and it takes more adjusting to, that's all." He didn't really see.

"I agree society is more *set*," Susannah said. "Heavens, it looks as if it will never move again. But it's not social machinery, it's *people*—and what they live by. Why, the workpeople here are more independent than the bourgeois. At least they're natural, they're themselves. Any laborer of ours would stand up to Mornac, and that's what matters really, standing up. You wouldn't have had that . . . that wretched scene in a working family. But the bourgeois! So shocked and hidebound. So paltry! Where's their spirit? You can't live life on the defensive. Look at your own business. The merchants and the brokers are throttling the growers, and the growers accept it."

"People don't see why they should be the sacrificial lamb, that's the answer. Let somebody else do it."

"Yes, better be safe than sorry. Well, I don't believe in that."

Next afternoon Francis brought Maître Carmontel out to La Guiche from Bordeaux. They had not been able to find anybody more suitable, and Carmontel had the merit of being a distant connection of the Archbishop. He was a brisk, sharp-featured young man with crinkly black hair, large hands and a magnificent voice. He only stayed an hour, asked Susannah the expected questions, was curt, quick, clipped, entirely noncommittal, and said they would await events.

Susannah was pulled up rather short by him. She was sorry she had not kept Mornac's cane, which she had forgotten about until the gendarmes' visit, but Carmontel dismissed it. Cane? He shrugged. Could she find the boy again? Susannah said she would try. Well . . . she might do that. Dryly he listened to her arguments, curtly nodded. And suddenly she was all confidence. She had been quite right—the affair would come to nothing. Carmontel's whole manner confirmed it.

That evening she chose a moment after supper and went through to the kitchen and told Joseph to saddle Red at six o'clock in the morning. Joseph was to keep him out of sight in the stable until she came for him. She had not taken the horse out since the incident and didn't want a great row over it again. But go she would, or every day would be more of a surrender.

It was a dull gray morning with threatening rain. She waited till Francis was out of the way, then walked the horse gently down the drive and, once on the road, prodded him into a quick trot. The horse had recovered from the fright he had had. He was full of joy to get out again and kept dancing sideways, wanting to gallop, but she held him in.

She chose the path by the river, let him go, and off he went like a thunderclap until he was winded; then she turned him west and set about finding the way she had come back that morning after leaving the boy. An hour later she hadn't found it and was not sure where she was.

The wide track she was on led straight ahead. Down came the rain in a great swish. She turned the horse off across the overgrown verge, taking him carefully in case there was a ditch, and guided him through an opening into the forest. The gentle hiss of the rain sounded all around her. She sat there, with the horse whisking his tail and shifting his feet on the soft pine needles lying thick on the ground. A footpath led from the opening she had used through the trees.

After a moment she began to think she ought to ignore the rain and get back. It was the sort of weather that could last all day here, and if she arrived at La Guiche too late there would be trouble. So she turned the horse and followed the path. About a mile on she saw an opening ahead and then, on the left, the dip with the huts where she had left the boy.

She could see at once there was nobody there. All the doors and shutters were shut, there was not a wisp of smoke from the chimneys, not a stray cat. She dismounted and went to the end hut. The door was held shut by a length of chain. She peered in through the crack but could only see the bare earth floor and empty fireplace. Was this the right place? She stood back studying the lopsided slither of huts, but there was no mistake. She saw how dilapidated the huts were, the woodwork rotten, holes in the roofs. They looked as if they had been abandoned for years.

She walked along leading the horse to the small group of cottages forming the hamlet and there, as if he had been struck by a spell, was the same old man with his spade looking up curiously at her from the patch of garden. Did he know where the people were from the hut? He shook his head and looked around toward his cottage. Out came a short elderly toothless woman. No, she didn't know either. No to all Susannah's questions.

Susannah thanked them and led the horse to a cottage farther on where another woman was shaking out a mat as a pretext to watch. Did she know where the people had gone? No. Nor when, nor anything about them. Surely they must . . . They would know everything that happened in so small a place. But they weren't saying. Fear?

Smiling to the woman, Susannah mounted the horse again. And just around the bend in the track beyond, a handsome ginger-haired young laborer was coming along with cart and horse. He pulled up at her question, shifted the match in his mouth, looked at her frankly and smilingly. Yes, he knew the hut she meant. Ah, the people? Where they'd gone? Ah, that . . . He couldn't say. That he didn't know. No, if they'd just gone, they'd gone. He didn't know. He smiled and his hazel eyes were friendly and admiring and she knew he was lying.

24

———————

A blue official envelope arrived three days later. It was a printed letter with name, date and hour filled in by hand and a big round blue stamp at the bottom—*République Française*—with an illegible scribble of signature. It ordered Susannah to present herself at the stated hour at the Public Prosecutor's office in Bordeaux. A shock! In spite of her confidence, she was upset.

There had been no warning, no hint from Carmontel. When Francis saw him in Bordeaux next day, Carmontel shrugged. He had heard something of the sort was likely. But why hadn't he told them? What did it mean? It meant that the Prosecutor had appointed an examining magistrate to deal with the case; the magistrate would examine the evidence, hear witnesses and hand on the indictment to the court. The magistrate now wished to hear her. He, Carmontel, would be there, of course, when she saw the magistrate, so would Mornac. Hearing this, Susannah had the impression that Carmontel knew more. She couldn't understand why he wouldn't tell, but that was the way of things here—secretive. Anything official was deadly secret. It helped to keep people afraid. She shuddered; she hated that.

On the appointed day she and Francis drove to Bordeaux and met Carmontel in the hall of the Palais de Justice. It was early afternoon and the hall was as busy as a railway station. People were waiting, wandering about, hurrying in and out—poor wretches in rags, police, lost-looking country folk intimidated by the place, busy fat lawyers in their black robes, laughing and at ease, mothers with bundles and children.

"Where's Dr. Cavan?" Carmontel said.

"I'm sorry, he couldn't come. He's been out since early morning with a patient and we got a message to say he couldn't leave." It had been arranged that Dr. Cavan should accompany her to give evidence about the blows she had received.

"Nuisance." Carmontel was obviously disappointed.

He led them into a short side corridor and left them; they sat on the bench, rather lost, and waited. They did not have much to say to each other. It was strange but they seemed to be pushed apart by something. Susannah felt this and she knew Francis felt it too, that was why they were rather silent. Perhaps it was the place, something threatening about it, something only lawyers and police could get used to, something sordid. She felt it overpoweringly, an aura that clung to the whole place, to everybody in it; it would cling to her clothes afterward. Was it despair? Despair? Something, at any rate, that got between her and Francis, pushed away their love, pushed their personal lives apart. She felt horribly alone. It was like being swept up by a great wave. You couldn't think of love then, and if you did it would seem trivial, irrelevant. These thoughts oppressed her and she tried to chase them away. She put her hand on Francis's. He looked at her and smiled, but so distantly.

Carmontel kept disappearing, then she would see him again, talking to another lawyer, whispering, joking. Now and then she or Francis would catch his eye and he would shake his head as if to say not yet. The magistrate's door was on the other side of the hall and she could see people going in and coming out, but they were not called. She dreaded seeing Mornac.

Four o'clock struck. She began to feel nervous. At last Carmontel came up and said to Francis, "I think we should be going in soon. The magistrate's arrived. You'd better go and come back later. You won't be able to come in with us anyway."

"I see." Francis looked a bit lost. He smiled at her. "Will you be all right?"

"Of course."

"Very well then." He gave her a kiss and took her hand. "Don't worry, it'll be all right. I'm sure it will."

"Yes, yes." She smiled as if she had to give him reassurance.

When he had gone Carmontel came and sat down close beside her on the bench. He looked at her and began to screw his lips tightly together as if he had bitten on a lemon or something equally sour, and she saw he had got rid of Francis because he wanted to speak to her alone.

"I believe you know Mr. John Blood, madame."

She stared at him, alarm filling her eyes, then she controlled herself and sat up straight. "What has that to do with the case?"

More sour lip-screwing. "It may have nothing. We can only hope so. But Mr. Blood is . . . ah . . . a notorious person and Monsieur de Mornac may try to blacken the case against us by bringing up your . . . ah . . . your acquaintance with him."

She looked at him in silence. Blacken the case against her? What did that mean? What did they know?

"It is something that we must at any rate be prepared for," he said. His eyes rested on her, rather small gray eyes, a size too small, she thought. His crinkly black hair made his head big, but he wore no beard or mustache. He was waiting for her answer.

"I know the gentleman slightly. He has been to La Guiche, we have met socially."

"Yet you have his horse."

"Really! Lady Canning gave me the horse." But she felt the sudden rush of color to her face.

"Yes, from Mr. Blood?"

"No! From herself. She couldn't manage him. Her husband bought him for her, but he was too much of a handful so she gave him to me. You can—" She was going to say that he could ask Constance Canning, then remembered that the Cannings were in England. "Mr. Blood lost him in a wager."

But she could see he didn't believe her, didn't believe her for a minute. He was used to hearing cooked-up stories. He was asking himself how it would sound, this story of hers, how he could dress it out, how he could make it sound convincing. *What else did he know?* She felt terribly uncertain now. Something must have got out about that day. He knew, he knew something, sending Francis away like that.

The small gray eyes were watching her and she knew her face was still red. He knew something. Then he put a hand inside his robe, brought out one or two papers from a pocket, selected one and put the rest back. It was a newspaper clipping. He unfolded it and handed it to her. Somebody had marked it in red ink in the margin and written *Times* on it and the date, and she saw it was part of a parliamentary report. She read it:

Certain recent events in Ireland (continued the MINISTER) had been of a nature seriously to disturb Her Majesty's Government. A movement led by a person well known at Dublin Castle and in Dublin society— (Interruption, cries of "Names!") He was reluctant to give names since he did not want to prejudice future steps against the ringleaders. (Renewed cries of "Names!" and "Give the names!") If hon. members insisted they should have names. The leader was John Blood of Limerick and his lieutenants were Michael Tulla of Dublin and Robert Curran of Kilkenny. (Cries of "Shame!") This movement had been a well-organized and dangerous conspiracy. He would say considerably more dangerous than the so-called Young Ireland Movement whose leaders had been so happily apprehended. During the recent famine period, Blood and his men had raided government food depots, attacked government cash offices, a Board of Works office and terrorized landlords and shopkeepers. He would give one or two particulars. On 7th April, hon. members would recall, a dastardly attack had been made on a light escort of six men of H.M. 7th Hussars accompanying a convoy of oats and oatmeal for export at Youghal, Co. Cork. Two men had been killed, the remaining four wounded and the export supplies, plus fifteen hundred pounds sterling in cash stolen along with them, distributed among a crowd on the spot. On 1 June twenty armed men, one identified as Blood, had attacked the government food depot at Ennis, Co. Clare, and distributed four tons of food to the population. On 14 September, Tulla had led a mob of 500 paupers into Castlebar, Co. Mayo, where they had plundered food shops and forced four prominent citizens to distribute money. On 9 December Blood and six men had raided the Longford workhouse and obliged the authorities to take in forty paupers refused admission that morning. On 18 September thirty armed men led by Blood had raided barges loaded with export grain at Waterford, but had been driven off by the timely arrival of 1st Royal Dragoons. On this occasion, four of Blood's men had been shot dead.

In addition, the band had murdered sixteen landlords on the pretext that they had disregarded warnings not to evict tenants and had terrorized whole areas of the country, often making nightly visitations on the gentry to intimidate them or extort money allegedly for the poor.

Of yet graver concern to Her Majesty's Government (the MINISTER continued) had been the movement's success in distributing arms among Irish sympathizers. Blood had exhausted his personal fortune to this end. The immediate aim of the conspiracy had been to sow such insecurity in Ireland as to drive the resident gentry out of the country. The longer-term aim had no doubt been a general rebellion leading to Repeal of the Union with Britain.

The Irish authorities had been on the point of apprehending Blood and Tulla when the intelligence had been betrayed. Blood had managed to escape, Tulla had been captured but wounded and died twelve hours later. The whereabouts of Curran were not known. There was reason to believe that Blood was now on the Continent.

She handed it back and turned her head away. Her lips were trembling and she began to chew them to hide it. She wished she could get up and walk away, avoid his eyes watching her so closely. Murder? A murderer? No, she couldn't believe it. There were surely other things to say, there must be another side. She struggled with her confusion. She remembered his face that day as he had said to her, "In these cases they see that a man's reputation doesn't flourish." She longed violently to see him now and talk to him. A rebel, yes. Oh, perhaps not blameless. "Obliged the authorities to take in forty paupers refused admission that morning." She could see him doing *that*, but that didn't sound like a murderer, did it? She couldn't relinquish belief in him. She was proud of him for the forty paupers. And a great gust of fresh life seemed to come to her as she looked at Carmontel who was taking all this in.

"It really hasn't anything to do with me, has it?" she said quietly.

"You are a friend of the gentleman's, madame. Like attracts like."

"Does it?"

"That is what people will say. Violence to a prominent man on his own land, after all"—he held up the newspaper clipping—"it's what you have here."

"I didn't start the violence."

"Public opinion in this city is very decided on such matters."

"You mean bigoted—hidebound?"

Carmontel screwed his lips tight together with irritation. "There are very strong dislikes, madame—particularly of impropriety."

No, no, no, she thought, she really must not quarrel with her own lawyer. She pulled herself up. "But good heavens, I really don't know Mr. Blood very well. I didn't, for instance, know those things about him until this moment."

"No matter."

"You mean I'll be tarred with this brush?"

He nodded, curt as ever. "If it comes out."

"It's probably lies anyway."

"I advise you not to say that if you are asked."

"Well, I don't believe it. Mr. Blood is not a murderer."

"Your loyalty to him may be natural, madame, but it is not judicious."

Before she could answer, he had suddenly swung around. An usher in a worn shiny old frock coat had come up behind him.

"Ah, we're ready? Good." He turned back to Susannah. "The magistrate is ready." They stood up, then as she prepared to follow him, he paused and looked at her gravely. "The examining magistrate is Monsieur Seriziat. He may have you arrested."

"Oh." The breath went out of her. She was terribly shaken and stared at him. "Arrested? Now?" She hadn't for a moment expected anything like that.

Carmontel nodded. "He *may*, it's not certain. He has the power. It is up to him. It depends on how he views the case, what he thinks of you." He was telling her to be careful again, to behave with "propriety."

"But on what?"

"He decides the charge, the indictment. He may not decide on anything today but . . . well, perhaps I shouldn't say this, but things have been done quickly."

She looked at him closely, frowned. "Do you mean he's under pressure? By Mornac?"

Oh, but Carmontel wouldn't commit himself to anything so open as that! "Monsieur de Mornac is a person of influence," he said and smiled as if he himself could be acting for Mornac tomorrow.

She felt horrible and was glad Francis wasn't there. It all seemed extraordinary and unreal. At the end of the corridor they entered the office. First a busy anteroom where they had to push their way through ushers and half a dozen lawyers and people talking together and consulting documents. Then through a padded door into a big overheated paneled room with red velvet curtains, Turkish carpet and a mahogany desk.

A man with a large head was standing talking with a bald elderly little clerk on the other side of the desk and nodding vigorously. He continued for a moment after she entered, then swung around, marched forward and waved a hand toward a chair. "Be seated, madame," he said and enthroned himself majestically at the desk. This was evidently Monsieur Seriziat, the magistrate. He had a presence; he sat at the desk as if he were commanding the whole town. His eyes were deep-set and gray like Carmontel's and just as flinty.

Susannah sat down, Carmontel next to her, and waited with a sickening nervous feeling for Mornac to come in. The door behind her opened. She felt herself go pale; but it was another usher who reached out, thumped a thick packet of documents on the desk and went out again. All at once the little clerk began to reel off an account of the incident, evidently taken from the gendarmes' report, speaking so fast she could hardly follow, and finally when he stopped, the magistrate threw out his cuffs, leaned back in his chair and looked at her.

"Well! You are represented by Maître Carmontel, yes? Well, now, madame, what have you got to say?"

"You have my statement to the gendarmes. I don't think I can add anything to that."

"You admit it then?"

"Admit what, sir?"

"That you rode into Monsieur de Mornac's vineyard and attacked him?"

"I admit *striking* Monsieur de Mornac in—"

"You do admit it?"

"—in self-defense and in defense of the child."

"I have seen Monsieur de Mornac, of course, and been through it thoroughly. He shouted at you, that was all. Does that warrant you using your whip on him?"

"He wasn't just shouting. He rushed up and started hitting the child. I shouted at him to stop, he wouldn't and when I rode up he hit me."

"He denies it—specifically denies striking you. He . . . er . . ." He looked down, consulting a document before him on the desk. "He 'repudiates it with indignation.' "

"Then he's lying!"

He looked at her narrowly.

"Monsieur Jaubert, the officer of gendarmes, saw the marks he made on me and so did Dr. Cavan. It is in my deposition and I can show you them now."

"You will do nothing of the sort, madame," the magistrate said sharply. "*I* will conduct this hearing and I shall allow no repetition of such a scene in this office. What you do in your own house is your concern, but I will not tolerate it here. Not for one moment."

"Then how am I to defend myself?"

"You will answer my questions." He paused. "I have noted Dr. Cavan's remarks. Since there is a conflict on this point, I intended to confront you with Monsieur de Mornac today, but unfortunately he is still indisposed." He turned to the clerk. "See if Dr. Boissy is ready."

The clerk went out by a door at the back of the room and Seriziat turned to Susannah. "I shall have you examined by the physician. In the meantime, we will continue."

"If I may," Carmontel said. "Why should Madame Gautier ride into the vines unless what she says is true? Simply to attack Monsieur de Mornac?"

"But Madame Gautier was already there, on the spot, when Monsieur de Mornac arrived." He leaned forward. "Were you not, madame?"

211

"Yes, I was."

"You knew there were young vines there, two-year-old vines. You could see them?"

"Yes."

"And you took no account of them?"

"In the circumstances, none at all."

"You were simply bent on amusing yourself with the child and the dog, playing some sort of game?"

"Of course not. The child was terrified of the dog, trying to get away from it."

"You were chasing each other around and around."

"No, no. I was chasing the dog *away*."

"But the child could easily have run away, say onto the road."

"He *was* running away, or trying to. He didn't know where to go next, and he could hardly run any more. He was absolutely winded."

The gray eyes regarded her skeptically. "Monsieur de Mornac had warned you to keep away from his property before, hadn't he?"

"No. He shouted at me abusively once, that's all."

"Why should he do that?"

"Haven't you asked him?"

A quick warning cough from Carmontel. Seriziat said, "You will not use that tone with me, madame. I ask the questions here. Why should Monsieur de Mornac shout at you abusively, as you call it?"

"Because he's a brute and a vulgar man."

"You are not helping your case, madame. I advise you not to continue in this vein."

"I'm unable to defend myself properly."

His face went deep red, his voice rose. "Answer the question!"

"I don't know the answer, sir."

"I think you do, madame. It is because you have been in the habit of riding about the country in a provocative and . . . and . . . scandalous fashion. In a way calculated to be an offense against good manners and decency."

"I think not, sir."

"You have become so notorious in the parish that Monsieur

212

de Mornac recognized you instantly. You were already on bad terms with him."

"I wasn't on any terms at all with him," Susannah said.

"You considered him brutal and vulgar, you have just said so. You believed he had shouted at you abusively before, so you did not welcome him coming up interrupting your game on this occasion, is that not so?"

"It has nothing to do with it. There was no game. I was trying to protect the child."

"You were not primarily defending yourself then?"

"No, the child."

Carmontel opened his mouth to speak, but the magistrate held up his hand. "All you had to do to defend yourself, after all, was to ride away."

"I would have been leaving—"

"Kindly answer the question. I said *to defend yourself*, all you would need to do would be to ride off?"

She sat clasping and unclasping her fingers and finally said, "With respect, sir, put like that . . . I . . . it does not reflect the reality of the situation. Monsieur de Mornac was belaboring the boy. He would have done him serious injury. How could I ride away?"

"Supposing, which I do not allow, since there is no evidence for it except your word, but supposing Monsieur de Mornac was chastising a trespasser on his property. Does that authorize you to interfere?"

"But a child!"

"Does that authorize you to assault Monsieur de Mornac so . . . so violently that he was stricken to the ground, unable to move, and then to attempt to trample him with your horse?"

"That is a legalistic formula, sir. In the heat of the moment I didn't ask myself about rights. I saw the child being hurt and I rushed to help."

"You flew into a passion and went for him?"

"I was in a passion, yes."

"And so you tried to kill him?"

"Oh, no—no!"

"He says he got that impression."

She was horrified. "It is not true. It is not true!" She covered her face with her hands, trembling. She was in a bad position and only seemed able to make things worse. Carmontel was being no help at all. She pulled herself together, got out a handkerchief, blew her nose.

There was a pause while Monsieur Seriziat made notes; then he turned his papers over and said, "Yes. You mention a cane. Where is it?"

"I threw it away, on the way back." It sounded terribly weak, but there was nothing else she could say.

"You threw it away." He eyed her steadily. "And the boy and the dog, you don't know where they are to be found?"

"No, sir."

"Didn't you inquire? You say the boy was hurt."

"I didn't inquire because I was too upset. I was . . . I was dazed. I found the cottage I took him to the other day, but it's empty. It is in a hamlet called Saint Amand."

He wrote it down. Susannah said, "Perhaps the child was one of the harvesttime workers. I don't know."

"But, madame, the harvest has been over for weeks! There are no workpeople here now." He glanced at the clerk, who had come back and was hovering at the desk. The man bent down and whispered something and Seriziat nodded and looked at Susannah. "Dr. Boissy is waiting to examine you, madame. If you will go now, then return here."

She got up and followed the clerk out through the door at the back. A corridor led to two small rooms, in the second of which an untidy-looking man with a mop of hair and thick glasses was waiting. He bowed, fidgeting.

"Madame Gautier? Dr. Boissy. If you will be so kind." He shut the door. Susannah waited, he turned and said, "You have certain marks?"

She took her dress off and showed him her shoulders and bosom. The marks were fainter now but still visible. He hunched over them closely, moving his lips inaudibly, putting his thick glasses close to her and fidgeting. He made her turn around, asked her to move closer to the window, peered nearsightedly while he said, "Hm . . . hm . . ." and made little fidgeting jerks. Then he said, "Thank you, madame, that is all. Kindly get dressed."

While she was dressing he sat down at the table and wrote rapidly on a slip of paper, then when she was ready he led her

214

back along the corridor. The clerk opened the magistrate's door. The doctor handed him his slip of paper with a nod. Susannah went in. The magistrate and Carmontel were both in their places and Jaubert, the gendarme, stood stiffly facing the desk. The clerk placed the doctor's slip in front of the magistrate. Seriziat glanced at it, then looked up at Jaubert again.

"Madame Gautier says she took the boy back to Saint Amand. You've tried there too?"

"Saint Amand? Y-yes . . . that is in the area I covered myself. No trace of the child there."

"But the hut is there!" Susannah said. "It's a tumbledown shack. They might only have stopped there a day or two, but I saw the woman."

The magistrate did not seem to like Jaubert. "I want more inquiries made. I want it pressed. You understand?"

Jaubert shifted his feet uncomfortably. Susannah looked inquiringly at Carmontel and Carmontel leaned over and said in a whisper, "Says he can't find the boy."

"And the dog?" Seriziat said.

Jaubert shrugged eloquently, pulling his mouth down. "We have had no reports of any dangerous animal at large."

"Reports? Reports? Do you wait for reports?" His tone was sharp. "I ordered a thorough search. I am not satisfied at all. Not at all. I want a thorough search made. And for the boy. Is that clear?"

"Yes, sir."

"Now send in Maître Odier, if you please."

Jaubert went out like a lamb. Seriziat was writing.

"Who is Odier?" Susannah whispered to Carmontel.

"Mornac's lawyer."

He came in, a large florid, slow-moving man with bushy side whiskers, a mustache stained with nicotine and a shrewd bleary eye. Two others in black robes were with him, presumably his juniors. He held out his hand familiarly to Seriziat and Seriziat glanced up from his writing and shook it mechanically. A bow to Carmontel, then he eased himself into a chair on the other side of the desk; the other pair remained standing. They all sat waiting till Seriziat had finished writing.

Finally, he sat back. "I have only one or two points to raise," he said to Odier. "Madame Gautier insists that Monsieur de Mornac struck her with his cane. She says—"

"But he had no opportunity!" A great bass voice. "He shouted and she charged him. She was upon him like a fury."

"She has marks on her which she says were made by Monsieur de Mornac's cane. I have had them examined." He looked down at his notes. " 'Bruising of the epidermis . . . undoubtedly the result of blows.' How do you account for them?"

"Nothing to do with us!" Odier said. "If the lady has some convenient bruises, they might have been done anyhow, some charming domestic scene—"

"Really, I protest!" Carmontel exploded.

"Some feat of horsemanship. How are we to know? The lady is aggressive, as we know, and a well-known amazon."

"Hm." Seriziat stared at him and seemed doubtful. Sometimes he seemed on Susannah's side, sometimes against her. He was foxy, wary.

"She is also positive that he struck the child repeatedly."

"He chased it away, that's all. Shouted at it," Odier said.

"It's your word against hers," Seriziat said. "Of course, in the absence of the child—"

"But it is quite clear! Quite clear! It is in our deposition. The lady was not in control of the horse. The horse was overexcited by the game of chasing the dog. It was nervous. It kicked the child once, to our certain knowledge, and Madame Gautier must have hit him herself when she hit Monsieur de Mornac."

"That's absolutely untrue!" Susannah said. "I—"

"If you please! If you please!" Odier's great courtroom voice overrode hers; he turned back to Seriziat. "The three of them were all mixed up, in a melee, at close quarters. The boy got knocked over and kicked at least once by the horse, because Monsieur de Mornac saw it. *At least* once, probably several times. She was careering the horse all over the place. You have only to study the ground to see that. Quite mad, quite out of control."

"I was entirely *in* control of the horse. There wasn't a mixup and I wasn't near enough to the boy to hit him. I'm not—"

"Madame! Madame!" Seriziat rapped on the desk. He paused, looking severely from one to the other, then said to Susannah, "You struck Monsieur de Mornac several blows. If he was, as you say, also belaboring the boy, you would all be mixed up, and you could have knocked the boy down or hit him accidentally."

"No. It wasn't like that. When I came to blows with Monsieur de Mornac, the boy had eluded him. Really!"

"You have recently acquired the horse, madame?"

"Weeks ago! I know him perfectly." She felt she was losing her temper and hoped they wouldn't go on about the horse.

But Odier leaned forward with a "May I?" to the magistrate and said to her, "You have already had an accident with it, haven't you, madame?"

"No, that was another horse."

"Oh, another horse. An accident with *another* horse." He made it sound as if she were constantly having accidents with horses. "And what occurred there?"

"The horse tipped a gig over, an accident."

"It was out of control? You could not control the horse, madame?"

"Really it has nothing to do with Monsieur de Mornac." She was exasperated. "The circumstances were quite different."

"But the lack of control was the same." Odier bobbed his head at the magistrate.

"Yes . . . Hm . . . Well, that's all for the moment, Maître," Seriziat said. "I will send for you if I need you."

Odier got ponderously to his feet. He and his assistants bowed and trooped out.

Seriziat began to sift quickly through his papers. Susannah sat waiting for him. Then he picked up a pen and twisted it in his fingers as he looked at her. "It is undisputed, madame, that you struck Monsieur de Mornac. You tell me you were defending yourself, yet you admit that Monsieur de Mornac did not attack you before you charged him on your horse. You maintain he assaulted the child; he denies assaulting anybody. On the other hand, you have marks on your person caused by blows. There were no witnesses." He shrugged. "You admit, however, that you were on Monsieur de Mornac's land without permission—indeed, in disregard of his earlier warnings to keep away. The presumption of blame therefore rests on you. By your trespass you provoked the incident. You ride onto his land, you defy him. He is entitled to use force to eject you, though not undue

217

force. But this he could not have done, since you were mounted on a horse and were in the stronger position. The fact that you left Monsieur de Mornac severely injured lying on the ground and rode away is evidence of that. And it must tell against you."

He tapped with the pen as if he were weighing his decision; he looked from her to the documents before him, then back at her again. She waited.

At last he said, "Madame Gautier, I am going to charge you under Articles 319 and 320 of the Penal Code with assault and battery on the person of the Count Jacques de Mornac, unauthorized entry and damage to crops." He paused. "It is left to my discretion whether or not to detain you in custody. In view of the nature of the case, I shall use that discretion in your favor and leave you at liberty."

"Then we shall come before the court this session?" Carmontel asked.

"I wish to consider the case further. You will be advised in due course, Maître. That is all. You may leave."

They went out. People stared at her, then she saw Francis pushing his way up to her. He took her arm, looked at her intently. "How was it? You look a bit washed out. Are you all right?"

"Yes, I'm all right," she said, though she felt exhausted. "They've charged me with assault. But don't worry."

25

Mist from the Atlantic hung over the landscape next morning, everything was transformed, everything was muffled. The trees loomed dimly, the world hung suspended in the opaque milk-like pool of mist, in the strange diffuse light from nowhere.

Susannah had crept out of the house with Red and had reached the black-earth track by the river. She wasn't going to give up her morning rides now, because it would look like admission of guilt. Francis had driven home with her the day before in one of those silent moods that came over him when he faced a problem he simply couldn't ignore. Later, Abel-Cherubin and Chabot had called and discussed the affair with him and Madame Gautier. Much head-shaking and disapproval. She had tried to go about her duties without paying too much attention, but she had been secretly wretched because it had given her another glimpse into her husband.

There was a hollow place in him. Just when she needed a response, when she longed for strength, she found a hollow place. He accepted what she said but without understanding, he listened to her, fidgeting, without much attention. It wasn't that he had any doubts about her story—she could have understood that. No, he just couldn't respond. And she found herself wondering if he had ever given himself up passionately, entirely, in a *deeper* sense. Perhaps the wonderful, unbelievable physical harmony, their closeness in that, had masked that hollow place.

Was it a lack of something spiritual in him? But then she hated herself for thinking that! Yet under his weakness was a strange, hard impermeability. Weak people often had fearful hardness underneath. He was like his mother, granite when it came to changing his way of thinking, when it came to receiving an idea he wasn't already half given to. And similarly she was beginning to see that his range of feelings was narrower than she had believed.

At first she had thought it was a curious contradiction in him that he could be so rigid in his mind yet hate to settle at anything very long; but then she saw it was an expression of his character. He simply would *not* do some things, refused to, usually on the grounds that they were too trivial for him. But let something take his fancy and he was off and away with it day and night.

And then she had begun to see that his marvelous refusal to harbor grudges, a quality in him she had so loved and admired, wasn't really highmindedness, wasn't generosity of soul. It was because he had never really committed himself. He had never really cared *deeply*. He wasn't resentful, because he had never really given his soul to anger or fierceness or yearning or even to love in the first place! Where she could hate and storm or weep with love, he was essentially . . . hollow. He had no capacity for deep attachment. Oh, of course his feelings took him up sometimes and he even raged, but it never lasted, because it had no grip on him. It didn't matter to him, and so he could throw it off so easily.

But . . . but . . . he was so sweet and kind and she loved him. She would tell herself she was being hateful and unworthy for thinking these things. They weren't true—of course he loved her. She would become disgusted with herself and ashamed. She would be extra loving with him. Then something would happen, some trivial thing, and the thoughts would return.

He wasn't ill-disposed, wouldn't do anybody harm. He had no resentment. He was sweet and loving and happy and optimistic. But he simply did not see the people or things outside his immediate interest and aim. It appeared to be a sort of harmless emotional absent-mindedness—rather sweet and engaging —but it was really something quite different. It was an inability to enter into a deep relationship with anyone else. A shallowness. Oh, at the beginning she had believed he felt deeply, as deeply as anyone. Yet gradually she had come to this knowledge of him. Time after time she had told herself she was wrong, but no longer.

Weren't many men like this? Weren't they? Why couldn't they respond? Why? Was it lack of imagination? Something fierce that they lacked? Or was it Europe, old and tired? Was she just under the influence of old tired Europe?

Well, she wasn't going to brood on it now. Above all, not now, in the misty morning.

She rode slowly on. She loved the mist, the strange muffled unearthliness it spread everywhere. Everything was softer, the world secret and turned inward and dreamlike. She seemed to move through the muffled landscape of a dream. The black earth was blacker with the damp and a little slushy and the trees loomed up suddenly out of nothing. She couldn't see more than a few yards ahead, so they just trotted along.

The gentle hoof-thud of another horse approached behind her. She looked around but could see nothing in the mist. She rode on. The mist seemed to be thicker here. She was somewhere about the middle of the track, where it narrowed, but wasn't really sure.

Presently she heard the jingle of a bridle and the soft thud again, then it stopped. She was fearful and pulled up too and sat staring around at the blank mist, her breath visible in the chill air. She shivered a little, chilled. Somebody following her? She thought of Mornac and knew it was ridiculous, but she was frightened all the same. She felt fright flickering in her. Red's ears had twitched, listening for the other horse, and for some reason this alarmed her. She eased him on and then in a start of fear urged him faster. They were cantering away into the white blankness, faster, faster. Now something took her and they were galloping. She could see nothing ahead save the white opalescence, the void of white. The horse was fearful under her yet trusting her.

A tree loomed, they swerved violently, galloped on into nothing. The chill damp air rushed past; she strained forward over the horse, strained to see ahead. They were wildly galloping into the void. She saw a flash of low bushes, at the last minute checked his rush and suddenly they were in the river. The yellow-brown water swirled up around them. The horse lurched forward, and as his hoofs sank into the mud she almost pitched over his neck with the jolt of his sinking forefeet. He floundered about; she tried to turn him but couldn't. His haunches were churning and plunging and struggling as he tried to get a firm foothold. She pulled him left, trying to help him back. The water was up to her boot. He was scrambling, driving with his legs, slipping and straining and churning. At last he lifted himself, rose, got onto something firmer and out onto the bank among the bushes again.

Great volumes of cold breath came out of Red. He walked out shaking and quivering. His hoofs touched the slushy black track, and she walked him around, bending over him, stroking and calming him. Really how mad! How stupid of her to have done such a thing. Some impulse had taken her, some nervous tension that burst into action and blinded her to everything. Some sort of electricity ran between her and the horse. The horse's nervousness caught her. Perhaps that was what John Blood had meant by Red's being difficult. She shuddered at her own foolishness. She let him stand quietly for a while, then gently walked him back along the track.

The mist seemed quite impenetrable here, a soapy ivory. She rode through it, trotting gently back. Then as she heard the sound of the other horse, the horseman suddenly appeared, almost on her. Mornac! She swerved to pass him, bent forward, prepared to give Red a dig, but he was across her path.

"Susannah! Susannah!"

It was John Blood. His face looked dark in the misty light.

"Oh!" She pulled up, her heart pounding. "I was so scared. I didn't know who it was. I heard you before, back there."

"Good heavens, woman, you go galloping in this and you'll kill yourself."

She was so relieved! Without turning his horse, he dismounted, came around, helped her to the ground and suddenly put his arms around her and kissed her. Her heart gave a great plunge. She resisted a little, then broke away, only aware of his closeness, his voice.

"I've been here every morning since I heard of your trouble," he said.

"I don't always come here."

"You must let me help you, my dear. I have friends here."

"No. No. Better not."

"Why not?"

"It's better not."

"What are they going to do?" She didn't answer, couldn't, she was feeling so uncertain of herself. "Tell me about it," he said.

He clasped her hand while she told him briefly.

"But we must find the child! It's the first thing to do, quickly. They can't have disappeared."

"I know, John, but . . . please"—she turned her eyes up at him pleadingly—"let me do it myself. I must. Don't you see, it'll only make it more difficult for me."

"How will it make it more difficult?"

"They already think you gave me the horse. They think we know each other . . . better than we do."

"They?"

"Oh . . . my lawyer, Carmontel, among others."

"Your husband?"

She didn't answer, looked down at the ground. Oh, yes, she had known already that Blood had guessed about that. He had guessed there had been a scene with Francis about the horse.

He said softly, "I'm sorry."

"Carmontel showed me an English newspaper report about you and Ireland. It was something said in the House of Commons."

"Ah . . . So you see I am not the sort of person to associate with."

"I've become notorious too, in my own way. Anyway, I didn't believe it. I told him so."

Suddenly his face became fierce and smiling, bright with recklessness and pride, and he caught her up and held her to him, his face close to hers. "Ah, I wish you'd been there. You would have ridden with us, eh? I wish I'd had you in my life before this. We'd have changed the world together. But I have you in my life now, my love." Their lips were close. She put her arms around him and they held each other in a kiss that lasted forever.

She broke at last and turned her face away, but he still held her against him. "I love you, Susannah." He spoke softly.

"It's no good, you can't, you mustn't." But he lifted her face and they kissed again, a long breathless kiss until again she pushed him away and took a step or two away, in the wild confusion in her heart. She felt weak, she felt like a child with him in some ways. She longed for him but was afraid of the longing. He came up behind her, took her shoulders, kissed the back of her neck, caressing her, and she had to say, "No . . . no," and break away again. At last she got control of herself and faced him.

"*Mes yeux bleus*," he said.

She looked at him, anguish and love and confusion in her heart, and she didn't know what to do. She needed his strength, she needed him. She bent her forehead against his shoulder and she felt the world was splitting in two. This was the man of her heart, her man, the man she loved; but she loved the other too. She loved Francis and she was his wife—the wife whom he loved and depended on, however she might see him now. And she did see him with love. She loved him.

"We'd better go before we're seen," he said.

She was startled to see the mist was clearing. "Ride with me to the end of the track."

They remounted and rode side by side in silence to the end of the track. A gap in the mist showed the road. He said, "If you need me, send me word at once and I'll come here next morning."

"Yes." She dug her heels into Red and rode away.

She had to keep her mind busy, she had to keep her attention occupied. She was in a nervous state of mind all morning, reproaching herself, uneasy. At eleven thirty old Madame Bechu appeared at the kitchen door.

"Oh, Madame Bechu, come in," Susannah said. It was the old widow who had given temporary shelter to Augustine after her miscarriage. Susannah often called at the cottage on her way to the village and chatted with her. Now Madame Bechu had brought a jar of her homemade quince jam and Susannah thought how kind of her it was, such generosity, for the old woman was miserably poor. "Thank you, Madame Bechu. I know it'll be lovely."

The old woman stood there talking, giving spaniel's-eye glances at Emilie and the cook, and Susannah saw she wanted a word in private, so she took her through to the back and sat down with her on the bench beside the path where she had planted the irises.

Ah! Madame Bechu shook her head. It was her son Emile, he was making life a misery for her. He was always drunk now when he came home to the cottage. The drink had got him, and he was maltreating her. Yes, his poor old mother. He had given her a cuff last night that sent her against the cupboard door and it was a wonder she hadn't broken a bone. And then he had cursed her and thrown the bit of soup she had gotten for his supper out onto the road, and she'd been afraid he would do her a mischief. What was she to do?

This went on with many repetitions and embroideries. The son was a mason and worked half the time at Blaye, on the other side of the river, and only lived at his mother's in the intervals. Susannah listened, knowing that the old woman hadn't come for advice but for something specific.

Ah, she had been happy in her little cottage by Sainte Hélène in the forest. Such a sweet little cottage and a garden where she had grown melons in the summer. It was empty now because the people who had been living there had gone away to Ares. To be sure, a witch had come to live close by, but she wouldn't even mind that if she could go back. It would be unfortunate to leave Emile alone, he wasn't a bad son, but she couldn't deal with him when he was drunk.

Then why didn't she go? Susannah asked. Ah, but it was twenty kilometers and how was she to get there, an old woman, alone, with her things?

"Why, Madame Bechu, don't worry about that. I'll send you with Joseph in the carriage. Or I'll have one of the hands drive you over one day. Tell me when you want to go." This was what the old woman had wanted, and after much polite refusal for form's sake she accepted and thanked Susannah.

They sat chatting, then as she got up to leave, Madame Bechu looked at Susannah gravely. "I heard about your trouble, ma'am. I'm sorry."

"Oh, thank you." Susannah gave an embarrassed little smile.

Looking at her intently, the old woman leaned forward. "You know where the boy is, don't you ma'am?"

Susannah's attention snapped up. "No. Do you?"

Madame Bechu nodded. "They're in Blaye."

"In Blaye? Whereabouts in Blaye?"

"Near the square. You must ask Madame Breton in the Rue Neuve—Emile's lodgings are on that side, and it was Madame Breton who told me. She knows the mother and the child. I said to myself, 'Maybe young Madame Gautier would do best to speak with the parents.' Maybe they could be a help to you, ma'am, seeing you've come to all this trouble."

"Oh, yes, Madame Bechu. Thank you. In the Rue Neuve?"

"The end house."

As soon as she had seen the old woman off, Susannah told Jóseph to bring Tom and the buggy—they called it a dogcart but to her it was a buggy—then she went quickly upstairs to change.

Excitement! She put on her dark blue dress with the full skirt and the little yellow embroidery on the bodice and her Dunstable bonnet. Then she didn't like the Dunstable and changed it for a plain mulberry one. Madame Gautier was in the drive as she came out. Susannah quickly pulled on her gloves and said she had an errand and wouldn't be home for lunch. Madame Gautier contented herself with watching her go in silence.

After the mist the November sky had cleared to greenish blue. Just like a duck's egg, she thought, the great duck's egg hovering over us all! She felt a great gust of exuberance and hope. Once she had found the boy, off to Bordeaux! If only Madame Bechu were right and the boy was still there.

No trouble with Tom and the buggy; he clipped along as if it were part of him. In the village it was past noon, so there were not many people about, but she got a good hard stare or two. A pair of women at a cottage door put their heads together and whispered quickly as she passed, and when she stopped to wait for an oncoming cart a curtain twitched. Oh, yes, they all knew.

Past the village the road dipped between lumpy grass banks topped by a few stunted willows. Then she was going through more vineyards, near the river, where they grew the vines against taller stakes but didn't get such good wine. Strange they were, all the same, the vineyards. In one field you could have patches of ground that gave magnificent wine and patches that gave wretched stuff. One man had a vineyard famous for its quality; another, his next door neighbor, who gave his as

226

much care and love, might never get more than a moderate wine. Yet the soil was apparently the same. And you couldn't change that. Nothing to be done. Simply nothing. No good bringing in new earth. In fact, that was the very thing not to do. Why, at Château Margaux they cultivated more than a hundred different patches.

How she loved the country here! The colors were now all winter browns and sepias and foxy reds and all the grays from ash and pearl to deep charcoal mingling with the dull green of the pine copses in the pale yellow winter sunlight. The dark stumps of the vines, rows and rows of them, rose just above the earth. A hare coursed across the vineyard to her right.

Lamarque was almost deserted, everybody indoors for lunch. She drove down toward the river. Nothing at the landing place, nobody waiting, only a group of young men sitting drinking at a table outdoors on the open space and a man with a red kerchief around his neck pushing a wheelbarrow toward the row of small houses back from the river. Of course she had come on impulse. She did not know if she would be able to get across.

She drove over to the man and pulled up. "Can you tell me if there's a boat going across today?"

"Boat?" He looked up at her, put his wheelbarrow down and pushed his hat off his forehead. He arched his back a little to ease it. "Eh, there'll be nothing as I've heard, ma'am."

"Not? Are you sure?"

He shook his head. "Not as I've heard."

"I thought there's been a crossing on Tuesdays lately. Hasn't there?"

More head-shaking. Really, she thought, it was too exasperating. You could never rely on getting across here. The little paddle boat seemed to be making its occasional crossings less and less often.

"It's winter now, ma'am," the man said, as if this accounted for everything.

She sat in the buggy gazing blankly and rather foolishly at him. Winter, yes, that would be enough to stop them completely. Lord!

"You could see if there's a notice posted up at the landing. Sometimes they leave word when they're crossing again."

"Yes. Thank you." She smiled and snapped the reins and

wheeled the buggy slowly around, wondering what she could do. She felt so baffled, so punctured. At the landing place she got down and walked over to the notice board. Nothing. Not a word. So she was stuck.

She looked helplessly down at the brown boats moored at the water's edge with their square casting nets on poles, then out across the great empty stretch of muddy brown water with the sky over it, past the islands in midstream to the low shore on the other side. To the west was nothing but water. The line of sky and water met, as if the immense river had found the sea already, everything liquid, the great liquid immensity. In some way it frightened her—the river, its yellow-brown immensity, silently surging, silently rushing, the sweep of the great tide—and it made her shiver a little.

The breeze coming in from the sea blew the wisps of her hair against her cheek. Back from the landing place by the tangle of bushes and tall straggly grass the group of young men sat at their marble-topped table. They sat tipped back in their chairs. Their laughter floated over. The wine in their glasses glinted red in the pale sunlight.

She started the horse and drove slowly away, back through the village, back along the road toward the vineyards again. What should she do? What *could* she do? She began to fret, to feel that the delay was going to be fatal, that the boy would be gone this very day. Then she began to wonder again if he were really there, if Madame Bechu hadn't made a mistake, if it hadn't been some bit of gossip which would turn out completely wrong.

Then, halfway home, she thought, wait! In the morning there would be the steamer from Bordeaux, which called at points on both banks of the river. She could take it to Blaye. And she would ask Dr. Cavan to come with her. Yes! Besides, she hadn't told him yet about the interview with the magistrate or how Dr. Boissy had examined her; and, strangely, in his testy, embittered way, Dr. Cavan was a support to her. She felt his affection, his understanding. Somehow in things like this she relied on him more than on Francis.

So she snapped the reins and made the horse trot faster. They clipped along through the empty countryside and reached Cantenac village again. At the doctor's, Madame Sicard, his servant, opened the door. The doctor had left on his visits. She shook her head. No, she didn't expect him back before dark. Another hitch! Susannah stood there in the hallway, frustrated again, and Madame Sicard watched with her sharp old eyes as Susannah chewed her lip with indecision. Would the doctor be free in the morning? The servant didn't know. In the end Susannah left a note saying the boy was in Blaye and asking if he could come with her next day; she would call for him in the morning in hopes that he could.

But the restlessness after that! All afternoon she was moving around inside the house and out, fidgeting, fretting, unable to settle to anything for long. She started to make some lemon tarts, then lost interest and told Octavie to cook them. She went upstairs and messed about with her clothes, then sat staring out of the window at nothing. It got dark and Emilie went around lighting the lamps. Susannah shook herself, took her sewing and sat in the salon; but each time she heard somebody coming down the drive she jumped up to see, hoping it was Dr. Cavan to say he would be going with her tomorrow. He did not come.

At last at seven o'clock Francis arrived. He came into the salon with a queer roguish look on his face, obviously pleased at something. He bent down and kissed her and she lifted her face to him and smiled, but she didn't want to tell him immediately about Madame Bechu and the boy, because now she was afraid to make too much of it. Really she was afraid it wasn't true. Something had eroded her confidence—the dull fretful afternoon, the delay, the dark, something. And she didn't want Francis to think she was relying too heavily on finding the boy.

Francis said, "Georges Gaveau is coming for dinner. He'll be here in about an hour and I've asked him to stay the night. We have some business to talk over."

"I'll tell Emilie," she said, head down, watching her needle. Gaveau was his shipping friend from Bordeaux, rather dull. She put the needle through the material, then looked up; he was still standing there looking down at her queerly with one hand behind his back and she realized he had brought something.

"I've got something for you."

She had a guilty pang at once. He had brought her a present; he was so sweet. She put the sewing down and jumped up.

"I bet you can't guess what it is," he said, still with the queer grin.

"No, what?"

"Ah, you must guess."

"Oh, do tell me." She laughed and reached out to put her arms around him, but he moved back with a laugh.

"Oh, come on, darling, please," she said. She tried again and he caught her and kissed her, still holding his hand behind his back. Then he brought it around and held it out to her with a little bow, his eyes on her face.

It was a silver-knobbed cane. She stared at it blankly and didn't understand. She looked up at him, then back at the cane again. It couldn't be Mornac's cane? Was it possible?

She took it from him, staring at it, then heard him chuckling. "Is it . . ?" she said. He was watching her in vast amusement.

"Yes! Mornac's. See?" He pointed to the coat of arms embossed on the silver, three oak trees forming a chevron with a boar's head beneath. "Those are Mornac's arms."

She was incredulous. "But how on earth . . ."

"You could never guess." He laughed with delight.

"It *is* his, I can see it now. Where did you get it, Frank?"

"Well, of course, not everybody can do these things," he joked.

"Oh come *on!* Where did you get it?"

He laughed again. "Well, it's a long story. And what do I get for it, madame?"

"Oh, darling, how clever of you, how clever. How wonderfully clever. You're wonderful." She threw her arms around him and kissed him, trying to blot out everything else in her love for him, to enclose them both protectively in her love. "But how did you *get* it? You couldn't have *found* it."

"No, *I* didn't. But I happened to see who did."

"Who then?"

"It was just chance. I was in the village and suddenly I see Museau prancing along the street bawling out at the top of his voice as usual."

Museau was the village drunkard and ne'er-do-well, a big still-powerful man, aggressive in some moods, and reputedly dangerous. She had often seen him in his two redingotes and layers of other clothing sprawled by the road with a liter of wine or lying drunk and dead to the world, sometimes far afield. For some reason Francis always treated him with amused indulgence and gave him a bottle of wine whenever he came begging at La Guiche.

"Naturally I tried to avoid him," Francis said, "but he saw me and rushed up wanting the price of a liter. And then I saw he had this under his arm. I didn't take any notice of it for a minute because—well, I don't know why—then I did because it looked so ridiculous, Museau, that scarecrow, with this. And *then* I noticed Mornac's arms on it, so I knew what it was straightaway."

"Heavens."

"I had the devil of a time getting it out of him, though. I asked him where he'd got it and he started to turn nasty. He wanted to know why I wanted to know and said I wanted to tell the gendarmes he had stolen it, wanted to get a poor man locked up—you know, his usual line—and then he started to rant and shout. He waved his arms and shouted, 'You're all the same, filthy bourgeois, filthy bourgeois!' He was really in a fury, shaking like mad, dribbling and glaring, and I thought he was just going to lurch off and that would be that. But I suppose he realized he wouldn't get the price of a drink if he did. At any rate, he started to gape and laugh and play the fool, as if it had all been a joke. And in the end he says, 'Do you like my cane, Javinet?' You know he calls everybody Javinet. 'You like my cane, Javinet?' and he shows it to me, just a little, then a bit more. He made a whole act out of it. I suppose he must have found it where you threw it away. He's always sleeping under hedges. Anyway, he finally says in a wheedling sort of way, 'You give me a bottle for it, eh? Hm? A good bottle, Javinet?' Five or six of the villagers were watching all this, and of course I didn't want them to interfere, so I said, 'You couldn't drink another liter,' and he sort of went 'Ho-ho' and threw himself back as if he was appealing to them. So I took him to the wineshop straightaway, bought him a bottle, and he handed the cane over. Can you believe it?"

"It's . . . it's incredible."

He was obviously happy and looked at her as if he had a new view of the whole Mornac incident now. Oh, he had never doubted her, but now he seemed more closely involved, seemed to feel more strongly with her.

"And I think I know where the boy is," she said—and told him. He thought she should tell Carmontel before making any move, but she wouldn't have that. No, she was going to see for herself, she was going tomorrow morning.

Carriage wheels sounded outside. It was Georges Gaveau arriving early, and Susannah flew to tell Emilie to prepare his room.

Over dinner they talked about Francis's idea of starting oyster beds in the Bassin d'Arcachon, and almost immediately afterward Francis took Gaveau away to his office for their mysterious business discussion. Susannah, rather relieved, read for an hour, then kissed Madame Gautier good night and went up to bed.

In the morning she was at Dr. Cavan's sharp at eight o'clock. The old man greeted her amiably. Yes, yes, he had got her note and he congratulated her on locating the boy. He whisked a big red snuff-smelling bandanna handkerchief back and forth under his rather red nose. Yes, yes, he would go with her, by all means, by all means. He had only one patient to see this morning and if Susannah would wait he would see to this at once and they could leave.

So they were ready to start before ten o'clock. The doctor climbed stiffly up with his cane into the buggy, settled his tall stovepipe hat, impatiently waved Madame Sicard away when she tried to wrap his redingote around him, and off they went.

It was bright and rather cold. Susannah talked busily most of the way, telling him about the interview with the magistrate, then about Dr. Boissy examining her. He flashed a craggy glint at her now and then. "Good . . . good." And when she told him about Francis and Mornac's cane he said dryly, "Capital."

They disembarked from the steamer at Blaye and walked to the house in the Rue Neuve. Madame Breton had a great white moon face and was draped in black with a black cloth around her head. She fixed Susannah and the doctor with mistrust and deep suspicion; but in the end she gave them directions and they made their way through the back streets of the little town in search of the boy.

And poor streets they were—mean little shops and courtyards, broken windows stuffed with sacking and rags. None of the sturdy nut-brown peasant faces she remembered seeing before. Some evil pall seemed to have settled on the district. She saw pasty emaciated creatures, many of them young. Old women were bowed under loads wrapped in rags. Three wizened blackened little chimney-sweep boys passed in their sooty caps, clogs and wooden knee pads. Men on crutches had wooden trays of combs and laces slung around their necks. Raw soldiers eyed her as she passed. Poverty! A different world from the great houses and the vineyards across the river.

They came to a little square with plane trees and crumbling houses, found the number, and Susannah saw with surprise that it was a tiny dark little shop hung outside with secondhand clothes. They went in, the doorbell jangled. More thickets of old clothes everywhere, then from behind a rampart of secondhand furniture a woman appeared.

"Good morning," Dr. Cavan said. "We are looking for Madame Sabra and her son. I am Dr. Cavan and this is Madame Gautier." Sabra was the name Madame Breton had told them to ask for.

The woman looked back at them steadily in silence. She was about thirty, with a wide face and small chin and dark liquid eyes. Thinking she didn't understand, Susannah said as simply as she could, "Madame Sabra? Is she here?"

The woman shook her head, still watching them. Something was faintly wrong; it wasn't simply misunderstanding. Susannah looked at the doctor, who was beginning to shift impatiently.

"I saw Madame Sabra's little boy not long ago," she said to the woman. "I took him home to his mother at Saint Amand. It's empty now, the cottage there, and I . . . I'd like to see them again if it's possible, with the doctor here."

Again the woman shook her head.

The doctor snorted and began to tap his cane on the floor. Then as Susannah looked into the gloom at the back of the shop, past the woman, behind more piles of old clothes, a door opened in the deep recesses, an oblong of light fell on a mirror, and there in the mirror she saw the face of Jacob, the old Jewish peddler. She stared at the face cut out against the little silvery frame of glass. Quickly she said, "Jacob! Jacob!" and turned to the doctor. "There's somebody I know there." She looked at the woman. "Please tell Jacob it's me. He knows me; he's been to my house. Please tell him. He's back there."

And then as the woman turned there was a little pause, all of them standing expectantly looking toward the back of the shop, and Jacob came forward out of the gloom and saw her. He

233

was bent over as if he still had the bundle on his back and he looked at them with anxious eyes. He said something to the woman, who retreated, and then he came up to Susannah and gave his little bob.

"Madame," he said in his tinny voice and, turning to the doctor, "Monsieur."

"You remember me?" Susannah said. "La Guiche at Cantenac? Look." She had the little seed necklace on and pulled it out and showed him.

"Yes." He smiled and nodded. "What can I do for you, madame?"

"This is Dr. Cavan from Cantenac. We're looking for Madame Sabra and her son. We were told they were here." Jacob continued to eye them steadily, anxiously, inquiringly. Seeing no reply coming, Dr. Cavan intervened. Briefly he explained the incident with Mornac, how Susannah had taken the boy to Saint Amand, had returned there to look for him in vain, and how anxious she was to find him now.

Jacob kept nodding and saying, "So . . . so . . ." but he was constrained, anxious.

"So you see, I must find him," Susannah said as the doctor concluded. "Is he here?"

Jacob hunched his shoulders, he spread his hands. "He is sick . . . He is sick . . ."

"Then won't you let the doctor see him?"

Jacob swayed from side to side as if he didn't want to commit himself, then turned around as a younger man came from the back of the shop, a sharp-looking man of thirty with brilliant dark eyes. He was wearing a long brown wool coat and he at once said something quickly to Jacob, then looked brightly at Susannah and the doctor. He was like a dark handsome brightly flashing male bird.

"This is Sabra, my son-in-law," Jacob said. "He is the boy's father." He spoke to the young man in Hebrew, and Sabra nodded brightly several times.

"Can we see him?" Susannah repeated.

Jacob hesitated, looked uneasily at Sabra, then turned with a sign for them to follow. The door at the back led into a corridor. They passed a room where she glimpsed the woman from the shop sitting with a second woman and two men. Jacob turned into the room beyond.

234

It was a poor place with bare plaster walls, two beds, a line of washing hanging up. And there in bed was the boy.

Susannah felt a shock seeing him again, the recollection of the scene flashed up. He was wearing a wool cap under which she could see a bandage and one hand outside the covers was also wrapped up. He lay there with his head drooping to one side, one eye watering, mouth open and dribbling a little, his plump pleasant face blotchy and flushed. A bowl of soup stood on the chair by the bed, and his mother, whom she had seen at Saint Amand, was standing there with another woman.

Susannah leaned over him. He looked up at her listlessly, then turned his eyes away. Dr. Cavan pushed her aside, waved to them to take the soup away and sat down by the bedside. Very gently he took off the cap and bandages and the boy's nightshirt and bent over examining him. He clicked his tongue, handled the child with great care. The boy's back and shoulders were badly bruised and the raw cut on his forehead looked yellow and festering. Susannah saw he had another cut on his neck.

The boy was apathetic. He answered Dr. Cavan's questions in a dull, weak way and seemed to have trouble with his eyes. Very gently Cavan shifted his position in the bed, raised his head a little, examined his eyes, mouth and neck, gently turning his head this way and that. He took the bandage off the boy's hand and clicked his tongue again. "Broken finger." He called over the Sabras and questioned them about the boy's behavior and what he had complained of. Then he asked for warm water and fresh bandages and turned back to the child again.

It all took a long time. Susannah, Jacob and the Sabras stood together by the window. They spoke in low voices, glancing occasionally over at the bed.

"You were at Saint Amand too, then?" Susannah asked Sabra.

"All, all of us," Jacob said.

Sabra said, "Sometimes we used that place a little bit in the summer, maybe a little later on. We are moving about, we are selling, buying, sometimes here, sometimes away." He wanted to give the impression that moving was nothing unusual for them, a family of peddlers.

But Jacob saw she understood they had moved away because of Mornac. He saw she understood that. He lifted his eyebrows sadly, made a little shrugging gesture with his hand while explaining. "It is trouble there already. It is bad already, you understand. If the gendarmes come there, we are sure for more trouble. For sure, for sure. This man is an important man. We have once before had trouble from him. I am just a peddler. My family . . . this shop . . . you understand? And the boy, he is all right then. His head he has cuts on, his shoulders he has beatings on, aie, yes, and his back; but more or less he is all right. So we move away. And a good boy he is; he does not complain. Always a quiet boy he is. It is best to move away. So we come here, the family. Here . . . and then the boy, he gets sick. He is not complaining, but he is sick. You understand?"

"Yes." She looked at the old man, a sort of patriarch, and she could understand. They knew Mornac. And they had an instinct for trouble. After the kicks and curses they had received, even from people like Josserand, when it came to the Mornacs . . . Yes, she could understand.

They stood together speaking softly, glancing across anxiously at the bed from time to time. They had had a doctor they knew in, but the medicine he had given had done no good.

At length Dr. Cavan got up and came over. He turned his sleeve cuffs down. "I shall have to move him. He needs care without delay."

"Is he going to get better?" Susannah said.

"I don't think his life is in danger, but . . . I don't know. He has had a bad beating. I don't like the head injury. I . . . I'm afraid there may be damage there. His reactions are not favorable. But that's all I can say without expert opinion. I shall have to move him."

"Not to the hospital," Jacob said and both the Sabras shook their heads decidedly. Not the hospital, the poor here hated the hospital, even the maternity hospital. Susannah had learned that.

Cavan got his coat on, tetchily refusing Sabra's help. "There is a good hospice here," he said. "We can have Dr. Arnoud from Bordeaux to attend to the boy. He will have good care, good care. But I must move him today."

Jacob and the Sabras conferred together, then Jacob said, "Yes, please."

They all knew it would be a Catholic hospice, but that was left unspoken. There was a tacit understanding that it would have to be accepted. Dr. Cavan put his coat on, went over and looked at the boy again. He told Sabra he would arrange for the hospice to collect the boy. They were to prepare his things but were not to move him until the hospice people came. "He's not to be moved, you understand?" He glared at them. Then he took Susannah's arm firmly and led her out of the room. He said nothing as they went through the shop, simply nodded at Jacob's expressions of thanks. Then in the street he pulled up.

"What do you really think?" she said.

"Think! Listen to me, young woman. You have one thing to do. Go and see your Monsieur Seriziat. Go now. Tell him I wish to see him at the hospice here at noon tomorrow *with* Dr. Boissy—promptly at twelve noon, if you please, at the Hospice Saint Jean—or I am going to make a scandal he will not forget. And I will— No, wait. On second thought, leave it to me. I know how to do it. Yes. Leave it to me. You be at the Hospice Saint Jean here yourself at noon tomorrow and ask for me. That's all. And now go. I'll get back on my own. What? Don't argue with me. I have been getting about this countryside for forty-five years without your help, madame, and I don't need it now. Now go. Go. And good day to you."

He was furious.

Whatever he said or did or whose ear he reached she never found out, but he had many old connections in Bordeaux and the department. At all events, when she arrived with Francis at the hospice next day it was evident that his method had been effective. Carmontel was pacing the courtyard and came up to them with a self-assured air, as if it had been his doing. He bowed to Francis, kissed Susannah's hand. "I am happy to see you here. I was too late to advise you last night that the magistrate would be here today, but we have managed to get him here."

"You mean Dr. Cavan got him here."

He hitched up a quick little smile. "The doctor's intervention, dear lady, would have been quite ineffective had it not been for the work we had already done. Quite ineffective. It was merely a support."

Of course. Faces had to be saved. And she saw how it would be. They would manage the thing so as to preserve everybody's dignity. They would all come out of it with superb dignity, no-

237

body to blame, everybody a model of energetic sagacity, rectitude and high moral principle. Naturally.

"Is he here already then—Monsieur Seriziat?"

"Yes, they are all here. They have been here an hour. They are in seeing the boy with Dr. Boissy and Dr. Cavan."

There was a quiet bustle in the courtyard—the nuns of the hospice, medical staff, visitors, porters. Carmontel had been eying the cane Francis was carrying. "What have you got there?"

"Mornac's cane."

"What! Is that it? You . . . you found it?"

Francis explained briefly.

"Well! You'd better let me have it," Carmontel said.

"No, thank you." Susannah took it. She wasn't going to let him have the credit.

"Oh, well, shall we go in?" he said. "If I can find the way." He led them inside.

Stone corridors, stone stairs, great stone-flagged rooms with gothic windows and rows of beds, the smell of carbolic, the nuns in their nursing aprons and cuffs and the great white sails of their bonnets and their sweet remote smiles. It was all archaic. There was a whiff of the Middle Ages, of men struggling with the unknown, of mystery and awe. Carmontel got lost, had to ask the way and finally they came to the wing where one or two old stone rooms had been adapted to offices. Two gendarmes stood outside a door. "Here we are," Carmontel said. They went in.

She was surprised to see so many people, quite a little gathering—two more gendarmes, Seriziat's clerk busy writing at a table, the Sabras and Jacob standing by a window, and several men she didn't know.

"We were asked to wait here," Carmontel said and pulled up a chair for her.

But she had hardly sat down when a whole troop more came in from the next room—Seriziat, Dr. Cavan, Dr. Boissy and three other middle-aged men in formal black coats and side whiskers, doctors from the hospice, presumably, all talking together, and a senior officer of gendarmerie. The process seemed to demand a lot of people! They glanced at Susannah, crossed the room and stood in a close group by the window talking in low voices together. Then they moved apart.

The clerk came over. "If you please, madame."

Susannah got up with Carmontel and advanced to the chair in front of the table where Seriziat was now seated flanked by Dr. Boissy and the hospice doctors. Dr. Cavan stood a little apart, looking on. Susannah sat down.

"As a result of a communication from Dr. Cavan here, I ordered a medical examination of the child Jacob Sabra, who was admitted to the hospice yesterday," Seriziat said. "I have also heard testimony from the child's parents, who are present here . . . Are they not?" He craned around.

"Yes, yes. Present."

"From which it appears that the child was involved with you in the incident in Monsieur de Mornac's vineyard. You yourself saw this child at Monsieur Sabra's domicile, did you not?"

"Yes, sir."

"And you affirm that this Jacob Sabra is the child who was present on that occasion?"

"Yes, he is the one."

"You knew the child before the incident?"

"No, I did not."

He grunted, rubbed his chin. "The medical officers' opinion is that the child received multiple blows about the head and shoulders which . . . ah . . . which could have been inflicted in the way you describe and—"

Cavan's voice broke in. "No, which are *perfectly consistent* with the manner Madame Gautier describes."

Seriziat gave him a look and said mildly, "Please allow me to conduct my case, Dr. Cavan."

He turned back to Susannah, but before he could speak, she said, "I have something to say, sir, if you please, before you go on."

"Madame, I cannot—"

"I have Monsieur de Mornac's cane here, and I should like to put it in as evidence. It was found the other day where I threw it away."

The magistrate jerked his chin in abruptly with surprise, and in the silence she turned around, took the cane from Francis's outstretched hand and laid it on the desk.

Seriziat hesitated, then picked it up. The clerk, the senior gendarme and two of the other men came up from behind to look at it. Seriziat turned and held it up to them. They went into a little huddle of murmured consultation, holding the cane between them, fingering the silver knob, examining it, flexing it. Finally Seriziat turned back toward Susannah. He reflected a moment, glanced at his clerk, who immediately bent forward, and they had another whispered exchange. Then Seriziat folded his hands on the desk and looked at Susannah.

"You have been charged, madame, under Articles 319 and 320 of the Penal Code. As I intimated to you at your examination, I have been continuing my inquiries into the case. The child in question, missing at the time, has now been found. He has given verbal testimony to the best of his ability. There being no witnesses, I am obliged to make up my mind on the evidence as it stands, which up till now has been against you. I say up till now. In view, however, of the previous medical evidence, the medical evidence I have just heard and a comparison of the two, in view of what the child has said and also having regard to the fresh evidence now submitted—having regard to all this, I am prepared to withdraw the charge. I shall rule that the case be dismissed."

Dismissed! It was over, it was finished? She could hardly believe it, she seemed to have lived with it for so long. She felt relief and yet something behind the relief. Carmontel was speaking to her. Francis caught her arm from behind, pulled her up and kissed her cheek.

"Yes, but wait a minute." She was still staring at the magistrate. "Wait a minute." But Seriziat was on his feet and her voice was lost in the general hubbub as the others moved around the desk. "But wait a minute!" They were all talking at once and passing around Mornac's cane.

Susannah pushed roughly through them and faced Seriziat. "But what about the boy?"

Dr. Cavan's angry voice came from behind the others. "He is going to be blind."

"Is it true? Is it true he is going to be blind?" She felt the cold fury coming over her and she could see on their faces it was true. They had tried to conceal it. "Why isn't Monsieur de Mornac here?"

Seriziat gave her a level look. "Madame, I advise you to take your good fortune and go."

"Why isn't Monsieur de Mornac here to be proved a liar and a scoundrel? Why isn't he here?"

"You may think yourself fortunate, madame, that you have got off so lightly."

"Fortunate, sir? Does one need luck to get justice here then? It was monstrous that I was charged at all, so I cannot be grateful to you. Monsieur de Mornac is a murderous blackguard. Why isn't he here to answer for maiming the child?"

Carmontel tugged at her arm, but she shook him off.

"I warn you, madame, I will not tolerate improper reflections."

"Because the boy's a peddler's son? Why is Monsieur de Mornac not brought to account, if you please?"

"Susannah, please!"

"Are you trying to dictate my duty to me, Madame Gautier?"

"Dictate it, sir? I am pointing it out to you. You are a public servant, I believe."

"You go too far, madame."

"But you charged me on a fraction of the evidence you have here against Monsieur de Mornac! He accused me of trying to kill him—a lie. He denied striking the child—a lie. And you have the proof. Why isn't he here? Why isn't he being charged here and now? I demand an answer."

Seriziat was so beside himself he could hardly bring himself to speak. "You demand! You demand, madame! You forget yourself. My duty, madame, is not a matter for your appreciation. I am not to be questioned by you or by anybody else. Your impertinence is . . . is . . . beyond all bounds. I have warned you once. If there is any more, I shall charge you with insulting a magistrate in the performance of his duty. And I will add this. I will add this. If I hear any whisper, you understand, a whisper in future about the conduct of this case, then, depend upon it, you will answer for it. And now, madame, off with you or I shall have you removed!" He was shaking.

Francis dragged her away. She was white-faced. Vaguely she heard Francis and Carmontel speaking to her as they went down the stone corridor outside, but she didn't take in what they said.

All at once, she pulled up. "I must see the boy. No, no, it's no good. I want to see him. Where are the Sabras? Don't, Francis! I'm going to see him before we leave here."

She looked back and saw Dr. Cavan in his tall old hat com-

241

ing after them. She turned and ran back to him. "Thank you. Thank you. You did everything. It was wonderful of you." She took his hand and pressed it in hers.

"Eh, madame, you did a fair deal yourself." His old face wrinkled into one of his rare wintry smiles.

"I want to see him. Will you take me in?"

"No, my dear, I cannot. He's tired. He has had them all examining him and asking him questions and he is too tired for any more."

"Please. For a minute. I won't say anything."

"Not for a minute. I won't have an emotional scene with him now. You can come in two or three days. It'll be time enough."

"Is he really going blind?"

He nodded abruptly. "Arnoud is coming from Bordeaux. He is a specialist, a good man. Perhaps something can be done."

"And what about Mornac?"

He grunted and looked angrily away. "They'll do nothing. They'll shelve it. What can you expect? We did what we could." Then he lifted his hat and bowed goodbye to her as if anxious to get away. Along the corridor she saw the Sabras and Jacob coming and she waited for them.

On the way back, after they had crossed the river and she was driving between the vineyards with Francis in the buggy, she cried. It was pain and relief and frustration all intermingling. Francis put his arm around her and held her against him. It was like the evening she had arrived.

She felt a phase of her life was ending and a new one beginning. The dark was falling, a soft evening, so marvelously soft for November, so full of peace and calm, the last streaks of green across the sky brilliant emerald above a long strip of silver and then the rest deepening, deepening to purple and brown, and the silent vineyards and the trees looming deep brown and misty gray and black. Everything was so quiet and soft.

The stars were coming out. Part of her life was ending. Yes, she felt that. It was ending. Ending and renewing, like the waves of the sea, the flux and reflux of life. Mysteriously it caught her up now as she sat there next to her husband. The horse's hoofs clopped on the road and they went home through the peaceful evening.

PART TWO

1

A blustery March wind swept around the curve of the Bordeaux waterfront. It swooped up the gulls like scraps of paper, lifted white crests in the river, snapped the flags of the ships off the Quai des Chartrons. The bright crisp sun sparkled on bright-work. The glass of rocking portholes flashed like semaphore lamps. Everything was in sharp, blustery, lively movement and Francis, waiting on the quay, felt full of bright, crisp expectancy, as if the weather had got into his blood.

The waterfront always excited him—ships and cargoes from exotic places, rough-looking tykes in mates' caps ashore for a stroll and a spit, the smell of gunny bags and linseed oil, the smell that meant the sea to any true deep-sea man, and simply the bustle and movement, the sense of departure for something new. And this morning he felt more than usually aglow, because if everything worked out, he would shortly be a ship-owner himself.

His father's spirit, the spirit of old Pierre Gautier and his impossible dreams, had at last awoken in Francis. Curious that it should be ships and shipping with him too, as if the pair of them, father and son, had been two benighted seamen longing to feel a lurching deck under them, whereas neither had had any but a landsman's experience. It had been a vision that had drawn the old man on; with Francis it was bright boyish eagerness, the sudden weakness for an idea that, if only it were handled in the right way, could lead to great things. And as he always believed the best, success always looked so bright, so likely.

It was this eager freshness that was so attractive in him. He had none of the old man's crankiness and dogged downrightness. With Francis it was all eagerness and sparkle. Yet the same essential spirit was there. It really was a sweet sort of longing. One of old Gautier's favorite ideas had been for a great rail and water system across southwest France joining the Gulf of Lions to the Gulf of Gascony. A shortcut from the Mediterranean to the Atlantic! All the long haul around the Straits of Gibraltar eliminated, and all the rich trade of the area drained off through Bordeaux—trade from Italy, Greece, Central Europe, the Middle East and beyond.

And Francis took it up with a sort of laughing affection. Why not? What was so impossible about it? He laughed, but he was laughing because the scheme was so feasible, so grandiose and marvelous. And he would pull old Gautier's maps out and show the start of the waterway already, the Canal du Midi. All it needed was a link with the Garonne, the Mediterranean terminal would be the port of Cette—and there you were. So perhaps his father's dream of maritime glory hadn't been so outlandish after all.

One night he and Georges Gaveau, his schooltime friend, now a Bordeaux shipping agent, had dined together in Bordeaux as they did from time to time, and in the course of the evening Gaveau had mentioned a Nantes man named Robic, one of his clients who had just died leaving a fine little sail-and-steam vessel called the *Amiable Rose*. Robic's widow didn't know what to do with the vessel and was going to sell it; and since she was an impatient woman, somebody was going to get a bargain. Francis had listened, they had passed on to other things—and then the idea had struck Francis.

Wait a minute. Why shouldn't *they* join forces and buy the *Amiable Rose?* What? Gaveau had frowned. What for? Why, to operate her, of course. And all at once it had blossomed for Francis, like all the ideas he fell for, as a sort of special happiness. It was a magnificent opportunity, a chance they simply must not miss! His face glowed; he was all eagerness for it. To begin with they would start a passenger and freight service from Bordeaux to La Rochelle and Nantes, then—

Wait a bit, wait a bit, Gaveau interrupted. A Nantes shipper already had two steamers fitted out to start a thrice-weekly Bordeaux–Nantes service on Tuesdays, Thursdays and Sundays.

But that wouldn't matter! Francis brushed it aside. They could run their service on different days. And if they put their first profits into buying a second steamer, they too could soon be running thrice-weekly and making a handsome thing of it. There was a fortune in it.

Gaveau was struck by his enthusiasm, quite carried along by it. He got out pencil and paper and worked out a few figures. They ordered another bottle of wine and began to talk about the scheme. Gaveau had a better idea. Instead of running north to Nantes, why not turn south to Spain? There would be no sea competition there, there was no railroad, and passengers and freight from France to Spain still had to go lumbering in wagons and coaches by road. They could be pioneers, run from Bordeaux to San Sebastian, call it "the short route to Madrid." Gaveau was beginning to warm up.

And then Francis had had the most inspired idea of all. Instead of starting from Bordeaux at the base of the Médoc triangle and steaming all the way up the Gironde to the Atlantic, rounding the Pointe de Grave at the top of the triangle and then turning south again to Spain—a route which meant steaming 120 useless miles and waiting for tides to cross the sandbars in the river—why not start the steamer from La Teste, the little seabathing resort on the Bassin d'Arcachon practically on the Atlantic?

Eagerly he drew on the tablecloth the tall triangle of Médoc, with Bordeaux in the right-hand bottom corner, La Teste in the bottom left-hand corner. Why steam all the way around the triangle when they could take the shortcut across the bottom? For, of course, there was the Bordeaux–La Teste railroad, all ready to take passengers and freight to and from the steamer. Marvelous! That was the idea that had decided them.

The little Bordeaux–La Teste line, running out across the empty moors and marshes of the Landes, was a comic anachronism. It had been one of the very first railroads in Europe, built in 1841, not in a spirit of pioneering enterprise but simply because it had proved impossible to keep up a road over the waste of sand and swamp. It was a primitive little line that carried summer bathers and loads of wood and resin from the forest and had never turned a profit. But it ran daily services. It was served by omnibuses that picked up and put down passengers at five different points in Bordeaux. And it was known to every Bordelais. It was what decided them.

"It's a magnificent idea."

"Handled right, there's a fortune in it."

They had clasped hands on the bargain, raised their glasses and plunged into excited discussion of their new enterprise.

Now as he waited on the quayside Francis was more confident than ever. A tall hat came rolling along in the wind; he shot out a foot and stopped it and the owner came puffing up. Then, beyond, Francis saw Gaveau approaching with his vigorous arm-swinging gait. Negotiations for the purchase had been lengthy, but Gaveau had been to see Madame Robic today to conclude it. They shook hands as he came up.

"Well?"

Gaveau's eyebrows gave a little twitch. "She's asking for more."

"What!"

"Wants ten thousand francs more. I said I'd have to ask you."

"But it was settled!"

"I know, but she wants this now."

Francis looked at him, his face still bright and boyish and eager. The dream couldn't vanish now! Absolutely impossible to let it all go now, the vision of the golden future. "Well, we'll just have to pay it."

They turned together toward the quayside café where they had been meeting to discuss the business and sat down at one of the little tables outside. A hurdy-gurdy man was cranking a little organ, playing a plaintive tune. They each ordered a glass of Sauternes.

Gaveau gave a sigh and cocked an eye at Francis. "You know, with the best will in the world, I don't think I can find any more. Much as I'd like to, I'm just too short of funds."

"But I'll put it up," Francis said eagerly. "I'll find it. It's all right. Heavens, we can't lose the ship for ten thousand francs! Absolutely no question of it. How soon can we take over? I tell you I can't wait any longer." He laughed.

"As soon as she signs the promise to sell." Gaveau tapped his pocket. "I had it with me all ready for her."

"Then do see her again this afternoon, won't you? Do. Tell her of course we'll pay the extra. I'll get it."

"All right," Gaveau said.

"I mean, this is a chance in a thousand and we can't miss it." Francis was boyish with hope, his eyes shining, gazing out at the sun-dazzled river. "Think of it!"

The little organ played its plaintive tune. The wind tapped the ropes of the boats against their masts, and beyond the flying clouds the sky was blue as blue. The waiter poured the wine and it caught the sun like gold in their glasses. They looked at each other and laughed with excited happiness.

2

As the spring came Susannah began to see herself more clearly in relation to her life at La Guiche. Something had been released in her; she was becoming more fully herself. She felt a strength in herself she had not had before and a spirit of self-reliance.

She didn't want to defy convention for the sake of defiance, but she wasn't going to conform for the sake of being like everybody else or just to be accepted. She wasn't going to yield to social taboos if they stifled her. And she wouldn't kowtow. She wanted to be herself—genuine, generous, free. She didn't care two sous about accusations of "vulgarity," and though she was only aware of it as a sort of instinct, she felt the active principle of life in herself.

Francis was more and more often away, and his absences began to make themselves felt. He was as sweet and cheerful as ever, often bringing her presents, once an expensive Cashmere shawl.

"All the other women have one, I don't see why you shouldn't." So kind and sweet. But if she told him, for instance, that Josserand had been asking for him in his absence, he would say, "All right," and she would often find later that he had not seen the man. Josserand, in his ill-tempered way, began complaining to her about small things, though nothing of great consequence. A woman, to his way of thinking, had nothing to do with things of consequence.

So she began to worry about La Guiche. She thought of asking Monsieur Laverne for advice and watched for an opportunity. Laverne was a quiet, decent man whom she trusted, and perhaps by talking to him she would find her worries were groundless. So one day when he had been showing her how they racked the wine in the cellar, she said, "Won't you tell me, Monsieur Laverne, if there are things I can help with?"

He understood at once and smiled, obviously feeling awkward. His ruddy face took on a tinge of purple. "Thank you, ma'am, but it's the master I need to talk to."

"Why don't you then?"

Smiling and red-faced, Laverne rubbed his hands on his apron. "Oh . . . he's busy . . . always on the go." He laughed good-humoredly, as if it were understood that the master was like this, always on the go, busy, too busy. It was plain he had a lot to say, but he wasn't going to say it to her. She saw that he couldn't get hold of Francis for long either.

This disturbed Susannah. She felt sure it was wrong to leave the running of La Guiche to the workpeople. Francis should be out there himself and working with Laverne. She waited, chose her moment and spoke to him. "You know Monsieur Laverne relies on you an awful lot. So does Josserand. They need you here."

"What?" He gave her a quick, rather resentful look. "Of course they don't, they're all right. They know what to do." He was immediately defensive and she saw he was piqued. He looked aggrieved and went silent and a moment later he got up and left the room. She looked after him, sorry she had upset him. But it always passed off quickly, often within a minute or two. He couldn't harbor resentment, but neither could he accept criticism. She had noticed it before. With the outside world he was always soft and pliant; with her he flared up sometimes, but it never lasted.

However, it left things at La Guiche as unsatisfactory as before. Francis couldn't be bothered by the administration of the estate, the details bored him. She saw that his interest had shifted elsewhere, and since he was sensitive about being questioned too closely she didn't press him. She decided it was some temporary thing, something to do with Georges Gaveau, and that he would come around soon.

251

But she loved La Guiche so much now with the spring here and the vines coming into leaf that she set herself to learn. She watched the men and women at work, she asked questions, she followed Laverne and his men around the vatting room and the cellars.

She already understood a certain amount. The Bordeaux wine brokers in their daily buying and selling graded what they considered the finest wines of the area in five classes. This listing represented their professional judgment of the best wines of the Bordeaux vineyards. It was a trade opinion, nothing official. And it wasn't invariable, for the brokers didn't all agree with one another in their comparisons of the wines; they didn't all have the same opinion about this or that wine. But by and large they arrived at the same general estimation, because from experience they knew that certain great estates, through the nature of their soil and the care with which their wines were made, produced better wines than the rest. So there were these five classes.

Three wines from Médoc—Château Lafite, Château Margaux and Château Latour—and one from the Graves area —Château Haut-Brion—made up the first class. In the second class the brokers listed about eleven wines, all from Médoc; in the third, fourteen, again all Médocs; in the fourth, eleven; and in the fifth class, seventeen.

This did not mean that a wine in the fifth class was *fifth rate*; it meant it was in the fifth rank of the aristocracy, for all these classified wines were far above the common run. Among the white wines, the brokers acknowledged that the Château d'Yquem of Sauternes was so outstanding that it was in a class by itself. After it they usually listed about nine first-class whites and ten or eleven second-class.

All these, known as "classified wines" or "classified growths," were the aristocracy of Bordeaux. Each went by the name of the château or the estate on which it was produced. Below them were all the others made in the Bordeaux area, all the unclassified wines ranging from very good to poor.

Most of the aristocratic wines came from the Médoc. But within the Médoc area the finest vineyards were intermingled closely with the unclassified, so the same village or parish that made a first, second or third classified wine also produced unclassified wines. A great wine, one of the nobility, might be a next-door neighbor to a poor or middling wine. Pauillac, for instance, in upper Médoc, produced wines of the first, second, fourth and fifth classes and large quantities of unclassified wines.

All the unclassified wines went by a generic name. This could be either the name of a region—Médoc, Sauternes Graves, Entre-Deux-Mers, Côtes de Bourg and so on—or the name of the village or parish where they were made, Saint Julien, Pauillac, Saint Estèphe and so on. So that if you saw a wine simply called Médoc or Saint Estèphe, you knew it was an unclassified wine from Médoc which the brokers and wine merchants did not consider good enough to be classified and sold under the name of a château or an estate, yet although it was below the top, below the aristocracy, it might still be a very fine wine indeed. It might have come from a vineyard with good soil and have been made with extreme care.

The brokers, therefore, graded these unclassified wines into several carefully graduated sub-categories—Superior Bourgeois, Good Bourgeois, Ordinary Bourgeois, Superior Peasants, Ordinary Peasants and Artisans. A Superior Bourgeois from the village of Margaux or Saint Julien or Pauillac was only just below the aristocratic fifth class, whereas an Ordinary Peasants of Blaye was a low-quality wine.

Susannah knew that Château La Guiche had at one time, a few years before Pierre Gautier's death, been among the nobility, a fourth classified growth. But the old man's neglect and poor management had cost it this place, and it was now graded Superior Bourgeois.

Médoc was the great red wine region; then came the Graves area, lying in an arc to the west and south of Bordeaux, which also produced white wines; then Saint Émilion, an area on the other side of the Garonne to the east.

But, of course, the quality of any wine did not depend simply on the vineyard it came from or how carefully it had been made. It was the weather that mattered so much—in other words, the year, the vintage. A bad year's Château Margaux might be less drinkable than good year's Bourgeois. And one year you might only be able to buy Lafite at a tremendous price and then, two years later, find a barrel from the same vineyard

253

going for a mere fraction of that price—because it was a bad year.

One morning Susannah found Laverne clarifying some wine they had bought from a local peasant who owned a little strip of land nearby. The peasant's vines only produced about six barrels, but the wine was of good quality and would have been better if the man had taken more care with it. So at Laverne's instigation, they bought it up whenever the man was inclined to sell and tried to improve it. This particular morning Laverne was fining it down and Susannah asked him about the process. They were watching the workmen in the outbuilding beyond the vatting room.

"Well, ma'am, if you leave wine cloudy there's a danger it will ferment again, and it tastes common. If it's been perfectly made and properly racked—that is, transferred to a fresh cask to get rid of the deposit or the lees as we call it—and if it's kept in the right place, you can simply leave it and it will become clear naturally. Otherwise you have to do what we're doing here."

"Yes, but what in fact are you doing?"

"Well, you might say we're throwing a very fine-spun filter over the wine. As this sinks from the top of the barrel to the bottom, it catches the impurities clouding the wine and carries them down with it. You leave it for two or three weeks, maybe a month, and as soon as you see the wine is perfectly clear, you draw it off."

She watched the workmen start on a new barrel. They took the bung out, drew about ten liters out with a siphon and poured some ready-prepared mixture into the barrel. Then one of them took a stick with one end split into four, like an egg whisk. He put it into the bunghole and violently whipped the wine and the mixture up together. Finally they poured the ten liters back into the barrel, topped the wine up, replaced the bung and moved on to the next. The finished barrels were immediately moved away to be stacked.

"What do you use for the filtering?" Susannah asked.

"Oh . . ." Laverne lifted one hand as much as to say there are all sorts of things. "Some people use thick gray paper, for instance, or fine sand."

"*Paper?*"

"Yes. It's something like blotting paper, acts as a filter. You take five or six sheets, tear them up and soak them in a couple of liters of wine. Then you mash them all up, pouring water on them as you go, until you get a sort of paste and you pour this into the barrel."

Susannah made a face.

"Then some people use ground-up oyster shells or powdered marble or chalk or alabaster or wood cinders, which are what you call alkaline clarifiers. You get a little spontaneous effervescence with them and they work like sand, carrying the impurities to the bottom. You use about a liter to a barrel, or about a third of that if you mix them with gelatin. Then some people swear by albumin clarifiers, like animal blood."

"What! You put animal blood in wine?"

"Plenty of people do, to clarify. It's used either fresh or dried. Ox blood, cow blood and sheep's blood leave a disagreeable taste. Pig's blood's the best."

"Oh, no!" Another grimace.

Laverne nodded. "Plenty of people do it. *I* think there's a disadvantage. The alcohol in the wine only partially coagulates pig's blood, and the rest, the watery part of the blood, remains in suspension; and it *can* give it a faint taste which only disappears after a while. In my opinion, you shouldn't use it on fine wines or wines of any age. But if you do use it, fresh blood's better than dried. You pour out a liter, mix it up well with a liter of wine and pour it in like the other stuff."

"Horrible!" Susannah said.

"Then there's whey, gum arabic, starch paste, butcher's morsels, gelatin, calves' feet, sheep's heads. Monsieur Marchet over at Lormont soaks some calves' feet or a couple of sheep's heads in water for twenty-four hours. This gives a jelly with a lot of gelatin in it, and he uses that. Then you can use fish glue."

"Fish glue? You're joking."

"No, ma'am." Laverne laughed pleasantly. "It's used above all for white wines. It's what you call isinglass in English, I believe. A lot of people use it to clarify their wine. It's really taken only from one fish, or should be, the sturgeon, from his air bladder, and it's got a lot of pure gelatin in it. You buy it in little sheets. You beat the sheets on a wooden platter, break them up as small as possible, put them in a jar with white wine and let it stand for a day or a night. When the glue is soaked, you squeeze it out with your fingers, beat it up in a small quantity of warm water until it's all dissolved, and then strain it. Finally you dilute it in half a bottle of white wine for each barrel and proceed as with the other things."

"Is that what they are using, fish glue?" Susannah indicated the workmen.

"No, ma'am. That's white of egg, that's what we use here. It's best because it's pure albumin, it doesn't leave any soluble residue, it doesn't leave any taste and it doesn't change any of the constituents of the wine. Mind you, fish glue, pure gelatin and the gelatin you get from calves' feet or butcher's morsels don't leave any soluble residue in the wine either, but they do precipitate the tannin and part of the color, so they're really best for white wines that are weak in alcohol. With eggs, you just beat up the whites of six to eight eggs with a quarter-bottle of the wine you are going to clarify and pour the mixture into the barrel like the other things. If the wine is new and difficult to clarify you can beat the eggs in a little salt water instead of wine."

On other days Susannah tackled the men working outside.

"What are you doing here now?" she asked a plowman one day.

The man grinned awkwardly and shuffled his feet. "This is the second plowing, ma'am."

"You plowed once already, a few weeks ago."

"Yes, ma'am. It was uncovering then."

"Why do you do that?"

"Ah . . ." He gaped at her, grinning. "It's what you have to do."

She was patient and gradually got the explanations. They did four plowings a year: one in February to uncover the foot of the vines and loosen the earth to promote germination, one again in April to cover them up again, two more in the same way in May. They needed two different plows for this, one turning the earth one way, one the other.

But the tilling itself had always amazed her. It took two oxen to drag the plow, oxen like elephants, so big they could not get between the rows of vines together. So one with the actual plow had to walk in one row, and the other in the next row, with harness and plow attachments dangling between them over the top of the vines. This was why they grew the vines so low in the Médoc, the stock or stem hardly more than six to eight inches above the ground, the branches making the whole about a foot tall. The harness wouldn't pass over them if they were taller.

At every tilling the women and children would follow the plow down the rows, either pulling the earth out from between the vines where the plow couldn't get or shielding the young shoots to prevent them from being covered up.

Pruning was the critical thing outdoors. The locals had a saying that the winegrower's fortune was in his pruning hook. This pruning hook was more like a medieval battle weapon, a bill hook, than a farm implement—a great slab of steel with a razor-sharp edge and a point sticking out on top and another at the back, a murderous-looking affair. It was the same tool they had used in the vineyards since the Middle Ages, and here in Médoc they would use no other.

But when Susannah asked Josserand anything he usually gave her sour answers. She caught him outside one evening and he began complaining about the ham he owed. This was a ham he had to supply to the house once a year under his contract. The peasants lived in wretched privation, and old Pierre Gautier, no more benevolent toward them than other owners, had decreed that it was better to encourage his workpeople to keep pigs than to pay them more money.

"I can't kill the pig now," Josserand said. "You can't have it; there's no help for it." He was unsteady with drink. "When do I get my plows repaired? How can I do the work?"

"The plows are being repaired, you say?"

"They'll be repaired when the blacksmith's paid, not before. He won't do a thing till then. Yokes and harness and hoes are waiting to be mended—how can I work in these conditions?"

"Tell him to send me the bill."

"That I won't. You'll see him yourself or the master will, for I'm sick of it." He thrust his neck out. "I've got a contract, ma'am, signed by the master."

"I know that." All the price makers worked by contract, which set out the various tasks they were to do, together with the prices for each task and whatever else they were entitled to.

"It says I'm to have two barrels of first-grade piquette and two of second, a hundred fagots of branches and fifty fagots of small wood. Aye, and a pound of soap, a hundred sardines at Lent and two pints of cooking oil. All I've got is three barrels of second piquette. Where's the rest of it? Oh, says the master, it's all the same."

Piquette was the drink made for the workmen from the skins and stalks of the grapes and it was made in two grades, the first slightly stronger than the second.

"The contract says I'm to get medicine when there's sickness," Josserand went on belligerently. "Here my wife's been in bed for a month come Saint Anselme's and never a call from a doctor. I'm supposed to have my house kept in repair—and the roof's all holes and there's not a window'll shut. You wouldn't keep a pig in the place."

Susannah said, "I'll see your wife has the doctor. As for the rest, I'll speak to my husband."

"Pah!" He made a dismissive gesture.

Susannah threw back her shoulders and said sharply, "You will keep a civil tongue in your head, Josserand!"

"Nay, ma'am. It's no good this way." He stood shifting from one leg to the other, eying her with his little eyes, then he waved his hand toward the vines. "Half the laths is rotten. We use eight hundred and fifty an acre and it's eighty centimes a bundle they cost. Work it out. You need new stakes all over, eighty-four hundred an acre, seven francs a thousand. Soon there'll be insects, and who's going to pay the women to pick them off? It's not my job, not in my price, so don't think it is. But it'll be Josserand's fault if it's not done. Well, you can get on with it!"

He stalked off and she watched him go, angry with herself for listening to him.

This conversation, however, set off others. Perhaps something Josserand had let fall encouraged the other workpeople to come to her. Next day it was Balavoine, the maître bouvier, who looked after the oxen. He had nearly as many complaints as Josserand, but he was a big genial slow-moving man, like one of his beasts, a nice fellow. He was always lacking fresh straw, he said, for his animals, his carts needed mending, the blacksmith was asking for fifty francs in advance to shoe a pair of oxen.

"I need two new beasts, ma'am. We can't carry on with the ones we've got. I'm using an old ox that's half blind and he breaks the new shoots sometimes. It's tricky working close to the vines."

"And how much is a new ox going to cost?" she said.

He bobbed his head about. "You have to reckon eight hundred francs."

"Good Lord!"

"We have to keep the beasts seven months in stable, ma'am, and they've been poorly fed."

"But Monsieur Josserand should have reported all this before."

He looked at her kindly. "You'll pardon me, ma'am, but it shouldn't be left to Josserand. There's a place for a master vigneron here, someone who's in charge, someone we can look to."

What was she to do? Francis must know all this.

"I don't mean it unkindly, Madame Gautier," Balavoine said.

She smiled and nodded. "I know. Thank you."

That afternoon she waited for Francis, but he was not back at dinnertime. It was a cool bright evening and she walked out past the garden into the vines. She could see faint whitish traces on the leaves. The vines at the ends of the rows looked well tended, but toward the middle of each row they were neglected, surely a sign of careless work. She wished she knew more about it . . . but she didn't trust Josserand. Josserand had plots of wheat and oats that, she suspected, encroached on the land where vines had been. His attitude was to put his own interest before the work. And she simply didn't believe his story of being kept short of piquette. If there was one thing all the workpeople were sharp about it was their piquette.

That night in bed she told Francis about Josserand's complaints, about the oxen and the repairs that needed to be done.

"I know, I know." He put his arm around her. "My dear Sue, what are you worrying about it for? There are always these things outstanding, you can't do them all at once. They've been trying to wheedle things out of you. They're all the same. I'll deal with them. Don't worry, leave them to me." And he kissed her.

She felt uncertain. Perhaps they *had* been trying to get

things out of her that they knew they couldn't get out of him; perhaps they had exaggerated.

"Darling, I'm sorry. I shouldn't have meddled," she said. They snuggled together in the bed.

A week went by, then another. She discovered almost by chance that the blacksmith had not been paid. She tried to tell herself it was simply forgetfulness but she knew in her heart it wasn't. Two weeks later nothing had changed. She saw now that things would drift on. It would be pointless to speak to Francis again. He would be sweet and smile and be reassuring. Everything would be all right. He wasn't willfully deceiving her. He believed it.

So her worry grew.

3

And then a great blow—the blight reappeared.

All through the winter, growers, price makers and laboring men had talked one another into half believing it had run its course or persuaded themselves it had been a passing malady, some seasonal weakness that had spent itself within the year, since the vine stocks were healthy. A few scientifically minded growers and estate managers had disagreed, but the others weren't listening. For how could the disease survive the winter? If it was an insect the eggs wouldn't outlive the cold, and if it was vegetable in origin the first frosts would kill it off.

And then to see the greasy gray powder on all the vines again—a fearful shock!

By early May it was everywhere. Vineyards that had partly escaped the year before were covered with it; a few cranky owners who had painstakingly plastered their vines or burned smoky fires all through the winter to make sure the disease was killed off found their vines as bad as the rest. *How* could it have come through the winter? It was baffling; there was something malevolent about it. And here and there the older people talked of witches and of seeing evil phosphorescent lights playing low about the vineyards, and heads were nodded.

Susannah watched Francis going around with Josserand trying one new remedy after another; she saw that his impatience communicated itself to the other man and that, as soon as his back was turned, the work slacked off. Francis wasn't actively impatient. He didn't get angry, he merely turned passive and dull and uninterested, as if things didn't matter. And he went to Bordeaux more often than before, either saying he had business or had to find out what other people were doing against the disease. Now and then he was in a moody silence after one of these trips, which she knew meant he was shutting himself off from some unpleasant fact, but when she tried to find out, he evaded her.

Sometimes she took the opportunity and went along with him so that she could see young Jacob Sabra, who had been moved to Dr. Arnoud's clinic in Bordeaux at the doctor's insistence. The clinic, where Arnoud treated about thirty poor children and where some of them lived, was a raw, uncomfortable place; but everybody was cheerful and positive and Jacob was well cared for. He was now blind and Arnoud was teaching him to read and count by his own method of embossed letters, based on Captain Charles Barbier's well-known system. Susannah was fascinated to sit with the boy as he touched the little raised shapes and said the letters; it was slow, patient work, but he was a sensitive child and Susannah loved him. She used to bake him cakes and cookies and take them to him, and they were close friends.

That spring the first of her irises bloomed—a great sweep of them, blues and yellows, maroon and violet. The blues were so pale, so delicate with their yellow-dipped tongues. At the front of the house she had pink saxifrage and pansies, lupins and larkspur, the orange trees in their tubs and an unexpected newcomer which she had thought wouldn't bloom—a beautiful camellia. And in the forest she picked the thornless broom and brought great armfuls in and put it in vases in the house.

One morning Susannah rode up to the Marquis de Talabu's house and he came out and greeted her smilingly. "You are neglecting your old friend. It's weeks since you have come to see me."

"Yes, I'm sorry. How are you? I hope you are well."

"Oh, yes. I have been hoping to see you. Have you a little time to spare this morning? I would like to show you something."

"Yes."

"Then please come in."

She tethered the horse and followed him inside, full of curiosity. They went through the small cluttered room where they had sat talking and drinking tea on her earlier visits and out into a dilapidated hall. Nimbly he led her through the ruin of the old house, through sagging doorways, along galleries awash with broken floor tiles. He kept turning around and saying, "This way, follow me. It's all right. It's quite safe. Just put your foot there, that's right."

The place was a madhouse of plants. Festoons of creeper hung everywhere and elephant leaves quivered in their path. Thickets of plant life swooped on them from pots and jars and tubs. They brushed past swordlike spikes. Fungus sprouted on the rotten woodwork. Now and then the little old Marquis would pause for an instant, twitch a leaf, glance at a bulbous growth and pass on. Once he picked up a can and watered a thing with pendulous evil-looking mauve blooms.

At last at the back of the house they came to a long narrow room, part conservatory, part laboratory. A long tiled workbench with a stone sink in it faced the door. It was littered with bottles of chemicals, jars of cultures, tray after tray of strange blue and white moldy growths, a pair of brass microscopes, slides and notebooks. The rest of the place was a proliferation of tortured greenery, tanks of water plants, monstrous toadstools and furry things, a tank of green water full of frogs. Books of pressed plants lay open beside piles of magazines, *La Revue Horticole, The Gardener's Journal, The Gardener's Chronicle.*

"This is my plant laboratory," the Marquis said with the funny little dip of his head.

Outside she could see the two greenhouses she had glimpsed before. "You're a naturalist?"

"A botanist and a cryptogamist chiefly," he said. "Now come over here, my dear. I want to show you something very interesting."

He pulled a stool up to the workbench for her, bent for a moment over one of the microscopes, adjusting a slide in it, then placed the instrument for her. "Can you use a microscope? Well . . . here, you adjust by this screw to focus, and this one here when you want to move over the surface of the slide. Now look and see what you can see. . . . That's right. Have you got it?"

263

She peered into the eyepiece, worked the focusing screw. It remained a blur; he showed her again and after a while a clear image came. She saw a thing like a vein running across the bottom of the slide and, rising out of it, several strange wormy tubes, each rounded at the tip like a finger. Some were long, some short. The longer ones were divided into four or five compartments, like long four-jointed or five-jointed fingers. Inside the two top joints of the fingerlike tubes she could see several light spots that seemed to be cavities. The rest of the fingers and the vein at the bottom were filled with tiny granulations. Also, on the underside of the vein was a little protuberance like a wart. She took her eye away and looked at the Marquis beside her.

"Do you know what that is?" he said.

"No."

"That is the oïdium."

"The oïdium?" She looked again. The top joints of the longest fingerlike tubes seemed almost ready to fall off. She looked back at the Marquis. "You mean this is the disease?"

"There is no disease, young lady."

"How do you mean, no disease? Everybody's seen it. The vines were all sickly, the leaves fell off, the grapes split open."

"You must be careful not to confuse things. There is no disease. It is this little vegetable, a sort of mushroom, what we call a fungus, that causes all the trouble. That is all there is. It is a new fungus we haven't seen before, one of the genus *Botrytis*. This is the *Oïdium tuckeri* that forms the grayish-white powder on the vines and makes the leaves and grapes drop off."

She frowned, puzzled. "But, Monsieur de Talabu, how can that be? The white powder only comes afterward. It comes *because* the vine is already diseased."

"No, young lady, that is the mistake people are making. This tiny vegetable organism, this little parasite, is what causes everything. There is nothing else. Let me show you how it lives and spreads. Have you got time?"

"Oh, yes, please. Yes." She was all eagerness.

He reached out for a large sketchbook and turned the pages. It was full of drawings of monstrous tentacled creatures, things like nightmarish insects with multiple legs and feelers.

"Heavens. What are those things?" she asked.

"They are Cryptogamia—different kinds of fungi. Aren't they beautiful?"

"*Beautiful?* Well . . ."

"Here is ours, *Oïdium tuckeri.* I have made some drawings of it in various stages. And let me hasten to say that of course I am not the discoverer. That honor belongs to Mr. Tucker of Margate, after whom it is named. The Reverend Mr. Berkeley of Northamptonshire in England has done very distinguished work on it, and so has my friend Dr. Montagne of Paris, who discovered the potato murrain, the potato blight. Dr. Montagne and I have worked closely together for many years and correspond regularly with each other and with Mr. Berkeley and other gentlemen. Now here, you see . . ."

The drawing showed a tangled nest of filaments crawling in all directions over a leaf, and rising vertically from the filaments were dozens of the little fingerlike tubes she had seen under the microscope.

"This system of filaments is what we call the mycelium. It's the body of the fungus, if you will. The filaments crawl all over the surface of the leaves, the vine shoots, the grapes, over all the *green* parts of the vine, and branch out and ramify and crisscross in all directions." He pointed to the little wartlike protuberances on the underside that Susannah had noticed under the microscope. "These little things are the suckers with which the mycelium feeds itself, sucking up nourishment from the leaves and the other green parts."

"I see."

"Very well. So first you have this network of little filaments, the mycelium, crawling over the vines in the springtime. Then, out of the filaments grow these little oval-tipped shoots. They are tiny tubes, the same as you saw there under the microscope."

"Rather like fingers?"

"That's right, minute fingers. They grow out of the mycelium in thousands. And as they grow, little partitions form inside them, dividing them up into sections, usually three or four sections but sometimes as many as six. Gradually, as you see here, the top section matures. First a number of tiny cavities, like little white spots, form inside it. Then it gradually takes on an oval shape, the cavities join together into two or three big cavities, and then the whole oval section—the tip of the finger, as it were—falls off. Then it is the turn of the next section, which has now become the fingertip. It too matures, becomes oval and falls off. Sometimes you see several sections almost ready to sep-. arate, and they look like little oval glass beads strung together.

"Now these little oval sections are seed spores, what we call conidia. When a spore falls on a leaf or a green part of the vine, it germinates, as you see here. It sends out a tiny thread-like filament, which in its turn starts ramifying and branching out in all directions. In other words it soon becomes a new my-celium, which begins sending up its fingerlike shoots, each with more spores. And so the process goes on and the oïdium spreads. The spores are so light that the lightest spring breeze sends countless millions of them flying about the vineyard, each one able to generate millions and millions more. You see? It is beautiful, is it not?"

He gazed at her, then turned aside and fitted another slide into the microscope. "Look, here are four spores just germi-nating on a morsel of leaf."

She peered down and saw four oval spores, rather like tad-poles with long, long tails. The cavities looked for all the world like big round eyes. "Those tails they have, they are the new filaments?"

"That's right—the beginning of new mycelia."

Susannah studied them a moment longer, then leaned back thoughtfully. It all seemed very strange to her, hardly credible. "You mean this tiny mold is the cause of it?"

"Yes." He nodded, obviously delighted.

"But how can it be?" *Was* he a little odd, after all? A crank? He spoke so beautifully and clearly, and yet the notion seemed so outlandish. "How can it?"

"By its external action on the plant—destroying the leaves, killing the shoots, splitting the grapes and exhausting the plant," he said.

"But do you really *know* it's the cause, Monsieur de Ta-labu? I mean, I've heard them talking about the disease so often and everybody says the mold appears *because* the vines are sick. They say the mildew or the mold or whatever you want to call it is a manifestation of the sickness, like boils or smallpox pus-tules or feverish sweating. But it isn't the *disease*. How can you be sure?"

He smiled, lifting his eyebrows. "Well, we can't prove it yet, but that will come."

Oh, she thought, *that* was an admission, wasn't it? A distinct retreat. "So it's really only a guess, a theory?"

He didn't seem a bit put out and nodded, still smiling. "Until we can prove it scientifically, it is only a hypothesis, a conjecture put forward to account for the facts. It's what has been called the fungal hypothesis."

She considered, then looked at him again. "But things that are decaying and decomposing often get moldy, don't they? Isn't it part of the decaying process?"

"You are forgetting the little suckers, madame. If the mold were just a part of the decaying process or decomposition, it wouldn't be feeding itself on the sap in this way."

"Oh, wouldn't it? . . . I don't know." Susannah looked doubtful. "It might only live on dead or decaying matter, mightn't it? I mean the suckers might not be strong enough to penetrate a living plant."

Talabu laughed delightedly. "You would make an excellent botanist, madame. As you say, the suckers do not *prove* the oïdium is a parasite on a living plant but their existence is very significant. They tend to show it is one."

"But you don't know which comes first, the decay or the mold."

"We can't yet prove scientifically which comes first, but I am sure of it in my own mind. After all, every sickly vine has got the oïdium mold on it, every one. And if the mold doesn't cause the sickliness, where does the mold come from? Even a tiny plant like the fungus doesn't just spring spontaneously to life from nothing. However decaying the leaf tissue may be, it can't produce life, even so rudimentary a form of life as a mold. Not so far as we know, at least."

"Well, then, where *does* the mold come from?"

His eyebrows went right up and he made a little grimace. "That we don't know. We think it must have been imported."

"Yes." Susannah was impressed. "You say the mold is a tiny plant, but a plant has roots and flowers and fruit. Doesn't this have any?"

"We don't know yet. There are all sorts of things we don't understand—how it survives the winter, how it is fertilized, where it has come from."

"But how are we to cure it? That's the most important of all."

"You are quite right, madame. But alas we don't know that either yet. From my own observations I am inclined to think Mr. Berkeley is making a mistake when he says that the fungus penetrates the leaves and lives partly inside them. I believe the mycelium, the whole fungus, remains on the surface. This may help us to find a way to kill it off, but for the moment we don't know."

Was he a crank? Was it just a crazy theory? Somehow she did not think either of these things. Riding home, she felt a curious sort of elation. It was just as if she had participated in a discovery. Something about the world had changed for her. She looked around her with new eyes. And think of it, all those myriads of tiny threads creeping everywhere. It was amazing . . . terrifying.

She was strangely excited. She didn't think the Marquis de Talabu was mad at all. He was a great scientific spirit, perhaps one of the great discoverers of the age. She couldn't get over it. She saw the images in the microscope again, the weird and frightening creatures in the Marquis's sketchbook. She couldn't get over the feeling that there was something amazing and revolutionary somewhere in all this, all mixed up with what people called disease, the idea of parasites causing sickness.

And they were helpless, they could do nothing.

4

Yet Susannah's life refused to flow back in the old even way. In spite of her new strength, her self-reliance, her secret vows to herself, the deep, sweet assuring flow of the early days was gone. Gone for good, she knew it.

She had days when she was fretful, in a state of nerves, ill at ease with her body. Behind her vitality was longing now. She reached out with longing. And then she would force herself out of it, become exasperated with herself, force herself to practical things, the realities of the house and the vineyard and her marriage. But she longed to see John Blood.

Several times since that morning in the fog they had met on the path by the river. And once, madly, in the blue winter dusk in Bordeaux, they had wandered across the empty, silent snowbound Place des Quinconces and he had declared his love for her again. Sheer madness, sheer insanity. The snow-laden evening was so fleeting yet so time-laden, so marvelous to her. The corner of the great silent Place where they had stood for a moment was remote from everything in the silence, the ramparts of snow everywhere, the dim yellow lights, the feathery trees, the smoky slate-blue void of the river beyond and their breath on the air and his cloak around her and *him*, his arms holding her.

Absolute madness. Yet how could it be otherwise with him? Caution seemed so old to her, so crabbed. Carefulness would destroy something in the essence of their love. Somehow it must be headlong or not exist, like his mad galloping horse, like him. And at these moments when she was swept up she felt that she would be betraying the truth of herself if she didn't respond to him in this headlong way—a wildness meeting a wildness. That was how they loved each other. That was the essence of them.

Ah, but there were other moments too. Life couldn't be all one mad impulse, she knew. But knowing it didn't make it any easier to accept. That was the trouble. It didn't stop her being swept up with John Blood and carried beyond herself. She couldn't sit herself down stolidly, dully on earth because life wasn't all mad impulse. You must live on the assumption that it could be. You must live as if it often were. You must. Or life wasn't anything. If you couldn't be mad you were dead. Yes, really, she felt that.

She knew he was an adventurer. It hadn't all been simply patriotic gallantry in Ireland, but she didn't love him any the less for that. Sometimes, in the other moments at La Guiche, when she wandered about the house trying to keep him out of her mind, trying to smother her longing to see him, she told herself she was developing a taste for doubtful men. She even told herself it was atavism, since wasn't she, after all, the niece of Aunt Maxine and Aunt Ady. When he wanted to make love to her, it was terribly difficult to say no; and she wanted to give. Life was giving.

Yet the blind force of convention still checked her, held her back in spite of herself. She struggled against it, clinging to her love for John Blood yet unwilling to sacrifice Francis. She did love Francis, deeply and sincerely, as she loved his trust and faith in her. It was just that her love for John Blood was different, another thing. It involved another self in her. And so she was torn and tormented.

Blood had told her in a fragmentary, disjointed way about his doings in Ireland, and beyond a few general questions she hadn't pressed him. And then they had met one March morning on the horses and he had told her he was leaving for Paris next day. The unexpectedness, the haste, his sardonic lack of explanation, gave her the impression that it was something risky. It was surely something to do with Ireland. Perhaps some emissary had arrived, or the English government was taking some new step for his extradition?

When he had gone she turned to the vineyard, the work in the cellars, learning all she could. She was busy, engrossed. But after a month, oh, she missed him. Not a word came, nothing. She didn't even know where he was. And instead of forgetting him, she thought of him with more love than ever.

And now, with the spring and the fine weather, she roamed about longing to see him. A girl in love, she drifted out to the garden plots or walked out among the vines in the fine spring rain thinking of him. She sat up late by the lamp sewing, then staring out of the dark pane wanting him back. Once when she went into Bordeaux with Francis she had contrived to drive past his house in a cab simply to gaze at it.

She was sweet and loving to Francis. And sometimes at dusk or in the night the old Methodist guilt crept upon her, tormented her soul even more, made her kneel by the bed and pray. And in those moments of prayer she was different from the woman who stood out against convention, who was going to be free in her life. She wept and was a young innocent girl again. She loved two men, yet she did not feel impure in heart. Her love was large enough for them both.

Then Regis and Abel-Cherubin came out to La Guiche one day in mid-May, and in the course of the evening Regis mentioned having seen John Blood at a private house. So he was back! Susannah waited a week without a word. He did not appear on the riverside path. Gradually she became more fretful.

She had promised to see Jacob Sabra at the clinic the following week, and when Francis announced that he was going to Bordeaux on the Saturday, she said she would go with him. Perhaps there was some half-formed intention in her mind to go to the house.

It was a clear sunny day, the first Saturday of June, and they started out early. Francis talked away happily about a ship one of his friends was interested in, about ships' engines, the new steamers coming into Bordeaux. And he absolutely must take Susannah out to the bathing beach one of these fine days. They could go by the little railway to La Teste, it would make a fine excursion. Ridiculous they had not been before. He was cheerful and talkative.

Susannah listened absently. She sat back in the seat looking out at the vineyards going by where men were at work dusting the vines against the oïdium, spraying them or smoking them. Francis had received her account of the visit to the Marquis de Talabu and the oïdium theory with amused indulgence. He thought the explanation that it was simply a mold was entertaining. Still, old Talabu was harmless. And he wasn't worried about the blight. They had seen the worst of it. When they got into full summer it would go, especially with a spell of dry weather. She would see. And for once his confidence irritated her. She sat silent, then caught herself guiltily and took his hand. He was a sweet man.

They rattled over the cobbles into Bordeaux. Susannah had some shopping to do after seeing the boy, so they arranged that Francis would take the carriage on and either meet her with it at three o'clock in the Cathedral Square or send Joseph with it to say if she should go on home alone, for sometimes now he stayed the night in Bordeaux on business.

"What shall you do for lunch?" he said.

"Oh, I'll go to Louise's."

"Yes, all right."

Dr. Arnoud's clinic was in a quiet back street, an old stone house, bare and uncomfortable inside, but it had a good area of walled garden. All the staff knew Susannah now. And today she found the boy surrounded by his family, old Jacob and half a dozen cousins whom she didn't know. Madame Sabra introduced her. The boy was better, quite talkative and showed how quickly he could now read with his fingers. He laughingly pushed about a couple of other boy patients who came charging up among his visitors wanting attention. They all moved about with surprising assurance.

Old Jacob was sweet and said Dr. Arnoud was hoping to train the boy as a shoemaker. Susannah stayed talking with one and the other of them; but she knew the old man couldn't come often and she didn't want to spoil the family's visit, so after half an hour she said she had to go. She put down the things she had brought, said goodbye to the boy, promising to come again soon, and left them.

Outside in the corridor someone came hurrying after her. It was one of the nurses. "If you please, ma'am."

Susannah halted and the girl came up. "I was asked to give this to you."

Susannah stared down at the envelope. "For me?"

"Yes, ma'am." The girl's blue eyes were on her and she was smiling gently and kindly.

"Oh, thank you." Susannah felt herself blushing. She took the blank envelope and stuffed it hastily into her pocket. She smiled back at the girl and turned away down the corridor. Her heart was beating madly. She knew it was from him. She turned into the dim little vestibule leading to the entrance hall, glanced quickly around—nobody coming—tore the note open and read it.

I must see you, only for a moment. My life stops without you. If you receive this on Saturday come at eleven o'clock to the market in the Place des Grands Hommes. J.

In a flash she had read it, folded it, put it away. She was like a girl breathless with her first love note, and she stood there looking down, pretending to rearrange a fold of her dress, unable to think of anything. Then she managed to compose herself, lifted her head and walked on out. A group of large bearded men were talking quietly in the entrance. The little hunchbacked porter bowed, and she caught herself in time to give him a smile in return. Outside, she realized she didn't know what time it was and had to go back.

"Five minutes past eleven, madame," the porter said.

"Thank you." She couldn't miss him now! Nothing in sight at the end of the street. She hurried along, then saw a cab putting down his fare. After it she flew and caught it just as it was moving off.

The streets were crowded. She sat on the edge of the seat mentally urging the horse on as it crawled. The big general market in the Place des Grands Hommes near the Cours de l'Intendance would be bustling at this hour on a Saturday morning. It would look natural for her to walk around studying the stalls; and he, of course, had arranged it so. She drew him to herself in her thoughts.

At last they got there. The big circular Place with the high canvas canopy in the middle was a confusion of stalls, barrows, piles of food, straw, crates, carts and horses and crowds of people. She paid off the cab, stood looking around, then pressed in

273

among the crowd. The vendors shouted their wares; the cheese smells and fish smells and dung smells drifted over her. She squeezed between backs and shoulders, craning for a glimpse of him. She couldn't see him anywhere.

The market overflowed into one or two side streets. She scanned these, then went back into the main crowd. She stood on tiptoe to see over intervening heads. Then her heart gave a plunge. He was a little ways away, passing slowly among the stalls, glancing here and there. She started quickly toward him, then caught herself and half-turned aside, trying to look casual, but watching him and moving toward him.

He didn't see her for a moment, then looked over in her direction. Their eyes met, and she saw him become still with the shock of love. Their eyes lingered, then without another sign he turned away.

She pressed toward him. He moved away through the crowd, past the market women, the red-faced vendors, and Susannah followed. She supposed he was leading her somewhere. He went on at random, as if he were simply looking at the market, not glancing at her. But people got in her way, pushed her. She began to lose distance. She was going to lose him.

She pressed on. The distance widened and he didn't wait. She could still see him in the thick of the crowd, going on as if unaware of her. She didn't understand and forced her way through the people, trying to keep up with him. One or two stared around at her. And then he turned and looked straight at her and gave a quick shake of his head. The next instant he had turned his back and was moving away again.

She pulled up, jolted, perplexed. Why? It had been an unmistakable sign. Don't follow. Why? She stared down unseeing at the mound of poultry on the stall in front of her, lifted a strand of hair away from her face. What did it mean? Was he being observed? Was *she* being followed? Had he seen somebody behind her and meant to warn her not to come to him?

Her heart began to hammer. Not one of the family? She tried to seem natural as she looked around. She couldn't see anybody she knew among the nearer faces. But it would be easy to hide here, and perhaps they were somewhere behind? There must be somebody. And now she had lost sight of him. He had gone.

Vaguely she was aware of the market woman speaking to her, holding up a fowl. She shook her head, turned away, caught up her skirt and pushed her way out.

She felt wretched, guilty and hot as she reached the edge of the crowd and walked down a quiet street, her thoughts in confusion. Her spirit drooped. The relatively empty street seemed to expose her, and she wanted to hasten away. Who could it have been? What did it mean? She kept asking herself over and over. She walked on in the dazzling sunlight, not seeing where she was going, then all at once the crashing of drays pulled her up.

Heavens, she was hot! She lifted the loose strand of hair from her face, eased the neck of her dress with her forefinger. The light was dazzling; her dress was too heavy. There was dust and grit everywhere and she had brought no sunshade. She was on the quayside, going toward the Quai des Chartrons, completely out of her way. And it must be nearly noon.

Not knowing what was behind it—*that* was what was unsettling. Yet she reasoned with herself. After all, they had not even spoken to each other and it *could* have seemed chance to anyone looking on that they should be there in the square together.

In the meantime she was so hot! She didn't want to go to Louise's. She was feeling lost and forlorn, feeling abandoned. The quayside stretched before her, full of noise and bustle. Not a cab in sight. Oh, Lord, what to do? She thought there must be a rank farther along and the only thing was to go on.

The sun came down, the streams of vehicles rolled noisily by in both directions. She walked on down the endless quay. Gradually, the uneasiness began to subside in her. After all, they had avoided each other, hardly looked at each other. She longed to see him. And now she realized that for all his apparent casualness, he had struck her as unusually watchful. Yes, watchful, the impression came back to her now.

On she walked. So hot it was, and shadeless. Oh, for a little cool shade. Never a cab came by. She could see the immense quay curving away in the distance ahead. She walked on. Once she stopped in a doorway and stood fanning herself, then out into the glare she went again.

Presently, in her half-abstraction, she noticed that a smart gray landau which had just passed her had slowed down a few paces ahead, and she was vaguely aware of the passenger turning around. Still preoccupied, she paid no particular attention, then she saw it was John Lovell. The carriage pulled to the curb, he got out, lifted his hat as she came up.

"Good morning." She smiled, so glad to see him but thinking she must look a sight in this heat.

"This is a hot morning to be walking, madame. May I offer you a lift?"

She was delighted to see him. "I was only going as far as the cab rank."

"Cab rank? There's not one for half a mile yet. Pray allow me."

"You're very kind, Mr. Lovell." She climbed in and sank thankfully down onto the seat with a little "Oh!" He sat beside her and the driver whipped up. Lovely, the breeze. She sat back, lifting her face to it, feeling better already.

"I hoped you were coming to look at my cellars," he said with a smile.

"Oh, of course, you're just along here, aren't you? How is Collard and Sons?"

"Doing very well. You promised to come and see."

She smiled back at him, aware of the admiration in his eyes. "I really will. I'd love to see the house."

"Then come now."

She looked at him, a little unprepared for that and taken aback.

"Let me persuade you on the spot, since we're so close."

"Now?"

"Won't you?"

Decidedly today was full of surprises. But she was glad of the encounter. It helped her; she clung to it, to his quiet ease and assurance.

"You haven't got an appointment, have you?" he asked.

"Not really. But, well, I was on my way to my sister-in-law's."

"Then change your mind. I'll confess that, apart from the pleasure, I have another reason. You would be doing a poor bachelor a service. One of my good clients is here, an American gentleman by the name of Stockton. He never travels on business without his sister, but today he is busy elsewhere and I am engaged to give Miss Stockton luncheon. She is a most estimable lady but a little . . . a little formidable alone. You would help me over the occasion. I promise it won't be unduly prolonged. She is very businesslike."

Susannah looked at him. It was as if he knew. And she thought he could probably see it in her face, and this made her suddenly color. She was going to tell him she couldn't accept his invitation, then abruptly she changed her mind and said, "Yes, I should love to."

"Good." He nodded. The carriage was slowing down to turn under a porte-cochère. "And here we are."

5

In the months since he had taken over Collard and Sons, John Lovell had been working eighteen hours a day. First he had exerted his organizing talent to revive the famous old firm—hiring new staff, seeing the brokers and buying fresh stock, sending out agents and generally getting the business on its feet again. Then he had applied himself to learning the business of wine-making, the complexities of the trade, the tricks of his fellow merchants, the foibles of customers, and he had begun to train his palate to the subtleties of the various vintages. He knew it would take him years to acquire a sound knowledge of all this, but he went at it with energy, method and a level-headed application. Outside of mealtimes he spent every spare hour of the day and half his nights teaching himself or getting Thornton, his cellar master, to show him how things were done. He was good at getting the men to explain their craft, and they liked him because he willingly rolled up his sleeves and worked with them. He had a gift for handling his staff and saw that the older hands received respect from the younger.

One of the first things he learned was that claret, as Bordeaux wine was called in England, was largely a manufactured product like most of the wines shipped under high-sounding names as Château This or Château That or "Médoc" or "Fine Old Bordeaux" to the United States. It amazed him at first to find the merchants pouring spirits of wine or raw brandy into a vat of fine Médoc, mixing it with Hermitage wine from the

Rhone, strong black Cahors, Beni Carlos from Spain, cheap wine from the Roussillon.

"Why? To make it more powerful, sir," Thornton explained. "The English and the Americans have been taught to judge wine by its potency—how quick it gets them drunk."

The Hermitage destroyed the flavor, the Beni Carlos destroyed the bouquet, so the merchants added orris root, dashed in a little raspberry brandy and coolly shipped the result as Château Latour.

"Make them sick, sir?" Thornton said to his question. "They lap it up! If anything, they complain it's 'too light.' Why, Lord bless you, sir, you should see some of the good old blackstrap port that goes to America and England—*and* is drunk. I've seen a cask of port made out of forty-five gallons of cider, six gallons of raw brandy, eight gallons of port wine, two gallons of sloes stewed in two of water, tincture of red sanders to give it color and catechu powder to crust the bottle. And I've seen worse port made with oak bark, cider, Brazil wood, privet, beet and turnip—and they lapped *that* up!"

Lovell laughed. Thornton was always cheerful, a wonderful help to him.

"When you've been in the trade a bit, sir, you'll wonder why they need wine at all. If you mixed up some rough brandy with sugar and tartaric acid and put some logwood and alum and elderberries in, why you wouldn't be able to tell it from a vast deal of what's drunk for wine in America and England."

"God help us."

"I've mentioned port and you might think I'm a bit off the track, but you see, sir, that's where the idea comes from. They've got so used to their port, which is anything *but* pure wine, that they think they ought to have their Bordeaux just like it. Their taste's been spoiled. The merchants believe they have to compete with the Portuguese and there's only one way to do that—make their wine stronger."

"You mean American taste has been spoiled too?"

"It's going the English way, I fear, sir. Going the English way—unless it's stopped. The cheapest, rottenest Bordeaux gets passed off in America as fine claret. Only common stuff, most of it. Why, sir, French Bordeaux and the Bordeaux that's shipped over to the United States wouldn't scarce recognize each other.

When some of these merchants here get an order from a Boston customer for say, Château Lafite or Beychevelle, well, sir, there aren't many who'll say they are out of stock. Some will but most won't. They'll send what they've got and they'll put it down as Château Lafite or the vintage ordered—*and* charge according."

"Don't the Lafite people complain?"

"How can they, sir? Their harvest has probably been bought up for years ahead by the merchants. Why, Château Margaux produces four hundred casks a year. A few years ago, a poor year, the merchants sold easily four thousand casks."

"Yes?"

"And never fear, sir, the London and New York merchants are worse. They'll ship in casks of cheap Queyries or Palus— Palus, that's the wine from close by the river here—they'll dose it with rough cider, color it up with turnsole and sell it as fine-quality Médoc. In England they make champagne out of raw sugar, tartaric acid, water, homemade grape wine and French brandy. And if you want it pink, they'll color it with strawberries for you in a trice."

Lovell laughed again.

"If you're thinking of supplying the Americans or the English, sir, what they want is something rough and strong, something to catch the throat and make them gasp. They don't want to hear about flavor or softness. For them, the stronger the better. And the merchants here will tell you an intelligent man studies the taste of his customers, however strange it may be."

"Well, that's where we won't be following suit," Lovell said.

Thornton looked at him and a grin came slowly and broadly onto his face. "Good, sir. I'm glad of that. I'm with you there."

Other things Lovell learned. He learned that wine needed constant attention, that if their vigilance lapsed for only a brief interval he would be the owner of a fine stock of vinegar.

Casks of new wine had to be topped up to the bung every two or three days or the level would fall, and if it did they would get the "flower," a white mold on the surface of the wine which soon made it undrinkable. Sometimes in the early days he would look around the cellars at those hundreds of casks of wine just waiting to go sour if he turned his back too long. After a while the topping up could be spaced out to once a week, then once a fortnight and finally once a month. A simple task, yet it had to be supervised because it was essential to top up a cask with the same wine, never a different one, and the organization of half-casks and quarters for the wine left over needed an eagle eye or there would be losses. Casks being topped up at short intervals were always placed bunghole up, with a glass bung in them; older wines were bunged normally and turned on their side.

The wine had to be treated with the delicacy of a young girl.

He learned that it had to be regularly racked off the lees, an operation which meant transferring it gently from one cask to another, leaving behind its deposit. If this wasn't done the lees would turn it acid or ferment it. Ruin again! The racking had to be done three or four times the first year and once at the spring and autumn equinoxes for the older wines.

"Never do it in hot or stormy weather," Thornton said. "You always try to rack in dry clear weather with a north wind and a waning moon."

Lovell looked skeptical.

"You may smile, sir, but you'll find it's good sense. I don't rightly know how to explain it, but a south wind means it's warm and that seems to make liquids dilate and the lees rise easier. When the wind's dry and cold, it has a contracting effect. You've only got to look at those little streams with lime in them next time you're up in the Dordogne. When the wind's in the south you can't see the bottom, and when there's a north wind you can spot a collar stud in ten feet of water."

Blending, however, was something quite different from adulterating wine. One of the first things he had seen in Collard's were the great blending vats at the entrance to the cellars. No crime to blend a wine weak in alcohol with a stronger one, provided the two were of the same nature, carefully selected and preferably from the same vineyard or close by. You blended a wine lacking in one quality with one possessing it to excess. A fine vintage was unique and would not bear any mixing. But ordinary wine of a bad year might be blended to advantage with a more generous growth—not to cheat the customer but to improve a wine that would otherwise be dull or too sharp for the palate. New wine with a high color might have an earthy taint, but blend it with an old wine, let it mellow, and it was excellent. You could lighten a white wine which had turned yellow by pouring it over the lees of a red, but you would have to wait to bottle it. Sometimes an old wine of good quality that was getting a bit tired could be blended with a younger one, provided the wines had a natural affinity and the operation was done with care.

"Some of the firms here blend their finer wines with lesser growths to cut down the price," Thornton said.

"Do they? Well, that's another thing we shan't be following," Lovell said. "How about sugaring?"

"Oh, common enough, sir. Maybe I'm prejudiced, but it's not to my fancy. People here, when they get a common wine with no aroma, very poor color, only seven or eight per cent alcohol and a bit acid, the sort of wine that's very difficult to keep, why, they just go ahead and sugar it. Sugar will certainly bring up your alcohol content; but it won't make a thin wine more robust, it won't destroy acidity, it won't give you aroma—and it'll push up the cost. So where's the sense?"

"How *do* you get rid of acid?"

"All wines have acid, sir. It's essential to them. The thing is to have just the right amount."

He learned that at any given time he would have his capital heavily locked up in Collard's, for he had to keep good Bordeaux wines two full years in the cask and the Médocs and finer wines three or four years before bottling them. And then they wouldn't be fit to drink for another two years at the earliest.

The firm's bottling expert was Elie Mathurin, Thornton's chief assistant, a quick half-English albino of thirty-two with a huge pair of shoulders and dangling arms who could move a cask of wine like a toy.

"I thought you could keep a good wine in the wood for donkey's years," Lovell said to him.

"Ah, no, sir. Some of them very full-bodied ones you can leave for five, and I've seen some Queyries in the cask for six, but they're exceptional. If you leave it too long in the wood, y'see, a wine goes into a decline. It loses its velvet and fruitiness. Goes dry. If you try to mature it in the wood, you'll find it won't last as long as wine that's matured in the bottle. Of course, the bottle don't give a wine qualities it ain't got, but it keeps better in bottle than in barrel. And you've got to leave a good wine in bottle for at least two years and a fine wine five or more."

"And you're going to tell me you only bottle when there's a cold north wind blowing," Lovell said with a grin.

"Yes, sir, that's right. About September if you can or October."

"With the moon on the wane?"

"Why, yes, sir." Mathurin blinked his sandy-lashed albino eyes. "How did you guess that?"

"Oh, I had a feeling." Lovell felt he was learning!

He watched Thornton and the men operating and learned about the mysteries of wines that were earthy, flinty, green, greasy, harsh, woody or lacked color. He learned to find his way in the master cellar book where the number of each lot and each cask and its place in the cellar was inscribed. He acquired a constant "feel" for the temperature as he went about the cellars. He learned never to rack a fine wine into a cask that had contained a common wine, or it would be spoiled. And he quickly saw that, with all this, a good deal of ordinary foresight was essential to the business. Collard's would be sending out orders at all times of the year—they could hardly wait till the moon waned—so they must plan to rack, fine and bottle enough wine in advance.

He learned the great years for Bordeaux: 1798, 1811, 1815, 1847 and 1848; the good years: 1819, 1825, 1831, 1834, 1844 and 1846; and the bad years: 1813, 1816, 1817, 1820, 1821, 1824 (the worst ever), 1826, 1830, 1836, 1843 and 1845.

But it seemed it took a longish time before you could make a sound judgment about a vintage, sometimes four or five years; and it happened often enough that a vintage was only appreciated when it had begun to run out.

"Now you take the 1841 and the 1842, sir," Thornton said. "They're a good illustration of an important point. The whole summer of 1841 was damp, rainy and cold. Then at the beginning of September it turned dry and very warm, with a southerly wind. The harvest was about the twentieth of September. Result? A good wine—fine color, robust and velvety. The next year, 1842, we had the whole summer dry and warm. Looked ideal. On the fourth of September it started to rain and it came down cats and dogs all through the harvest on the twenty-first.

The result? A bad wine. It just shows you that it's the weather for those few final weeks before the harvest that makes all the difference to the quality of the wine."

And what of his fellow merchants? Pillars of society, hand in glove with the brokers, entrenched in the Chamber of Commerce, controlling the finest estates, the most powerful of them laid down the law and would have no interference. Most of the growers they treated as lesser beings, mere subordinates; and a grower who considered himself disfavored by the classification had no recourse, no appeal. For the price the merchants would pay for a wine depended on its place in the classification. And it was the brokers, who worked closely with them, who fixed the classification. The growers grumbled. What was the good of their improving their wine? A fine wine classed as Bourgeois would still only fetch a Bourgeois price from the merchants. The merchant could buy it under its real value, label it as he wished, sell it to the public at a fancy price and net the profit. And who could afford to challenge the power of these mighty men?

Well, John Lovell will see what he can do, said Lovell to himself.

That day after luncheon he showed Susannah around the cellars. Miss Stockton, a neat apple-faced woman of forty with tight-drawn black hair, had expressed decided opinions about things European and announced that since her brother was undoubtedly being robbed at that very moment she would have to hasten to join him when luncheon was over to redress the situation. So when she had gone Lovell took Susannah around.

They walked through the whitewashed upper cellars where the blending or "assembling" was done in the big oak vats marked Saint Émilion or Côtes de Bordeaux or Graves.

"What happens when they come out of there?" Susannah asked.

"They go down to the cellar below to get used to the cask a bit. Then we look at them again."

"And how much does this hold, this vat?"

"Nine thousand liters."

She smiled, her eyes gleamed. "I say! Aren't you up on all this!"

"No. It's marked up there on the vat, look." They laughed.

"Oh, is this what Miss Stockton's brother bought?" A dozen

casks were grouped for removal with Stockton's name stenciled on them.

"Yes. He wants to take it back in the ship with him and he's quite right. If we sent it in cask they'd put it in bond in New York and just let it lie there till they got around to advising him, and it'd have a good chance to spoil. I haven't reorganized my New York agency yet."

By Stockton's casks was a crate of magnums chalked "Mr. John Blood."

"Another of your customers?" she said.

"Yes."

She was going to say she didn't know they were acquainted, then thought better of it and the next moment he was saying, "This way. Mind the step."

He led the way down to the cool dim cellars below, row after row of vaulted passages with blackened walls where the barrels of wine stood in double rows, one on top of the other.

"It's lovely," she said. "I had no idea it was so big."

"It used to be part of an old monastery. There are three miles of this."

"Monastery? What did they *do* down here?"

"Don't ask me." He took his keys and opened the heavy grille and they went into the bottle cellars—tall black iron bins from floor to ceiling supported by iron arches, a maze of passages and bottles, bottles, bottles—blackened, cobweb-hung magnums, jeroboams with the crust of the ages upon them, hoary old pieces that looked as if they had been there undisturbed for centuries.

"Ghostly," she said. "But beautiful."

It was like some black mossy subterranean grotto, the thick black furry cobwebs clung to the bins and looped like nocturnal blooms and fronds from the walls and ceiling. He wiped off a bottle. "Gruaud-Larose 1834."

"Um. Delicious."

"Time the cork was changed, though." He took a stub of chalk from his pocket and made a mark by the bin. "They say they have to be changed every twenty years to be on the safe side."

They made their way through the passages between the bins, each holding up a candlestick. They looked here and there. Susannah dropped behind to peer down at two crusty imperials,

285

trying to make out a name on the sooty enamel plaque above the bin. Was there a coat of arms? Lovell came back. The plaque hung at the beginning of a side passage narrower than the rest.

"I was wondering who this was," she said.

He wiped off the plaque and she leaned forward and read, "Monsieur Paulmier de Lunaret. It's a good name, whoever he was." But when she looked up at him she saw he hadn't been listening; he had a slightly perplexed frown and was peering past her down the passage. She followed his look but saw nothing.

"Curious," he said. "I don't remember this."

"Remember what?"

"This section. Do you mind, a minute?" He raised his candle above his head and walked down the narrow passage. Susannah followed; it was decidedly more cobwebby than the rest, as if nobody had come down here for a long time. Lovell paused now and then to glance at a bin, wipe off a bottle, then went on. And at the end he stopped. She peered past him and saw a step down, an angle and a grille at which he was pushing.

"What is it?"

"I don't know. It's locked."

Lifting their candles, they could see only darkness on the other side.

"Would you mind waiting here a moment?" he said. "I'll have to force it."

She waited and he came back with an iron bar. While she held both candles he pushed and prized at the grille and finally after a good deal of effort got it open. It screeched as he pushed it wide and they went forward. She could see there wasn't a big space. The candlelight fell on festoons of cobwebs and then on bottle ends—rows of bottles in old stone racks. She kept brushing the cobwebs away from her face while Lovell peered into one bin and then the next. He fished out a length of wood, shook the dust off and held the candle to it.

She heard his exclamation of surprise. He put the wood back, went excitedly to the next row of bins and, after searching, found a similar strip of wood, which he examined likewise. At first he couldn't make it out, then he said, "What!"

"What is it?" Susannah said. But he was moving on to the next bin.

"Good God!"

286

"What *is* it?"

"Do you know what this is?"

"Heavens, Mr. Lovell, I keep asking you!"

"This is the old Collard private reserve. I've looked for it on and off, but I suppose I didn't really believe it existed. But this is it, all right, the family cellar. That"—he pointed to the first row of bins—"is Lafite 1798 and 1802. And all this, if you please"—indicating the second wall of bins—"is Lafite and Latour 1811, the Year of the Comet, a fabulous vintage, the greatest Bordeaux ever made."

"Oh." She smiled with pleasure. "How marvelous. How lovely. It's like finding a great golden treasure. It *is* treasure, but better, much better."

"And it's your discovery, my dear. You'll allow me to send you a dozen."

"It's a happy augury. I know it. Now I really feel Collard's is alive again."

6

_____

It was three o'clock in the afternoon when Regis Gautier walked through the quiet lobby of his club toward the door. The sunlight gleamed beyond the heavy portal, the spring warmth filtered in with the smell of madonna lilies. Regis had every right to feel pleased with himself, and yet . . . his unsettled mood would not lift.

As the porter handed him his hat he caught his reflection in the tall glass—his handsome dark-complexioned face with its straight nose, black hair, deep-set eyes and rather angular eyebrows, the smart long-skirted coat in a youthful tone of gray, the gold watch chain with dangling cornelian seal. He paused for a moment before lifting the hat to his head to admire the lofty dome of his forehead and turned slightly to see it in half profile. Intelligence there, who could doubt it? He was putting on a little weight too. Well, it suited him. Sign of prosperity.

The porter's bow as he turned for the door was deferent, if not downright obsequious. It had amused Regis to watch it deepen from a mere jerk to this low obeisance—the inverse to his own rise! With a curt acknowledgment he stepped out into the late-spring warmth, conscious that, framed there, he cut a figure for any passerby. And the passerby would do well to pause, for the groom was just bringing his new phaeton around to the door—and if *that* wasn't enough to give a man pride, Regis would like to know what was.

It was light, it was high sprung, it was dashing; it looked

ready to fly off on the instant, the devil of a phaeton. The sun flashed on its rich magenta panels, on the contrasting black of the box, on the brass fittings and the harness. The only thing it lacked was his own groom rigid on the box behind. But that would come, never fear. That would come. That was the next stage.

The man held out the reins. Regis had him wait while he slowly pulled on his lavender-colored gloves. Then he took them, sprang up and, with a scarcely perceptible flick of his wrist, started the horse. Yes, satisfactions indeed. Life *was* very satisfactory in many respects just now. Keeping the horse at a slow trot, he smiled at the recollection of his triumph at Barret and Ratier's auction the day before. He had picked up the prize lot of three dozen Latour 1815 from the old Count de Coquerel's cellar right under Mawdistly Baynes's nose.

"These thirty-seven magnums, full two quarts each of Latour 1815 bottled at the Château in 1818. Going once . . . Do I hear another bid? Thank you, sir, from the gentleman in the lavender-colored gloves I have . . ."

The auctioneer had known perfectly well who he was, standing there half hidden by the column, but Mawdistly hadn't woken up to "the gentleman in the lavender-colored gloves" until it was too late. Regis chuckled with pleasure. It was a presage of good things to come with Mademoiselle Aurelie Hagenbach, he felt. And Mademoiselle Aurelie had yet to see the phaeton! He was planning to call on her tomorrow and, he hoped, take her for a drive in it. And yes, he would hire a liveried groom from the stable for the occasion.

Nevertheless, these solid satisfactions were offset by other annoying things. The Mornac affair had undoubtedly damaged him, was still damaging him. The mere family connection was enough. Mornac had a lot of friends in Bordeaux, influential friends, and whatever pains Regis took to disassociate himself from the woman, some of the opprobrium stuck. The Hagenbachs, of course, knew; he had had to redouble efforts to counter the effect on them. He *had* countered the effect, but it had not been easy. And with others it was harder.

Francis and his wife were now being ostracized, and no wonder. Some of the gossip came to him through Sophie de Monteiro: Madame de Hennicourt saying she could not have

Susannah in her house with her young daughters, the Baroness de la Bouchardiere saying that Susannah had been in some sort of scuffle in the Rue Sainte Catherine well before the Mornac episode.

Regis reined in at the boulevard crossing while a squadron of dragoons, all horsehair plumes and perspiration, clattered past.

Then there was James. He was annoyed with James. Really extremely annoyed. James had arrived unexpectedly from Paris and said he would be staying a week. He had spent two nights at La Guiche, apparently talking to Francis in the office at some length, according to what Aunt Victorine Gautier said, and then had gone haring off to visit some theater people at Arcachon, promising to return. Regis himself had been laid up with his liver. The doctor had called it food poisoning, but Regis put it down to liver. He had really been devilish poorly for a few days and couldn't get out. Nevertheless he had sent James a private note saying he particularly wanted to see him. And the next thing he knew was Abel-Cherubin reporting that James was back in Paris! It was too damned annoying for words.

And finally, the most exasperating of all, there had been Chabot today.

Regis had carefully arranged their luncheon, secured a quiet corner at the club where they had been able to talk without interruption—and Chabot had poured cold water on his idea of replacing Francis at La Guiche with an estate manager. Simply turned it down. Wouldn't have it for a minute. Oh, he had been smoothness itself—flattering, unctuous, the perfect courtier, Chabot—but in his opinion a manager for La Guiche was *not* the solution.

Regis didn't think you could suspect Chabot of tender feelings for Francis. Regis had pointed out that Francis was more and more often away from La Guiche, that the place was being run very slackly. But no, it wouldn't do. A manager, said Chabot, was definitely not the right idea. For one thing there would be legal difficulties, probably insuperable legal difficulties if they tried to force the issue. And apart from that he didn't think it was psychologically the best way to proceed. Well, what *was* the best way? They all agreed that Francis was running the place badly and the arrival of this wife had not improved things.

But Chabot didn't know and he wouldn't budge. So the maneuver had been fruitless. And Abel-Cherubin wouldn't do anything against Chabot's advice.

Regis couldn't get over the impression that Chabot was playing some game of his own. Of course Chabot always gave that impression, it was his manner. It was in his face. A born intriguer.

The last of the dragoons went by and the crossing cleared; he snapped the reins and drove on. The afternoon traffic was heavier here, and he kept the phaeton at its steady slow trot, anxious to be seen by as many as could see. His eye caught Madame Michael Scully, the wife of the chartron merchant, approaching in her open carriage with her daughter. He waited until they were level, then raised his hat and was rewarded with an inclination of the head from Madame and an interested glance from Mademoiselle. Alas, the child was only eleven years old. He could never wait that long! A little farther along he glimpsed a hat being raised to *him* and saw it was Uzer, the jute and cotton merchant, and responded in turn with a nod, not too curt but curt enough.

Really, it was annoying about Chabot—that smooth, cynical manner. Secretive, Chabot. Oh, yes, and clever. Regis knew now that Chabot and his friends had been involved in the slave trade; he had the proof of it. It happened that La Monteiro knew the captain they had used on the last voyage and voyages before, a Captain Kergo. This was how she had got the original hint that it was slaving. Regis hadn't inquired too closely how she knew Kergo, but she had not lived exactly a sheltered life. Kergo, she had told him, had been "a good friend" to her when she was sixteen and just striking out in the world of men. And, from the hint, it appeared that Kergo had been led to speak more openly to her. On the last voyage, he said, Chabot and company had bilked him. He had taken the risk and they had bilked him of his promised share, knowing he couldn't denounce them without implicating himself.

Interesting. He wouldn't have thought that of Chabot, but he had probably been pushed by his partners. Faget de la Saigne was a creature. At all events the embittered Kergo had confided that when he suspected they might spring some dirty trick on this last voyage, he had had all the slave sales on the other side made in the names of his Bordeaux principals. He had given Monteiro a paper to this effect, telling her to use it if anything should happen to him. These Bretons with their wild fancies! The fact remained that some ugly business had been done.

A pair of eyes from the olive-green landau across the way encountered his—Madame Albert Joos, the banker's wife. Elegantly, Regis raised his hat. Pretty Madame Joos dimpled a smile and dipped her head. Charming, charming. And all at once Regis's unsettled mood flew away. Here it was, a spring afternoon, he was driving a spanking new phaeton, his prospects were blossoming and any number of glancing tributes were coming his way as he moved along, and he was damned if he was going to feel down in the mouth. He knew how to wait, after all. He might have an angry outburst now and then, but he never let them affect his general conduct. By nature he was a long-term planner, a patient burrower. Things were not to be rushed. He must continue to play his hand quietly and all would come out in the end.

He turned into a quiet, fashionable street near the Public Gardens and wheeled in under the porte-cochere of Number Four. The porter, who ran out at once, knew him well, since it was Regis who paid the bills. Regis threw him the reins, told him to see to the horse and turned in through the glass-and-iron-framed door. It was a roomy three-story house with its own stables and excellent reception rooms, and Monsieur de Monteiro, the nominal owner, was never in residence except on the rare occasions when it suited Madame to have him there for a day or so.

Regis took out his key and let himself in. In the entrance he hung up his hat. He glanced into the main salon, saw it was empty and went upstairs to the floor above. Here he knocked at the door of her boudoir, heard her answer and went in. The odor of her perfume floated over him, and she looked around from the pots and creams of the dressing table holding a small white cup of Turkish coffee in her hands. The maid was tidying in a corner.

"Oh, there you are."

He disliked this little room, overfurnished like the rest of the house and now fashionably stuffed with Algerian poufs and cushions and ottomans.

"My dear." Regis bent down to kiss her. She made a defensive movement with cup and saucer to say Careful! and held up her face gingerly. He touched it with his lips. The robe showed her arms and neck; she had just got up.

"How are you?" she said coolly. They had not seen each other for four days.

"All right." Regis nodded, looking at her and thinking she was slimmer. Her blue-black hair was tucked up, showing her ears but leaving a black wisp beside them. Her long slender neck rose out of the robe, her perfect black eyes with their blueish whites under the black eyebrows looked at him, her whole pose as she held cup and saucer in front of her expressed most enticingly the unattainable. Sometimes he wondered if she didn't have some Oriental blood in her, some distant touch of the Javanese. Today she was especially beautiful.

The maid left the room. Madame de Monteiro put the cup down, and he gently kissed her neck, caressing her.

"Have you missed me?"

"You know I never miss you," she said, and the little sarcastic fold appeared by her mouth. "I am able to stay alone. You aren't."

Alone! He turned away and sat down on a pouf, recognizing this as another day when she had the upper hand. Sometimes the mood varied and he dominated, felt that she was smaller, weaker, following him—but these were rare days. Nearly always he felt at a disadvantage with her, almost naïve. As if she didn't need him. As if there were a mysterious deep self-sufficiency in her, attained somehow from her experience with men.

He watched her as she turned back to the mirror to attend to her face. Sometimes he thought she was a pure cocotte—one of those women for whom men were meant to be used, managed, manipulated, at the most to be enjoyed as a temporary bedmate provided he did not interfere with other business, but not to be loved.

Love was rather childish to them. The notion of love was childish, a little ridiculous, not a sentiment for the mature. Love did not enter into their calculations. And, one way or another, life *was* all calculation, wasn't it? Clever women, women who knew what they were about, used men. Otherwise men would use them quite ruthlessly—that was their point of view. That

293

was the cocotte. That was the successful woman.

And these, of course, were the terms his friends accepted their mistresses on. Most of them knew they were being used and manipulated. They accepted it as part of the "amusement." Sometimes it was rather forced, the amusement, but that they accepted too. It was part of the convention, like the convention that to cut any figure as a male you had to keep one of these women. To be ruined by one was devilish dashing.

And yet, tormenting as she was, La Monteiro had heart, she had passion. She was tormenting, but it wasn't all coldness with her. She behaved like a cocotte but she didn't have the icy core.

And, of course, as a man about town Regis was imbued with the need for mistresses. There was justification for the system. Ample justification. For at forty a bourgeois woman stopped being a woman—sometimes long before. She became a domestic item, a bit of furnishing, a spouse—very comfortable and useful but no *fun*. She became a matron, she lost her shape, she became dowdy, if not pious, and her allure vanished. Oh, she was probably sharp as a needle, but she couldn't join in male amusements. She no longer wanted to behave like a girl; she no longer wanted to please as a *female*—perhaps as a hard-eyed business partner, yes, but not as a female. By the time she was thirty-five or forty all she wanted was to be left alone. And so she spent her time with her children, her interminable household affairs, her family, her curé, her bourgeois women friends and her good works.

A terrible bore. Terrible. Above all, as a wife she wasn't interested in being desirable. Which, of course, was where women like Sophie de Monteiro came in. Desirability, a distinctly suspect attribute to any bourgeois woman, was supremely the mistress's business.

And so things were kept apart: the man's wife, his family, his social life on the one side; his "private" life, his mistress, his extravagances, his amusements on the other. A man never took his wife to the races, for example, or on a shooting trip. It would be absurdly out of place. He took his mistress because she was part of his fun, whereas a wife was part of his duty. He never committed a folly for his wife or gave her a really costly piece of jewelry. That was for his mistress, and the mistress took care to show it off to demonstrate her success, her standing. And since husbands and mistresses only mixed with other husbands and mistresses, they moved in their separate worlds.

But Madame de Monteiro had a husband and many influential friends. She wasn't, after all, in the strictly professional ranks. And so she was privileged and got invited to bourgeois social functions where a large attendance would enable the men to flirt with her discreetly. The bourgeois women did not consort with her on these occasions any more than on any other. They merely looked her up and down and wondered if *their* husband had bought her necklace and said, "That woman . . ." And Sophie de Monteiro laughed and enjoyed both worlds.

"Have you got your new turnout?" she asked Regis, meaning the phaeton.

"Yes."

"Is it smart?"

"Very. It's downstairs. I drove around in it."

"I must drive it." She laughed.

Regis lit a cigar. He had no intention of driving out with her until Mademoiselle Hagenbach had had a first spin. Madame de Monteiro put her face close to the mirror, applying something to her eyes.

"And did you see Dumouriez?" she asked.

Regis paused, handling his effect carefully. "Yes," he said in an offhand way. Through a friend she had heard of an unusual cargo of Peruvian wool and American skins in the port which could be had cheaply, provided the sale were quick and did not attract attention. Regis had speculated, bought it up and almost immediately found a buyer at a handsome profit.

"Well?" Still close to the mirror.

"I looked at it, I bought it and sold it yesterday."

She looked quickly around at him and her black eyes flashed with pleasure. "How much?"

"Thirty-eight per cent." He took a purse from his pocket, got up and put it on the dressing table, the expression of his face unchanging. "The rest of your share is in my safe."

"How clever of you, my friend," she said, smiling. "How clever."

He felt the balance had tipped slightly in his favor, though the "my friend" was meant to mark a limitation. She was looking up at him and he kissed her tentatively, careful to show no ardor, which she would only repel.

A moment later, when she had made him resume his seat and had turned back to the mirror, she said, "By the way, I hear your cousin Susannah is with John Blood, did you know?"

" 'With' him?"

"His mistress."

"Is it true?" He was astonished . . . yet he wasn't; and then he was shocked and indignant.

"It's an established thing, it seems."

"Established? Not that I know of. Who did you get it from?"

She didn't answer, as he had known she wouldn't, and he said, "Are you sure it's true?"

She shrugged, a feminine shrug which might mean anything. "I tell you, it's established."

Regis was silent. She continued attending to her face. He sat thinking, shocked in spite of himself, shocked and indignant. Soon *this* would be around the town, if it wasn't already.

Sophie de Monteiro said, "You know, I think I shall take to that riding style of hers—astride."

"What?" he said absently.

"I'm going to start riding astride, like your cousin Susannah."

"Don't be ridiculous."

"Why not? It'll set a new vogue—so eye-catching!" And she pealed with laughter.

After ten days of silence Susannah couldn't help herself and went to Bordeaux again. She had to. There must be some word of explanation. He would surely have left word. But at the clinic the young nurse wasn't on duty and Susannah began to feel panic. Jacob was happy to see her and taught her a game with pieces like checkers, and she stayed with him for an hour and a half, watching for a glimpse of the girl. At the end she got up in despair and said goodbye. And then at the last minute the nurse appeared and gave her a note.

Susannah walked out trembling without looking at it. The streets were hot and dusty. She would have to see Louise before going back—it would look more natural—so she took a cab.

The note was six days old.

I'm sorry. I noticed I was being followed and thought
it best we should not speak. Did you understand? I
trust I did not distress you? Did Tom Mowbray by
chance speak to you? He was there. I also glimpsed
him in Paris unexpectedly, and it is curious. So be
watchful in that quarter. I long to see you. But for the
moment—discretion. J.

Tom Mowbray? She stared out of the cab window. She
hadn't, of course, seen him that day. She hardly ever saw him
nowadays. Once Francis had brought him to the house, saying
they had met on the way. On another occasion he had asked
Mowbray to look at Lad, the dog. Oh, yes, and they had run into
him one day in Bordeaux. What did it mean? *He* had been following John?

She had come to Bordeaux by the Messageries coach and
couldn't stay long with Louise because of the service back. On
the way home she tore up the note and scattered it on the wind.

7

Toward the end of June Francis arrived home at La Guiche one evening after a day in Bordeaux and found Abel-Cherubin waiting for him impatiently. Abel-Cherubin was pacing the hall with his chin up as Francis came down the drive from the stable.

"I must say! I said seven o'clock."

"You said . . ." Oh, Lord, he had forgotten. Abel-Cherubin had sent a note three days before saying he wanted to talk business and would be there at seven. "I'm terribly sorry, Abel-Cherubin. I completely forgot." He smiled ingratiatingly.

"Seems to amuse you."

"No, no."

"I haven't time to waste, even if you have."

"Have you had dinner?" Francis said to placate him as they went in.

"An hour ago! If you wouldn't mind, I have a heavy day tomorrow and I'd like to get our business over right away."

"All right. I'm so thirsty I must have something to drink first. Oh, Mother." Francis took his hat off and kissed his mother. "I'm sorry you've been waiting for me. Yes, I've had dinner. Where's Susannah?"

"Upstairs. Writing home."

"I see." Francis heaved a contented sigh, glad to be home in spite of Abel-Cherubin. He picked up a carafe of water from the dining-room sideboard and poured himself a glass. "Lord, I'm parched." He emptied it in one draft, then refilled the glass from the bottle of white Graves standing there and took an appreciative sip.

It was one of the evenings when he was in a state of blissful exhaustion. He had been up and away since five o'clock and had loved every minute of the day, felt as if he had soaked up the sea! Slowly and steadily the *Amiable Rose* was being refitted. Every day there was some interesting new point to discuss, and even when it was settled he stayed behind, doing nothing in particular, just hanging about happily, telling himself his presence might be useful. The days seemed to drift by in a golden haze while he chatted with the workmen, discussed things with Gaveau, walked around the ship for the thousandth time and stood about on the waterfront dreaming. Often Gaveau could not get away from his ordinary business affairs and had to leave things to Francis. And Francis was happy to attend to them.

"Do you mind?" Abel-Cherubin said testily.

"Oh . . . yes." Francis smiled and came out of his reverie. "Thinking of something else. Let's go into the office." He took a lamp and led the way.

Inside he shut the door, put the lamp on the desk and sat down while Abel-Cherubin ponderously took the armchair and folded his hands.

"Well! I'm here to discuss your wife's situation, Francis."

"What?" A frown.

"Your wife's situation in regard to the property. It's some time since we talked about it. You'll agree we have left you ample time for reflection."

So this was it! Francis felt his happy mood was going to be punctured after all, and after such a good day. Why did they have to bring this up? They had not mentioned the subject for so long he had hoped it was buried. Nevertheless, he tried to look cheerful. "Well, yes . . ."

"The time has come to regularize the position."

"How do you mean, 'regularize'?"

Abel-Cherubin settled himself in the chair. "We have now gone into the matter and, up to a point, the conclusions are clear. The property is in France and therefore comes under French law. So far so good. Equally, under French law, your wife does not, upon your death, automatically inherit your share. That you know?"

Francis nodded.

"The law prescribes that on your death your share shall revert to the family, in other words to Mother, to James and myself. That is quite clear, is it not?"

"Well, yes, but Monsieur Parenteau says I can make a will and leave it to Susannah," Francis said.

Abel-Cherubin looked annoyed. "Parenteau knows perfectly well you can do that. Parenteau *also* knows, as he has told you, that Father wished to make the property indivisible, so as to keep it in the family. The law, of course, provides for that —the law of joint estates—and so Father wrote instructions to Parenteau to draw up the papers. Unfortunately he did not live to sign them. But his intention was crystal clear. And we are now advised—I say we are now advised on excellent legal authority—that these instructions in our father's hand would be ample basis for contesting any will which flouted those intentions of his—in other words a will by which you left the property to your wife. *I* say it would invalidate it. Apart from family duty, your *moral obligations*, we must trust your good sense to avoid such an issue."

The lamplight cut across Abel-Cherubin's heavy face. His eyes held Francis's across the desk. Francis didn't know what to say, but he felt more and more depressed.

"What we are *not* sure about—you see I am being quite frank with you—is the American side," Abel-Cherubin went on. "What is the American law on the point? Opinions differ. We have therefore thought it wise to draw up a deed by which the lady renounces her rights in perpetuity. This is for the American side, you understand. It will save any legal entanglements from the American side. It may not be strictly necessary, but we prefer to make sure. And we shall have it notarized and registered in Philadelphia so that there may be no dispute later on."

One plump white hand went inside his coat and came out with a document tied up with red lawyer's ribbon. Abel-Cherubin undid the ribbon, leaned forward and flattened the document on the desk. His finger pointed to a place. "Your wife signs here—her maiden name, of course—and on this second copy. In addition you must get it signed by two witnesses, not members of the family, with their occupations. Very simple. We will have it notarized forthwith."

Francis felt a sickening lump in his chest. He hated all this. "But really, Abel-Cherubin, I—"

"Francis, I will *not* have any more shilly-shallying! We have wasted time enough. This deed should have been signed a year ago. And if it hadn't been for Chabot's finicking insistence on every word and phrase, that's what it would have been— signed and done with! I am sick and tired of pressing for it. But I am not having any more of it. It has gone on long enough. You will now kindly get it signed and returned to me!"

Francis was flicking the pages back and forth in his fingers, making the thick paper crackle. "But how can I? Can't we just leave it? Do be reasonable, Abel-Cherubin. How can I ask my wife to sign a thing like this?"

"How *can* you? You entered into a solemn moral obligation with our father, which means with each one of us. And now you ask how can you keep it?"

"It wasn't quite like that and you know very well. It's so damned awkward."

"Awkward? *I* signed the equivalent. I signed a marriage contract excluding *my* wife. I did not find it awkward—and it might have been *much* to my advantage the other way around." Abel-Cherubin gave a self-righteous sniff but did not mention that it had been his wife's family that had insisted on their having a marriage contract so that, having had Louise's dowry, Abel-Cherubin should not get his hands on her property.

Francis squirmed unhappily.

"And in Louise's family there are more responsible members than in your wife's, let me tell you that," Abel-Cherubin threw in.

"Oh, really!"

"There's no 'really' about it. Why should this . . . this American, this brazen interloper expect favored treatment? In the name of what?" The jowls quivered. "As if she hasn't caused enough trouble. All she is waiting for is to get her hands on the property, you may count on that. Well, we are not having it!"

"We?" said Francis in a gloomy voice.

"Mother is of my opinion. And so is James. He confirmed it while he was here, if you want to know. And I may say that the recent deplorable events . . . her . . . her whole conduct has resolved us to push this to the very end, Francis. So there

301

will be no getting away from it. Make up your mind on that."

"I suppose Chabot's in it too?"

"We are all resolved to go to the utmost to protect ourselves."

"That's more like it—to protect yourselves, as you call it, not to respect Father's wishes."

"Both!"

"I think you're all being damned unfair to Susannah. She is not like that and she certainly didn't marry me for La Guiche."

"Then she can prove it by signing this."

Francis threw it off. He said nothing to Susannah, and after a couple of days he had forgotten it. He was really so absorbed in the *Amiable Rose* that it went out of his mind. Then by chance he met Abel-Cherubin and Chabot together in Bordeaux, and when he had to admit he had done nothing Abel-Cherubin made a scene.

Francis sighed; he saw he would have to take some step. So at the beginning of July he decided to take Susannah off to Arcachon to get it over with. It was a Sunday, the weather was fine and he told her he wouldn't wait any longer—she must see the seacoast. They would leave next day.

"You really want to go tomorrow?" she said, a little astonished at the sudden decision but happy.

"If we don't go now we never will."

They found a seafront room at the Pension Boniface, and for a week they had a lovely time. They took the sea baths, buried themselves in the sand like children, ate oysters by the dozen, and paddled out over the sand flats when the tide was out to hunt cockles. They rode donkeys and watched the jugglers and mustachioed acrobats in striped undershirts who cried, "Hop!" and clapped their hands at each trick they performed.

On the third day they went to Pilat, where they struggled laughing up the great dunes and stood on the knife-edge top in the whipping breeze. The sand blew off the top like wave spume. Susannah hardly dared stand upright, so high it was and so narrow their foothold. At her feet the sheer side of the dune dropped steeply to the water's edge—one step and she would go pitching down.

How beautiful it was! The sun flashed on the sea. There below them lay the great tidal inlet of the Bassin, all blue and white and tossing. At the seaward end the narrow pass was choked with golden-brown sandbanks, and there was a tide race where the Atlantic came surging in, pressing and ripping in in roaring breakers, even in this weather. And beyond all this the dark olive-green of the pine forest stretched far, far off, as far as you could see, north to the Pointe de Grave, south, behind them, to the Pyrenees. Beautiful!

They found jellyfish of palest blue-white, and he taught her to catch razor fish by sprinkling salt into a little slit in the sand and waiting, still and breathless, till suddenly up popped the fish. So foolish, they always laughed.

From the café terrace they watched the fishing boats with their dun sails following one another out down the channel to the pass.

"Dangerous place, the pass, if you don't know it," Francis said.

And at night when it was still they could lie and hear faintly in the distance the long continuous boom of the ocean.

Francis was especially happy when they were inspecting the vessels on the slipways or watching the men caulking boats or repairing rigging or nets. He talked to all the crews.

"You've missed your vocation, Captain," Susannah said to him and he laughed.

"I think I have, you know." He had told her nothing yet of the venture with Gaveau; time enough when the *Amiable Rose* was ready. And he waited all week, delaying the moment when he must speak of the legal business. For why spoil it? Why spoil their holiday? Yet in the end it had to come.

On the last afternoon they picnicked on the beach at Cap Ferret, the long spit of sand on the other side of the Bassin where there were only a few fishermen's huts. They had crossed in one of the narrow local boats called a *pinasse* with a high curved bow. Then they walked along the empty beach to the point where they had the Atlantic on one side and the Bassin on the other. Nobody in sight. Not a soul as far as they could see. The long straight ocean beach ran north out of sight into the heat haze. In the distance the sand seemed to lift and fill the air with countless particles. Only sun and sky and sand.

The breeze was gentle and they were glad of the shade of the big black umbrella Francis had brought along. Susannah had unbuttoned the front of her dress and had her skirt to her knees, as there wasn't a soul about. The sun beat down. They paddled and ate their picnic lunch and watched the gulls diving for fish and the silver backs of porpoises flashing far out.

"Sleepy?" Susannah said.

He was lying on his elbow on the sand, half under the umbrella. "No. Why?"

"You're rather quiet."

"Well, to tell you the truth, Sue, there is something I have to talk to you about."

She looked at him; she had guessed it since morning. He was staring down and scooping up the sand, not looking at her. "It's . . . it's to do with you and La Guiche. I mean . . . You see, Father's idea was to keep the property intact and keep it in the family, and by rights we should have signed a contract when we were married."

"We should?"

"Yes. I mean a contract to keep my property separate from yours. You understand?" He scooped up more sand and let it run through his fingers. "It's a legal thing. I didn't remember it at the time, but, well, it puts me in an awkward position. They could cause all sorts of trouble if I went against it and tried to make over my share to you in a will, so—"

"Who could?"

"The family—Abel-Cherubin and the others."

"But how do you mean cause trouble if you make a will?"

"Sue, I tell you they'll make trouble. I don't want to discuss that side of it. I just don't. I can't go against them there. It'll only stir up a whole lot of trouble if I disregard them—I mean if I try to ride roughshod over them. I . . . I can't help it. I've decided and that's all there is to it." He was strange and distant to her as he spoke.

She gazed at him with anger coming into her eyes. "You're saying you can't leave me your share of La Guiche in your will, is that it?"

He nodded glumly, looking down at the sand.

"Well, I suppose it's just as well I should know, isn't it? It's sweet of you to choose a lovely day out here to tell me."

He looked miserable. "They're within their rights."

She turned her head away. Then he said, "There's some-

304

thing you do have to do. They want you to sign a paper. It's really nothing—just renouncing the property from the American point of view. I've got the paper in my bag at the pension. You can sign it when we get back. It's really only so there won't be a legal mixup." He suddenly looked up at her and gave a quick hopeful smile.

"Because they're afraid I might claim under American law, is that what you mean?" she said.

"They want it kept in the family."

"And I'm not the family?"

"The Gautier family."

"My name is Gautier, but I am not one of the family."

He scooped up the sand unhappily, as if she were making it unnecesarily difficult for him. "I'm simply repairing an omission."

"To keep me out? Perhaps I'm too notorious?"

"It won't change anything between us."

"Have you agreed to it?"

"Yes. I had to. Best for you to sign it."

It was like a smack across the face. She got to her knees and brushed her hair from her face with the back of her hand. "You can't disregard them, but you can disregard me," she said with anger.

"Look, Sue—"

"It always *is* your family before me, isn't it?"

"Sue, for heaven's sake—"

"I think it's disgusting. Disgusting! Why do they hate me? Because I won't be like Louise? They're all horrible! It's not that I want La Guiche—it's just the meanness. Their mean spirit. They hate me."

She jumped up and swung away down the beach, hot and furious and sickened. She simply saw nothing, she was so furious. It was too much for her. She couldn't bear this meanness and narrowness. As if she wanted to claim their property! She would rather do anything than make a claim on any of them. She had some pride in her soul. Did they know what pride was? To think that she would scheme for a piece of their property!

Property—how they loved it! It was their god. And she was hurt, deeply hurt, that Francis should share this meanness. They were forming their defenses against the outsider. Watch

305

out! Here's a foreigner, an American. Sure to be after our property. Careful! Keep her out. She's your wife? All the more reason to be on your guard. That's why she married you. You're one of the family, so close the ring around our property—*our* family and *our* property. They would do anything to stop her getting their property. They would scheme, they would lash out, they would make life impossible for her if they thought she might get La Guiche. Never would they let an outsider in—least of all a woman.

The wind blew her skirts and her hair. And when she realized he had stored this up all week, all their happy week, she was hot with anger.

He came trudging through the sand after her. "Sue. Sue! Be reasonable."

She swung around on him at the water's edge. "You've decided. *You've* decided! You mean *they've* decided! Why can't you stand up to them? Why do you let them treat me like dirt? Because you're one of them! You agree with them."

"They've got grounds. They've got their rights."

"And what about *my* rights? What am I to you? A piece of furniture you can brush aside when it suits you, when it comes to your sacred property! *Your* rights! But my rights don't exist! You're all the same. I hate you. Get away from me."

"Sue, listen to me." He took her arm.

"Leave me alone!" She wrenched away and walked off, but he went after her.

"Sue, listen to me, will you?"

"I will not!"

"Listen to me. If we don't fall in with this, do you know what's going to happen?"

"I don't care!" She screamed at him and walked away.

He walked along beside her, persisting. "They'll consider themselves free, and they'll all sell out, d'you hear? Abel-Cherubin is already itching to sell out. He'll sell first and persuade the others to follow. We'll be left with a bit of land that'll cut us right down—right down to the knuckle. We'll have to let the house go. And then what? Then what'll we do? I don't know. I've got one or two irons in the fire, but I'm not ready. It'd be . . . it'd be terribly awkward. We've *got* to keep them in. We've got to just now. It's bad enough as it is with the oïdium ruining the property."

306

"But the oïdium is the very reason why Abel-Cherubin *won't* sell out. The market's dead. Do you understand? He wouldn't get any price at all. Nor would the others. And they know it. And they'd rather die than get a small price for their property. It would hurt their meanness too much."

"You'll have to sign that paper all the same, Sue."

"I will *not*. I will not sign it! You can't force me to. That's one of my rights, to say no! You can tear it up. And I will tell Abel-Cherubin to his face."

"Susannah—"

"Oh, leave me alone!" She flung away and walked angrily down the beach alone.

8

The following Thursday was Louise's biweekly visiting day, and she arrived for tea with her niece Berthe, a pretty auburn-haired girl of eighteen. It was a warm day and not too sunny, so they had tea outside. Madame Gautier was away visiting, the second time this had happened lately on Louise's calling day, and Louise was rather nervous about it, as if it were a sign of displeasure, a warning that Madame Gautier suspected her loyalty.

When tea was over, Berthe went off to explore, and Susannah saw that Louise had arranged this because she had something to say. It was a long time coming. Louise twisted her fingers, talked of everything else, but at last she leaned forward and said quietly, "My dear, you must forgive me. I can't help mentioning this. Perhaps you'll think it indiscreet of me, but I do want to tell you that . . . that I'm on your side."

"Oh, Louise, that's sweet of you. Thank you. It's nice of you." Susannah smiled, a little puzzled all the same.

"I know it's been difficult for you. I just wanted you to know I do understand. And I think you behaved splendidly."

"Louise, how kind you are." She took the other woman's hand and squeezed it in sympathy. Yet there was something else, something more to come, she saw that.

"Now please don't think it indiscreet of me, my dear, will you? You won't, will you? You see, the other day I overheard Abel-Cherubin speaking to Chabot about . . . about a paper they've given you to sign."

Susannah sat quite still. "Yes?"

"They have given it to you, haven't they?"

"No, because I won't have anything to do with it. I know what it's about though. Why?"

"You do know? I've been feeling so uncomfortable about it. So wretched. Ever since that day last year, you remember, the first day I came to tea?"

"Yes, when Mother asked me to leave the table because she had something to say to you in private."

Louise nodded. "It was about that. She told me I mustn't speak to you about the paper they were drawing up."

"So that was it." Susannah looked at her, then gazed out across the flowerbeds. All that time ago? All that time? They had been carefully preparing it all this time without breathing a word to her? But how secretive, how petty. She shuddered in her heart.

"Oh, it's made me feel so unhappy I couldn't tell you. So miserable." Louise was gazing at her with anxious distress. "I've cried to myself sometimes. I've thought I must tell her, but . . . I didn't. I was a coward. I'm sorry I didn't, my dear. Will you forgive me?"

"Of course. I understand, Louise, and it's sweet of you to feel like that. I'm not going to sign it anyway. I wouldn't dream of it."

"I advise you not to, my dear."

Sympathy she found also with the little Marquis de Talabu, a silent communion of spirit. He was such a nice man, always kind and sweetly considerate and courtly, and she felt that he understood her situation, he who had known and loved America when he was young. He had a sweet gentle way with her, and his active mind, his scientific curiosity stimulated her, took her mind off her trouble. His was the European spirit she admired, the Europe of the great encyclopedists, not the cautious old crabbed Europe it had become. He saw she was tormented and tried to distract her.

She called on him often now; his house had become a refuge to her. Sometimes she found him in the plant laboratory shining with excitement at some fresh drawing he had made from the microscope, sometimes submerged in letters and magazine articles. With his encouragement she studied his sketchbook of fungoids, peered at them under the microscope while he taught her what to look for, and she read the spirited exchanges about the oïdium and the potato blight in the English horticultural magazines. She grew to find the fungoids fascinating; the weird unearthly tentacular shapes no longer repelled her.

"They are all God's creation," he said to her with a beautiful fervor in his face. He really loved creation; the smallest parasite was beautiful to him. And she became convinced he was right—the mold made the vines fail and nothing else.

Now the oïdium was worse than before and everybody in the vineyards was in a panic. All over the wine country, growers, peasants, the smallholders and the rich were calling meetings to try to find some way to fight it. They formed defense committees, they petitioned the government. But in their fear and anxiety they couldn't agree. This man knew better than that, the third scoffed at both, the chorus of voices rose. So the meetings were often rowdy and wrangling. Men who were losing their livelihood were desperate, angry, looking for a scapegoat. Susannah asked Francis to take her to one of these meetings, but he either forgot or was away and nothing came of it.

And *she* now was having to make the decisions at La Guiche. What to do about the oïdium she didn't know. Wipe the mold off all the leaves and grapes? Impossible. Yet how else could they destroy it? Josserand and Laverne and the other people kept coming to her for this or that, and she couldn't always put them off till Francis was there and so she had to decide. Josserand always shrugged his shoulders and went about the work slackly, and Susannah would find herself going after him, pointing out that the vine leaves had not been thinned out or something else had been done badly.

"What's the good of me thinning the leaves out? The grapes are all rotten with mildew."

"We may save some. And you're paid for it, so do it."

He glared silently at her, hating her.

Once or twice Madame Gautier got Raynal over from Libourne to look at the work, but he evidently had no desire to interfere and said nothing to Susannah. Susannah loved La Guiche too much to mind; the stricken vines were a terrible sight to her.

On the first Friday in August she was sitting at breakfast when a great clanging and beating on tins came from the road.

Emilie, who went to see, came back with a leaflet saying a big meeting on the oïdium emergency was being held in the village that evening. Susannah decided she *must* go and told Joseph she would want the buggy at seven o'clock. When she mentioned it to Francis he said he had to go to Bordeaux, and directly after lunch he drove off with Madame Gautier, whom he was leaving at Blanquefort on the way. Susannah didn't really mind. What was she to do? Half the workpeople looked more to her now than to Francis.

At six thirty she went up and changed into a plain brown dress and her simplest bonnet. It would be best to look as modest as possible, for she was determined to speak at the meeting if she got the chance, to make them see the mold as the cause of the trouble and try to find some means of attacking it. Downstairs there was no buggy. She sent Emilie for it and Emilie came back saying it was by the stable with one wheel off, and the wheelwright who had been working on it was nowhere to be seen.

Susannah stamped her foot in vexation. The wheelwright was a tippler, a great drinking companion of Josserand's. She thought she really couldn't go on horseback. She waited impatiently while they searched for the man again, but in the end she had to send Jean, the garden boy, to bring a carriage from the livery stable in the village. However, by the time Jean had come back with it and they had set out, it was forty minutes late for the meeting and she was in a bad temper.

The cool silvery evening was soft and still. The vineyards looked terrible. Death was passing over them; the stillness was death. Even the birds kept away. Hardly a workman to be seen, as if they had all given up the ghost. It cast a pall over her— everything, the stupid delay, the decaying stillness of the vineyards, the empty landscape. It made her shudder. It threw her back on herself, on her own trouble. What was she to do? Her husband was a weak man, kind and loving but without iron in him, without the will to stand for himself. In his strange blind way he wasn't aware of anything but his fancy of the moment, which it was always urgent to pursue. Urgent! Like a child. It had to be now, this minute. Yet he couldn't stand alone. He hated *being* alone physically and was always horribly restless unless he was with other people. And above all his class and family overwhelmed him, cowed him.

311

She, on the other hand, hated the idea of immersing herself in conformity; the bourgeois narrowmindedness stifled her. Living forever on their guard! She hated their lack of imagination, hated their crabwise approach to life, their fear of emotion. They had no passion in their thin blood. She had to be her own individual soul. This was what being American meant to her, the refusal of these old inbred fears and confinements and constraints, this terrible guardedness.

Riding the horse had been the physical expression of it, her physical need for space and freedom to run. She felt it in her body, the physical need for space. It was very strange, but the actual geographical limits here made her ache, made her feel cramped. She needed the sense of space, the sense of wildness and passion that went with space. It was in her blood. It must be in the blood of every American, she thought, this sense of space and freedom and a certain dangerousness in life, a rawness, an edge. Yes, dangerousness!

As against this other world of Europe she felt in herself the force of something almost primitive, the principle of *energy*, of vitality, perhaps of immanent evil but also of every immanent good. Perhaps it was the meeting of these two worlds, America and Europe, that made her aware of it so keenly. The civilization of America was shallow, crude, corrupt and coarse, full of vice and money-consciousness and slumbering force and will, but open, passionate, vital as a young animal, the real life-force and still far, far behind the old hereditary cunning, the deep inbred hatreds and aloofness, the holding away of Europe. One world crude and barbaric, crossing the prairie with the sun in its face, the other effete and bloodless, going to the grave. History! Everything before one, the shadows falling on the other.

And this was why she must listen to herself, why she must listen to the voice of her American soul. She would fight, she would not be submerged.

In the village the square in front of the Mairie was full of tethered horses, dogcarts and carriages. The Mairie was also the village school, the best they could do in the way of a meeting hall. Local youths, women and servant girls were hanging around giggling outside. Susannah told the driver to come for her after the meeting, got down and walked to the door. The groups stared at her. There was a woman's laugh and a quick "Hush!"

Susannah went up the steps and opened the door. A solid row of male backs blocked the way. She could hear someone speaking and being interrupted. By craning her neck she saw a banner at the far end with *Defense Committee, Cantenac* on it in red letters. The committee, a solid row of bourgeois men, was seated underneath, and one, a fat red-faced man, was on his feet trying to make himself heard.

"Excuse me, can I get in?" She pushed. Faces turned, and the men standing in the back moved an inch or two. She pushed between them and others beyond and found herself inside. A good deal of noise was going on, men interrupting the speaker and others talking on their own. The place was full of tobacco smoke and male faces—bald heads and beards, top hats and paunches of the bourgeois, the red faces of the intermingled workpeople and estate managers. She saw she was the only woman there and sat down on the end of a bench, aware that every man present was staring at her as if she were an interloper, that the groundswell of voices had died away as they craned around to see.

But up again it rose next minute. A running discussion was going on. The fat speaker, a local grower named Janivel, was telling them that the oïdium was caused by excess humidity and it could all be cleared up by proper drainage; and men in the audience kept wanting to know who was going to pay for the drainage. Among the seated committee Susannah saw Legros, one of their neighbors; the Mayor of Cantenac, who was a local landowner; Dr. Davenne and Monsieur Fraissinet, two more from the parish. Fraissinet, a large florid man, glared at her.

She sat listening. It was the usual floundering among hit-or-miss remedies, pseudoscientific explanations, reports of cure-alls elsewhere. One man after another stood up and expounded the virtues of some treatment or other. Spray the vines with copper sulfate and all would be well. Douse them with soapy water and they would thrive. Sprinkle them with nitrate of potash, dust them with cinders or chalk, wash them with diluted oil or tar water, cut a ring around each vine stock—it was endless.

A tiny ferret-faced man bawled out that the smallholders were being "sacrificed," and he was noisily acclaimed by one section of the audience and denounced with heat by the rest. Several men demanded a deputation be sent to the Préfet. Somebody else tossed in the Bordeaux merchants, and a spate of angry recrimination followed.

Susannah sat there. The men stared at her, they turned around and openly looked her up and down, some farther forward stood up and turned to see her. They joked together, nudging one another. It was the collective male in all his cockiness, his self-assurance, his superiority. They resented her presence, as if it were a defiance of their prerogatives.

Finally Dr. Davenne stood up. Ah . . . they all knew that the oïdium was a form of vegetable dropsy, not unlike the potato blight. The vines had in some way contracted a weakness which made them unable to eliminate the excess water. The result was that in wet or foggy weather their systems became swamped and decay set in. This decay quickly spread through the leaves and grapes, which naturally turned moldy and dropped off. Hence . . .

Dr. Davenne was tall and thin with an aquiline nose. He gestured with his delicate long hands. As he went on, the hall became restless. Susannah was impatient. Why were they so footless? A man interrupted Davenne with some quibble about "wet putrefaction" and Davenne answered him.

At last Susannah could bear it no more. She jumped up. "The vines are perfectly healthy. They are not diseased. And the proof is they don't die but grow new shoots each year."

Davenne stopped speaking. A numbed, amazed silence fell on them all, as if they were stunned. Stunned by her interference. There they were, in all their power, their position, their maleness, and this woman, this notorious *American* had interrupted. Was telling them their business! They stared at her.

"You are all looking for something which is in front of your noses," she said. "The oïdium is the mold. That is what's wrong. There is nothing else. Get rid of that and you've got rid of your trouble."

A rumble came from the gathered men and she had to raise her voice. "The mold is a fungus. If you study it under a microscope you can see it spreading its filaments all over the leaves and shoots. From these filaments it pushes up tiny stalks which are spore containers. These drop off by millions, and each one of them germinates as soon as it falls on another leaf or grape. The vines are not diseased. It is the fungus and nothing else. We have to find a way to kill off the mold, that is what all our efforts must be bent to. And I don't see any use petitioning the Préfet."

A confused murmur from the hall, a murmur of disapproval. Davenne was holding up his hand. "And what claim have you, madame, to teach experienced men what to do?"

"I have studied the fungus at Monsieur de Talabu's laboratory."

"Talabu!" It rolled out like a hoot of amusement. They rocked with laughter, laughter tinged with scorn. But Susannah faced them, looking around defiantly. "Have any of you taken the trouble to do that?"

"Be about your proper business, madame," somebody yelled.

"Get home to your sewing!"

"Quiet! If you please." Davenne quieted them down, lifted his chin to Susannah. "You appear to think you have made a discovery, madame. You and Monsieur de Talabu."

"We don't claim anything of the sort," Susannah said.

"But we have known all about it, this famous fungus of yours, for years," Davenne said. "For years, madame. It was described two years ago by Dr. Leveillé. Two years ago, in the *Horticultural Review*."

Susannah *was* a little taken aback by that. She had seen Leveillé's name but no more.

"It is the same sort of fungus as we find on rose leaves, on peach leaves, on peas—"

"No, I don't think so," she put in.

"And Dr. Leveillé is quite firm. Absolutely firm. It does *not* feed on the vines. It does *not* cause the vine disease."

"Then where does it come from?" Susannah said. "Every ailing vine has mold on it."

"Naturally—because it is ailing!"

A general jeer at Susannah's expense.

"The mold comes from the diseased tissue of the vine," Fraissinet called out.

"But that's spontaneous generation!" Susannah said. "You are saying that life can spring from nothing."

A chorus of "No! No!"

"No. From decay. From the decay!"

There were movements of impatience, dismissive gestures. Somebody bawled out, "Leave a pound of meat in the cupboard and see if it doesn't generate life. You get a pound of blowflies—that's life enough for you."

A murmur of approval. They were all against her. Somebody else called out, "Sit down!"

Susannah raised her voice. "People were saying not long ago you could generate mice if you left a bit of cheese and some old paper in a box. Do you believe that, Monsieur Fraissinet?"

An elderly man in the audience stood up. "If it's the mold, how does a little mold live through the winter? Answer me that."

"I can't. We don't know yet."

Derisive hoots. Dr. Davenne spread his hands. "It is obvious to everyone here, madame. There is no need to confuse things. The mold lives on the decay caused by the disease. You can study the mold till you're blue in the face; it won't help cure the disease. The disease comes first and the mold after. You are only confusing things, madame."

"But I, sir, can point to a cause—the fungus. You can't point to anything. All you can say is 'disease.' But you can't show any evidence. You have no evidence."

"No evidence!" A rumble of protest went up.

"No evidence, madame?" Davenne was indignant. "When the vines are stricken all around you? No evidence?" They all bristled with indignation.

"I am speaking of scientific evidence, sir."

Angry shouts from them now. "We have all the evidence we need."

"Listening to a woman!"

"Sit down, madame!"

"Get on with the meeting."

Susannah stood her ground and Fraissinet raised his voice. "We have discussed this enough, madame. It is perfectly clear. I will repeat what we all know. As soon as a plant begins to die all sorts of parasites fasten on it. It happens with every living thing that decays. It is part of decomposition. All mortifying things go moldy. And now, madame—"

"But it's not true!" she called out. "You cannot get fungus to grow and thrive on a decaying plant. We have tried it and it can't be done. It only attacks healthy plants, because it feeds on them."

"No. No!"

Cries of "No!" from all over. They did not believe her.

They would not have it. Their voices were angry. They didn't like it and she had got their backs up by coming here, invading this male domain. But she was determined not to give way. Another bellow from the hall. "Why should your mildew come here all of a sudden? Why hasn't it come before?"

Cries of "Yes, what about that?"

Susannah said, "Nobody knows. But I should say—"

But they wouldn't have any more. They shouted her down. They waved her away.

"Get back on your horse!" A roar of amusement greeted this sally.

Susannah looked at their laughing, jeering, indignant faces and lifted her head and called out, "All right, and I'll race you a mile for a hundred francs, whoever you are. Is it done? A mile and four jumps for a hundred francs? Are we on? Get up on your feet if you're not a coward. Who is it? Some clodhopper who can't sit his horse like a man? Not man enough to beat a woman?"

The mingling laughter and jeers swelled to a roar as the men craned around to see her. She could see a scarlet face to one side, his friends urging him to get up. Yet they weren't on her side. They didn't like a woman taking it out on them like this. A woman publicly calling one of them a coward? There was something against all of them, collectively as males, in her challenge, and they disliked it. It was undignified. She had no business here in the first place. Male activity—what had it to do with her? The older men were shocked. Some of them stared at her as if she were out of her mind and plenty of them scowled.

"Be off to your home, madame!"

"Go about your business."

"Away with you, woman."

She had made a mistake in coming alone. Now under the banner the Mayor was on his feet booming that he was going to put a motion to a vote.

Susannah saw it was no use. No use at all. She turned for the door. Other men had pressed in since her arrival and she was hemmed in. Thick ranks stood between her and the door. She began to push her way out. They looked at her with disdain, as if she had made an exhibition of herself. She was no longer a *woman*—not like their wives and daughters. She was tainted, something they despised.

She pushed past them. To one side among the faces she saw Dufaud, Mornac's bailiff, the man who had come to La Guiche with the gendarmes. On the instant it was merely an unpleasant reminder, but as she saw him she noticed him exchange the flash of a glance with two young men nearby. The two began to push their way through the crush toward her. She stared. Would they dare?

She had a sudden fear of some grossness, some insult done under cover of the crush—her hair cut off, her dress, something horrible. She shrank within herself. She tried to push a way through the strong heavy bodies of the men, but they hung back sullenly. They were there in their collective male strength, she had defied them, and they were not getting out of her way. They would show her her place. The two were moving toward her. She saw she couldn't reach the door before they got to her.

"Let me through!" She pushed with all her strength.

"Just a moment, madame. This is not a circus!"

The two were only a few feet away now. One was moving to come behind her. They kept their hands down, as if they were hiding something. Surely they wouldn't injure her, cut her face.

She struggled blindly against the stolid, resentful packed protesting men. Somebody on the other side grasped her arm; she caught her breath and wrenched madly away. Two tall heavy men blocked her path, and as she tried to force a way past them she saw the nearer of the pair would reach her.

"Susannah!" She hardly dared turn, but she flashed a glance over her shoulder and saw John Blood a yard away pushing through to her.

"John." She reached back to him, still watching the other two. The next moment he had caught her hand and was beside her. The two men had seen him and simply stood still, facing the far end of the hall where the Mayor was speaking.

Susannah drooped with relief. "Please let's get out."

"Yes."

"Keep close to me, John." She was breathless. He eyed her closely, glanced suspiciously around. Holding her near him, he pushed a way through and in a moment they were outside.

It was nearly dark in the little square, only a band of pale yellowish light above the roofs. He stood looking at her intently. She was breathing hard and could feel the sweat on her face.

"Are you all right?" he asked.

"Yes. So hot in there. Lord!"

"That was no place for you."

"There were two men. I saw them with Mornac's bailiff. I was frightened they'd hurt me."

"Two of Mornac's men? Which ones?" He blazed up at once and swung around toward the hall, but she caught his arm.

"It's nothing. It's all right."

"What did they do? Did they insult you?"

"No, nothing. John, don't, for heaven's sake, make a scene. Everybody knows me here."

They stood there while she pushed the hair from her face and straightened her dress.

"Where's your carriage?" he said.

"One from the stables is supposed to come, but it probably isn't here yet."

"Well, here's mine." His driver had seen them and was coming up with the carriage. Susannah was aware of the idle groups watching, missing nothing. And who else might have slipped out of the meeting? They always saw, in so small a place, and spoke of it afterwards.

"John, I can't go with you. Everybody knows I'm here tonight and I can't be seen going off with you."

He stood facing her, the shadow half across his face, and she loved him so much she didn't know what to do. "You understand that?" she said.

"Yes."

"How did you know I was here?"

"I went to La Guiche. They told me."

"You went there!"

"I knew your husband wouldn't be there. I saw him in Bordeaux."

Duplicity! Oh it stung her all the same and she averted her face.

"I thought we would go to Bordeaux tonight—now, the two of us," he said.

Her breath was short; it seemed to come out of her in gasps she could hardly control. There was a sort of electricity between them, and she could not stand too close to him, hardly dared look at him. She was afraid he would take her hand; she was frightened of the weakness in herself.

His carriage drew up beside them, he opened the door and

bowed to her formally. "Let him take you home. He'll come back for me."

"Thank you." She got in.

He shut the door, stepped forward and spoke to the driver while she sat in the carriage and raged in her heart, raged at herself, at her weakness, her cowardice. This was how she fought—this was how she steered her individual soul—look at her! She wasn't brave enough to defy them even for love. She raged at her own mean narrowness of heart. A mere exhibitionist, coming to meetings like this, showing off, talking like a man. But when it came to the courage to follow her heart— look at her! She was disgusted with herself. Be careful, worry what they would think. She was as bad as the rest of them.

She sat and fumed. He was still speaking to the driver, and she wished he would get it over with, whatever he was saying, so they could drive away. She loved him and she didn't have the courage to take him. She was ashamed of herself. Love a man, but love him truly and fully. Not this half-love of looks and frightened longings. Drifting about the house for days thinking of him, dreaming about him, unable to get him out of her mind; and then, when it came to it—no! She was disgusted with herself.

The carriage began to move, she saw him lift his hat and he was gone. She sat back in the carriage, slumped back moody and wretched, her face sullen and dark, her soul brooding, furious with herself, furious at everything, furious at the thought of the men at the meeting, the stubborn, sullen stupidity, the rejection of a mere woman's word. Oh, God, what was she to do? The most dangerous thing a married woman could do here was to have a love affair with another man. It would brand her for good. It would destroy her forever with these people. She would be contaminated, finished. They would never let her live it down and remain in bourgeois society. And if she tried to, they would humiliate her. The defense of society, that was what they would invoke. We must defend society, they would say. Their precious small-minded society might be wrecked by a little love! She was tortured and maddened at her failure to grasp life as she felt she must.

So she raged as the carriage jolted through the village streets. They lurched over the cobbles. Presently, out of her sickened fury, her blindness to everything, she was aware that they were in some difficulty. The carriage had stopped, and she glanced out and saw that they were in a narrow dark street which seemed to be a dead end.

What was happening? Oh, she didn't care! Then after a minute she looked out the window again. The driver was trying to maneuver in the confined space and had got the carriage stuck. She didn't see how it had been possible to miss his way in the village, but he had managed it. More rocking about as he tried to work free, then he got down and came to the window, a short young man with a lock of black hair over one eye and his hat tipped back.

"I'm sorry, ma'am, I took a wrong turn. If you'll get down a minute I can turn around." She got out, her mood not improved by it, and stood a few yards away by a blank wall while he took the horse's head and seesawed the carriage around to the accompaniment of great creaks and crunchings. He was apologetic and now she was past caring about anything. She climbed back inside and sat there moodily, and they drove, slowly now, until he found the road and headed for La Guiche.

Wearily the prospect of sitting alone in the empty house loomed before her. Francis would surely not be back. Madame Gautier might return late. She would eat her solitary supper. Well, she must face it. She must face her lack of courage to live. Her fine free-roaming American soul would have to be soothed by embroidery!

They rolled on between the dark vineyards. The musty smell of oïdium came in on the night air. And she began to feel homesick. She ached for Philadelphia. For the first time since leaving she was genuinely homesick. Ah, homesick she was for America, yes. The disreputable side of her aunts' lives did not matter to her now, she saw them differently. Yes, the memory of that raffish, raucous, unscrupulous male-filled life gave her a touch of nostalgia tonight.

How she had hated it once, despised Aunt Maxine's and Aunt Ady's sordid careers. Some of it, in the early days, had been not much better than straight prostitution, until they had learned what a woman could do and must on no account do if she were to get on. Until they had learned how to behave, how to move in society, to use their wit, their originality, their native brass, as well as their bodies. And they had learned fast while their looks were still good.

321

She had always thought their manner with men and their flattering of them grotesque. How could any man believe in such shallowness for a moment? Yet men had. Numberless men! Men of a special sort, men who were strangely and willfully and deliberately blind to a woman's childish tricks and bogus caprices and ridiculous maneuvers and exploitation and faithlessness, the sort of men to whom consorting with successful ladies of the town like Aunt Maxine and Aunt Ady was irresistible—high life! They liked the gamey tang. And both aunts had proved their skill by making "society" marriages, both to bankers.

But they had been sweet to her mother and so generous. They had always accepted that her mother, the third of their trio of sisters, was different, was gentler. Oh, no doubt in her young days she had had adventures too, but not of the same sort. And though they had regarded her marriage to Robert Fielding as a disaster, because he was a charming, good-looking waster, they had not interfered; and when Fielding had deserted her and their daughter Susannah, the wife already touched by consumption, Aunt Maxine and Aunt Ady had come forward quite naturally and looked after them.

For years they had kept their pale, slender younger sister in and out of sanatoriums in Europe and at home. They had farmed out the growing Susannah between them or with acquaintances, taking her as a child on expensive holidays with them, once to Europe, to the mountains at Davos in Switzerland, always with some rich American or European male in the background.

Between them they had brought her up and paid for her education. To Susannah her mother had become a pale remote figure, seen only at rare intervals. Only after her mother's death in Europe, only then had the aunts made it clear that they expected her to follow the family calling, to become a male-hunter. And it was late in the day to begin her training, they had let her know! Her sheltered youth must now give way to serious business.

When she had refused, when she had spurned the men they pushed in front of her, they told her what an idiot she was. How they berated her. A woman's life had one aim—to get men. To use men. To carve herself a situation in "society" where she could continue to use men and to receive the peculiar male homage that came to men users—for some men would have no other kind of woman.

No! Susannah had said. And Aunt Ady had disgustedly turned her back on her. Aunt Maxine, the softer of the two, had continued to keep her. The chafing years of dependence on both aunts had often made her miserable. And then Francis Gautier had appeared and she had fallen in love with him. Marriage for love? Well, of course, it was a foolish notion to both aunts, but young Gautier seemed to be moderately well-off and what better could you expect for Susannah? And so it had gone through.

And now she wished she could see them both. She wished she were back for a while in that tall house full of plush and velveteen and frosted gas lamps on Spruce Street, listening to Aunt Maxine's whiskey-hoarse gossipy talk, being pampered by Miss Rosa, driving out to call on Aunt Ady and her comically grand snob of a husband who had a secret passion for high-buttoned boots.

All at once the carriage gave a jolt and swerved violently. She grabbed for support. Outside against the night sky a horse-man veered from the shadow across their path. The carriage jerked to a halt. She heard the driver's voice, the clatter of hoofs. As she leaned out, the horseman sprang to the ground, slapped the horse hard across the rump and sent it trotting back down the road toward the village. And before he had spun around and faced her she knew it was John Blood.

He pulled the door open, put his foot up and stood there, his coat open, neckcloth a bit undone, the shadow across his face —as he must have stood, she thought, on those wild raiding nights in Ireland.

"I think, madame, you lack an escort."

"Whose horse was that?"

"I borrowed him in the village, so I'm damned if I know."

And now, of course, she understood why the driver had "missed the way." She couldn't help smiling. Her heart was beating in a sort of triumph with subdued unbearable excitement.

"And now, my love, we'll ride to Bordeaux so fast the devil himself won't catch us."

He leapt in, slammed the door, and they started off. As he put his arms around her the horse broke into a gallop.

She woke up in the night and he was lying with eyes open in the dark watching her, one arm across her. The moonlight came in faintly through the window.

"Haven't you slept?"

"No."

A pause, then she said, "I meant to ask you about Tom Mowbray. What did you mean in that note?"

"He may be an English spy. As I told you, somebody was following me that day and it was best not to speak to you. I noticed Mowbray in a doorway there, on the Place—which was odd. And I'd already seen him in Paris when I was there. Perhaps he's been told to watch me. I don't know." He spoke quietly, without much concern.

He bent over and kissed her and she wound her arms around him and pressed him to her. "I need you. I need your strength. It's going to be much worse than before now."

"I want to overturn the world for you, to do great things. That's what you make me feel," he said.

Later she opened her eyes and saw him by the window. She got out of bed and went over and he took her by the shoulders, holding her hard.

"Get dressed. We'll ride to Nantes and get a boat for America. Go to the West and have a free life, away from this."

She shook her head. "You know I can't. I can't run away."

"The two of us, in the West. Across the Missouri. A mule train and a wagon out there. We'll conquer the world."

She pressed her face to his shoulder. "It's no good. There is no other country for us. Another country wouldn't mean freedom. It would be the same anywhere."

"You want to live. We'll live our hearts' desire—that's the only freedom there is. Here they'll shrivel you up and put you in black clothes and thin out our blood and your feelings. But we can strike out for a new world. Shed all this."

"We can't. I am married and I can't leave my husband. I pledged myself to him willingly, lovingly, and I won't go back on it." Then she added softly, "But it isn't simply the pledge. It's my heart too."

He lifted her face. "But we exist. You have to reach for life sometime or you'll drift. I love you. I want to take you with me, Susannah."

"And I love you with my heart and my body. I *am* yours.

I am yours absolutely. No . . . no, that's not true, because I'm his too. And I can't wreck his life to make mine. You can't live life like that. Other people are in the world with you. We met too late, you and I, that's all."

"You don't believe that. That's not you. Our life is together."

She held him tight, gripping his arms, unable to bear it. "Don't . . . don't." She averted her head, hiding her face, but holding him. Then she broke away. "What time is it?" she said.

"A little past three."

"Then I must go. I must get back before the house is astir. John . . ." She held him close to her.

It was still dark when they went down to the waiting carriage, a light closed fly. She wouldn't let him come with her. He held her in a long kiss. Then she climbed into the carriage and the driver whipped up.

"Hurry!" she called to him. She sat shrinking and huddled up and chilly in the early freshness, staring out at the dark as they flew back to La Guiche.

9

Francis was home all the following week. He was lively, good-humored and attentive to Susannah, which made the torment worse for her. And she, responding out of guilt, clung to him and they became closer than they had been for months. She loved him. And love can't be uncommanded any more than it can be commanded. And so in the night she clung to him as if she were afraid of being wrenched from him bodily, torn from him, and he was amazed at the intensity of her passion.

The days passed. He said nothing more about the deed of renunciation, but she knew he would speak of it again. It was something in suspense over them but held off by their new closeness. And yet in her soul she was afraid this might be a final flare-up of passion between them before its dying, and so she clung to him all the more.

The second week of August came, the weather was sultry with occasional early-morning showers. Susannah's garden was forlorn and rather neglected with only geraniums and petunias showing. In the vineyard Francis kept the men spraying or dusting the few grapes that remained, but they had little heart for it.

On the last evening of the week, Susannah was sitting alone sewing in the room upstairs. Francis had gone to talk to Josserand at his cottage after dinner and was still there. Madame Gautier had retired. It was a still, windless night; the house was quiet. Lad barked a couple of times, then stopped, and she paid no attention. The door to the stairs was open and she heard the clock in the hall below strike eleven. She decided to go to bed. As she put down her work and stood up she heard somebody cough hoarsely on the drive outside. Francis? She paused. Another cough, muffled this time. Probably one of the workmen coming in late.

She carried the lamp downstairs, turned along the hall to shut the front door and saw that the lamp over the entrance was out. The door was wide open as usual and as she swung it to, she saw two or three figures moving against the darkness beyond.

"Frank?" No answer. She held up the lamp and saw them on the grass on the other side of the drive, three men standing still, heads turned toward her, three roughly dressed workmen, two with straw hats and one bareheaded.

"Yes, what is it?" she called out. She stepped out onto the porch, then onto the gravel to see better, and turned up the lamp. They exchanged shifty glances. One had something in a bundle and she caught the dull glint of a pruning hook hanging from another's belt. She knew most of the workmen in the parish by sight and didn't recognize these three. She held up the lamp to get more light on them.

" 'Tis nothing," one of them said.

"What do you want?"

Silence, then, "We come to burn a fagot or two, my fine beauty, that's all. And a bit o' feathers." A rough peasant voice.

"At this time of night? What for?"

"Against the blight," called another.

She saw they were tipsy. "Come back in the morning," she called. They didn't answer but edged a little farther off into the dark.

"Where do you come from?" she called.

The biggest of them gestured vaguely. "Yonder, from the village." They halted again, facing her. The next minute the big man who had spoken last detached himself from the others and swayed toward her. She stood her ground and he pulled up. "Eh, ye want to get the blight off, don't ye?"

"Who told you to come here?"

"Who told us? Ah!" He stepped a little closer. " 'Twas here the blight started, wasn't it? The devil's hereabout, that's what. A light, low down, creeping down across the land here at moon-

327

rise. The people have seen it every night. It spreads the blight over in the night. It'll not go on when we're done."

One of the others turned away and called out a low monosyllable and Susannah saw two more men moving in the darkness beyond toward the vines. Was it some mad superstition? Had they been drinking and decided on an expedition to lay the devil? Or was there something else?

She glanced quickly around. The outbuildings beyond the house were in darkness, no sign of Francis or Josserand. Now the other two men had drifted back into the dark and she could not see the farther pair beyond.

A little breeze lifted out of the night and made her shiver. She held the lamp up, the foremost man had retreated a pace into the dark. He seemed to be edging away. She turned and hurried back to the house. Inside she swung the front door to and bolted it, then ran through to the back courtyard. She hurried past the vatting room and as she turned the corner ran into Francis coming back.

"Heavens, what's the matter?" he said. "Why aren't you in bed?"

Quickly she told him. He had been drinking. She could smell Josserand's rough brandy on him.

"How many of them do you say?"

"I don't know. I saw five."

"Oh . . . my dear . . ." he played it down at once, minimized it, put his arm over her shoulder and wanted to turn back to the house. "It's nothing. You must have made a mistake. It was probably some good fellows from the village having a joke with you."

But she wouldn't go, shook off his arm. "It wasn't a joke and they weren't from the village, I'll swear. They were strangers and it was something underhand. Get some of the men out and see if they're still on the property. If you won't I will. That dog! No good at all, hardly barked."

He protested that it was silly, but she made him rouse out Josserand and some of the hands. They went around with lanterns and their dogs and found nothing, not a trace of the men.

"I told you, just some of the good people from the village, that's all," Francis said. "You imagine things."

Two days passed. On the third morning Susannah was up

328

earlier than usual. She unbolted the front door, pulled it open and stopped still. Lying under the porch was an ugly mess—a black cock with its guts hanging out and next to it a dead bat, a toad and an arrangement of sticks and stones. She stared, thinking at first it was something brought there by the dog. The bright sensible morning sunlight shone down.

And then the import gradually came to her as she stared at it. It had been placed there deliberately and it was meant to be some sort of curse. It was horrible. And she remembered the man saying that the blight had started here, at La Guiche. Was this what they were saying now in the parish? Was this what they believed? In spite of herself she shuddered. La Guiche and the foreign woman. She could see their heads nodding, their weathered creased-up old eyes narrowing, the silent oblique glances.

She shut the door, went through to the kitchen and took a broom, dustpan and pail of water. Emilie, still sleepy, wanted to know what needed doing, but Susannah sent her about her business. She cleared the mess up herself and said nothing more about it to anyone. Yet it disturbed her. It was frightening to think of them creeping in at night, right up to the house.

And though she spoke of it to nobody, though it was unlikely that anybody else of the household had seen it, yet a strange atmosphere seemed to lie about the house and the vineyard. Susannah shook herself and told herself it was imagination. But it remained. All next day and the day after she noticed Josserand wandering about looking uneasy. And at dusk, when she went out to the vines, everything was so still in the leaden air, so silent and still, as if the place were waiting. The gray moldy vines were oppressive. She looked toward the workpeople's cottages; not a man or woman was outdoors, not a light was showing.

That night Francis was away again. Susannah had dinner with Madame Gautier, played piquet with her afterwards and they both went to bed at ten o'clock. Susannah read for a while, then blew the lamp out and turned over to sleep.

She woke up to deep silence. She did not know what the time was. Nothing stirred. She lay unmoving, aware that something had awakened her. She was wide awake staring at the dark room. Something had wakened her but was now still.

Silence. She sensed the open space of the night outside, as she had on the first night she had lain in this bed, the open dark space now full of decay, the decay of the vines. Everything was quiet.

At last she turned drowsily again to sleep, then heard a faint creak outside, like the creak of a wooden handle, and a quick whisper. Her heart gave a bump. She was awake again in a second, threw back the covers, got out of bed and peered through the crack in the shutter. Nothing visible in the dark.

Quickly she found her dress on the chair, slipped it over her head and, not stopping to button it, hurried on tiptoe downstairs. She felt the sick tightening of fear in herself, afraid for some reason they would try to set fire to the house. It was a horror to her, fire. At the bottom of the stairs she thought they might be there, just on the other side of the front door, and she stood poised and staring toward it, listening. Nothing.

Through to the kitchen she felt her way. It was pitch dark. She groped around, knocked something off the table which fell with a crash—the lamp. Blindly she groped for the mantel, found matches and lit the small second lamp. Glass and oil over the floor—couldn't bother about that. There, above the mantelpiece, was Francis's gun that he had bought in Paris. Often enough she had watched him load it—he called it "a newfangled breechloader"—and once, shooting at crows, he had shown her how to fire it. But now as she reached up for it and took it down it was awkward and unwieldy to her and she was uncertain what to do.

Somewhere ready here in the kitchen were the cartridges, she knew that, for now and then there were pheasants in the vines at the back. Impatiently she pulled open the cabinet doors, then she saw the box of cartridges on the top shelf.

Bent over the gun, she brushed back her loose hair. Wait a minute . . . yes. Now she remembered. You had to be sure to get the little pin on the cartridge pointing upward so that it would slip into the notch there. There—with trembling fingers she pressed the cartridges into place, shut the breech. The gun was full of menace to her and she handled it gingerly. Leaving the lamp where it was, she opened the kitchen door and slipped out into the dark.

The air was warm and still, the same oppressive stillness

everywhere. Her bare feet made no sound and her brown dress would be invisible. At the corner of the house she peered out into the dark. Toward the left the black mass of trees cut against the sky, farther left she could guess the outlines of the meadow and fences. To the right lay the low undulation of the vineyard. Perhaps they were close to the house again, setting one of their horrible curses, or a fire? Again the fire horror made her heart thud. She looked along the front of the house, straining to see anything moving, but could make out nothing. All was quiet and still.

Holding the gun across her body, she left the shelter of the house and walked out into the open. As she reached the grass she saw black moving on black in the nearer vines. Somebody there. Her heart was drumming. She moved forward a few more paces. The figure stood up—now she could see it—and began to move slowly away.

Susannah lifted the gun, took aim and pulled the trigger. The explosion blasted the stillness and the butt bumped back against her shoulder. When she looked again the black figure had gone. She stood there shaky but determined. She could hear movement somewhere beyond, and the price makers' dogs by the cottages had begun to bark. Then she saw another figure closer to on the left. She lifted the gun and fired again. Another echoing crash. She stared at the spot and saw a swift movement, then nothing. She had forgotten to bring more cartridges! She stood there a moment longer, no fear now, then turned, picked up her skirt and ran back to the house. As she reached the kitchen door she saw Joseph in his nightshirt at the entrance to the servants' passage.

"Madame!" He stared at her and down at the broken glass and oil on the floor.

"Go and get Josserand. Quick! And the men. There's somebody outside."

He stared and she realized her hair was loose and her dress undone. She clutched the front of her dress together.

"But, madame, you can't—"

"Do as I say!" she stormed at him. "And tell them to keep back till you hear me shoot or until I call you. I don't want to hit them. You understand?"

"Yes, ma'am." He disappeared into the passage.

It took her maddeningly long to reload the gun, then she hastened outside again. She crossed to the grass, ran along toward the meadow and the road, and almost at once saw someone moving away down to her right.

She pulled up, fired, stood watching. Silence. She squatted down, gun ready, scanning the dark. Everything remained silent and still except for the barking and yelping of the dogs, echoed by dogs farther off in other vineyards now. At last she stood up. They had gone; they must have run through the vines below.

She hastened back to the house, angry now. Joseph was waiting with Laverne, Balavoine, Jean and four of the other men with lanterns and dogs. Josserand had refused to turn out. They had all been alarmed by the shooting and pressed around her uneasily with questions.

"They were in the vines. Get out there, all of you. Some of you go down to the bottom, some at the back. And hurry!"

Laverne took charge, they spread out and searched all around. In the kitchen Susannah found Madame Gautier standing in her wrapper watching Emilie clearing up the spilled oil and glass.

"The whole household up in the middle of the night!"

"It's all right, Mother. I'm sorry you were disturbed. I heard some intruders but the men are out there now."

"Shooting guns! What is the meaning of it?"

"I heard somebody creeping about. They were here the other night, some men. Don't worry. It's all right."

Madame Gautier stood there, wrapped in her dark stony bitterness, her hair gleaming darkly red, her discolored lips clamped, her face blotchy with patches of tiny red veins. Her eyes were old and hating, centerless like the eyes of an American Indian. Her lips trembled. Why have you come here? Why are you usurping my place? she screamed in silence at Susannah. She turned. "Come, Emilie," she said and went out.

Susannah was still worked up by the excitement. She clutched the front of her dress to, went out and watched the moving lanterns, hearing the men's voices and the dogs barking in the stillness. At last she went indoors again, made some tea, sat down and waited.

It was three o'clock before the men trooped back. There had

evidently been six or eight interlopers, Laverne said, as far as they could judge in the dark from the bootmarks across the muddy patch by the lake. They had plastered one row of vines with blood, then hacked half of them down and broken a lot of laths. In addition they had spilled several bucketsful of bullock blood at different points of the vineyard, as if marking it out in some cabalistic fashion, and made piles of bloody feathers and sticks.

"Very well. Don't talk about it," Susannah said.

They eyed her, nodded silently. And of course they would talk about it, she knew. Inevitably.

"But what does it *mean?*" she said to Laverne after the rest had gone.

Laverne wasn't one of the superstitious kind. He seemed indifferent and shrugged. "I don't know, ma'am."

But *she* knew. At least she thought she knew. Somebody, in some insane way, was trying to make La Guiche the scapegoat, spreading tales of witches and curses on the place. Mornac? As revenge? Oh, he'd relish revenge, a man like Mornac. And all so sly, all this—spillings of blood, curses, rumors. All so shadowy. Didn't it smell of revenge? Bad for them, at any rate. Bad, bad.

She went up to bed but knew she wouldn't sleep, so she sat and wrote a letter to Maisie in Vicksburg. By the time she had finished it she was calmer, and with the sky lightening outside she got into bed and slept.

In the morning the sun shone gloriously. The air was alive with golden light; high golden curving light soared up as if the whole country were under a great high gleaming dome.

Francis arrived just before noon in a hired carriage, and when Susannah went out to greet him he threw his arms around her, kissed her, lifted her off her feet and whirled her around as if he hadn't seen her for a month.

"Stop it, you idiot!" She laughed.

He put her down and kissed her again. "Are you all right? . . . Eh? What? . . . Last night?"

He kept his arm around her waist as she told him. Only slowly did his happy smile fade. They walked together, heads bent forward, down the drive.

"You really did shoot at them?"

"Well, my God, I should think so! They chopped down half a row of vines. I don't know what they wouldn't have done. And this is the third time they've been here."

His eyes hardened on her, his face creased with doubt.

"I had them clear away the mess, the other things, since they're afraid of it," she said. "I've never seen such people for superstition. Octavie's half dead with it, even been hinting she'd like to go away for a while."

"Who else saw them?"

"Nobody. I was the only one."

He shot her another oblique glance, hating to face it. They pulled up at the corner of the vatting room and stood looking out over the vines while she told him about the things she had found under the porch.

"You didn't mention this before," he said, frowning again.

"I thought it was something isolated and we wouldn't hear any more. But, Frank, somebody is obviously spreading rumors in the village, and it's bad. What I'm afraid of is fire, some mad-man burning the house down while we're all asleep."

"No . . . no. They wouldn't do that. Too scared of fire here. I'll see Laverne."

After lunch Susannah changed into a thin muslin dress with half-length sleeves and went out behind the house where it was coolest.

She was in one of her ill-at-ease moods, impatient with her problems, her self-contradictions. She hated the idea of drifting, wanted her life to have direction—that was the old Protestant teaching that had been so incongruously grafted onto her up-bringing at Aunt Maxine's. Yet she clung to her essential wild-ness and hated the idea of turning into a bourgeois wife with her spirit flattened. She wanted to be able to submit to a rush of feel-ing and not be afraid of it. Damn reasonableness! Give her spirit and a bit of dash. Yes, and a raw edge to life—that was a touch Aunt Maxine would recognize! But she did miss it. It had all been there, in America. And only now, in this other place, did she feel its attraction, the rawness and danger of America, the sheer crude gusto and vigor, the space, the raw vitality. There was a great deal to that. Yes, she needed it, this American spirit, this simple yet mysterious compound which meant so much of America to her.

Here, in some way, it wasn't full-blooded life; it was half-measure, half-feeling. She was checked, pulled up short. Something kept saying, Don't! Careful! Don't! to her all the time. Perhaps it was the English influence, as John Lovell swore it was. "That's the legacy of the English, make no mistake," he had said to her. "That's England all over."

But La Guiche meant so much to her now. The skill of the winemaking, the striving for perfection, she loved that. She loved the house, the sunlit stone, the cool dim interior of the vatting room, the smell of the wine, the great gleaming vats. She loved this cool space behind the house where a garden should be laid out. In less than a month the broom would be out again, the forest and the Landes a blaze of yellow, and the ferns would be spreading their marvelous earthy smell. She thought of the great dunes and the ocean and the tossing waves of the Bassin. It was all beautiful to her, she loved it all.

She sat on in the cool shade. Gradually her mood changed. Jean appeared and did some desultory hoeing in the one flower-bed as he talked to her; he always liked to work near her. Yet, she noticed, he rarely asked her about the United States; he was essentially incurious and self-sufficient like most of the French. He would be quite content to spend his life in Cantenac.

A breeze was coming up, announcing a storm, and presently she went inside. From the salon she heard a carriage arrive, then Abel-Cherubin's voice and Francis saying, "Yes, come in."

A moment later the door of the salon opened and Francis came in. "Oh, Sue, here. I forgot to give you this. I met the postman on the way in this morning." It was a letter from Aunt Maxine.

Abel-Cherubin and Regis had followed him in, and when Abel-Cherubin saw her he checked. But he and Regis both came over and embraced her with cold formality—nothing could stop the kisses!—then Abel-Cherubin turned around to Francis, pulled a newspaper from his pocket and flung it on the table.

"What does this mean?" He glared at Francis.

Susannah went up and peered over Francis's shoulder. It was the *Courrier de la Gironde*, the Bordeaux newspaper, and ringed in red ink was an annoucement.

Regular departures alternate Mondays & Fridays
at 7 a.m.
by the steamship

AMIABLE ROSE

1st Class with bunk
1st Class without bunk
2nd Class

Tickets & Inquiries for freight & passage:
New Steamship Company
(Directors Geo. Gaveau & F. Gautier)
19 Place de la Bourse, Bordeaux

"Oh, you saw that." Francis gave his quick embarrassed little smile, cleared his throat. "Our new venture."

She looked up at him; his face had reddened. She was astounded. So *this* was it! This was the reason for the absences, the days in Bordeaux, the sudden interest in ships, his "vocation." Really! Susannah gazed at his bright cheerful face as if she were discovering him afresh, the eagerness, the enthusiasm, the voluntary blindness. Never face a fact! Oh, the capacity for self-delusion which she was still discovering. And the capacity for secrecy! After all, he hadn't breathed a word.

"Your new venture!" Abel-Cherubin shifted impatiently from one leg to another.

"As a matter of fact that announcement's misleading because it's. . . . it's premature. We've been meaning to announce it but we've had to put it off and the *Courrier* got mixed up—fools they are—and put this in too soon. But, well, yes, there it is. That's the idea." He put on a broad smile.

"We understand you *own* this vessel," Abel-Cherubin said carefully. His head was thrust forward and he glanced at Regis.

"Yes. And you know, she's a little beauty. You really must all come down and see her. I was waiting till we were ready, but you must all come."

"And where did the money come from?" Abel-Cherubin asked.

"Oh, well, you see . . ." Francis's eyes went quickly from one to the other of the men. "I'm only a sort of silent partner, practically nothing. Just my name really. I've known Gaveau for years, as you know. It's really his enterprise. He found the vessel; he's a shipping agent. Very quick fellow. Very able. I've just been helping with a few ideas, that's all."

They eyed him closely. "It's Gaveau's money, you say?"

"Yes. I mean, I . . . we . . . I'm just in nominally, as a friend."

"For how much?" Regis asked.

"Of course we're expecting to grow. This is only a modest beginning."

"For how much?"

"Bound to grow. And you must come and see her. I said to Georges the other day, 'We must always have one *Amiable Rose* in the fleet, just for luck's sake, to remind us of the beginning.' " He grinned again, but he was flushed and obviously bothered.

"The fleet?" Abel-Cherubin said. "Your business is growing vines, isn't it? This is your main venture, La Guiche."

"Allow me to know my own business, Abel-Cherubin."

"But it is, isn't it?"

"No, not necessarily. I don't see things like that at all."

"Then who is to run La Guiche?" Abel-Cherubin said.

"Run it? Why, it's running. It's running, isn't it?" Francis said pettishly. "I mean, all right, one has to keep a general eye on it, granted. But a fellow doesn't have to go around seeing if every vine's been properly pruned, check to see if they've taken the insects off, sit up all night hoping it won't freeze. Waste of time. I mean, one doesn't have to hang around everlastingly. We've got the staff, we've got the people. All they need is a general eye, that's all."

"And that is your idea of how to manage the property—a general eye?"

"Manage the property! Anybody would think it's a fine art." He was heated, his face pink.

"So that's the way you see it?"

"But why not? This is a going concern. Largely a matter of routine. I mean, I don't see why a man with a bent for other things, a bent for business—"

"Meaning yourself?"

"Meaning myself. Yes! I don't see why he shouldn't devote

337

himself to his business career and have his vineyard as a side interest. Don't see why not at all. What most people do, in fact."

Susannah was dismayed, she had never heard him speak like this before. Francis looked uncomfortably hot and worked up.

"Just have La Guiche as a hobby sort of thing?" Abel-Cherubin put in sarcastically. "It's very important for those who have a share to know."

"Nobody's saying that. No need to distort it. As for your share, I put enough hours in here and never get a sou for managing *your* share, Abel-Cherubin. Never a centime!"

Abel-Cherubin popped his lips in indignation.

"But La Guiche is now just a side interest to you?" Regis asked.

"But damn it, look at the neighbors! Half of them are in business in Bordeaux or somewhere else. You don't see the Pereires running down here every five minutes. You don't see the Scullys, you don't see the Laffan Jenningses. Other things to do. Busy with business. And I don't see why I must be limited to this if other opportunities present themselves." Now he was angry.

"So you agree that what we need here is a good estate manager?" Regis put in. "You agree?"

"And I may have to put one in. I may very well." Francis drew himself up importantly, lifted his chin. "If we expand the line fast enough, Gaveau and I. I may have to."

"Better do it now then," Regis said. "Save us a lot of time. I'll find a good man."

"I'll find a man when I want one, Regis, and not before. I'm in control of this property and nobody else, above all not you." He turned on his heel and stalked out.

Blank silence. They stood there, not often alone together the three of them. Abel-Cherubin stared at Regis. Regis stared back. They both glanced at Susannah, who looked away. She was bewildered, didn't know what to think. He had behaved like a boy caught at some mischief and had obviously been terribly embarrassed at having it come out like this.

From the far door Francis's voice bellowed, "Susannah!"

As she swept out she heard Regis say to Abel-Cherubin, "I told you we'd better get to the bottom of it."

Outside, Francis said pettishly, "You heard what went on.

338

Why didn't you come out with me?"

"I'm sorry."

"When I leave the room after a discussion of that sort I expect my wife to follow me! You understand?" He was angry, caught and angry. "Do you understand?"

"Yes."

"Then why not do it without being called, making me look a fool!"

"Don't take it out on me," she said quietly but firmly. He always had to have someone to turn on when he was angry, always a scapegoat. But she was sorry for him all the same. She looked at him tenderly, at his flushed, angry face, hating to see him unhappy. Quickly she put her arm around him. He shook her off, but she persisted, took his arm, pressed close to him.

"Frank, darling, never mind. Don't be upset. It's all right." Like talking to a sulky child, a child she loved. "Don't be upset, darling. They'll come around." She kissed his cheek.

He stalked out of the house, ignoring her, though she stayed at his side. He marched down the drive, a silent stubbornness over him now. He had wanted to give them all a happy surprise with his *Amiable Rose*, announce it to them with pride. He had obviously been so happy about it, but now his misery moved her. She couldn't bear it; she wanted to save him from it. "Dear Frank, never mind. Don't worry," she kept saying.

The storm wind was bucketing in from the west, banging in gusts, and the sky was surging with dark clouds. She clutched at her hair with her free hand. She kept asking him questions which he sulkily ignored.

"Do you think you'll be able to start the service soon?"

He shrugged, still silent and brooding.

"I'd love to see her. It's a lovely name, the *Amiable Rose*. Makes you think of a nice plump blond girl, happily unvirtuous."

He gave a little snort of laugh through his nose.

"It'll be good luck, I'm sure it will."

He looked at her quickly, looked away, then back again. His eyes shone. "Yes, isn't it a good name? Isn't it a *lovely* name? And I tell you, she's a beauty. You will come down, Sue, won't you?"

"Of course. I can't wait. So exciting!"

"They'll be all right, the others, when they see her. And it really is a chance in a thousand. She was a bargain, and ours will be the first steamer service to Spain out of Bordeaux. So we'll be pioneers."

"When do you start?"

"Oh, it won't be long. The Spaniards are being a bit slow, that's all. But they'll be coming through. They can't refuse us permission."

The wind was tousling his hair and he looked so boyish and fresh that she couldn't help loving him. He would have to be left to his *Amiable Rose*, she saw that. He would have to go through with it. And La Guiche was her responsibility now. Yes, she knew that. All his talk of being "in control" meant letting the place drift. She couldn't do that. She loved it too much. She was too proud of it. And she was too proud in herself.

10

The visit to the steamer, however, was put off. The *Amiable Rose* wasn't quite ready, Francis said; and he turned his attention back to La Guiche. It was really an acknowledgment that he had been neglecting the vineyard, which of course he would never admit openly. Never admit a weakness was his motto. And the fresh burst of interest was his way of saving appearances and gaining a little time; she was sure he would soon be wrapped up in the mad steamer scheme again. Meanwhile, the workpeople were arriving for the harvest.

The oïdium had devastated the whole Médoc, and La Guiche was as bad as the rest—hardly any sound grapes. They took on a few people and gathered what they could. Francis tried to buy from the local peasants but found that the Bordeaux brokers and merchants had got there long before him. And even when the wine was made, it proved to be sharp and thin, a bad year.

So money began to be tight again at La Guiche. Francis doled out a louis or two at a time. When Susannah said she couldn't manage like that, he told her to run up bills. She refused; they quarreled. And she began to feel that under the surface things were radically wrong. She woke at night with fears of imminent disaster. Why couldn't they have it out? There was no answer. He always eluded her about money.

And he insisted that Gaveau was financing the steamer scheme; but he obviously had *some* money in it. Where had it come from? They had had hardly any wine to sell for two years and no spare cash. She pressed him, and he shouted at her, told her it was his business, to leave him alone. Then he got moody and wouldn't speak to her. She screamed at him. They became strained and hateful to each other. At last she managed to get an answer out of him—his mother had lent him some money. And she wondered if that were true.

She was glad, therefore, when Constance Canning came back from England with husband and niece at the end of September and they resumed their friendship. She felt exhausted with Francis, as if at an end of something, and Constance's return eased her isolation. She liked Constance, though she thought her terribly lazy and spoiled. The Cannings had heard about the Mornac affair from friends in England. Constance called him a brute, said she loathed him, and from the way she spoke Susannah suspected that Mornac had insulted her on some occasion, perhaps tried to take liberties with her.

So now Susannah dragged Constance out of bed on fine mornings to come and ride. The early October days were glorious in the forest, with the brown and ocher ferns against the gray-green pines. Constance rode well, though rather demurely. She wouldn't jump but did let rip now and then in a gallop when Susannah shamed her. Susannah hoped they would get closer, for she had no woman friend except Louise, who was really too old and too crushed, poor thing.

But too often Susannah would call for Constance, walk Red into the Cannings' forecourt in the early morning, and Constance would send her chambermaid down to excuse her. Sorry, not today, not this morning. One whole week, then most of another. Susannah put it down to her indolence, but gradually it dawned on her that there were other reasons. She called for Constance one last time and Constance "couldn't come." That afternoon, when they happened to meet in the village and Susannah joked about it, Constance confessed that Byam, her husband, had put his foot down. "It was . . . well, he has his notions, but it was the riding style, really."

"The riding . . ." Susannah frowned. Oh, of course, the riding *astride*. Indecent! Susannah understood. As Susannah knew, Constance said, they had Byam's young niece staying with them and Byam was responsible for her. She *knew* Susannah would understand.

Constance was quite cool and self-possessed about it, not at

342

all embarrassed, which was rather a sign of friendship, if any-thing, Susannah decided. Oh, yes, Susannah said, she under-stood. She tried to shrug it off, but it was a blow. Obviously the word had gone around. Also, her appearance at the village meet-ing had aroused shocked comment.

The Cannings, she knew, were friendly with the Onslows in the cliquey English way. And Coote Onslow, for all his apparent bonhomie, was a great snob. "Frightfully keen on good form," his wife had said to Susannah one day. Once in the Onslows' drawing room Susannah had peeped into the little brown-paper folder marked *House Rules* kept for guests.

All guests staying in the house are asked to read the House Rules and initial the attached chit.
1. Careful with water.
2. If there is no water, ask Host or Hostess to have cistern filled. No one else uses the pump to cis-tern.
3. Please do NOT pick the grapes. Table grapes will be served, in season, at dinner.
4. Promptness at meals will be appreciated.
5. Hours of quiet. Quiet please on the back terrace after lunch until Hostess appears.
6. People staying in the house are asked to respect local customs. We live here.

And one afternoon she had seen Coote Onslow round on Sarah, his fourteen-year-old daughter, in a fury when she ap-peared in a favorite little frock which had got an inch or two too short for her. "Get indoors and change those clothes at once! I will not have it!" Purple and shaking. In a high passion! The social consciousness. What would people think. *We live here!*

But oh, Lord. Finally Susannah couldn't be bothered about it; life was too short. Why should she take notice of the English? And so she accepted Coote Onslow's buoyant outward display of cordiality as if it were genuine, knowing quite well he con-sidered her a blatant, vulgar creature, a mere American. And Constance Canning called at La Guiche now and then.

One evening Francis came back from Bordeaux and told her laughingly that John Lovell was in a great row with Simcoe Baynes. "Do you know what he did, friend Lovell? He up and complained about Baynes to the Chamber of Commerce."

She smiled. "Like complaining about the Pope's secretary to the College of Cardinals, I should think."

"Accused Baynes of mixing cheap Spanish stuff with Médoc and 'damaging the good name of Bordeaux.' "

"Good. About time!"

"Had it all chapter and verse too. Apparently he bought a consignment of Baynes's 'fine old Médoc' and submitted it to the Chamber. Pretty poor mixed stuff, it seems. They discussed the complaint today. Baynes was there, so was Lovell. Lovell wanted to go in and give evidence, but they wouldn't let him. Naturally they threw his charges out, supported Baynes, but the pair of them met outside in the courtyard. I got there just in time to see it.

"I thought Baynes was going to have apoplexy. He nearly set on Lovell. There was a most tremendous row. Lovell was as cool as the devil. I went up and congratulated him and I didn't mind Baynes seeing it either. Lovell just laughed and said he knew he had had no chance of scoring against Baynes but it was a first blow at them, the first nail in their coffin, and he hopes his complaint will encourage others to do likewise and break these people's power."

"You must ask him out here," Susannah said. "I want him to market Château La Guiche for us in the States—if ever we get over this oïdium."

He gave her a look as if to say one more year of that would finish them. And he forgot to ask Lovell.

Susannah at this time began to get into a state of frustration. Francis was away in Bordeaux. She was left to moon about the house and garden with nothing even to occupy her in the vineyard, since this was the slack period of the year. She wandered about longing for John Blood. Nothing satisfied her; nothing held her attention. She was impatient, got angry with the cook, angry with herself. She felt she was drifting and she hated it.

She knew how much she had changed; she saw that. And her mind went eternally on the same track. She thought of the girl she had been when she had first arrived and could hardly recognize herself. Was she, after all, becoming hard like the rest of them? Allowing herself to drift and yield? Was she gradually becoming one of the people she had despised? Soon she would be plowed under, indistinguishable from the rest. And when she thought this she would jump up, throw the embroidery on the chair and sweep out of the house, furious, restless and frustrated.

All during this time she was struggling with the desire to go to Bordeaux. It seemed madness to her, for what would she do there? Go to him? Simply go to him as if she were his mistress? Her pride wouldn't let her. Then she said to herself, Why not? If she were honest in her feelings, why not? Ah, but *convention* held her back. She heard the mocking laughter. The convention she despised mocked her. She was no stronger than that! So she hated herself. And then, on impulse one day, she caught the morning Messageries coach to Bordeaux.

At the clinic she found that Jacob had been transferred to a training center at Royan. No, the young nurse had no message for her.

A great gray void opened to her. She walked out into emptiness. She *had* to see him. He meant everything to her. She felt utterly wretched and alone. She wandered through the shops, her attention only half on what she was doing, trying to suppress her longing to go to him. She wandered about, tormented and hungry, one minute swearing in suppressed rage that she would never see him again, the next minute longing for him like a schoolgirl.

A black cab horse appeared on top of her; she started back. "Cab, ma'am?"

She climbed up, gave his address. She sat back in the closed cab, hardly breathing, in a state of disbelief at herself, trying to shut her mind to what she was doing, not to see herself, as if she could extract these few minutes of transit from reality. And then, when the cab turned into the street and began to slow down, she leaned forward in a panic. "Don't stop! I've changed my mind. Go on."

The drive shrugged indifferently and went on. Around the corner he craned back. "Where to then?"

She rode with him back to the center of the town and paid him off, aware of his stare. She felt a sort of madness had come on her. Ten times she thought she saw John Blood in the crowd. She walked down the arcades she had seen already, into shops she had seen an hour before. She was in torment. The afternoon was passing. Everywhere she turned she seemed to see big clock faces with black hands showing the minutes passing. Soon it would be too late to go back. Half-consciously she was trying to miss the coach.

Why didn't she take what she wanted? No courage! She was always telling herself that Francis could never face a fact. Let *her* face the fact. Here she was wandering the streets like some moonfaced village girl. She wanted direction to her life. Then *she* had to give it direction. It wasn't going to get direction out of the air. Life didn't drift in the direction you wanted. Still, she couldn't do it.

Have it out with Francis? Or tell him she wanted to go home for a visit? Once the break was made she could judge if she wanted to come back. Wouldn't that be more honest than this? But the thought of leaving Francis made her feel worse. It was not possible.

She forced herself to go to the public coach station, dragged herself there feeling blank, worn out and empty now. No coach —it was late. She took her ticket, turned and looked across at the bustling café where she had sometimes sat with Francis, but of course she couldn't go in there alone. It would put a mark on her right away. Nor, alone, would they even serve her; it would offend the respectable customers. And she had to conform to that, didn't she? What a failure she was in her nonconformity— a cowardly failure. This was all her soaring American spirit stood for.

Oh, God, she was wretched.

She began to stroll across the square while she waited. A closed black cab was standing a little distance away and her glance caught the driver's eye. He lifted his chin and made a little "Cab, ma'am?" sign with his hand, and without thinking anything more she walked straight to him.

Take what you want for once in this life. She gave the address, opened the door, grasped the handrail, and as she lifted her eyes to climb in saw John Blood in the other corner.

She got in. The door slammed. He took her hand, pulled her to him and she was in his arms as the cab began to roll over the cobbles. She clung to him with passion in their kiss and was breathless when he released her.

"How was it you came there?" she asked.

"That's the Messageries coach, the one you always take. I've been there every day."

"Why didn't you leave a note at the clinic?"

"The boy's gone. I thought you wouldn't go there any more."

"Oh, God, John, I've been wandering about Bordeaux all day wanting to come to you. What are we going to do?"

"I've told you. We're going to the West together."

Across the roofs came the sound of the cathedral clock striking the hour. One o'clock.

She leaned back, half sitting, against the arm of the chair, one leg stretched out, and looked down at the little red lacquer box on the bedside table. Her hair was loose; the peignoir, caught loosely at the waist, fell back from her nudity. She leaned forward, lifted the lid of the box and looked down at the little Spanish cigars lying inside like dark brown pencils. Then she took one, reached for the matches, pushed her hair back and lit it. Aunt Maxine! The bitter smoke curled up. Ah, she hated herself.

And to complete the picture he kicked the door open from outside and stood there, bare-chested, trousers tucked into knee-boots, carrying two glasses of drink. He stood looking at her in the peignoir smoking the cigar. He came in, put the glasses down, and moving to her side, bent and kissed her neck, caressing her. She turned her head impatiently, made to break free, but he held her strongly. His arm around her, inside the peignoir against her skin, made the robe fall open. Fiercely he pulled her against him. She curved back from him, struggling silently, then he let her go.

She flung away across the room, one arm across her breast, hand tucked under armpit, hair loose, then turned and looked at him almost with hate. And when he came again to her she turned her back. "Leave me alone. Leave me alone." She rocked her head. "Leave me *alone*." Gently he laid a hand on her shoulder. She flung it off and rounded on him.

"Why do I come here? Why do I come? Some physical madness. I hate it. I despise myself."

He looked at her patiently, said nothing.

"Weeks and weeks at the house, waiting . . . silence. Then this again. I hate it! It is going to destroy everything. Destroy me and destroy you."

"Then break. I've given you the choice."

347

"How can I? How can I leave him? He's a child. Somebody has to be strong, somebody has to have some strength."

"You want a chance to make your life, a chance at happiness."

She blazed at him. "Happiness! Do you think I want happiness? I loathe the idea of happiness. Mush? Like a sow wallowing happily with her litter? Happiness, my God! I don't want my days filled up by some mushy sowlike happiness. I'm not a receptacle, a belly for mush happiness. Take your soft mushy happiness, the mud of humanity. I don't want love and sweetness any more. Yes, I wanted them when I was first married but not now. I don't even believe in that sort of love any more. Because it's love-happiness, it's all one, all mush. Love-happiness mush. Love will make you happy. Get love and you'll be happy ever after. You'll become a sow and never know anything but filling your belly with mush. Get love and your life will be perfect! And it's all false. All false. It makes me sick! An absolute lie. I'm tired of love. My husband loves me and he can't give me honesty. I love him—and look at me!"

"If you open yourself to it you accept all these things. You accept suffering. And to suffer hell is better than not to feel," John Blood said.

"I desire you, I want your maleness, I want to be consumed by you, swept up by you. But above all I want *strength* from you, not love. I don't want goodness—I want guts. Maleness. Dauntlessness! I want strength and courage to fight. I'm a fighter and that's what living is about. Contending! Let me have some sense of having fought and fulfilled myself. Don't pledge me piddling happiness."

She broke off, put the cigar to her mouth and drew in some smoke.

"But you hate yourself?"

"I hate myself because I haven't got guts enough, strength enough to fulfill my own destiny, to fight properly. Because I'm false to myself—I was struggling all afternoon to come here—because I'm drifting, because I'm still torn, because I'm still afraid of convention. Oh—" She turned impatiently away and stood with her back to him. There was silence. Then she said quietly, "And because I don't know what to do."

11

The golden liquid in the two deep goblets gleamed above the brilliant mahogany of Chabot's desk. The glow, reflected by the lamp, fell on the red-backed filing cases, spilled over onto the green tooled-leather inlay and struck a yellow glint from the diamond in Chabot's neckcloth. His foxy visage faced Regis from the chair, chin lifted, forehead sloping at the same angle as his nose, eyes sharp as knives. His lips, which were well-shaped, formed his cynical smile.

The wine was an Yquem 1844—Chabot never drank *poor* wine—and Regis knew it was all the return he would get for his luncheon to Chabot in the spring. However, he had not come for that but for a business consultation, and it was, in fact, unexpectedly generous of Chabot to produce even this.

The office was hot and airtight, though the coal fire in the grate was low, this being the end of the day. But the rumble of evening traffic outside hardly penetrated the quiet and no sound filtered through the padded door leading to the office beyond. Delicately, Chabot lifted his goblet and drank. Regis did likewise and they nodded wordlessly to each other in the manner of men who knew that to appreciate wine was a matter of silent ingestion.

Warily they eyed each other across the desk as befits members of the same family. At length Regis said, "So you'll put out a feeler about the house?" He had come to discuss a house property which he had heard might be had for a private sale and wanted Chabot to inquire about discreetly.

"I will," Chabot said.

A knock on the door and the ancient clerk looked in. "It's nearly six, monsieur."

"Ah, so it is. Well! Must leave you, dear boy. Appointment at six fifteen." Chabot got to his feet.

"I was just going." Regis rose too. He took his lavender-colored gloves out of his hat, picked up the hat and his cane, pulled down his waistcoat. When he turned around he saw that Chabot was opening a small door behind the bookcases to one side.

"Don't go," Chabot said. "Shan't be a moment." The lamp flared up inside and Regis's curiosity was piqued. He had never glimpsed this cubbyhole before. So, as nonchalantly as he could, he stepped across and stood in the doorway.

"You realize it will be costly, that house," Chabot was saying over his shoulder. "Extensive renovations, replastering. Cellar in poor state, I believe. You realize that?"

Regis's eyes took it all in. It was a little private *cabinet de toilette* equipped with washstand, water jug and basin, towels, slop pail, a mirror. Bottles and pomades stood on a side table, and against the wall was a leather sofa. Ho-hum, thought Regis. So convenient for special clients.

"Yes, I know. What do you think they'd ask?" His face betrayed nothing of his beguilement.

"No idea. No idea. Depends if I can get to the old woman. Dodge around the son. Son looks soft, but hard as nails."

Briskly, as he kept up his quick patter over his shoulder, Chabot was titivating himself. Bent forward, he washed fingers, dabbed face, combed eyebrows, pomaded hair. Regis watched fascinated. Chabot dabbed something on his cheeks, took a hand mirror and studied himself from behind, adjusted his neckcloth, gave it a dash of scent. Regis's nose identified attar of roses as Chabot turned around and asked, "Can I drop you?"

"Ah . . . thanks, no," Regis said.

They put on their coats, emptied their glasses, and in two minutes had passed through the cluttered outer office and were outside. They turned up their coat collars against the fine rain falling past the streetlamps. For a moment they stood facing each other on the sidewalk, then each raised his hat and they

parted, Regis turning away down the street and Chabot jumping
into his waiting tilbury.

As the carriage rolled away, Chabot rubbed his hands
briskly and dryly together. His mind, always sharpened by a
hint of weakness in another, worked swiftly over the details of
the interview. Interesting, very interesting. Regis must have
plenty of money all of a sudden. What had he been buying
lately? Clever on the Bourse. Needed watching.

Faintly the scent of attar of roses floated inside the carriage.

Simcoe Baynes's house was on the Cours du Pavé des Chartrons, an elegant curve of matching eighteenth-century man-
sions where the aristocracy of the wine trade lived and did their
business. A stone balcony with delicate ironwork ran the width
of the first floor, stone garlands graced the façade above, and
the upper windows of the private apartments were fittingly sur-
mounted by crowns of bay leaves.

As Chabot's carriage drew up to the high porte-cochère, he
saw the lights gleaming from the three tall first-floor windows
of the salon and caught a glimpse of white-aproned servants
passing to and fro preparing for a reception. Baynes was "fitting him in" before a soirée. And it was a measure of the social
distance between the two men that Chabot had been glad to be
fitted in, even though it was *he* who, for the time being, was
doing a service for Simcoe Baynes. But Baynes's turn would
come. Chabot's dry hands rubbed together and made a sound
like the rustling of paper. Baynes's turn would come, no doubt
of it.

He alighted and walked down the long high entry under
the porte-cochère to the second door on the right. *Baynes and
Sheehan. Office*, said the brass plate. He turned the brass knob
and went in. The square high-ceilinged office was windowless
and badly lit, with six or seven clerks behind the counter still
bent at their desks.

A weedy man of forty looked up over his glasses, stuck his
pen behind his ear and limped over. "Evening, Monsieur
Chabot."

"Mr. Baynes is expecting me."

As the man took Chabot's coat and hat, the heavy mahogany door behind him swung open and Simcoe Baynes appeared, watch in hand. He straddled the doorway and stared at Chabot. "Ye're three minutes late, my good sir."

"Pray excuse me. Traffic was heavy."

"Another two and ye'd have been *too* late, Monsieur Chabot." He moved back into the room and Chabot followed, leaving the clerk to shut the door behind them. It was a big room with two tall windows looking on to the street. Its furnishings included Baynes's desk, a Turkish carpet, heavy plush-upholstered chairs and a marble column with a portrait bust of Thomas (Bordeaux Tom) Baynes, co-founder of the house. A fire was blazing in the handsome stone fireplace. Baynes took up a position on the hearthrug, back to the blaze with his hands under his coattails; and Chabot, catching the touch of informality, was encouraged. A seat at the desk would have meant a stiffer mood.

"I've no time to beat about the bush, Chabot. You told me ten months ago you needed time. You've had it. And now I want a straight answer. Can ye get me La Guiche or can't ye?"

Chabot uncovered his long teeth. "I promised it to you, my dear Baynes, and I keep my promises."

"Then I want delivery, man."

"The thing has to come to fruition."

"Fruition be damned. How do I know ye're not playing me off against somebody else? Ye're as slippery as a bag of eels, the lot of ye."

Chabot put his fingertips together and swayed backward on his heels, affecting to find Baynes's words funny. Baynes put on his bluff manner to be able to insult people, but Chabot considered him a man of no finesse.

"Come to that, *I* might look elsewhere. And how would that suit your book?" Baynes asked and shot him a quick glance as much as to say two could play that game.

"Ah, but how would it suit Mawdistly's book? That's what you have to ask yourself, my dear Baynes."

There being no adequate reply to this, Baynes grunted. "Mawdistly will do as I tell him."

Chabot smiled again, this time in the knowledge that Mawdistly Baynes could give his father lessons in bluff and craftiness, a fact Baynes senior was quite aware of.

"And how would it suit the Baron's book, my dear sir?

Hm? That's what we have to consider."

"Eh?"

"I hear Mademoiselle Hagenbach has taken a fancy to La Guiche."

"Ye hear, do ye?"

"Won't be put off with anything else. And what Mademoiselle likes, her father likes."

Baynes shifted irritatedly. "Ye hear a lot of things, don't ye?"

"It's a confidential profession, you know, the law." Chabot smiled, feeling he had the upper hand. "Human weakness, my dear Baynes."

Baynes regarded him pugnaciously. "See here, Chabot, I'll tell you this. Mawdistly or no Mawdistly, marriage to Mademoiselle Hagenbach or no marriage, it's the whole property I'm after. The whole property. And no fifteen per cent in the hands of Monsieur Abel-Cherubin Gautier. That's understood?"

"Understood. Understood. And you *will* have his fifteen per cent. But I need time. He has to be led."

"Led, by God, ye could lead a man-eating shark by the nose, y'could."

"Delicate work, my dear Baynes. If he guessed it was you it would be no go. No go."

Baynes grunted again. "What about the widow, Madame Gautier? What about her share?"

Chabot made a gesture. "We've been all over this. Once we have Abel-Cherubin's share, the rest follows."

"Ye sound mighty sure of yourself, man. I hope ye're right. I've laid out a bit o' money on this and it won't do to go wrong. You understand *that*, Chabot?" He gave Chabot a hard look.

"Come, you haven't laid it out because of me. You've laid it out because Mawdistly and the future Madame Mawdistly Baynes are set on having La Guiche. And you have my promise. I will *deliver* you La Guiche. Can't say fairer than that."

A wheeze came from the speaking tube by the desk. Baynes ignored it, then when it sounded again he stepped over, answered briefly and marched back. He stood reflecting a moment, then said, "Aye, so it's a confidential trade, the law, eh? Ye wouldn't have heard any confidential tidbits about our upstart young friend Mr. John Lovell by any chance?"

"Mmmmm, I . . ."

"Anything he'd particularly like to keep confidential?"

"For the moment, no. But you never know."

"I hear he's thick with Mr. John Blood lately."

"So it seems." Chabot nodded. "Birds of a feather."

"A fine pair of scoundrels."

"May hear something." They looked at each other and Chabot nodded as if to say that all manner of things came his way. "You never know."

Ten minutes later the interview was over. As they walked to the door Baynes stopped, tucked his chin into his chest and looked up under his eyebrows at Chabot. "I'm a blunt man, Chabot, and I believe in a blunt way of dealing. You scratch my back, I scratch yours. That's what ye're after and ye needn't smile, for it's a sound business principle and I dare say the Holy Father in Rome uses no other. You get me La Guiche for my son, I support you for the Munipical Council. That's our understanding and let's have it all clear, straight and aboveboard."

"*And* the support of your political friends," Chabot said.

"Aye, ye get that too. That's understood."

Chabot nodded. "That is our understanding."

"Good. I like a man who knows his mind."

"And I, my dear Baynes, like a man who speaks his," Chabot said, and the trace of irony in his smile was gone in a flash.

The smoke from Abel-Cherubin's cigar spiraled gently up in the warm air of the study. It was after dinner and he was wearing a plum-colored velvet jacket, and on his bald head was his favorite little evening cap, a shallow pillbox with a long green silk tassel that fell to his shoulder.

Facing him, Chabot eased his legs on the hassock. "I don't say it's impossible. Nothing's impossible. But it's ve-ry ve-ry difficult," he said.

Abel-Cherubin let his melancholy gaze drop to the glass of brandy in his hand. "And who's going to give any price with things in this state? Even if you find somebody."

"Price? Don't talk about price." Chabot shook his head. "Bad lookout for you. Capital locked up. No return. And shrinking—shrinking."

Abel-Cherubin looked up at him with pained eyes.

"Going moldy," Chabot said. "Need the money elsewhere but can't get at it. Bad lookout. Unproductive capital. Worst thing in the world. Against nature. Puts years on you. Years."

Abel-Cherubin sighed.

"Thousand pities you didn't sell out to start with. Could have used the money to extend the refinery," Chabot said. "You'd have been nicely placed now."

Abel-Cherubin swirled the brandy in his glass, fortified himself with a mouthful. He looked at Chabot with a glimmer of appeal in his eyes. "People come to you. You could find somebody, Léon."

Chabot shrugged eloquently. "Find? Thing is to find a price. Any sort of price with things as they are."

"That's just it."

"Nothing's impossible. Have to be luck. Pure stroke of luck." Suddenly he stabbed a forefinger at Abel-Cherubin's waistcoat. "*And* you'd have to jump at it."

"Yes." In spite of the melancholy tone, Abel-Cherubin's eyes gleamed a little.

"No argument. Just jump at it when I say so. Grab. Both hands."

"Yes."

Chabot stared hard at the carpet. He seemed to be wrestling in moral perplexity, and when at last he spoke his voice was one of deep regret and almost philosophical resignation. "Pity, great pity."

"Pity? What's a pity?"

No answer.

"You mean you've missed somebody?" Abel-Cherubin asked.

Chabot looked up with a hangdog expression. "Afraid so."

"No!"

"He's in the market, but—"

"Couldn't you make an approach?"

Chabot turned his mouth down and sat there in morose silence.

"But couldn't you *try?*"

"Well . . ."

"Nobody I know, is it?"

Chabot considered, stared at the carpet some more, at last looked up with resolution. "Baynes."

Abel-Cherubin jerked upright as if stung. "You know I'd never sell to that scoundrel!"

A pause. Silence. Abel-Cherubin regarded Chabot. Chabot contemplated Abel-Cherubin. Chabot cocked his head to one side and somehow his muzzle looked longer than usual; in the glow of the fire his hair took on a reddish tinge. His eyebrows rose. "Not even to get your own back on him?" he asked.

"Own back? How do you mean?"

"You could take his eyeteeth."

"Ah?"

"You have him cornered."

"How?"

"Mawdistly."

"Mawdistly?"

"Caught the Hagenbach. And she wants it."

A coal in the fireplace collapsed with a metallic tinkle like the clink of gold. Chabot laid a finger alongside his nose. Solemnly he winked. Abel-Cherubin's eyes enlarged, his mouth opened and shut silently like a goldfish's; he sat shifting his feet about and staring at Chabot. Then he began nodding slowly. "Ah . . . well . . . in those circumstances . . ."

"You think you could bring yourself?"

"Ah . . ."

"*Force* yourself?"

"For the top price, yes."

"Leave it to me. Then when Baynes bites I can jump on it."

Abel-Cherubin nodded slowly again. A look of quiet calculation had replaced his former eagerness, as if he were thinking now that he would make sure it *was* the top price by keeping Baynes dangling till the last minute.

"Mind you, you'll be damned lucky," Chabot said.

"Yes . . . yes," on Abel-Cherubin's flushed face the beginnings of a smile appeared.

Two wild ducks had alighted noisily on the lake at sundown and immediately after lunch next day Susannah put on her cloak and went out to see if they were still in residence and hadn't scared off the moor hen and her family. As she reached the water's edge she heard a carriage arriving, looked around and saw it was Constance Canning. She walked slowly back. It was unusual for Constance to come at this hour. They exchanged kisses.

"Oh, isn't that sweet!" Susannah said, stepping back and admiring Constance's dress.

"And I found it in Bordeaux, would you believe it? New Galleries."

"Yes, they're getting some smart things there lately. But I thought you were going to Poitiers."

"Byam changed his plans. His aunt is coming down."

"Shall we go indoors? Is it too late for coffee for you?"

"No coffee. Can we stroll a minute? I . . . I'd like to talk."

"Yes, all right." Susannah glanced at her, thinking that Constance looked serious, and she wondered what was on her mind. And rather insistently Constance was steering away from the house toward the trees, as if she were anxious not to meet other members of the family. It was obvious she had come to say something.

They reached the bench, brushed off the twigs and dust and sat down. For a moment they talked of families and plans. Constance was sitting up very straight and spoke in her usual quiet, calm manner. Then she said, "Susannah, I really came to see you to tell you something. I hope it won't upset you too much but you must know."

"What, pray?"

"I don't make it my business to repeat common gossip, but it can't be kept from you any longer. The common gossip is that you are John Blood's mistress."

Susannah sat quite still and looked at her steadily; it was a shock and she felt herself coloring, but she kept her self-possession. "And who is saying this?"

"I don't think it will help to repeat that. It is common property. I wouldn't make it any business of mine, and I confess I might not have told you now, except that it has had consequences which you cannot fail to hear about."

"Consequences?"

"Mr. Blood heard the gossip being repeated in Bordeaux last night by a man named Calonne. The result you may guess. Mr. Blood challenged him and they are to fight—if they have not done so already."

Now the shock was making her breath come short. She sat

357

staring in front of her, her heart filled with a confusion of alarm, pride and despair. "Is there any way of stopping it?"

"None, I think. These things are best left to run their course."

Common gossip. She was filled with consternation and with anxiety for him. "To . . . to what?" she asked, bringing her attention back to Constance.

"They must fight with each other. Mr. John Lovell is one of Mr. Blood's seconds in the affair. I do know that."

"I see. And the other man, who is he?"

"Calonne? I'm told he is a notorious duelist."

"Oh . . . but—"

"I wanted to tell you this so that you shouldn't hear it in some way when you were not prepared."

"Yes. Thank you, Constance. It's kind of you."

"I hope you won't be too upset."

There seemed nothing more to say. They sat in awkward silence, then Constance rose and Susannah walked with her to the drive. At the door of the carriage Constance turned around and pressed her hand. "I'm sorry," she said, then she climbed in and the carriage drove off.

Susannah walked into the house with her heart in tumult.

12

The three carriages were drawn up under cover of the trees. The horses' breath was white on the morning air and they shook their heads occasionally, making the harnesses clink. Pale, smoky orange-red November sunlight splashed the gaunt trunks of the pines and touched the farther edges of the open space beyond where the three groups of men were standing.

John Lovell—between Blood and his other friend Philippe Jourdain, who was his principal second—looked across at the two men conferring in the center: Baron Louis de Lavertumel, director of the duel, and the surgeon Dr. Huys, a small worried-looking gray-haired man in steel spectacles. Lavertumel, who was stout and fresh-complexioned, was perspiring in his heavy coat.

Lovell's gaze went past them to the trio beyond—Calonne and his two seconds. Calonne was about thirty-five years old; he had a narrow little black mustache, prominently bunched cheek muscles and the smooth skin of a woman. Lovell knew the type —a dull-witted, reckless and slightly irrational Frenchman who went around almost longing to be insulted and finding any excuse for it to get up a fight. One of his seconds was a small man with a dab of beard named Edmond Rigaud, a Bordelais; the other was a blond silent man with a lantern jaw, said to be Austrian.

Lovell turned as Blood said, "Lavertumel's a fusser."

"I think he's got it right now."

"Coats off, we said?"

"Yes, it's agreed." Lovell glanced at Blood's face, clear-cut in the morning light, his dark eyes, lined at the corners, were slightly puckered up as he watched the others. He had his white ruffled shirt open at the neck, sleeves rolled up and his black trousers tucked into kneeboots.

"They like a deal of ceremonial, by God."

"Here he is," Jourdain said.

Lavertumel strode up, the skirts of his long heavy coat flapping. "Are you ready?"

"We've been ready for—"

"Quite ready," Jourdain cut in firmly.

Lavertumel walked over to Calonne's group, who signified they were ready too, then he called the two groups together. They marched up, stood a few paces apart, Lavertumel facing them.

"The conditions of the combat have been agreed upon. I have set out the marks, as you have seen. They are forty paces apart. Two balls will be exchanged. I will give two commands. First 'Ready,' then, ten seconds later, 'Fire!' At the command 'Fire!' each gentleman will be free to fire at once or advance up to ten paces in direct line toward his opponent and to fire at will. That is understood? I repeat, at the command 'Fire!' he may fire at once or he may advance toward his opponent. If he advances, he may fire at any moment he chooses—at one pace, at three paces, at six paces, at ten paces, as he chooses. But he must not advance more than ten paces toward his opponent. Understood?" He looked from one to the other.

They each nodded.

"No questions? Very well. The pistols?"

Calonne turned to his seconds. Rigaud opened a green sha-green-covered case with a brace of pistols inside. Calonne took one. Rigaud stepped up and presented the case to Blood, who took the other.

"Then, if you please, gentlemen," Lavertumel said.

Calonne, who had his coat draped over his shoulders, threw it negligently to the Austrian. Lovell watched John Blood walk unhurried across to the mark while Calonne took up his position at the other end. The sun's rays fell across the ground, so neither had an advantage. The two men faced each other, motionless in the clear morning light, pistol arms at their sides.

Lovell had been in a brawl or two in his life in the East, but had never witnessed a duel before and felt uncomfortably tense. Blood, he thought, looked cool enough. The two white shirts stood out against the dull gray-green of the trees.

And abruptly, in the pause, Lovell felt it was all damnable and ridiculous. Why couldn't they get it over with with a good fist fight, a good satisfying bare-knuckle fight where they would each get their hands on each other and knock each other down instead of this stiff, cold-blooded affair. He blamed himself for encouraging it. He had allowed himself to be carried away by the thing and by Blood's temperament. However, if he had refused, Blood would certainly have got somebody else.

"Ready."

Pause. Lovell counted to himself.

"Fire!"

Lovell expected a shot at once and flinched; his eyes, fixed first on Blood, went quickly from one to the other. Everything seemed to go with agonizing slowness.

Each man stepped toward the other. One . . . two . . . three . . . They were both advancing at about the same pace, their eyes steadily fixed on each other. Calonne had a slight quiver of a limp, an affectation. Four . . . five . . . six . . . It seemed interminable. Seven . . . eight.

At eight, Calonne's right arm came up. He paused to steady himself, aimed and fired. The report crashed around the clearing. A startled jingle from the horses, a puff of smoke in the air. Lovell saw Blood check and make a slight movement with his left shoulder. Hit? At the same moment, Blood aimed his pistol and fired. There was a snap. The pistol had not fired.

Blood stood with his arm half extended. Not hit! Lovell could see no mark on him. Instantly Lavertumel was pointing his cane at Blood and bawling, "Stand where you are, sir! Stand where you are! You are at eight paces." To Calonne's seconds he called out, "Bring another cap."

Rigaud fumbled for the cap, hastened forward with it and handed it to Blood. Blood fitted the cap to the pistol, made a sign to Lavertumel and, holding the pistol at his side, waited for his order. Calonne stood glaring at him defiantly.

Lovell's eyes were going from one to the other, waiting in the sickening interval for the order.

"Fire!"

Blood raised the pistol. Another snap.

With an oath, Blood threw the pistol on the ground and called out, "Mr. Lovell, fetch the sabers."

Lovell hesitated, looked inquiringly at Lavertumel, then he stooped for the pair of sabers they had brought with them. He heard Blood call out to Calonne, "Will you have it out with sabers, you dirty blackguard?"

"I am directing this duel, sir," Lavertumel bawled out to him before Calonne could answer. He marched forward. "Stand your ground, sir! Stand where you are!"

"Just one moment. If you please!" Jourdain and Rigaud were both hurrying over to Lavertumel. Lovell strode up too.

"The conditions of combat—"

"The only thing is to begin again," Rigaud said.

"Your man has already fired."

"Your man has fired twice!"

"I will not have an argument—"

"He has *tried* to fire twice."

"He has been given two chances to fire."

"The conditions of combat were quite clear," Lovell said. "Only one ball has been fired."

"That's not our fault!" Rigaud said.

"Silence, sir, will you!"

"Nor ours."

"Silence!" roared Lavertumel. He glared at one and the other. "Mr. Lovell is correct. Mr. Blood has not yet fired."

"I demand another pistol," Jourdain said.

"Yes. Let Mr. Blood have another pistol. You have the others?"

"We have." Lovell hastened back to where he had left the weapons, picked up the pistol case and took one out. He walked over and as he handed it to Blood saw the stain on Blood's shirt at the left shoulder.

"He hit you."

"Just a touch. It's nothing." Blood's face was dark with anger.

Lovell picked up the pistol that had not fired and retreated. Calonne was still standing on the same spot. Lavertumel retreated again and there was another awful pause.

"Fire!"

Blood turned his back on Calonne and began to walk away. Head down, looking at the ground, he walked almost casually away from him. One . . . two . . . three paces . . . Lovell gazed in amazed silence. Four . . . five . . . Was he going to give it up? *Give it up?* Abruptly Blood wheeled around, brought the pistol up and aimed in one swift movement and fired.

The shot reverberated. Calonne took a step back as if to move away. Not hit, thought Lovell. Then Calonne made a jerky little movement with his pistol hand, buckled at the knees and fell heavily.

The seconds and Lavertumel rushed forward. From behind, Dr. Huys came hurrying with his bag. Lovell and Jourdain ran up to Blood, who was craning his chin around to see the wound on his shoulder.

"Are you all right?"

"Let me see that."

They tore the shirt and examined the wound. It was bleeding a good deal now, but the ball had simply scooped out a furrow above the bone.

"It's all right, I think. Not serious."

"I was afraid Lavertumel was going to stop it," Blood said.

"I thought so when you walked back. You had him puzzled. I don't think he knew what to do."

"That needs cauterizing, though," Lovell said, meaning the wound. He had seen too many superficial wounds go bad in India to take chances. And who knew with a pistol ball. "Here, if you don't mind. Old-fashioned method." He applied his mouth to the wound, sucked out the blood at the surface, spat it out, and did it a second time. "Now press your handkerchief on it. We'll get a dressing to stop the bleeding."

"Much obliged to you, Lovell."

With surprise, Lovell found himself sweating and surreptitiously ran his sleeve over his forehead. The other group was still bent over the fallen man. Jourdain, who had gone over, came back rather pale. He waited till he was up with them.

"Where's he hit?" Lovell said.

"He's dead."

"Dead! God . . ." Lovell was shaken. He saw the angry glow in Blood's eyes, saw his face darken again. Then it was gone. They regarded each other in silence, then looked over at the small huddled group outlined against the trees. Everything seemed very still. Lavertumel straightened up and raised an arm, signaling urgently for a carriage to come over.

Blood said, "Let's go and get our breakfast."

Half an hour after Constance Canning had gone Susannah was in her room when Emilie knocked and came in. "A gentleman calling, ma'am. Mr. Thornton."

Thornton? Oh, yes. "Very well, I'll come down."

Thornton was standing in the salon, hat in hand, and bowed as she came in. "Good day, ma'am. I trust you are well."

"Thank you."

"Mr. Lovell asked me to bring you this message. He said it was confidential."

She took the envelope. "Pray be seated, Mr. Thornton and excuse me." The letter said:

> You will have heard of the affair this morning. I write in haste to apprise you of the outcome since I imagine your anxiety. I regret I have not had time to do it before. Mr. Blood is unharmed, the other dead. It has caused a stir—no doubt there are some who secretly wish it had been the other way round—and half an hour ago, Mr. B was arrested. As I understand it, killing an opponent in a duel here is now strictly speaking punishable at law. I had urged him to pay a timely visit to another part of the country, but he would not hear of it. Pray try not to be upset. I don't know what the outcome will be. The authorities used to shut their eyes to affairs of honor, even if one of the participants was killed; but for about ten years, I'm told, they have been somewhat stricter. However, there's no knowing what any particular magistrate will do. Quite a few stick to the old way. At all events, we are not absolutely without friends! I shall be in touch with him and you may rely on my devotion and discretion. You may give Mr. Thornton, who is my cellar master and valued employee, any message you wish in the assurance that it will remain in strict confidence.
>
> Your devoted servant
> John Lovell

She folded the letter and turned away to the window. She longed violently to go to him, to tell Thornton she would go back with him now, but that was not possible. She stood staring at nothing. After a moment she controlled herself and turned around.

"Mr. Thornton, will you take some refreshment while I write a reply to Mr. Lovell?"

"Thank you, ma'am. A small brandy and water, if you please."

She had Emilie fetch the drink and sat down, trembling now, and wrote a brief note to Lovell.

> Thank you for your kindness. I will try to come and see you tomorrow, late in the morning, but you will understand I may not be able to. I am worried in case the English ask for him to be given up to them. Please think of this and try to consider what we can do. S.G.

But she had not faced telling her husband. She had not faced the admission that she had lovingly, willingly, given herself to another man. And it tormented her.

It wasn't shame. Not that. It was too strong and too natural for her to feel shame. How could she deny that passionate feeling that swept her up with him? She could not.

But she *had* transgressed the sacred law of marriage, and there was the old awe of that, whether she liked it or not. And it was the pain it would cause Francis and her own lack of courage in facing the issue that afflicted her now. She hated herself more than before, now that she was up against it. What had she imagined—that she could go on with John Blood, deceiving her husband, comfortably living in that falsity until it had become routine? Until she stopped having any moral feelings about it because nobody found out? Until it was nice and comfortable and eventually Francis more or less perceived what was going on and it all became accepted and snug? The complaisant husband and so on. Was that what she had imagined?

She hated it. She hated herself. Was this her fine free-roaming American soul again? So it merely meant taking what you wanted and hoping you wouldn't be caught? Her old Methodism rose up in her with all the wrath and dark damnations and railings against sin, but she put it down.

The *real* sin was in the failure of her courage. For herself she didn't give a damn for society or for social blame. Besides, the duel, according to their male code, had formally disposed of the question. But Francis's feelings were another matter. She had had the courage of her own passion, but she had flinched from the final step it entailed—facing him with it.

She hated her lack of courage. This was the very thing she found so woeful in Europe—the compromises, the half-acceptances, the half-shames, the thin-bloodedness, the willingness to live on half-shares, the great European bourgeois habit of thinking small! Taking care! How it depressed her. And here *she* had begun to fall into this same miserable smallness of mind.

The sound of a carriage below made her start. She turned around from the dressing table and listened, then quickly fastened her hair and stood up. The afternoon light was fading, the portraits made dark holes on the somber wallpaper. She braced herself as steps came along the corridor outside. The door opened and Madame Gautier stood there, her mauve dress and jet beads darker in the fading light, her eyes on Susannah.

"I wish to speak to you."

"Pray come in."

Madame Gautier shut the door behind her and advanced into the room. She clasped her hands in front of her. Dark and biblical was her face, the stone lines of her neck and head. "You have heard what has happened?"

"Yes."

"You know the man is dead. And the other arrested?"

"Yes."

"And you know that it is a public scandal? That Bordeaux is full of it and your name is an abomination?"

"I am sorry if it is so."

"An abomination!" Madame Gautier shook with accusing wrath. "You also know why they fought?"

"Gossip, I believe."

"Gossip?" The old eyes were upon her, full of knowledge. "Which you deny?"

Susannah wetted her lips.

"You deny the man is your lover?"

For a moment Susannah wavered. Her breath coming deep and fast, she pushed back a strand of hair from her face. "No," she said in a low voice. "I do not deny it."

"So it is true."

"Yes."

A harsh wrathful whisper came from the old woman. "Have you no shame?"

Susannah lifted her head, though her voice trembled when she spoke. "I am not ashamed of it, because I love him."

"Love? Do you know what love is?"

"And I love Francis too. I . . . I don't expect you to understand it."

"You may indeed not expect it!"

Susannah turned convulsively away to the window, still breathing hard, then she faced Madame Gautier again. "Yet everyone has several selves. And to me it's sweet and natural when I am with either of them. They are both mine. I love them both as if I had two hearts, two souls. Francis is one thing and I, loving him, am one self. And another me loves John Blood, another self. It takes nothing from Francis. A woman may love two men."

"In marriage a woman is given to one man, and one only!"

"I am bound to Francis stronger than ever. But there is another reality, another self which has awoken in me, which I did not know then, or only dimly."

"And after this another—why not? So that you may deceive your husband at your pleasure."

"No. It's not deception. Deception would mean I calculated, and that I did not do. I don't want to hurt Francis, but I have been a coward not facing it, not telling him. And now I shall."

"You will not!" Madame Gautier made a convulsive movement with her hands. "You will not speak a word. I forbid it!" A sort of dark will flowed from her.

"But it is stifling for a woman in this atmosphere. Don't you see that? It is impossible to breathe. I need openness, the American sense of space, a bit of American courage. 'He who desires and acts not breeds pestilence.' " Susannah was recovering her presence of mind.

"And you, for your famous American freedom, have sacrificed your husband!"

"No."

"You do not care about convention, but he does. We do! And it is your duty, your bounden duty as his wife, to follow him."

"To sacrifice myself then? To sacrifice myself to convention? To deny myself? I must deny my own existence as a woman? In the name of what?"

"It is no sacrifice. Duty is duty. It is your bounden duty."

"My bounden duty to narrow my life? To kowtow, always to hold myself up for the approval of . . . of dried-up, soulless people? My bounden duty to watch out, to conform, to think carefully, with reserve, and to think small? To stifle myself? How can any man demand that? And unconditionally."

"You have one duty as a wife—to obey!"

"In the name of what?"

"In the name of society. In the name of all that is decent. In the name of the sacrament of marriage."

"Which means in the name of male domination, does it not?"

Madame Gautier glared at her.

"And why must the woman accept this sacrifice? Why the *woman* and not the man? Why should the woman always have to bend?"

"It is the woman's part."

"But why shouldn't the man make some sacrifice to allow the woman to live fully and honestly? Isn't that *his* duty? Otherwise the man has all the rights and the woman has all the duties. Life is broad and rich and generous, and I am young and I want to meet it with passion."

"And in pursuit of that you have broken the most sacred law of marriage." The old unyielding rock of her.

"But marriage here makes a piece of property of me!" Susannah cried. "That's what women are here—property. Property of the men. Look at the women here—male amusements for a few years. Breeding machines for a few more. Then of no more importance than . . . than the family chest of drawers, the family silver. Less than the family house property—less! Much less. Their sacred property! As *women*, they're finished."

"A woman's fulfillment is in her husband."

"But a woman is also herself. I love my husband, but I've got to breathe. I've got to be myself."

"Then you must go from here. You must go!" Madame Gautier's eyes were hard with her old strength.

"Ever since I came here you have hated me. Rejected me. Why? Why do you hate me?"

"Because you do not belong to this house. You have no place here."

"Because I want to fight, isn't that it? Because I won't conform, because I won't be treated as you have been." She checked herself as her anger rose again. She turned away to the window.

"You know nothing of me, nothing of how I have lived. Nothing." The voice was hard yet it trembled, and Susannah faced her again. Madame Gautier's hand clutched tremblingly, convulsively at the beads around her neck, and in the half-light of the room the lines of her face seemed to have changed strangely. Her mouth sagged, her chin trembled in a pathetic, almost childish, helplessness. She caught hold of the back of a chair to steady herself.

At that moment the crunch of carriage wheels came from the drive.

In a shaking voice Madame Gautier said, "My sons are here. You will come down now." She had recovered. She steadied herself, picked up her skirt and went silently from the room. Susannah remained staring after her through the open doorway, hearing her footsteps going down the stairs. She felt horribly shaken and oppressed. What was she to do? Somehow the interview had shaken her resolution. She knew she could not tell Francis. It was the sacrifice *she* had to make, not to tell him. She was stronger than Francis and she must use her strength to protect him.

She glanced out the window. Below, Francis and Monsieur Parenteau were getting out of one carriage and from the second Abel-Cherubin and Louise had alighted with Chabot and Raynal following.

Susannah stood gnawing her fist in wretchedness. Tears trembled on her eyelids, her heart was torn. It was the end of John Blood. All that she must give up. She knew it, had known it for weeks, had struggled against it but knew it must be. Her husband had his claim on her heart and that, whatever else she might long for, she must yield to. Must! Must—no other way. One could not make impossible demands on life.

The snowbound evening on the Place des Quinconces came to her. She saw all that and longed for him with a terrible aching. Below, she could hear them entering the house. The tears ran down her cheeks. At last she shook her head, brushed the tears away with her fingers and crossed to the mirror. She dabbed her face, straightened her hair and, bracing herself, turned to the door and went downstairs.

"Well, madame, and what have you got to say?"

Posed like a family portrait group in their tall collars, their stiff clothes, they faced her, Abel-Cherubin, the speaker, seated with Madame Gautier on his right, then Chabot and Raynal. Parenteau was next to them, slightly behind, then came Louise and Francis. Their faces were set and grim except for Francis, who sat with wrinkled, unhappy brow, and Louise, who was twisting her fingers anxiously.

"I have nothing to say to you, sir," Susannah said.

"What!"

"Why, pray, should I explain myself to you like a . . . a naughty schoolgirl?"

"Schoolgirl, indeed! Rather more than a schoolgirl's prank, I think, madame. An accusation of adultery, a man dead and a public scandal! A fine schoolgirl."

"I am not answerable to you, sir."

"On the contrary, madame, if I may say so," put in Chabot smoothly, "I should have thought your *family* would be the *first* to whom you owed an explanation. To whom you would wish to give a frank answer about these unfortunate events."

"But why am I to answer public gossip? Called down here as if I were on trial!"

"No smoke without fire."

"This is not Paris, madame. There are serious responsible people here who do not launch accusations lightly."

Susannah said, "And in any event, I am not considered one of the family."

"A quibble!" Abel-Cherubin brushed it aside. "Since we are all affected, I think we are entitled to know the truth of the matter between you and Mr. Blood."

"I don't think we need to have this out in front of everybody," Francis said.

Susannah's eyes met Madame Gautier's. Abel-Cherubin persisted. "But on the contrary, Francis, as we have told you, there are facts you may not be aware of. And we are all concerned."

Francis wriggled uncomfortably. Madame Gautier opened her mouth to speak, her eyes still on Susannah, but before she could do so Susannah said, "Mr. Blood has answered the accusations and I dare say he will dispose of any repetitions in the same way."

"Oh, pouf! Bravado, madame. Sheer bravado. You do not deny you have met the gentleman?"

Hastily Francis said, "That's a matter between Susannah and me."

"Your private relations are one thing, Francis, but this is now public. You, madame, have been seen with the man."

"People see what they want," she said wretchedly.

"You have been seen with him on horseback. By the river."

"Indeed, I have seen Mr. Blood there."

"Ah. You have met several times, I believe."

"Believe what you will, sir."

"And perhaps in Bordeaux also?"

"It is not your affair and I decline to answer your questions." She was struggling with tears.

"I think that'll do, Abel-Cherubin," Francis said.

"It doesn't change the fact that Madame is at the center of a grave public scandal by which the whole family is affected. And you have agreed something must be done."

Madame Gautier moved her hands in her lap, clasping her fingers and looking at Susannah. "You have brought nothing but trouble to this house. It would be better for us all if you went away. This would allow the scandal to die of its own accord."

"Yes, till the scandal blows over," Abel-Cherubin said.

"And we shall all breathe easier," Madame Gautier said. "All of us."

"We are thinking of your good, too, madame," Chabot said.

"We consider you should go back to the United States for a prolonged stay and perhaps you could then reflect if you wish to return here."

Susannah stared at Francis's unhappy face; he was staring at the floor, jiggling his foot nervously. "You mean you've agreed to this, Francis?"

Anxiously his head came up. "No, not to that. I only said for a short trip, that's all. And then come back. I only thought it's going to be very uncomfortable for you here, Sue, while this scandal is on. It's going to be very awkward, people talking . . . I mean, pointing at you. I really, I—"

"It would be best for everybody," Madame Gautier said.

Susannah drew herself up. She stood erect before them. "Well, I am not going. You can't get rid of me like that. Nor will I sign any deed of renunciation, Abel-Cherubin."

They gazed at her in stunned silence. Then, with a scraping of her chair, Louise got to her feet. She was pale and obviously apprehensive, but she stepped forward to Susannah's side. "I think Susannah is right and I'm on her side."

Abel-Cherubin's face became congested. He swelled with indignation at his wife, who was twisting her hands and gazing at Susannah with a thin smile.

"Louise! Sit down at once!"

"Come, Louise," Susannah said, taking her arm. The two women turned their backs on them and went out.

"Susannah!" Francis jumped up and hurried after them. "Listen, Sue, I don't want you to go."

13

Three mornings later John Lovell stood in the window of his office at Collard and Sons and watched the Baron de Lavertumel approaching along the quayside in his long coat. The weather was sharp, with a crisp northwest wind coming down the river, but Lavertumel's face was red and perspiring as usual. A choleric man, and on this occasion, thought Lovell, justifiably so.

The day after the duel, Lavertumel had burst fulminating into this same office, thrown down his hat and banged his cane on the floor, saying he had just been questioned by the police for one hour on his part in the duel. For one hour! It was an outrage. He would not stand for it. And now the police were poking into the whole affair. It was scandalous enough that Mr. Blood had been detained after his arrest, as if he were a criminal. But if a man could not go out over a matter of honor without these gentry of the police poking their dirty noses in, then it was the end of everything. Conducting an investigation, were they? Then they, the gentlemen in question, must form a committee of honor and conduct their *own* investigation with which they could confront the police, or heaven knows what monkey business there might not be. An affair between gentlemen must remain between gentlemen.

Lovell had agreed, because some aspects of the affair had struck him as strange, and he was anxious to help Blood. So they had formed the committee—Lovell himself, Lavertumel, Philippe Jourdain, and two other friends of Blood's, a young Irishman named Alexander Hanna, who was in the Bordeaux wine trade, and Jacques Bontoux, a dealer in jute and cotton whom Lovell knew himself. And they had agreed to meet at Lovell's office this morning after making their first inquiries.

As Lavertumel reached the entrance door below, a tilbury pulled up on the quayside and deposited Jourdain and Bontoux. They greeted Lavertumel and shook hands, Jourdain slim and natty, and Bontoux a large man with bristling black eyebrows who towered over the others. A few moments later they were all being ushered into Lovell's commodious office and Lovell himself was shaking their hands.

"How are you, my dear fellow?"

"Morning . . . morning."

The bulk of Lavertumel and Bontoux together was impressive.

"Well, how is our friend?"

Lovell had been to see Blood in jail the day before. "Oh, he's all right. In good spirits. No complaints about treatment. Mind you, I think they're all being pretty careful over him. Handling him with kid gloves for the moment."

"So much the better."

"He told me one or two interesting things which I'll report in a moment."

"Yes. Yes."

A comfortable fire was blazing in the hearth, Lovell had had spirits, lemon and hot water set out on a side table along with brandy, port, three bottles of 1844 Calon-Ségur and one of Yquem 1846. When they had got rid of their coats they helped themselves.

"By the way, Lovell, I thought of asking Mowbray to join us," Lavertumel said. "Be the thing to do, wouldn't it?"

"Mm. As a matter of fact, I did so, but he . . . he couldn't see his way to it."

"What?" Lavertumel looked surprised.

"He couldn't do it."

Lavertumel's glance sharpened, then he stared down frowningly at his glass of toddy. "Hm. Thought they were friendly enough. Did he say . . . ah . . . did he say why?"

"No. But I think we can draw conclusions."

"Conclusions? What the devil do you mean?"

"Well," said Lovell. "This was one of the things I was going to report to you from our friend. And it does seem to bear on the affair. Blood told me yesterday that on his last visit to Paris he happened to see Mowbray, or rather he happened to *catch sight* of Mowbray, one evening, very unexpectedly, when he was about to have a meeting with one of his friends from Ireland. He had arranged the meeting carefully—by which he meant secretly—and suddenly seeing Mowbray there made him break it off. A couple of nights later, in Chantilly, our friend was shot at."

"Blood was?"

"What? Shot at?"

"Yes."

"You mean Mowbray might have been mixed up in it?"

"I do. Blood says there have been three or four other small incidents which make him suspect Mowbray."

"Suspect him? What do you mean? Mowbray's an English agent?"

Lovell nodded. "No proof, but Blood's convinced of it. Apart from the fact that Blood's a wanted man for the English, he's a continuing nuisance to them over Ireland, and they would obviously like to . . . to eliminate him. They can't get any open measures taken against him here because of his friends in Paris —Morny and others—so they are using other methods. As I say, all this has a bearing on the affair with Calonne."

They were all looking at him intently. Jourdain rubbed his chin hard. "You mean . . . ?"

"Damn it, this puts the whole thing in a new light," Lavertumel said.

"Do the police know this yet?" Bontoux asked, twisting an eyebrow in thumb and forefinger.

"No, and this is just what they *won't* find out. And if there is any threat of putting Blood on trial, this is what we must put before the magistrate."

"Where the devil is young Hanna?" Impatiently Lavertumel pulled out his watch. "I'd like to get on with our meeting. Most unsatisfactory dealing with things in dribs and drabs like this."

"Then let's begin. He can't be much longer." Lovell moved

to the large oval table and pulled out chairs for the others. They carried their glasses over and sat down.

"Philippe, you were inquiring about the man Calonne," Lovell said. "What result?"

Jourdain sat forward. "I can't find anybody who knew Calonne."

"Nobody?"

"Not a soul. Apparently he arrived here from Paris knowing nobody. He struck up an acquaintance or two at the Army Club, particularly with Edmond Rigaud, who was in the Hussars at one time, but he got himself thoroughly disliked—I'm talking about Calonne—because of his arrogance and boasting. Somebody or other had heard of his having killed two men in duels, but nobody *knew* him. Rigaud was the only one who could stand him even as a drinking companion, and even Rigaud knew nothing about him except what Calonne himself volunteered, which was hardly anything."

The others were all leaning forward listening closely.

"Calonne seems to have been hanging about Bordeaux for weeks," Jourdain continued.

"Weeks?"

"Yes."

"Doing what?"

"That's just it, doing nothing. Drinking mostly and playing cards with casual acquaintances. I've been to his lodgings, and his landlady said he never had any visitors. Altogether a mysterious bird. He got Rigaud to introduce him to the New Club as a visitor, and it was there he insulted Blood. And the curious thing is that it was the first time Blood had been into the club for weeks, in fact, the first time since Calonne had arrived in Bordeaux. Sort of the first opportunity Calonne had had of catching Blood there. That's all I can find out."

"That seems to fit, doesn't it?" Lovell said. They all looked at him. "What about his seconds, Rigaud and the other fellow?"

"Oh, Rigaud's all right," Lavertumel said. "Family's an old Bordeaux family. Don't care for the fellow, but he's honest. I don't question his good faith. Says he simply struck up with Calonne. Calonne asked him to be his friend in the affair and sent him to the other, the Austrian, a man named Wolters. Rigaud found Wolters and Wolters said he would join him as sec-

376

ond. Rigaud learned precious little about the man, it seems. Hangdog sort of fellow, I thought."

"I'm told the police can't find him," Bontoux said.

"Who, the Austrian?"

"Yes, Wolters."

"What do they intend to do about Blood—the Public Prosecutor, I mean?"

"I can't get any firm information." Lavertumel fingered his glass. "They don't seem to have made up their minds. Want to find a way out, of course. A man like Mr. Blood, a foreigner with influential friends. Damned awkward for them. Be only too glad to find a decent way out."

"Then shouldn't we step in now and press for his release?" Lovell said.

"How do you see that?"

"Well, I mean, in the past, as I understand it, the authorities have shut their eyes to affairs of honor, and even when one of the parties was killed they've managed not to take cognizance of the matter. At least, if a man has been arrested he has soon been released and not sent up for trial."

"Well . . . unfortunately, that's not quite true." Bontoux twisted his other eyebrow. "There was that affair between a couple of students at Poitiers in January 1843 when they sent the whole caboodle to trial, seconds and all."

"Bah, sir! They were all acquitted," said Lavertumel hotly. "Acquitted unanimously. Enormous crowd. Cheered the verdict. Damned right."

"True, but strictly speaking a duel comes under the Penal Code now."

"Bah, damned scandal! Interference, that's all it is. Can't think what things are coming to. All the same, I think we'll have to wait a day or two before we do anything. See if the Austrian turns up."

"You won't see him again, I'll warrant," Lovell said. "And I doubt he's Austrian either."

"Well, that's as may be. I'm sorry Mr. Hanna is not with us to complete our information."

"He's supposed to be seeing the gunsmith, Augier, the man we got the pistols from," Lovell said.

"Well, he's not here and we can't do anything more for the

moment." Lavertumel heaved himself heavily to his feet. "I'll have a little more of that excellent toddy of yours, if I may, Mr. Lovell. Damned cold outside."

"By all means, sir. Another glass, Philippe? Bontoux? Help yourselves."

It was half an hour before they broke up, having agreed to wait for another forty-eight hours before going to the Public Prosecutor. Then, as they stood with their coats on shaking hands, a fresh-faced young man in a puce coat with velvet lapels appeared in the doorway.

"Hanna! Well, there you are."

"Damn it, sir, you're an hour late."

"We've been waiting for you."

The young man in the puce coat had curly blond hair and light blue eyes and he was smiling, a little out of breath. "Sorry, sorry. I couldn't find a cab. How are you?" He shook hands all around. Lovell shut the door again and poured him a glass of the Yquem.

"Well, have you found out anything of interest?"

"Yes, I have. Your good health." He took a drink of the wine, savored it. "Mmm, excellent. Let me guess the year."

"Get *on* with it, sir!" Lavertumel fumed.

"Sorry. Well, I finally got hold of the gunsmith. And do you know what he says? He says when you took the pistols back to him afterwards, one was still loaded."

"Yes, that was the pistol that wouldn't fire."

"The one Blood threw on the ground."

"Correct. Well, he says he found a bit of rag, a scrap of rag, under the ball and the powder."

"A scrap of rag?"

"What, it stopped it firing?"

"You mean the cap couldn't fire the powder?"

"Exactly. Because the rag was in the way, the cap couldn't fire the powder. There was no shot."

"Yes. And we changed the cap and it still wouldn't fire."

"But how did the rag get there?"

"Augier says it *might* have got there when somebody tried to clean the pistol before loading it, got torn off. It *might* have. But he says it's a neat oval shape, hasn't got ragged edges like a bit of rag torn accidentally would have."

"And they loaded those pistols, didn't they?"

378

"Yes."

They all looked at one another.

"I think, all told, it looks like an attempt to murder Mr. Blood," Lovell said quietly.

"Yes." Lavertumel nodded and his eyes went from one face to another. "I think so too."

Relations between Susannah and Francis were cautious now. Francis felt they were close to a break and must feel their way carefully with each other. He slept in the dressing room and did not speak much to her. Yet he didn't sit with his mother in the evening playing piquet as he had always done. He wanted to avoid seeming to side with her. He was wretched at not having stood up for Susannah more with his family. And the idea of her going away frightened him now. If she went he would be lost.

Whatever Susannah might have said, he sensed in his heart that something had happened between her and John Blood, but he did not want to see it, did not want to admit it to himself, and he turned away from it. It made him quiet and cautious. He lived as if by being too vigorous he would destroy his own defenses, so he was quiet. Even with his limited understanding of his wife, he could see how greatly she had changed from the girl he had brought to La Guiche. How she could have changed so much was a mystery to him. He sensed the depths in her, the mystery, though he understood dimly that he could not reach her there. To him she was almost another woman, and he was afraid now in case he should lose her.

This quietness went on for three or four days after the scene with the family, and then she came to him one night after he had gone to bed in the dressing room and knelt by his bed and kissed him and asked him to come back to her in the bedroom. He clung to her as if he were going to lose her. He buried his face in her bosom and held her as if he were a child, as if they were both going through fire, and, clinging to her with tears, he kept saying to her, "Don't go. I can't live without you, Sue. Don't go," and she couldn't help it and wept too.

They went back to the big warm bed and she held him to her, giving herself with love, not being swept up but giving herself lovingly, sweetly and yieldingly, wanting to give him her strength.

379

Afterwards she lay with her head on his shoulder while he stroked her. The peaceful night was around them, and she felt they had gone through the fire and reached peace in the deep darkness. Francis felt there was a mystery about her he would never know. But it was not an enemy to him, the mystery. He felt he could lose himself in it as in the deep darkness. He lost himself in her; she was all things mysterious to him now. She was outside him and beyond him and around him as her body was when he went to her in love. There were distances and mysteries in her which he could not comprehend. With the change that had come over her she was really the mystery of life to him.

They both woke early in the morning. The spell of cold weather had given way to a mild greenish sky without a cloud, and pale yellow sunlight came into the bedroom when he pushed open the shutters.

"Sue, you must come down and see the ship today. Look, it's going to be a fine day. Let's go and see her. Won't you?"

He was all boyish eagerness again. She watched him from the bed as he slipped into his trousers and thought what a well-made man he was, slim and supple with good strong legs, flat belly and good shoulders and velvet-smooth skin.

"How about it? Let's go right after breakfast and have lunch in Bordeaux. You must see her."

She didn't answer, still eying him. In the bed she stretched.

"Sue, will you? What . . ." Hopping on one leg, half into his trousers, he grabbed the bedpost and looked at her as she lay back in the bed with her blond hair spilling around her, watching him with a little smile. He knew what that expression meant, and with one leg out of his trousers he went awkwardly over to her.

"Oh, *cold*," she cried at his touch.

Off he kicked the trousers as the warm odor of her body and the odorousness of the bed came to him. He took her strongly in his arms. "Oh, Sue, I love you."

So after breakfast they set off for Bordeaux and the *Amiable Rose*. The ship was moored in the river off the right bank of the Gironde opposite a district new to Susannah. They were ferried out in a small boat by two red-faced longshoremen, apparently old friends of Francis's.

Francis, in fact, seemed to know everybody on the waterfront, exchanging greetings and nodding sagaciously when men called out some salty remark. Quite at home! When he introduced her, she caught the peculiar look in the men's eyes, the snap of attention. For, of course, they all knew about the notorious Madame Gautier. But Francis was happy and she couldn't help thinking he looked just as he had on their first day together in Bordeaux, so young and fresh and bright-eyed. Georges Gaveau, summoned from his office, appeared in haste, and with one or other of the half-dozen crew on board they inspected the *Amiable Rose* from stem to stern—the tiny saloon, the few little cubicle-sized cabins, the galley, the rigging, the great winches and sails, the engine room. They poked about and squeezed in and out. There seemed no real space for anything.

She was a neat little ship, sticky with new paint. But Susannah couldn't help thinking how far it all was from La Guiche. Francis opened the door to one of the tiny cabins no bigger than a closet and said proudly, "You see? First class with bunk. Isn't it neat?"

She said, "Yes, lovely." But she kept thinking, What has it all got to do with your real business, La Guiche? It was like a toy to him. It was a game, a fantasy. It was a barrier between him and reality. He didn't want to see too much of reality, and to have something like the *Amiable Rose* was sheer joy to him. Escape!

Once or twice she caught smirky glances from the men of the crew when Francis had just finished speaking with them and had turned away again or when the three of them passed by.

And Gaveau. Gaveau, she thought, didn't behave at all like the one who was the leading partner in the enterprise. Not for a single solitary minute. On the contrary, as they walked around and talked about the ship and what they were going to do, he was reticent. Sometimes he seemed ill at ease, though maybe that was just an impression. Too bad the captain was ashore, Francis said, and asked Gaveau several times where he was, but Gaveau didn't know. It was Francis who did the talking and suggesting and explaining.

What was holding them up? Susannah asked. Oh, it was nothing, Francis explained, simply permission from the Spaniards to take passengers and freight to and from the two Spanish ports. They were tiresome and infernally slow, the Spaniards, but it would be coming through. Fortunately there weren't all that number of passages in the winter months. It was spring and summer that counted.

When they had inspected the ship, Gaveau produced a bottle of Sauternes in the little saloon and they drank their toast to the New Steamship Company.

"Isn't she a beauty, eh?" Francis said to her. "Admit it, you didn't expect this, eh?"

"She's lovely." She gave him a kiss on the cheek.

Ashore they had a late lunch in a quayside café where Francis and Gaveau were greeted like habitués. During the meal the two men talked about one of them going to Madrid to try to shake the Spaniards up, while Susannah watched the patron of the place going around surreptitiously pointing her out to his male friends. And she sat under their stares taking no notice. Fortunately they didn't linger in the place, since Gaveau had to get back to his office.

It was beginning to get dark as they drove home. Francis was so happy! He hugged her and kept talking about the ship, plans for their next vessel, plans for their new service, and so on. And because they had come through their trial so recently she couldn't cast a doubt on any of it, couldn't even seem not to share his enthusiasm. So she smiled and hugged him as if he were the cleverest man in the world.

But she thought of the freshly painted little ship with its improvised air, the absent captain, the indifferent Spaniards, the smirky glances of the crew. She thought of what it had cost and must still be costing, and she shuddered inwardly and was worried.

She lay in bed that night and stared into the dark while Francis slept beside her.

No word of John Blood. Now that he needed her most, she was cut off from him entirely. Too difficult to go to him, and too cruel to Francis. She felt a coward, but she couldn't help it. She ached to see him, her other self reached out for him, yet she knew all that was over. It was all gone, and yet she thought of him with terrible fierce love, the fierce longing she had always had for him, the sort of battle pride he stirred in her, the hard bright fearless love of that other self of hers behind which was tenderness overflowing.

She lay there biting her lip, then brushed away her tears and turned and saw Francis's sleeping face in the shadows. She laid her hand gently on his brow, smoothing it, then she leaned over and gently kissed him.

Six days passed. It was a strange interlude, timeless it seemed to her afterwards, as if everything were waiting, and even the new closeness between her and Francis was in some curious way foreshortened and tangled so that she did not see it clearly in retrospect for long afterwards.

They saw none of the family, and she and Francis seemed to exist alone in the universe, with Madame Gautier only dimly present. A strange empty period. Yet Susannah was fretfully uneasy without news of John Blood. All she knew was that he was still detained, but of course no one gossiped to her and she had no source of information beyond the newspapers, which simply said the police inquiries were continuing. One afternoon she met Constance and Byam Canning, but Constance either knew nothing or wouldn't say in her husband's presence and they were rather awkward together.

The morning after this she was driving to the village in the carriage when a horseman cantered past going in the same direction. It was John Lovell. Susannah called out to Joseph to pull in to the side of the road, and when he had done so Lovell, who had turned his horse, came up.

He doffed his hat and dismounted. "I trust you are well, madame?"

"Thank you. And yourself, Mr. Lovell?" Smart he looked in his damson-blue coat, she thought, and his smile was attractive.

"A lucky meeting this. I have been wanting to see you for several days. Forgive me but I thought it too delicate to send you a letter and I confess I was at a loss to know how to see you alone. I trust I am not embarrassing you here." He scanned the road discreetly, but there was only a peasant's cart approaching.

"No. Not at all."

"I came up today to devise a means of getting a message to you at La Guiche."

"Thank you, Mr. Lovell." She appreciated his care. A call at La Guiche was out of the question for the moment, since everybody knew he had been Blood's second at the duel.

"I have seen our friend, of course. He is well and I am glad to say the authorities have decided to release him."

"Oh." She felt a great gust of relief. Her hand tightened on the carriage door and she stared at him. "He is going to be free —not charged?"

"His friends in Bordeaux saw the authorities and presented some evidence which had not come to their attention. With the result that they have ordered his release."

"I'm so glad."

"In fact, he is being released today. And he asked me to give you a message, if it were possible, to say that he will be by the river this evening."

She knew she would have reddened at that not so long ago, but now she was so relieved and grateful and so full of gladness. "Thank you, Mr. Lovell. It is truly kind of you."

"Then I have done my commission and"—he gave another glance down the road—"perhaps it is best I should be brief."

"Yes. I . . . I hope in a little while when this has passed over we shall be able to meet as before."

"I truly hope so, my dear." He swung into the saddle, raised his hat and the next minute, even before the peasant's cart had lumbered up to them, he was on his way.

The old tumult was in her heart! She was like a girl waiting again for her first love meeting, could think of nothing else. She moved restlessly about the house for the rest of the morning doing unnecessary things, paying sudden grave attention to trifles, nervously aware of Francis, of Madame Gautier, watching their movements, watching the hours before she could set out.

After lunch she told Francis she had an appointment to see Dr. Cavan and he nodded vaguely, then his attention sharpened. He frowned, eyes on her. "What, is something . . . ?"

She was studying the big silver cruet, twisting and turning it in her hands, her heart beating fast in the intensity of the moment. Then, with his gaze resting on her face, he said, "Oh, yes." His tone left the unspoken conclusion that it was one of those "women's things" for which she saw the doctor from time to time and he said no more.

It was a dull afternoon with darkening clouds. At three o'clock Joseph came around with Tom and the buggy with the hood up and she started off. Halfway there it began to rain, and by the time she reached the path the rain was driving down, masking the river, cutting the path with little rivulets and filling the landscape with its gray curtain.

The path was deserted. She turned down it, peering through the rain, thinking of that morning in the fog when he had told her he loved her. So long ago, it seemed, and yet so close. The wildness of their love, it was all going, all going. She drove down the path and saw him on his horse a little way off, coming toward her.

She pulled up under a clump of pines where there was a little shelter and got out as he sprang down from the saddle. She was in his arms. He held her and the world was gone for them. They stood there for a long time without speaking, held close in their kiss and their embrace, and her heart poured out her love for him.

At last he said, "I hope you haven't had too much trouble."

"No."

"I thought you'd come on Red."

"Why, do you want that race at last?"

He smiled. "Why not?"

They were silent again, they took no notice of the rain. He said, "I'm leaving tomorrow and perhaps it will be some time before we see each other again."

"Where are you going?"

"Oh, I don't know. Somewhere. I'll make up my mind at the last minute. But I'll be back. I'll be back for you."

She looked at him. "You know you're the man I want to follow. You know I'd follow you anywhere because you're strong, you want to fight and you live your life like a true man. The real men are getting fewer and fewer. I love you and I always shall, you know that. You helped me see myself, be myself. You remember that night when I raged at you about happiness—I'd got some of that from you. You made me see I must be myself no matter what the rest of the world does and that's the sort of man I want to follow. But I can't come with you. I can't leave him, because I love him. I'm bound to him, and now I can't even think of it because I'm going to have his child."

He was still for a moment, looking at her gravely, then bowed his head. But he looked up again. "I shall always remember you that night standing there smoking that cigar. You were wonderful."

She couldn't bear it; she pressed her face against him.

"And on the Place des Quinconces, that night in the snow."

She put herself away from him. "Who knows, perhaps next time it'll be in Ireland?"

"Aye, in Dublin Castle."

"Yes!"

"And I shall ask you to dance."

"Oh, John, I love you."

"And I too, you, always, Susannah."

She held him again, she couldn't let him go.

The rain came down and dripped from the trees and they stood against the buggy in silence. Slowly the light faded and they couldn't part. It was almost dark. The rain went on and they stood there. At last she said, "I must go back."

He held her strongly and kissed her, and then as she stood there he turned and sprang into the saddle and was quickly gone in the rainy dusk.

14

Christmas passed and the New Year came with its round of family visits. Susannah went along dutifully with Francis and sat quiet and unobtrusive, folded in on herself, ignoring their disapproval. She was withdrawn and silent and submissive, took no part in their conversation and was simply dutifully present. But she was loving to Francis. Francis was overjoyed at the prospect of a child—which they did not announce until Susannah had seen Dr. Cavan again at the end of January—and fussed about her, insisting she take care of herself. Madame Gautier was watchfully neutral and old Monsieur Parenteau, on the day they drank their New Year's toast at La Guiche, took her aside and confided that it would probably dispose of any more talk about deeds of renunciation, since her child could not by law be disinherited.

With the quiet in her also came the listening. Under the surface, during these calm days of January and February, something menacing was working, and each day seemed to bring it nearer. She could hear it. She sat very still in herself and could hear it gnawing like a deadly insect at their life.

Work started in the vineyard. The gossip and evil rumors had died away as mysteriously as they had arisen. They had no more nocturnal visits at La Guiche, and Octavie, the cook, who had been so frightened, was almost her old self, only a little subdued and nervous sometimes. Susannah watched herself growing heavier, her waist thickening. Physically, she was blooming, the colors of her face all deep golden-brown and cream, hair thick, ocher-yellow and glowing. At the end of February Francis came home one day and announced with triumph that the Spaniards had granted permission and the *Amiable Rose* would be making her first voyage in a week's time.

Yet . . . Susannah could hear the secret gnawing. And like the dust from a wormeaten beam, tiny grains began to fall. Money was short again and the men, particularly Josserand, complained they weren't getting their due, couldn't get repairs done, couldn't prepare the outdoor work. Balavoine, for one, came to her and said they couldn't do the rest of the spring tilling unless he had new plows and harness. Susannah drove to Bordeaux, saw Monsieur Parenteau and borrowed three hundred francs. The old notary was reluctant, said the loan must be her personal responsibility and made her sign a paper; but when she tried to get something out of him about the general finances of La Guiche he became tetchy and closed up.

Whenever she spoke to Francis about any of the practical matters of the estate, he cheerfully put her off and did nothing. So Susannah had to take it all on herself, and finally she stopped consulting him and simply gave the orders herself. And always the ticking of the deadly beetle.

And so the weeks went by, the spring began to open out before them. The child moved in her. She let her clothes out, became slower in movement, began to collect baby linen and knitted small things. Louise was always turning up with something new—tiny socks, bonnets, embroidered bibs and so on. Susannah's mind was quiet, as if she were resigned, in her withdrawn silence. Francis was happily occupied with his career as shipowner, reporting that passage and freight bookings were as good as could be expected for a new line—in fact were surprisingly good—but would be picking up considerably when the service became better known.

And all the time Susannah listened to the tiny gnawing approach of disaster. It was plain that Francis had borrowed money and that another year's failure with the wine would be fatal to them. No good old Parenteau trying to hide it. Abel-Cherubin was unnaturally complacent and offhand in the way he inquired about the work, and Susannah couldn't help feeling that something was working surreptitiously there too—something *else*. Dr. Cavan noticed her inwardness and lectured her impatiently. And walking out into the vines one evening as April arrived, she looked quietly down at the long freshly tilled rows, almost *waiting* for the oïdium mold to appear.

Suddenly she reacted. Her will, her American will, exploded in her. She thrust dread away from her. Energy came back into her like a charge. It was the prospect of defeat that moved her. Impatience flowed from her like electricity. She couldn't bear to sit still for a moment longer.

A Committee for the Malady of the Vines had been set up in Bordeaux. She drove in to see them, found a busy, rather disordered set of offices with posters and notices pinned up where people were charging about and looking important. A large bearded man gave her leaflets and harangued her about local distress and the committee's efforts to arouse the government in Paris, while other men kept passing and looking her up and down. She thought they were a feeble lot of shufflers and wasted no time on them. Back at La Guiche, she sat up late reading the leaflets and found the advice, as she expected, was mainly a repetition of the "remedies" she had listened to at the village meeting and read about in the Bordeaux papers. She threw them away. She raged in impatience.

Three mornings later Josserand came to her and reported the oïdium had reappeared on a section of the vines.

She was in a fury. All her quietness had gone now. She walked back taut with impatient anger and anguish to the house. Francis had left for Bordeaux. And she realized that six months back she would have wanted to scream at him to stop playing with his damned *Amiable Rose*, would have screamed at him that La Guiche was more important, but that now she couldn't be bothered. She couldn't waste time with him. The whole business of the *Amiable Rose* was footling and ridiculous, even the name made her sick. Oh, God, for a man! A *man*.

She shook with impatience. She must do something, even if it were wrong, since nobody apparently knew what the right thing was. She could not sit and watch the oïdium destroy the vines again. She must take some action. First she would go and see the Marquis de Talabu. It was months since she had seen him. And if the visit produced nothing—well, she would see. But act she must.

She sent Emilie to have Tom hitched to the buggy and hurried upstairs to change her dress. Joseph was away and Emilie didn't like her driving the buggy alone, wanted her to take Jean with her, but Susannah impatiently shooed her off.

It was a fine warm April morning. All the way through the vineyards men were out tilling or tending the vines. The little old Marquis de Talabu greeted her in the courtyard of his house with his courtly bow. He was wearing a mole-colored velvet coat and a little skull cap to match, and when she had tied up the horse and buggy he gave her his arm and led her indoors.

"You have heard the message I have been sending to you?" he said.

"Message? What message?"

"Telepathy, my dear. I have been wanting you to come here for days. I've been sending thought vibrations to you every day."

She laughed, but he looked so serious she pulled herself up. "Why?"

"Come to the laboratory, I'll show you. I see you are expecting a child."

"Yes. In July. I already feel enormous."

He smiled, nodded. "Keep hold of my arm as we go through."

In the laboratory he sat her down at the bench, then carried over several trays of fungus growths and set up two microscopes. He leaned his arms on the bench and interlaced his fingers; his face with its odd high forehead looked stranger than ever. "I've been experimenting with various things against our friend *Oïdium tuckeri*. I forced some little plants in the greenhouse because I wanted them nice and fresh, then infected them and tried different remedies. And I will make my confession at once for a particularly bad piece of observation, because until the other day, when Miles Berkeley called my attention to it, I did not take sufficient account of a remedy which Mr. Tucker— the discoverer of our parasite—used himself in his greenhouse at Margate at the very beginning."

"Used himself?"

"Yes. I have looked up Mr. Tucker's original communication to the *Gardener's Journal* of the twenty-second of September 1847." He reached out for the paper. "Here it is. And you

390

will see that in his letter Mr. Tucker explains that he destroyed the oïdium in his greenhouse by the use of sulphur and lime."

Susannah glanced at the paper where he had ringed a letter signed "Progressionist."

"He took flower of sulphur and mixed it up with lime in cold water. He had been using sulphur on his peach trees, so it wasn't new to him. Well, he dipped a sponge in the sulphur and lime mixture and wiped all the leaves of his vines with it. And the oïdium disappeared."

"Mm. Another 'proven remedy'?" Susannah said skeptically.

Talabu smiled. "Well, this one I have tested myself and it is effective."

"But why haven't we heard of it before? Here we are in 1854 and Mr. Tucker's letter is dated seven years ago."

"With the remedy there all the time!" Talabu was smiling at her. "Isn't it strange?"

"But how is it possible?" She was still skeptical.

"Well, I think I can explain it," he said. "Mr. Tucker had only the small closed space of his greenhouse to worry about. He could easily wipe down all the leaves himself. And you will not need me to tell you that to wipe every leaf and shoot of a vineyard of even thirty acres, let alone a bigger one, is impossible. Nobody has done it. Nobody will ever do it. Of course, not enough notice was taken of Mr. Tucker's remedy, that is certain. They were in too much of a panic. But, as you may have noticed from the newspapers, a few growers *have* been experimenting with sulphur in different forms and in combination with other substances. The results have been disappointing—people think it doesn't work properly. But it is only because an *effective method of application* has not yet been found that these experiments have not fully succeeded. Either because the applications have not been heavy enough or persistent enough or for some other reason, I don't know. But the agent itself has been known all along—sulphur."

She gazed at him, at the elfin face, the bright intelligent eyes. "Is it possible?"

"Not only possible but proven. Look. Take this microscope. There you will see the portion of a leaf on which the oïdium is flourishing."

Susannah looked through the eyepiece, adjusted the instrument and saw the tiny fingerlike stalks of the oïdium on the leaf.

"Now look at this one. It is a leaf from the same plant, but it has been treated with sulphur."

Susannah saw that the patches of mildew were dried up and none of the oïdium active. "And how did you apply it?" she asked.

"Mashed up sulphur and water and applied it with a brush to the hot pipes. Also I burned some. In a greenhouse the fumes are enough to kill the oïdium. You, alas, cannot use either of those methods because you have to work in the open. You have got to find some way to get the sulphur onto the vines and shoots."

That was the upshot. They went out to the greenhouses and inspected the sulphured vines. Not a trace of the white powder. Susannah was excited. But when it came to nailing him down to a method that could be used outdoors, that was another matter. Having made his demonstration, the little Marquis wanted to talk about other things. They were, he said, on the track of the fruit of the oïdium by means of which it managed to survive the winter. This was a tiny round pod with long tendrils lying on a bed of silky filaments. He would show her one. No, wait, he would draw her one first to demonstrate.

She tried to drag him back to the sulphuring problem, but he was off on his fungus fruit. Then on to his experiments with things called oospores and zoospores. Then to the potato blight. Then to his and Berkeley's idea of founding a new branch of science to be called vegetable pathology. Impossible to get him back.

It was midafternoon when Susannah left. But now she felt she had got hold of something. She must find a way of sulphuring the vines; and she would try first by spraying them with water and blowing the sulphur over them. Begin with that. And if it did not work, then try something else. It *must* work.

In the village she stopped at Marcilhac's store, bought four pairs of hand bellows, all they had, and had them load a tub of sulphur into the buggy. It *must* work. She wanted to force it to work by her will. She felt she was the only one to stop La Guiche drifting away into dissolution. She *had* to save it. She loved it and would not let it go.

At six next morning Susannah was up and out waiting as the men and women appeared; she had told Josserand the night before what they would be doing, and he drifted up now in his miserable rags of clothes looking bad-tempered. She faced them. "This morning we are going to start destroying the oïdium with sulphur. I can tell you it works because I have seen it myself. So you can be sure you are doing the right thing. Every vine has to be treated. Every one. The object is to get the powdered sulphur, which we have here, on to all the green parts, leaves and shoots. To fix the sulphur, to make it stay on, we first have to spray the vines with water. Then we blow the sulphur on. On every vine, you understand? It's going to take a long time. It is going to be hard work, but we've got to drop everything else to do this first."

" 'Tis not in our price," came Josserand's surly voice.

"You'll get ten centimes a row. And don't expect any more." She wasn't really sure they'd accept it from her; she had never fixed a price with them before. They looked at one another. Josserand shuffled and muttered, and she knew she would have to give him a little more than the others. The price was good—half as much as they were paid for the pruning—but of course they argued, for the principle of the thing, complained it hadn't been foreseen. In the end they gave way. Perhaps because they thought it wouldn't last. A woman's whim!

So that morning Susannah began the fight with the oïdium. And almost at once they were in difficulties. Laborious enough carrying out buckets of water and spraying each vine with a garden syringe; but trying to blow the sulphur on so that it stuck to the leaves and shoots was maddening. One man or woman held some sulphur on the end of a spade while another worked the bellows. Hopeless! The men coughed, got it in their faces; a little in the eyes stung badly. A puff of wind blew the sulphur anywhere. But she made them persist. She stood over them and made them persist. They shrugged and went on skeptically, rather resentfully, but thinking, no doubt, that they might as well earn the extra ten centimes a row at this as at anything.

And Susannah stayed with them. She went from one team to the other, keeping them at it, making them go back over the vines they had not done properly. In midmorning she went indoors for half an hour, but when she came out again she saw they were larking about and making a joke of it and found they

393

had got tired of spraying the water on and had barely been dusting with the dry sulphur, which, of course, had blown off.

She called over Josserand and told him dryly they wouldn't get paid unless the work were done properly. He waved his hand dismissively, said they were wasting their time.

"I'll decide that!" she yelled at him. "Do what you're told!" And her sudden violence, the look on her face, silenced him. All the men and women turned to stare. Josserand slunk back to them, swore at them and told them to get on. And that was the beginning of her fight with Josserand.

So they labored. Every step she watched them. She helped them, she summoned them back down the rows, lifted the leaves, made them begin again. They eyed her resentfully, snorted down their noses. She would say, "Well? If you've got something to say, say it! If not, shut up and do your job." Then they turned silently back to the work and went on.

But of course they took it out on her by slacking off as soon as her back was turned, and she had to be there constantly to watch them. Her back ached with bending to the low vines. She got a pain in her side and had to go and sit down for a while. But she got to her feet and walked out to them again.

So slow it was. By evening they had only done a small area and she was dog-tired. She saw they would never succeed with this clumsy method. She would have to find another way. And she saw that the task was going to test her will to the utmost.

That evening after dinner while Francis was with his mother she sat at the dining-room table with pencil and paper, her head propped in her hand, trying to stay awake and to think of some alternative method. But what? The bellows were obviously unsatisfactory. Sleepily she stared at the big silver cruet on the sideboard before her. Wait a minute. What if they sprinkled the sulphur on from something like a big pepper pot? Perhaps it would work.

She drew two models. It would surely be an improvement. She wished she were more inventive, but she was too tired and in the end she carried her pepper-pot idea up to bed with her and had hardly laid her head on the pillow before she was asleep.

At six in the morning she was up again seeing the workpeople begin. An hour later she had breakfast, changed her clothes and had Joseph drive her to the tinsmith in the village.

The tinsmith's wife, who kept his shop, studied Susannah's drawings of the enlarged pepper pot about eight inches tall with the lid end punctured with holes and said it would be simple enough to make. Her husband could let Susannah have four the following afternoon and two more the day after. Susannah's idea was to fill the canisters with sulphur and have the men shake them over the wet vines.

As soon as she got back to La Guiche she saw that the men had been blowing the dry sulphur dust on with the bellows again without wetting the vines, and four of the women had disappeared. Another row with Josserand which resulted in black looks and mutterings. The other men had been rather infected with Josserand's claim that it was a waste of time. Antagonism was in them and she felt Josserand set them against her. But she kept them at it.

"Well, what have you been doing all day?" Francis said at dinner.

"Oh, I've been out in the vines. Sulphuring them."

"Sulphur?"

She was dropping with exhaustion and didn't want to talk to him. She was in a period of exasperation with him and had no patience with his blindness, his voluntary blinkering of himself. And on impulse after dinner she asked him to sleep in his dressing room because she was uncomfortable with him in the big bed. He looked at her with a faint, slightly patronizing smile as if it were one of the pregnant woman's fancies with which he was supposed to comply. Let him believe it, she didn't mind. All her energy, her thoughts, her will were concentrated now on the vineyard, and he was only an encumbrance to her in that so she was better without him. She was glad he stayed in Bordeaux one or two nights a week now.

And then in the night—rain! She woke to it blustering against the shutters, wiping out all their efforts. Oh, God! Two full days of work gone. They would have to begin all over again.

In the cold gray light next morning the men and women trooped out, but it was so obviously threatening more rain that she had to call it off. Josserand sneered; it had all been a waste of time as he had said all along. More oïdium had appeared in another part of the vineyard. She said they would resume as soon as the weather cleared.

395

So Susannah went on from day to day. The pepper-pot canisters proved a failure. The men complained that they had to keep shaking them hard to get the sulphur out. And when it did come out, she saw that it spread very unevenly.

Back to the tinsmith. Had she tried this patent bellows, asked the tinsmith's wife—a bellows with a little tin container for the sulphur fixed on just where the nozzle of the bellows joined the flat wooden sides. They tried it. And Susannah found herself tramping from one group to another the whole day to refill the little containers, for as soon as they found them empty, the men slacked off or stopped work. Then they complained that the bellows was too heavy, the weight of the container was badly distributed and the thing made their arms ache. They had to abandon it and try another kind.

Susannah came back to the house in the evening exhausted, her limbs leaden, her back aching. She changed her clothes, sat at the table while Francis, when he was home, chatted gaily about the *Amiable Rose* and life in the Bordeaux shipping world, about which he was not very knowledgeable. He was shutting his mind to the vineyard, to what she was doing there all day, and his questions simply skimmed it all and passed on. Often she was too tired to eat but would rather have died than show it. Her will sustained her.

She threw the patent bellows away, made Balavoine pierce a hole in the flat side of an ordinary pair of fire bellows, poured the sulphur in, corked the hole and tried that. It worked fairly well. She had Balavoine make six pairs. But if the workpeople tilted the bellows, the sulphur inside accumulated at the nozzle end and blocked the hole. And so, over and over again, relentlessly over and over, she had to go to them. "Hold it level. No, don't tilt it. Level. Like that. No, *level*." Over and over they threw the things down in disgust. "It doesn't work," and she had to show them once more, once more and again. They holed the leather sides and the sulphur puffed back over them. Patiently she had the things patched. She willed them to it. She lifted them up with the strength of her will. They wasted too much time going to and fro for the sulphur, dawdling whenever they could, so she had shoulder bags made for each of them to carry his own supply—which they resented. Still the women went back and forth with the buckets of water. A storm would wipe out all their work and she would drive them back immediately to blow the sulphur on the vines while they were still wet from the rain. Ah, the struggle! Slowly they worked over the vineyard.

At last one evening Josserand came to her, looking at her loweringly with his little reddish eyes. "There's a patch down by the hut with new leaves out and two more on the far side, and they've all got the oïdium. I'll have no more of this game."

"But it's what you'd expect! The vines are growing and naturally the oïdium fixes on the new shoots and leaves. We'll have to go over them again."

"That I won't. You can get on with it."

"Josserand, I've had enough of your grousing."

"Then you'll hear no more, for you'll do without me on this fancy bit of woman's nonsense."

"You'll do what I say! And I'm not having your damned impertinence either, do you hear?"

"Eh, and you take yourself for the master here?"

She lost her temper. "Yes! And you'd better understand it! I'm the master here and you'll do what I say or get out. Do you hear me? I give the orders here, not you. If you're not out here tomorrow morning to do your job *as I say*, to do exactly *what* I say, I'll have you thrown off the property. By your neck! Do you hear that?" She screamed at him, livid.

"Eh, there's no—"

"Now get away. Get off with you!"

He turned away. She glared after him, blazing. Then she went back to the house. She was exhausted.

15

———————————

Regis Gautier walked up the Allées de Tourny with the peculiar feeling of not being quite present in his surroundings. You must, he imagined, feel something like this when you had sunstroke, a little dazed and lightheaded yet with a strange sensation of being elsewhere. As if reality were muffled behind the curious cotton wool of the present moment.

He had not drunk more than usual, rather less in fact, and there had been no sun to expose himself to. He was having trouble adjusting to the painful scene that had just taken place between himself and Mademoiselle Aurelie Hagenbach. She had listened to him, allowed him to present his suit, allowed him to make a bit of a fool of himself with his ardor—he had been on the point of dropping to one knee but hadn't, thank God—and then had coyly told him she had given her promise to Mawdistly Baynes.

Mawdistly Baynes! The name alone made him sick. The thought of her preferring that gangling creature to himself was bad enough. The further thought that she had intended it all along or that he had been outmaneuvered, outdistanced, outrun by that stoop-shouldered oaf of a Mawdistly was worse. But worse still was the impression that it had all been a bit of a confidence trick, a bit of a joke. He flushed deeply again at the thought of it. Mawdistly, he believed, had induced her to lead him on, had concerted with her to encourage him up to the last minute as a kind of entertainment. There had been something in the set of Aurelie's mouth . . . Mawdistly might have been behind the door listening.

All in vain the assiduous campaign he had plotted so carefully for the last three years. All in vain the watchful attentions. All in vain the phaeton, the projected town house. And all, surely, observed by Mademoiselle Aurelie and her Mawdistly as a huge joke.

Perhaps even worse than the actual scene with Aurelie had been the ensuing moments with the Baroness Hagenbach, the mother. The high condescension of her manner! The boiled stare! The set of those mighty elbows which said he must have realized the absurdity of his pretensions all along. Awful.

But it was the sudden void in his prospects which had really stunned him. That was what was making him feel lightheaded. That was the worst of all—the knowledge that, except for some unexpected death which might create an eligible widow in the chartrons' ranks, the gates of social bliss were closed to him, that he could not aspire now to becoming one of the elite. Dead men's shoes! Or to wait till a little eleven-year-old became a twenty-one-year-old, and then . . . then to find himself competing with the young Mawdistlys of that day? Ah, no! No.

And so he walked up the Allées de Tourny with less than his usual jauntiness. The phaeton he had taken straight back to the stables after the interview; he simply had no heart to drive it. And now at the corner, checked by the flow of afternoon traffic, he paused, at a loss. He felt himself adrift, he who usually knew so firmly where he was going, and it made him wretchedly uncomfortable.

Sophie would be out. With the interview with Aurelie in mind and, as he thought, eminently promising, he had told Sophie he would be busy all afternoon, all evening too probably. And now here it was, barely four o'clock and everything over. His office he could not face. His club he could not think of. His male friends he shrank from.

A familiar face caught his eye, Madame Boehmer in her carriage with her bloated eight-year-old daughter. Repressing a shudder, Regis lifted his hat and bowed.

Even the weather was depressing his mood, a great blue-black bag of storm cloud hanging above. What to do? He felt lonely, dispirited, in need of sympathy. And so, almost mechanically, his steps took the direction of his mistress's house. There at least he would be able to nurse his chagrin undisturbed, there where one creature at least gave him love, accepted his caresses, found him clever, he could brood until Sophie herself came back and could minister to him. Difficult she might be, but she had warmth. Yes, and more physical beauty in her toe than the whole tribe of Hagenbachs and Bayneses assembled. Ah, she was a true woman. She was a consolation to a man after all.

He made his way to the quiet streets by the Public Gardens, quickening his pace, for the storm clouds above were lowering now and the wind had dropped. The weather had discouraged the afternoon callers and there were not many people about. As he turned down toward the house, the first few drops of rain spattered the sidewalk. He hurried and as he reached Number Four a tremendous cannonade of thunder crashed out above. In a trice he was under the porte-cochère, and down came the flood.

A cloudburst, very spectacular as they sometimes were here. For a moment or two he paused, contemplating the blinding force of the storm, then turned into the entrance and mounted the short flight of stairs to the door. As he inserted his key and opened it another terrific thunderclap sounded above, making him start, and this was followed by a continuous rumble overhead. Even with the door shut he could hear the swirling drumming of the rain outside.

Peeling off his gloves, he crossed the gloomy storm-darkened entrance. He put his hat on a table and was about to lay his gloves on top of it when he caught something faintly familiar in the air. What was it? He stood blinking, gloves in hand, puzzled. Then he shrugged, dismissing it. He placed his gloves on his hat, moved aside to see himself in the mirror, peering in the half-dark space at his reflection.

He fingered his hair, touched his cravat, sighed. Again he caught the faint, vaguely familiar something. Of course, a smell. What? Perfume. Yes. His nose twitched. No, gone again. He turned his head, sniffing. Couldn't get it. Wait a minute. Yes. Wasn't it? Attar of roses. Now where the devil had he come across attar of roses lately?

He stood stock still. Crash went another thunderclap above. The rain poured down, intermingled with the spouting and gurgling of innumerable unseen gutters, the swirling swish of drainpipes.

In the dim mirror his eyes enlarged with recollection. He looked around and perceived in the corner another hat, another pair of gloves. In a flash he snatched the hat up. He couldn't see a mark in the dimness, reached out and took the gloves. Gray, with red pigeon-eye buttons and three rows of black stitching on the back. Maker's name but no mark.

Standing there, he lifted one to his nose. No mistake, no possible mistake. Attar of roses. The vision came to him of the little private cubicle, the washbasin, the mirror, the pots of pomade, the leather couch.

Chabot.

Moving like a ghost, he replaced hat and gloves and glided across the entrance, past the empty salon, through the vestibule to the stairs. Another crackling snarl, like the laughter of cracked lips, came from the storm outside and a new rumble.

He reached her bedroom door. Impossible to hear a sound. Wraithlike he floated along the landing to the room beyond, entered and passed through to the small dressing room which gave on to her *cabinet de toilette*. The door to the bedroom was shut.

The boom of thunder overhead, the gurgle of gutters, the ubiquitous sound of water. Then, from behind the door, a different sort of gurgle. Regis felt his face reddening, his skin prickled. A rain-filled spouting moment passed, then, distinctly, her laugh followed by a male chuckle.

Regis was breathing hard. Gently he took the doorknob in his hand, waited, and as another roll of thunder came he eased the door open a crack. It was, he knew, half hidden by a screen. An inch or so more. Chabot's coat and trousers on the chair, natty boots below. He could just see the edge of the bed reflected in the mirror, one bare foot. Then, in a momentary lull in the drumming of the rain, her voice said something he could not catch and Chabot answered, "Must say I'm partial to it myself."

They laughed together. The bed creaked as weight shifted. He hung there, torturing himself, then retreated from the *cabinet de toilette* and gained the farther room.

As he went softly along the landing outside past the bedroom again, a gasp, familiar enough, came from behind the door. Down the stairs he went, as if pursued, and across the dim hall, shoulders bent with dejection and rueful self-righteousness. Chabot! Of all people. The indignity of the exchange was what hurt so much. Chabot!

Another rumble of thunder. Somewhere a broken gutter was spouting and splashing.

She had never locked the door. And strictly he had no grounds for complaint. She had told him quite plainly he didn't own exclusive rights over her. He simply had the privilege of paying the bills, for which he got the latchkey; and if he didn't like it, she had said, he could give the key up and she would pass it to somebody else. That was the sort of imperious mistress relationship she had imposed. And he had accepted. And never had he found a visitor until today. So officially, so to speak, he had no grounds for complaint. But Chabot! It was cruel.

He took his hat and gloves. A spare umbrella stood in the stand and he contemplated taking it; then he decided not to. Best he leave her no clue that he had called. He was tasting the subtle pleasure of personal martyrdom today.

But already he was beginning to recover. He would come back later, in the evening, give her warning of his impending arrival by sending around some flowers in advance. He would behave as if he knew nothing. And he would observe her. Yes. He knew how to play the waiting game.

He crossed the entrance and let himself quietly out.

It was like fighting an invisible enemy. The oïdium had reappeared. All over the vineyard they had gone with the back-breaking sulphuring, yet there was the gray mold again. Susannah drooped. Intermittent rain had destroyed their efforts; and then the vines had been growing, pushing out new green surfaces for the spores to settle on. The sulphuring did seem to have checked the fungus—there were clear patches—but the persistence of even a small area of oïdium meant that it would soon be all over the vineyard again. All the workpeople were disgusted.

Susannah remembered that Talabu, following Tucker, had mixed lime with his sulphur for the greenhouse. She got two big caldrons, put sulphur and lime into each, added water and boiled them together in the kitchen. The mixture would have to be sprayed on with syringes, but it would eliminate the tiresome process of wetting the vines and so save time.

But the stench! The stink of bad eggs hung all over the house. Francis complained, Madame Gautier told her to take the stuff away. Susannah had Jean and Joseph carry the caldrons out to one of the outbuildings and there, on the old stove used by the vintagers, she continued to boil the sulphur and lime until they were thoroughly mixed. It gave a brown-colored liquid which smelled very powerful—bad eggs still—so she diluted it with water and boiled some more. She begged four small barrels with spigots from Monsieur Laverne, filled these and had the men cart them out to four different parts of the vineyard as supply points. Then she told Josserand to turn the workpeople out for a fresh assault next day.

"Can't be done," he said.

Each time she spoke to him now he was obstructive. Always some difficulty, always some reason why what she wanted couldn't be done. This time the men were busy removing surplus earth from the ends of the rows where the oxen turned and water collected; and others were tilling, since they had postponed the fourth tilling this year till June.

"Never mind," she said. "They must stop all that and spray this new mixture on tomorrow."

He uttered an oath, dropped the bundle of laths he was carrying and walked off.

"Josserand!" He took no notice.

At the midday break she went to his cottage. His wife was outside and called through the open door for him to come. He came out with a tight mouth. Susannah faced him. "We are going to start spraying at five thirty in the morning," she said. "You'll see everybody is there, if you please."

He spat on the ground, wiped the back of his hand across his mouth. "You'll not go on making fools of folk. They've had about enough of you."

She felt herself going pale but kept her temper. "I'll decide what we do here. They will turn out tomorrow morning as I say. And when I speak to you, I expect an answer, not your turned back." He made a scowling grimace. "What's the matter with you, Josserand?" she said.

"Nothing the matter with me. You can be asking that question about yourself."

"I don't understand you."

"Eh, you'll not see a woman going on suchwise in these parts, that's all."

"Then all I can say is the quicker you get used to it the better, for that's how it's going to be."

He looked at her with hatred, the deep old peasant hatred, old as the land itself. She turned and walked away.

So next morning in the rosy light they began once more. All day, back and forth along the rows they went, bending down spraying the low vines with the stinking mixture. The garden syringes were pitifully inadequate but were all they had. The workpeople did not need Josserand's bad example to get their backs up. They protested it wasn't their work, was making them sick, affecting their skin and eyes and so forth. They got the fine spray on their clothes. On their skin. In their hair. They kept grimacing and stopping to wipe it off. They looked like horrible bedraggled scarecrows and she was sorry for them. She knew it was only by being there with them, sharing their pain, that she could keep them at it. And as soon as she went indoors for a few minutes, they found a reason to break off. Back she came and put them at it again.

The weight of the child dragged on her. She carried a stool out from the house and sat down at intervals; but it was a form of surrender, it set her apart from them, and she took it no more. She had seen those women at the harvest during her first year working all day in the rain and then coming in at night, caring for their children, doing their share of the kitchen work, seeing to their men and then larking and joking to the tunes of the old fiddler. Heroic! If they could do it, she could.

And the fat good-natured Balavoine supported her, helped her. One afternoon when she had a dizzy spell and nearly fell, he made her go back to the house and rest and he himself kept the workpeople at the spraying. Two days later, when they had gone over the whole vineyard again—more rain. But this time when she walked anxiously around in the early morning, she saw that the sulphur staining on the leaves and shoots had not been washed off. And the gray mold was dried up! If only she had beaten it!

And still, underneath it all, a little louder now, she could hear the ticking of disaster. On some days, as June went by, she

404

was indifferent to it, engrossed by her body, her heaviness, the approaching term of her pregnancy. On other days she worried or secretly raged, knowing that Francis would dissimulate to the last.

He spent days at a time in the vineyard now, walked around with Josserand, who, she knew from Balavoine, complained to Francis about her; and it seemed as if his interest in it were reviving. Then just as she began to hope that the steamer folly had passed, off he would go to Bordeaux again and come back with a little present for her which would secretly exasperate her, since he was still keeping her short of money and they owed bills everywhere. But when she gently tried to discourage him, he would laugh and say, "Well, if I can't afford a brooch for my wife, it's a pretty poor lookout," and kiss her happily. And he meant it. He could always afford things. Bills didn't matter, people would wait. By being careful and making small payments to first one then another out of what she could save, she kept the tradespeople and others from the door. He still paid the workpeople, but she suspected he owed wages to Balavoine and one or two of the single men.

But those silent moods of his when he had come up against some unpleasantness that he had been unable to avoid were growing. So were his bouts of bright nervous energy. One evening she overheard him talking about the steamer with Madame Gautier. The Spanish port and customs authorities at the two ports were causing long delays with their formalities. But when Madame Gautier said shrewdly that perhaps the Spaniards were being awkward because they really didn't want the steamer calling, he couldn't face the idea. He laughed, as if that were a comic remark, and quickly brushed it off.

"It's all being settled, really. It's nothing. Now, Mother, you promised me, you know, we'd make a round trip together. Now the fine weather's here, you've got to let me arrange it. I'll book a first-class cabin for each of us and you'll see how pleasant a little sea trip is. Hm?"

"Well . . . I'll see."

"We really must. I want you to give me a date."

And Madame Gautier—strange the subtle change in her. She was softer to Susannah now. At times in the afternoon and evening Susannah felt her eyes resting on her, and her mother-in-law spoke to her in a gentler way. It was like a whisper, a hush, the change from the old harshness. Was it the child? Her son's child? Was there going to be a new battle for the child? Susannah asked herself. But no, it wasn't that.

And the strange thing was that Susannah herself, all *will* now, found it hard to receive this new mood in her mother-in-law. She held herself from it. Didn't want gentleness from any of them. She liked the fight better! She didn't want marshmallow softness! And so she was brisk—as brisk as she could be, so heavily pregnant—and unreceiving. She couldn't help it. Now *she* was hard. Hardness was her strength, her integrity.

She wanted, even in her cumbersome swollen state, to cling to her individuality, her passionate rebellion against the narrowness of life here. She longed to see John Blood again. She told herself she had thrown away the chance of daring—that she should have gone with him. She had bowed down instead of grasping at life. She had been false to herself. She should have dared.

In the cool of the evening she would wander out, drawn by her beloved Red, and call to him, watching his lordliness, his grace, the deep glitter of his red-orange coat and the whisking of his tail as he turned and came to her. It was cruel to keep him confined. She had tried to teach Jean, who could ride a little, to handle him. But it was no good. The horse was too proud and touchy, and all she could do now was to get Joseph, who understood the horse with a natural instinct, to take him out for a little trot now and then. She suffered for Red in his paddock, hearing him whinnying; and in the early morning, seeing her come out of the house, he would trot alongside the enclosure, lifting his nose at her.

Now the grapes hung in bunches on the vines, their green in fresh contrast to the rather scorched look of the strongly sulphured leaves. Not a sign of the oïdium on the leaves—success there for the moment. But Susannah walked along the rows gazing at the fresh green bunches with a terrible anxiety. They looked so vulnerable. She wanted to cover them, protect them. She thought of the myriad spores being blown about on the breeze, for all the surrounding vineyards were full of oïdium.

And, sure enough, one morning behind the house she saw the mold again—on the grapes themselves now. It was like a mockery of all their efforts. She was in a panic. She made Josserand take the men around spraying again; but at the end of the morning he came to her triumphant—the sulphur would not stay on the waxy surface of the grapes. She made them go along a row again while she watched; no difference. Ten times they sprayed the bunches, the smooth surface of the grapes remained dry. In a rage of impatience she took a bucket and dipped entire bunches into the sulphur mixture. It slid off them.

So a fresh torment began. She remembered Octavie telling her that the old peasants wetted a goose's back by dousing the bird with soapy water. She fetched Madame Josserand and Balavoine's wife and had them boil up soapy water in the outbuilding with the sulphur and lime. Then she had to go at Josserand again, argue, raise the price to fifteen centimes a row and finally storm at him.

And in the morning when they turned out to do the work they found that the soap had curdled and rapidly blocked the holes in the syringes. They had to keep shaking and poking at the syringes to get a squirt of liquid, then they would block up again. There was cursing and swearing all around. Susannah made them persist. After a while she realized that at Josserand's urging most of them were quietly and slyly faking the work, squeezing a few drops out of the syringes and moving on.

"No, no. This won't do. You'll have to go back. Look at these grapes, look at them. They're not getting sprayed. Go on, go back."

They protested, they stood arguing. She went from one group to another.

"What's the good of this thing?" Raboutet, a stumpy little man, a great friend of Josserand's, threw down his syringe.

"A whole lot of damned nonsense, all this." Josserand spat.

Furiously Susannah turned on him. "Get out of here, Josserand! I don't want to see you. We're better off without you and your sniveling. You give up before you start. Go on. Clear off!"

Josserand stood tight-lipped and scowling at her, not liking the humiliation in front of the others.

"Clear off, do you hear?" she screamed at him.

Josserand took a threatening step toward her, then checked himself. He swung around and stalked away muttering. She put Balavoine in charge and they went around shaking and pumping at the near-useless syringes. For a few moments the syringes would work then they would choke again. It was maddening work. All day she stood with them, driving them. But by evening they were disgusted, surly and weary, and she saw she would not be able to keep them at it much longer. They were going to be defeated. Even as they tried to spray, the oïdium was gaining.

She went back to the house. She felt so tired she could hardly walk. She felt if she sat down she wouldn't be able to get up again. It was a cool evening, the sun going down in a blaze of silky orange. The dog ran up, but she was too tired to take any notice. The hall was empty and she longed to sit down, but she began to climb the stairs. She went slowly, she was so tired. Every step seemed a foot high. Her legs quivered with the effort. Up she went, breathing hard, knowing that if she paused it would only take a greater effort to start again. She looked up and saw the curve of the staircase above, rather menacing, the landing immensely high.

The weight of the child dragged at her groin. Sweat came out on her face and she felt uncertain of her strength, as if she had taken on more than she could manage, and unless she *did* manage it she was going to kill herself. She labored up, breathless. She knew she had to place her feet carefully, for the polished wood of the steps was slippery. The weight of her body was pulling her down . . . down. Her legs began to shake horribly. She gripped the banister with both hands. Another step. She could not lift her feet.

Her heart was hammering. If she could only sit down, but she dared not let go of the banister. She felt cold sweat all over her. Her hands were slipping sweatily on the banister rail. She looked down; the hall was far below, so small now. And she knew she was going to fall.

She shut her eyes and put out another effort, rose another step. She was almost at the top. The landing was just above her. She hardly dared look up, it made her dizzy. Only three more steps . . . but she couldn't. She had to stop . . . had to. She felt clammy and vaguely sick. Below, the black and white stone squares of the hall swayed and merged into one another. The light seemed to dim as she stared at them. She could feel her grip loosening. Her head drooped over the banister, her grip was shaking and slipping. One hand slipped away, she drooped over. A cry came to her throat, but she could not utter a sound.

And something held her. Strong and firm, something around her back held her. A distant voice was there. With a great effort she lifted her head and in her breathless gasping saw Madame Gautier's terrified staring face, felt her strong arms, dimly heard her calling for Emilie.

Firmly Madame Gautier held her. Emilie did not come. They stood there, both shaking, at the top of the stairs, Susannah bent forward now, gradually coming back to herself, catching her breath. Slowly her shaking subsided, the sickening clamminess passed. Presently she said, "It's all right. I think I can get to the top."

"No! Wait. Not yet."

They hung there. Susannah said, "I'm all right now."

"Are you sure?"

"Yes, I'm all right."

Slowly, with Madame Gautier's arm around her, she went up the three top steps and stood shakily on the landing. In silence Susannah clung to the other woman, head on her shoulder, shaking again, tears coming. She couldn't help it. She sobbed like a child and Madame Gautier's hand stroked her hair. She held Susannah to her.

"Oh, Mother . . . I . . ."

"Hush now, my dear. We'll get you to your room and you must lie down."

"Please, I—"

"Hush, hush. Come along."

A sound from the hall below. Madame Gautier called out and a startled Emilie ran up to them.

She would not give in.

For a day she rested reluctantly while Madame Gautier came in and out of the room bringing her things, seeing that she did not move, attending to her. Both of them were still quiet and tentative with each other. In the afternoon Madame Gautier sat for a long time by the bed holding Susannah's hand, as if she were struggling with something she wished to say; but the old reticence was too hard to break down all at once. She had told Emilie to make up a bed for Susannah in one of the unused rooms below so that she would avoid the stairs until the baby was born.

But Susannah couldn't stay indoors, and the following morning she was out at six. She was too fretful, too tormented about the vines. It was win or lose now.

She stepped out onto the drive, with the scent of the lilies and pinks coming over on the freshness of the early day. The sun was making lovely pale gray morning shadows on the gravel, and the surface of the burnished lake gleamed deep greeny-black among the trees beyond. Red came lifting his head at the paddock enclosure and she walked across and stroked him. Down the dip she could see the men back at the tilling and others working in the vines. No sign of Josserand. A crisis was coming with Josserand, that she knew.

She turned back again and saw an unexpected figure in black Sunday suit, black gloves and tall hat by the stables. Oh, of course, Monsieur Laverne. He was waiting for Jean to hitch Tom to the buggy. Laverne's brother had died in Saint Médard and he had asked for the buggy to drive him over for the funeral. She went to him.

"Please give my condolences to your family, Monsieur Laverne."

"Thank you, ma'am. I will." A pause. He shook his head. "I see you're still in trouble there with the sulphur."

"We'll manage somehow."

"It's a terrible thing, the mold."

"Yes."

"I've been telling Balavoine. You don't remember old Dugas, that little old peasant who used to work along the road at Monsieur de Montferrat's? Little bent brown-faced old man, no teeth, white stubble? No, well, he had a little fruit garden, cherries and plums and so forth; and he always used to say when you want a lime fluid to take on a smooth-skinned fruit you add milk."

"Milk?" she frowned. Didn't sound likely.

"It's just come to me. He used to grow peas and they got a kind of mold sometimes, so I think he used lime or sulphur for

410

that. Got used to it. And that's where he got the idea. It's just come to me."

"I see. Well, perhaps we'll try."

Milk? She was skeptical. At the outbuilding she was greeted by the stink of the sulphur and lime mixture. Balavoine was inside with the caldrons boiling on the stove. There was a big steady confidence about Balavoine that she liked. He was a slow, sure-footed, patient ox.

"Good morning, ma'am," he greeted her. "I hope you don't mind me butting in. Monsieur Laverne's been telling me—"

"Yes, the milk." She nodded. "I've seen him. Is that what you're trying there?"

"Eh, I thought I would, if you don't mind, ma'am. Just a bit to see what it does, if it does anything. We can't be worse off than we have been."

"By all means."

She watched while he poured in more milk from a churn, then added some more lime and sulphur and stirred it all up with a stick. The fumes were sickening and she had to step outside. In any event they had to wait until it was cool, so it was not until midmorning that they tried it in the syringes. Besides his wife, Balavoine brought along two of the single men, Vitel and Poudic, among the steadiest of the workpeople. This time the syringes did not choke up—and the fluid remained on the grapes! She could not believe it. She stood there staring at the film of moisture clinging to the grapes. It was true. Excitedly she made them try several rows. There was no mistake, the waxy surface of the grapes was thoroughly wet. The bunches were soaked.

Still she hardly dared believe it. Had they come through it all at last? "Here, try it here. Try it again here." But there was no mistake. It worked. The fat Balavoine smiled at her, his pale-skinned knotty wife smiled her gap-toothed smile too.

"All right. Now we've got to do all the vines again. Every bunch," she said to him. "I want you to take charge. Mix up some more this afternoon, get the people out tomorrow morning and do the whole thing. I'll be out with you."

"You can leave it to me, ma'am," Balavoine said. "You'll not be out here all day in your condition."

"Oh, I'm not staying indoors if we are going to beat this."

411

Now! If only something didn't go wrong now, she believed, they had a chance to defeat the oïdium. She was exultant and dismissed all the rest, all the unknown and threatening rest hanging over them. Somehow they would come through.

Madame Gautier was going off in the carriage to Castelnau de Médoc in the afternoon to meet Raynal and her niece just back from Martinique. The two of them had lunch together, Susannah talking away about the oïdium, and Madame Gautier listening and then asking advice about clothes to take on the little steamer trip to Spain which she had now decided on. Francis was set on it and they would be leaving soon. Afterwards Susannah wandered out again to watch the preparation of the mixture, then at four o'clock she saw Madame Gautier off.

She watched the carriage turn out of the drive, then walked slowly across the grass to the trees and sat down in the shade. Lovely there in the somnolent afternoon—the deep cool shade of the trees, the smell of sun on grass and waterside reeds and the faint resinous odor of the pines mingling with the heavy pollen scent of the lilies drifting across.

In the deep slow afternoon the rhythm of her body seemed slower and she had almost a physical sensation of flowing away, downward, downward, everything slowing and deepening, and she wondered if the child weren't coming. Strange the flow of one's body and one's life, how they changed. She and Francis had drifted away from each other, partly because of her pregnancy, which he looked on, like other men here, with mingled distaste and indifference—though he would be closer again when the child was born. And she understood now that this curious drifting apart and moving together again was the flow of their life together. Yet even in this momentary distancing now, they were closer to each other, in a mysterious fashion, than before.

The change with Madame Gautier—that was something deep and mysterious too. There was a longing in Madame Gautier now, an inexpressible silent yearning, which even Louise on her last visit had detected. It all seemed at this moment to be deepening into a new rhythm, a new deeper flow of life; and she thought that it was surely the child in her that made her aware of it. She seemed to be in touch with a more mysterious side of her own nature, or with something beyond, in the universe, to which that side of herself responded.

She let herself drift toward it now in the quiet afternoon. The bees were droning in the flowerbed nearby. Presently through a gap in the trees she could see Josserand in the vines beyond. He was coming toward her. It took him a while to reach the trees, but as he got nearer something about him made her stir, then get up.

He came to her, head and shoulders thrust forward, his straw hat down over his eyes. "What's this about Balavoine giving orders to the folk?"

"I told him to."

"You did, eh? And what for?"

"When I think it is necessary to explain the orders I give here I'll do so."

"So we want to be high and mighty, do we?"

"No, just sensible, Josserand."

"Sensible! Well, I'll tell you one thing. I'm taking no more orders from you, and that's flat."

"You'll take my orders or I'll know why."

He lifted his chin defiantly. "Oh, if ye want to know why, it's no trouble to tell you. Because you're messing in other folk's business. Because it's want this, want that. Do this, do that. And ye don't know what you're doing."

Susannah said, "I'll decide that."

"Then you'll leave me alone to do my work and give your orders somewhere else. I was tending vines before you was out of your baby clothes. And I don't accept any advice, I don't accept any orders from the likes of you."

It was always the same with him; this was his song and she had had enough of it. "The likes of whom, then?"

"Eh." His tone was mocking. "And if I listened to you I'd be an apprentice. I'm too old to go to school with a . . . a snippet of a skirt. And what'd folk think of me, taking your orders, getting mucked and muddled about and made to do bad work. Aye, and then you'd say I was doing it on purpose. And I'll not have it, see?"

"In other words, you know it all and nobody's to tell you?"

"And what do you know of it? Nothing!"

"You notice we've got the oïdium under control—in spite of you."

"Oh." He threw his head back scornfully again. "That's to be seen, my fine dame. That's to be seen yet. Eh, and I'm hired for price maker here and not to be at your beck and call for whatever you fancy."

"Really, Josserand, I'm tired of your complaints. Whenever a job's outside your routine, you argue, you make a fuss, you object and you do it badly on purpose. Really I've had enough of it."

"I know my work, ma'am, and you'll not find the man to gainsay me. But you want me to do it your way. You want me to work at something else, something I don't understand, and I say no!"

"But *nobody* knows how to sulphur the vines. Nobody. And you've gotten a fair price."

"Pah for work I don't look for! And who's to profit by it?"

"If the vineyard does well, it's better for you than if it fails, isn't it?"

"Oh, if the vineyard does well, my fine dame, you'll take the profit and pay me as little as you wish and I'll still be the underdog. It's not a fine vineyard that's going to make you pay me a bit more, or give me a decent place to live in. I understand *your* interest, but where does mine come in? I hire myself to you as price maker and you want to turn me to something else to get more profit for yourself. Eh, no!"

She saw his reasoning and she wasn't unsympathetic—just as she had sympathy for his independence. He knew what he wanted and what he wasn't going to accept. But there couldn't be two masters.

"The fact is you've bossed this vineyard up till now and you want to go on bossing it."

"Aye, if it's bossing you call it, I intend to. Now you've got that into your head you can keep it there."

"Then you can get another place, Josserand."

"What!"

"You can go and boss somewhere else."

He moved closer. "Ye'd try to turn me out, would you?"

"You stay, you take orders from me like everybody else."

"I'm taking no orders from a woman. And a foreigner at that."

"Then you can go."

"Why, you . . ." He bent forward, his neck stretched out. "By God, to think I've stood for your fancy ways and all. And 'tis true what they say, ye're a bitch and a common whore."

She did not move. "Be off the property by noon tomorrow."

His mouth was working. "You'll pay me my due before you'll get rid of me."

"You'll get your due."

"There's forty francs I have coming to me."

"If I don't deduct the price of the wheat you've been growing where you'd no business to."

He stood with his fists clenched. "And do ye know who's child it is ye're carrying?"

"Get out! Get out! Go on, get out of here!" She screamed, beside herself, and he stepped back at her vehemence.

"Get out! Get out!"

He backed off a pace or two, baffled and deterred in spite of himself. He was breathing hard.

She blazed at him. "Get out of here or I'll have you thrown out!"

A sort of impotent sob came from him; and at the same moment she heard the sound of someone carrying tools approaching. Then Jean's cheerful whistling. Josserand backed off a little more, still facing her with hate, then he reached to his belt and brought out his great flat steel pruning hook. With a heave he jerked it up through the air, as if that was what he would like to do to her if he could, then he swung away. A few paces off he turned around again. There were tears of impotence on his face.

"You're not done with me, I tell ye that."

In a few moments he had gone again, behind the trees. Susannah stood listening to Jean's whistling and the small sounds of his rake on the flowerbed behind her.

16

———

The enclosed courtyard of the Bordeaux Chamber of Commerce hummed with the gentle murmur of voices. The light on this dull morning glanced in grayly, and the groups of black-clothed merchants scattered about the space of the courtyard resembled a colony of sea-elephants on an ice floe. Vast black-bound bellies confronted each other; moon faces and mustaches quivered over starched collars. But it was a subdued assembly, the stately figures being in the habit of conversing in prudently lowered tones.

In the corner by the exit Regis Gautier leaned on his cane and faced Léon Chabot. Chabot was leaning on *his* cane, but even in this unmoving stance, back hollowed, chest lifted, elbows tucked in, there was something wily, darting and just a touch mocking. Regis, on the other hand, was expressionless except for an occasional lift of the eyebrows meant to signify boredom.

"Pity," Chabot was saying. "Fine house. Price right. Old woman willing. Better state than I thought. Good piece of property. Sure you've made up your mind?"

"Absolutely. I shan't take it after all. Much obliged for your inquiries." Regis tucked his cane under his arm and pulled at his dark-green gloves, tightening them on his hands. He had given up the wretched lavender color.

"Pity. Did my best." Head tipped back, Chabot looked at him down his long nose, and his mouth twitched humorously.

"Wouldn't be anything to do with your disappointment over Mademoiselle Hagenbach?"

Regis's eyes sharpened with a look of irritation. He had not believed that the news was generally known yet. "No," he said.

"Ah? Wanted it for love nest, eh?" Chabot was screwing up his lips, having difficulty in keeping his amusement under control.

"Love nest?"

"You and Aurelie. Hm?"

"No. It was a bit of speculation, as a matter of fact," Regis said tightly.

"Oh." Chabot chortled, not taken in for a moment. "Pipped by Baynes, eh?"

Regis's face had darkened, but he kept his eyes on Chabot. "If you mean Baynes is going to marry the lady and not me, yes, it's true."

"Ah. Hard luck. Nice try, but pipped by Mawdistly. Not funny, eh? Maw-dist-ly. Ha-a."

"You seem to find it funny at any rate."

"Ho. Aha. I sympathize." Chabot's face was flushed with amusement. "Hear you're getting rid of your phaeton too. Any truth in that?"

Regis looked at him levelly. "Yes. I'm thinking of selling it. Why? Are you interested in taking it over?"

"Oh! Me?" For a fraction of a second Chabot looked genuinely surprised; between the two men passed a fleeting glance of interrogation and challenge. Then it was gone and Chabot's amusement had got the upper hand with him. "Ha-a. Might be. Why not? You never know."

"Expensive to keep up, you'll find. But think about it. Let me have an offer." Regis nodded and moved on.

Pivoting on his cane, his lips pinched up in exquisite enjoyment, Chabot watched him thread his way through the gathering and leave the courtyard.

By the first Monday of July, except for a small corner in the west of the vineyard, the last trace of the mold had gone. Susannah walked around with Balavoine examining the vines, and everywhere, apart from the one corner, they found the grapes in healthy bunches, free of the oïdium. The Josserands had gone and Susannah had put Balavoine in charge.

"We'll have to sulphur again before the harvest." Susannah glanced at him.

"Hm. There's a lot of things can happen between now and then," Balavoine said.

She found him a good workman; and the change from Josserand's grousing, backbiting spirit had affected the rest of the men. They were all brighter, more willing; and besides, the success against the oïdium had cheered them up. There wasn't a vineyard as healthy as La Guiche for miles. Abel-Cherubin had dropped by and had gone away quiet and preoccupied.

"I'll do the corner again now," Balavoine said.

"And clear away that wheat of Josserand's. We ought to replant there."

When they had finished, she walked back to the house and sat down on the stone bench outside to rest. There was the sweet smell of the pinks, and the little brown and cream guinea hen that Jean had given her picked its way shyly and delicately over the gravel, pecking here and there. Susannah had decided she wanted a peacock and peahen too.

Francis was in Bordeaux to meet his mother when she arrived back tomorrow morning from her trip to Spain on the *Amiable Rose*. Madame Gautier had had, after all, to go alone, because at the last minute Francis had been kept back to attend to an insurance claim at the Bordeaux end and had not been able to leave with her. However, everything had been arranged for Madame Gautier's comfort. The *Amiable Rose* was arriving back at La Teste in the morning. And now Susannah reminded herself that this afternoon she still had to make the cherry tarts that Madame Gautier liked so much.

She sat there a moment longer watching the groups of men and women working in the vines and thinking of Louise's visit the day before. They had sat on the lawn having tea, shaded by the big yellowy-white parasol that Emilie had put up. As usual Louise had brought some baby things, and Susannah had said firmly she must now stop, she had already accumulated too many. Susannah always felt comforted by Louise's presence. She was such a sweet, loyal creature, and whatever she had suffered from Abel-Cherubin after the declaration that she was on Susannah's side that day, she had never breathed a word of it.

418

The fringe of the parasol had stirred in the gentle breeze. Their talk had come around to Madame Gautier, and Susannah had said that she had seen a change in her lately. And Louise, saying, Yes, yes, had sat twisting her fingers together, agreeing and glancing at Susannah rather anxiously. Susannah saw that she wanted to tell her something but couldn't bring herself to do so. She waited. Another cup? Another piece of cake? The bees droned over the flowerbed. Still she waited. And at last, disjointedly, it had come out.

"Of course, she had such terrible trouble over Raynal," Louise said and shook her head sadly and reflectively.

"Over Raynal?"

"Yes. She was never married before, you see. That was just what was said. I really don't know if I . . . You see, she came from a good bourgeois family. Very good people but hard. And she ran away. You didn't know that?"

"No."

"Well, she ran away about a year after she and Pierre Gautier were married. Ran away with a young fellow, a peasant, a penniless young man with curly red hair and a brown skin. Just a peasant with a place as a laboring man in one of the vineyards." She clicked her tongue distressfully as if it had just happened.

"You see, when Pierre Gautier had married her he found her . . . well, rather quiet and closed in on herself. But he put it down to her parents. Good people but hard. And he wanted to . . . to open her out, you see. He loved her and was kind. And, my dear, her nature did open out. It was Gautier who thought he had awakened her.

"Well, it happened about a year afterwards. They were settled at Saint André de Cubzac. Gautier went away to Paris on business, leaving her to run the house and attend to his affairs. She was very capable, you know. Oh, yes, always. And, you see, that was when she ran away. While he was gone."

Her fingers twisted together, her light-brown eyes in their bony sockets glanced anxiously at Susannah, then away again.

"Gautier found out where they were and had her brought back quietly. Nobody knew. She cried and said she loved the man. Gautier did not harm the peasant. The man simply went away, out of the department. And . . . and then Gautier discovered that before their marriage she had already had a child by the man."

Up came the anxious eyes again, seeking reassurance. She reached nervously for her cup, put it down again. "It . . . it was such a blow to him."

"Did her parents know of it?" Susannah asked.

"Oh, yes, yes. They had known all along and they had concealed it, put the baby out with country folk."

"I see."

"You didn't know this?"

"No," Susannah said. "Don't worry, I won't tell anyone."

"Well, Gautier sent for the child. It was Raynal's. That was the peasant's name, Raynal. The child was his. Oh, there was no mistake. The cast of face, you see, the red hair. And it had been declared as her child by Raynal. Gautier made her keep it with them. And, my dear, he used the child to humiliate her. Made her keep it to humiliate them both—he for his trust, his blindness, she for . . . for . . ."

Nervously Louise's fingers pressed together. Her voice quavered. "When he bought La Guiche and they came to live here, people were told Raynal was her child by a former marriage. But the boy was treated apart, like a laboring man—worse. Gautier wanted him to be a peasant, a peasant like his father. It was silent and bitter. He ground him down, ground him to the earth. That was Pierre Gautier's self-torment. That was the other side to his dreaming, the darkness in him."

Tears trembled in Louise's eyes. "Oh, but she clung to the boy. She shielded him. She was strong. And in the end Gautier regretted it. In the end he asked her forgiveness."

Louise took out a handkerchief, sniffed and pressed her fingers together. "You promise me you won't—"

"No, no. Don't worry, Louise." Now Susannah understood. Bad enough in all conscience, society would say. But a peasant! The one unforgivable bourgeois sin was to go outside their class. She imagined the years of submission, the child being harshly treated, and his mother giving him her strength, sustaining him, a lifetime of that. Poor woman! And then her new daughter-in-law arrives, the stranger, *not* yielding, *not* submitting! The gall and bitterness of that! And the confession that she too had had a love affair! Not with a peasant, no, but she did not

420

deny it. Did not deny her nature but defended it. Ah, the poor woman.

Susannah reached across the table and laid her hand on Louise's. "I understand. I'm so sorry."

"Don't tell anyone."

"No."

They sat in silence, thinking about it. "And she's changed lately, as you say," Louise said. "She's looking forward to the baby so much."

"Is she?"

"Oh, she's told me so. So often."

It was such a revelation. Susannah looked out across the vines, moved in her heart. Looking forward to the baby. What defenses Madame Gautier had had to break down to reach that. Denied her own free life, she had lived in self-defense, poor woman. And Susannah had a pang of guilt at her own willfulness. But she couldn't help wishing that Madame Gautier had stayed with her peasant.

What would it have mattered? She would have been poor and regarded as sinful or mad by her class. To be déclassé— that, for them, was the horror. But once you had rejected that and left the horror to them, what could it matter?

But it was over now, her suffering for that. They would be closer in the time to come. She must try to make up to Madame Gautier for that painful past. That was her role now.

The swallows were wheeling above. Susannah sat there on the bench. The dog came up the drive wagging his tail and put his muzzle in her lap and she sat stroking him abstractedly. Her thoughts went to the letter she had received four days before from John Lovell saying he would be near La Guiche and would like to call if she would allow it. She had answered that she hoped he would. It was months since they had seen each other, and she liked his cool common sense. She wondered why there was no woman in his life; he was attractive enough physically.

All at once she remembered that her pastry for the tarts was waiting and got up.

At five o'clock that afternoon Jean brought the buggy around and Susannah came out tying the ribbons of her bonnet. Emilie, who had carried her basket out, said, "I wish you'd let Jean drive you, ma'am. I don't trust that horse."

"Not necessary."

"All the same, it'd be better," the girl persisted.

"Will you stop fussing, girl! You do it every time I go out now. I've been ten times to the village with him in the last month. Now go along with you. If Dr. Cavan comes by—I don't think he will, but he just might—tell him I've gone over to Madame Bechu at Lagrane and I'll be back about seven. If I don't go now I never will."

Old Madame Bechu had come back to visit her son at Lagrane, a nearby hamlet, and she had fallen and broken her leg. She was laid up in a cottage and Susannah, who had been over to see her, had promised to take the old woman some calf's-foot jelly.

"Very well, ma'am," said Emilie resignedly; it was no use arguing with the mistress. The buggy was low-built and Susannah climbed up carefully. She settled herself, started the horse and at the end of the drive turned toward the village. The afternoon had clouded over, though it was still warm. She kept to a slow pace beyond the village and through the countryside along the small dirt roads that led through the vineyards toward the forest farther on.

The vineyards were powdered with oïdium, some worse than others. In the forest the road ran empty between grass borders where she could see the pale petals of scabious and the blue of harebells and the little pink spikes of persicaria. She kept the horse trotting very gently, taking her time. On the far side of Lagrane she branched into the narrow track through the trees toward the cottage. At one point where the trees had been cut down and stacked alongside the track, she thought it best to pull up; but there was just room for them to get by, and the horse picked his way at a walking pace as if he sensed her care. The cottage was a little farther on. She hitched the horse and went in carrying her basket.

Old Madame Bechu was cheerful and talkative. Susannah sat and listened to her tales of her son, his work, her leg, the witch at Sainte Hélène and in her turn had to repeat all the news about herself, the family and the Sabra boy which she had already given on her first visit. The woman of the cottage brought out some little biscuits. It was essential to offer something to a visitor and impossible for the visitor to refuse without giving offense. Madame Bechu insisted that when Susannah's child was born she must take it to Saint Michael's church and pass it through the hole in the oaken partition to ensure it long life. On and on it went, and every time Susannah looked like going, Madame Bechu took her hand and held her there, and Susannah didn't have the heart to go away.

It began to get dim in the little cottage. Through the window the sky looked overcast and Susannah saw she was going to get caught by rain if she didn't go. At last Madame Bechu noticed too and said urgently, "Why, ma'am, I'm keeping you here with my gossip, and it's going to rain."

Susannah made her promise to come and see the child as soon as she was up and about and said goodbye.

Outside, the clouds were lowering, but the rain was holding off. Up she climbed, waved goodbye and snapped the reins. They ambled gently down the forest track. Among the trees the light was grayer, but she kept at the same slow pace. Never mind if she got wet, she didn't want an accident. Ahead she saw the narrower place where the felled trees were stacked, and as she reached it and pulled the horse back to a walk a figure came out of the undergrowth. He had a straw hat on and she saw it was Josserand.

"Eh, there, what's your hurry all of a sudden?" He was drunk.

"Get out of my way!"

He went for the horse's bridle. She tried to pull the horse's head around too late—he had forced it over toward the felled trees blocking that side of the track. Then before she could react, he had lurched to the seat and was grappling with her, trying to pull her out.

"Come out of there."

She screamed. She pummeled him. His fist came out of nowhere and hit her face. He was swearing at her and breathing hard with his mouth open. She beat at him with her fists and his hat went off. He lost his grip and she tried to grab the dropped reins but couldn't get them.

"Come out of there, y' hussy!"

"Get—away—from—me!"

"I'll teach ye to put me out."

They grappled. Her heart was beating in terror for her child. She screamed and clung to the rail, but he had hold of her with both hands and was pulling her forward out of the seat. She let go one hand and clawed wildly at his eyes. His foot slipped and he went down in a drunken stagger, but she was gasping too desperately to react before she saw him clambering to his feet again.

He gripped her leg to pull her out, and as she tipped back to resist, her hand touched the umbrella jammed between seat and frame. She wrenched it out and beat at him with it. He snatched at it, got it at the tip, but she jerked it free and jabbed the end into his face. He gasped and ducked drunkenly away, still keeping a grip on her leg.

She was stifling, could hardly breathe, her heart was going so fast. He grabbed at her again. She felt she couldn't hold on any more. A sudden gush of water came on her legs. As she hit at him his arm came up and knocked the umbrella out of her grasp. He got an arm around her to pull her out of the seat, and suddenly the buggy jerked backward violently once, twice, with a movement from the horse.

Josserand's face contorted as the wheel caught him. He went down, half pulling her with him. She was going to pitch out head-first, but at the last minute he let go and she caught herself. She clung to the rail, sick with fear. The horse plunged backward with his haunches as if he wanted to make a dash for it, then jumped forward for the gap in the track. Susannah felt the wheel go over Josserand. One side of the buggy bumped hard against the felled trees and slewed them around. Next moment they were on the other side.

"Whoa! Whoa!" She found breath enough to call out. The horse trotted a few yards with ears back, then pulled up. She thought she was going to faint. She could hardly move for the rasping of her breath and the contraction of pain in her belly. With one outstretched hand she clung to the rail.

Josserand . . . somewhere back there. Coming for her? She didn't know. She lay collapsed along the seat of the buggy, gasping, the pain gripping her. She lay there oblivious, couldn't help it. The core of pain spread through her and contracted. She lay there in fear in case the child came now.

Presently the pain ebbed away and she struggled upright

on the seat, pushed her hair out of her face with the back of her hand. She wanted to vomit. Her head swam and she had to sit still. Her bonnet was on the back of her head, the ribbons tight around her throat. She couldn't untie them and had to get her fingers under them and tear them away. The bonnet dropped to the ground.

She looked back. Nobody. Her underclothes were wet from the water she had lost and the front of her dress was torn. She knew the baby was coming and that she would soon have another contraction.

Vaguely, she looked around for the reins, then remembered they had fallen. She was shaking so much now she didn't know if she could get out of the buggy. Using two hands, she pulled the brake up, gripped the rail and put one leg over to the step. She put her weight onto the step, lowered the other leg and eased to the ground. Go back? No, she couldn't turn the buggy and he might be back there.

She tried to collect herself and thought she remembered a cottage—but how far? She didn't know how far she could walk. Yet she didn't know either if she would be able to manage the buggy, especially if the pain came again. But perhaps it was best to try. She stood leaning against the buggy, her body shaking, her hair falling over her face. At last she stirred, took the reins and managed to haul herself in. She started the horse at a walk.

Slowly along the track they went. After about half a mile she saw two cottages together in a clearing and a third farther off. The pain was beginning to shoot again. As she pulled up at the first cottage, a rosy-faced woman in a blue apron straightened up in the little front garden with a bunch of carrots in her hand. She stared across, alarm in her face.

Susannah reached for the brake but couldn't pull it up. Suddenly the pain was tearing at her. She leaned back, clutching the rail to stop herself from falling . . . heard herself scream and the woman's startled voice calling for someone.

John Lovell, in his new bottle-green dogcart, reached La Guiche just after seven o'clock. He had been making a quick tour of the Médoc vineyards to see the oïdium situation for him-

425

self in advance of the harvest and had found it disastrous. Here and there a perspicacious owner had managed to save his vines from the worst ravages of the mold, but the general picture was awful. Worse than the year before. So prices would be sky-high and a few more of the weaker merchants would disappear. He did not intend Collard and Sons to be among the casualties, but it was a cut-and-throat business, the wine trade, when it came to getting hold of wine in a year like this.

Yet none of this mattered at all to him at this moment as he turned into the drive at La Guiche. Lovell found himself in fact in a surprising state of emotion. He was half longing for, half dreading the moment when he would see Susannah, and he felt ridiculously unsure of himself. Something like dread was in him. All through these months he had told himself it was better for his peace of mind that he wasn't seeing her, but now that he was here he threw all that to the wind. He remembered her as he had seen her the last time, on the road, when he had given her the message from Blood, looking at him with her face lifted. So lovely and with such depths in her.

As he pulled up at the porch the girl Emilie came quickly out. She was obviously disappointed to see him, had been expecting someone else.

"Good evening. Is Monsieur Gautier at home? Or Madame?"

"No, sir. The master's away in Bordeaux. I'm expecting Madame but she's not back."

"I see. Are you expecting her soon?"

"Yes, sir. She should be back any moment," the girl said in a troubled way.

"Then I'll wait." But when she stood back for him to enter, he said, "No, I want to look around outside first."

"Very well, sir."

Lovell strolled over to the vines and as he went between the rows a big genial-looking man came up and introduced himself as Balavoine.

"Well, you seem to be lucky," Lovell said.

"Lucky, sir?"

"You've come off lightly with the mold."

Balavoine grinned. "You wouldn't have said so a while back. Bad as the rest we were."

"What've you been doing then?"

"Well, we've been using a mixture of sulphur and lime. With a drop of milk in it."

"Milk?"

Balavoine chuckled. "Aye. It's been quite a business, you can say that. We've had a fight, all right. A regular battle of it. But there's the result."

For the next half hour Lovell went around examining the vines and talking with Balavoine. As they came around from the back and he looked up again toward the house, he saw the maid standing in the drive facing the gate. Susannah arriving? He took leave of Balavoine and walked across, but nobody had appeared by the time he reached the drive. And now the girl seemed anxious.

"It's past seven thirty, sir, and Madame Gautier should be back. I do hope nothing's happened."

"What do you mean?"

"Well, sir, she went out with the little cart. She'll be having the baby soon, and I didn't want her to drive; but she wouldn't let Jean take her, and I don't trust that horse when he's nervous."

"I see. Do you know which way she's gone?"

"Yes, sir. She's gone over to Lagrane to see Madame Bechu. I'm sure she should be back by now." There was genuine worry in the girl's face.

"How far is it?"

"Not far, about four miles after the village. It's a little place in the forest. There's only one way she can come really, one good way."

Lovell looked at her, considering. There might be a hundred reasons for the delay, of course. Still, it was threatening rain now, not the sort of evening a woman would choose to linger on an errand. He could at least go and see. He longed to see Susannah. And if something was amiss, he'd never forgive himself.

"I'd better go and try to meet her. Perhaps she's been held up on the way."

"Oh, I wish you would, sir."

"Tell me how to get there."

She gave him the directions and described the buggy. Lovell climbed into the dogcart, swung around and drove out down

427

the drive. At the gate he half expected Susannah to confront him coming in. Every minute along the road he expected to see her arriving from the other direction. But no, no sign.

A few spots of rain fell. He kept the little cab at a steady pace through the vineyards and reached the forest. No Susannah. He began to wonder if he'd missed his way, then he came to Lagrane, where the trees gave way to open ground with a little vineyard. Careful about the right branch here. He drove through the hamlet and as he headed down the forest track on the far side he told himself with a rueful grin that she had probably arrived back at La Guiche by now. The track ran on, quite empty. Turn back? Just then he saw a little buggy drawn up outside a cottage ahead. Could that be hers? He got closer, slowed down. It looked like it. In spite of himself he had a stab of apprehension.

At the cottage he pulled up. Two peasant women and an elderly man were standing talking in front of the door and they all looked around as he drew up. Lovell got out and one of the women detached herself and came to meet him.

"From the doctor's are ye?" She had a rosy face and a blue apron.

"Doctor? What's happened? Is Madame Gautier here?" he asked in alarm.

"That's the name, sir, I think. Over by Cantenac way. Are ye the husband maybe?"

"No, a friend. Is she all right? What in God's name has happened?"

"Oh, nothing more tragical, sir, than a fine bonny girl she's had. And she's well enough herself. But she gave us a turn. Madame Lagunegrand delivered her and my boy's gone for the doctor. I thought ye was the new assistant he's got."

"Can I see her?"

"Eh." She looked at him a shade doubtfully. "If you'll be quiet. She's before her time and she's had a bit of a shock. First I thought she'd fallen off the cart. I can't get out of her what it was; but she got here in a state to put a body out of their wits, with her dress all torn and her bonnet gone and all."

"Is she all right now?"

"Right as rain now, but of course she's tired out. So you be quiet now and not be talking too much. Understand?" She was in command.

"Yes."

She led him into the dim little cottage, where he had to stoop, and there on the narrow bed at one side was Susannah, looking pale as paper, absolutely washed out. A white-haired woman with a warty face nodded to him from a corner, and beside her in a rough wooden crib on the earth floor he saw the child.

As he took the wooden stool by the bed, Susannah opened her eyes. It seemed to take her a moment to realize it was him, then she smiled faintly. "John. How did you find me?"

He put his hat on the bed. "Your maid told me you'd come out this way. My dear Susannah, are you all right?"

"Yes."

"What's that bruise on your face? One here too. Bruises all over. What happened?"

"It was nothing. I fell over and bumped myself. And the baby was in a hurry to arrive. Have you seen her?"

"Yes, she looks fine. Really, Susannah, what happened to you?"

"I've told you and that's all. You say you went to the house?"

He nodded; there was obviously something behind it, but it wasn't the moment to harass her. "Your maid was worried. I'll go back and tell Francis."

"He won't be home till the morning. He's bringing his mother back with him. If you'd just tell Emilie and say I'm quite comfortable here."

"They've sent for the doctor, I gather?"

"Yes, these women are splendid. They know exactly what to do. They've looked after me beautifully."

"Is there anything you need?"

"Just tell Emilie to bring my toilet things. And some of the small things for the baby. She knows where they are. Would you, John?"

"Of course. Are you sure you're all right?"

"Yes, really. Thank you for coming."

Her fingers crept across the coarse blanket and touched his and he looked at her with love. The door behind opened and a short, thickset man with gray hair and glasses bustled in, followed by the two women. The man nodded to Lovell, who got to his feet. "Dr. Duluc."

"John Lovell. How do you do." The doctor elbowed him aside and took his place on the stool.

"Hm. If you'd kindly leave us, sir. Thank you. Thank you." He put his little bag down, removed his hat, reached out and took Susannah's wrist. "Well, now, madame. . . ."

Lovell retrieved his hat and stole out.

The white-haired old woman moved gently about the cottage in the early morning. The dripping of rain came through a hole in the roof, falling ping-ping into a bowl on the floor. There had been a storm, but now it had passed over and Susannah lay watching the light brighten through the greenery outside. Now and then she glanced over at the sleeping infant. The old woman, who had helped the midwife, had slept in the room on a straw mattress and attended to Susannah in the night. She was called Madame Ferrand and was the mother of the woman in the blue apron, Madame Lartigue.

Lying there with her hands on her flat belly, Susannah felt marvelously light. Oh, the weight of those last few weeks—how it had pressed on her, even in bed. Now she felt relaxed and enormously relieved, and even the fight with Josserand didn't seem so terrible to her. She could feel the renewal in her body, as if a whole new cycle had begun in her.

The child was all wrapped up, legs and all. Emilie had arrived late the night before, driven over by John Lovell, with her toilet things and the baby's clothes and diapers. Susannah had said simply to tell Francis and Madame Gautier when they arrived back and they would arrange to have her taken home to La Guiche.

The old woman was cleaning the cottage, pottering about. She moved the crib next to the bed and Susannah looked down tenderly at the child. How beautiful it was. How wonderful. Pauline; she had chosen the name long before. It had a tiny down of blond hair, and Susannah had seen the open eyes were a tender dark blue. But the tiny hands—were they quite right? She reached down and touched one. The palm was half open and the little thumb seemed to be held across it as if deformed. The thumb was mobile, yet always went back into the same position across the palm. Susannah felt anxious.

"Madame Ferrand."

430

"Eh?" The old woman slouched over.

"Look at her thumbs. Do you think they're right? She's holding them in a funny way, isn't she?"

The old woman glanced down, shook her head. "There's nothing wrong with them. Are ye hungry?"

"Mm, I am, rather."

"I'll give ye a fresh boiled egg in a minute. And ye can have a drop of broth."

"No broth, but I'd love an egg."

"Eh, it's good chicken broth. Ye'd best take it. It's a bit early to give ye beer yet."

"Beer?"

"Aye, for your milk."

The morning drifted timelessly by. Susannah dozed and woke up. Sometimes the other women were there, sometimes only Madame Ferrand. Her breasts were beginning to hurt, and when she felt them they were hard as melons.

"Oh, Madame Ferrand, I'm sure my milk's come. Don't you think I should feed the baby?"

"Not yet," said the old woman and went about her business.

And then she woke up with the sun coming full into the room and the feeling that it was late. She was surprised to find it was only eleven o'clock. Another hour went by. Nobody came. They gave her more broth for lunch, a little white of chicken and a piece of the great country loaf, and she ate with pleasure.

Still nobody came. She lay there idle and began to feel it was strange. Then she told herself that she was like other people in bed who feel they ought to be the center of attention, whereas the world has other things to do. One o'clock passed. They would surely come by two. Two o'clock came and nobody appeared.

"Do you think your folk will be coming today, ma'am?" Madame Lartigue asked.

"I can't think why they haven't come already."

Then at two thirty Madame Lartigue came in from outside. "A visitor for you, ma'am." She held the door open. Louise.

"Oh, my dear, my dear. How are you?" Fervently she took both Susannah's hands, bent down and kissed her.

"I'm fine."

Louise turned and gazed down at the baby, exclaiming and touching the little hand. "So like you! But Francis's nose. Oh,

431

absolutely. And fair, of course. So sweet. My dear, I had such a fright when I heard. Are you all right? What did the doctor say?"

"I'm perfectly all right. She was just in too much of a hurry to arrive, that's all. Where's Francis?"

"Oh, he's . . . he's coming, dear. We'll have to get you back home. Good of these people to help you."

"They really have been kind. How did you hear I was here? I suppose John Lovell."

"Yes. He saw Francis in Bordeaux early this morning. Is everything normal?"

"Yes, absolutely. They got a doctor from Castelnau, a nice man—though the baby was here already. A woman in the next cottage was the midwife."

"Yes. I see."

"So what time is Francis coming?"

"He'll be here later. I don't know when. I said I wanted to come up and see you first. Just a selfish idea of mine." She laughed, but it sounded a little strange and Susannah gazed at her.

"No, but when *is* Francis coming? I—"

"My dear, if you'll just have a little more patience, I've got the big landau and I'm going to get some of the people from La Guiche to come and carry you out to it. And then you can get home."

Susannah gazed at her. Something was wrong. She saw that. Louise was not her usual self. "What's the matter, Louise?"

"Matter, my dear? Why nothing. Now don't you bother yourself one minute, we'll get—"

"Louise! What's the *matter?* Where's Francis? Why hasn't he come?"

"My dear . . ." Louise's lips quivered, but she quickly controlled herself.

"Louise!"

Louise straightened her back and sat very erect. "I didn't want to tell you, my dear. It would have been better later, but . . . there's been an accident."

"*Francis?*" Quickly Susannah sat upright, eyes staring.

"No. The steamer . . ."

Susannah caught her breath, hand to her lips.

"There was a storm this morning as the steamer was coming into the Bassin. They . . . they seem to have— Nobody knows yet, but they seem to have hit a sandbank in the pass, where it's very dangerous. They . . . the ship was lost, and—"

"Mother?"

"Everybody."

"Oh." Susannah covered her face with her hands.

"Francis will come home as soon as he can. But in the meantime we must manage on our own."

17

She looked down at the baby feeding at her breast. Such a funny little thing, such an expression of concentration on her face. Oh, the concentration! And the tiny fists clenched in the battle for life.

"There, that's enough," she said and gently took the nipple away. A momentary surprise and incomprehension on the little face and then, oh, what protest! My milk! A clutching of hands and little movements of the head, lips rounded, searching for the milky nipple again.

Susannah laughed. "Come on, you've had your share. That's all you're going to get."

She lifted the child and held it up against her, head against her neck, and gently tapped its back until it made the little belch. Then she wiped away the regurgitation and smoothed the wisps of hair. It always moved her to feed the child, she was full of milk and it came easily, pearling the nipple when she simply pressed her finger down the breast. That was the malt beer, they claimed, which she found she didn't mind. But she was *not* going to be misshapen, and she made Emilie bind her up tight.

The bedroom was bright with morning sun, and outside she could hear Balavoine speaking to someone on the drive. She reached out and rang the bell. In a moment Emilie came in and took the baby.

"She wants changing," Susannah said. "Is that the doctor already? I thought he said eleven o'clock."

"No, ma'am. Mr. Onslow's manager. Wants to see Balavoine."

Susannah watched while the girl dealt with the baby and put her in her crib. "Anything you need, ma'am?"

"No, that's all."

When the girl had gone she took the hand mirror, looked at herself, did her hair; then she resettled herself in the bed with a sigh. These were the little oases of peace, of oblivion, when she fed the baby. But the rest! Francis was away in Bordeaux for the second day of the official inquiry into the loss of the *Amiable Rose*. It was ending today, but it had been grim enough—the Préfet's representative in attendance, the Port Authority, the Maritime Superintendent, the experts and all the witnesses, the fishermen and local people who had helped, and the families. Francis, of course, questioned at length.

Doggedly they had gone through it all—the wrong approach, the wreckage, the fourteen dead. And only three of them passengers. That, in some way, made it worse. All for three passengers! For, of course, the service had been a failure.

And through it, Susannah could imagine those moments when somebody on board must have realized they had made a mistake, realized in the blinding storm that they were confused in that treacherous entrance between the north channel and the south, between the unnamed banks and the named—Arguin, Toulinguet, Pineau—and the whole mad half-invisible tide race and surge of wave on sand. And then the hit! And once on the sandbank the *Amiable Rose*, with never a chance, lurching and being slewed around like a toy, beam-on to the Atlantic breakers, and rolled over. Smashed up even before she could sink. Poor Mother.

Francis had sat there all day listening to them, living it over again. She felt so miserable for him.

So the shadow had fallen over her homecoming with her little daughter. For days Francis had hardly appeared, and she saw he was living in a sort of insanity, an unreality he could hardly cope with. He had had a gaunt wildness she would never forget, those first days after the tragedy. A feverishness and absence about him, staring through her as if she didn't exist. A wild hollow-eyed creature in whom she had seen nobility and a strange sort of strength, like his mother's.

And then gradually he had come to himself. Slowly, after the wreckage and the terrible details, the funerals, the memorial services had been dealt with, he had returned to life. Returned to her and seen her and seen the baby—like strangers. The child had soothed him. He had found comfort in her. And yes, he had recovered some of that irrepressible optimism. The inquiry was tormenting him again now, but once it was done with he would be over the worst of it.

Yet what else awaited them? He had told her in his offhand way that the insurance would cover the money to be paid out. Gaveau, he said, had handled the insurance side, and Gaveau had sworn they were covered for other parties. Indeed, the insurance people had appeared immediately and were, of course, attending the inquiry. The steamer herself? Well, that was their loss. They would get nothing there. She had listened to him and she had wondered, in great anxiety. And lying in bed, she felt restless in her soul and insecure.

The morning went by. The patterns of sunlight changed slowly in the room. Susannah lay sewing and listening to the sounds of the house, the occasional voices outside. At eleven o'clock Dr. Cavan came in with his stiff walk, his glance summing her up. He questioned her with utmost dryness. Really, she thought, what a manner for a doctor! Then he examined the child, and he was gentle and dexterous with her. The child screwed up her fists and yelled, furious at having been awakened.

"I'm fed up with lying here," Susannah said. "I want to get up."

"You stay where you are."

"But I've been here for nearly three weeks! I'm perfectly healthy, as you've seen. There are things to do and I've got to get up."

"Madame, I said no!"

"But why not?"

He stopped what he was doing. "You're a pig-headed, selfish woman when you want to be. And a touch of the temper, I notice today."

"No temper. I want to know why I can't get up."

"Because you exhausted yourself. Because you were up to some monkey tricks, which you prefer to keep to yourself, and

436

brought on your labor prematurely. Because you've had a shock. Because you are shortly going to be out there working till all hours again with the harvest—"

"Which won't kill anybody."

"Don't argue with me! And because, madame, in medicine"—he snapped his bag shut and stood up—"*I* give the orders. And I'll say good day to you."

She let him get to the door. "Doctor!"

He turned around; she smiled at him. "Come on now."

He stood looking back at her stonily, then his expression softened. He shook his head. "You know quite well where you stand with me, don't you?"

"I should be miserable if I didn't."

"How is your husband?"

"Oh, he's getting over it gradually."

"You'd better send him to me when he's free."

"I will. Thank you."

"I'll call again. Goodbye, my dear."

He went out. Dear old thing, all buckled up and armored inside himself in that strange way. But she couldn't waste any more time lying here.

She waited until the doctor's carriage had gone, then put on a little bed jacket and rang the bell. When Emilie appeared she said, "Send Balavoine up."

The girl gave her an oblique look and hesitated.

"Do as I tell you, girl." Each time she had Balavoine up to discuss the work, the girl acted as if it were the worst impropriety.

"Yes, ma'am," Emilie said quietly and went out.

Balavoine clumped in cheerfully with his straw hat in his hands, looking huge but quite at ease and natural. "Morning, ma'am. I trust you're well today. And the baby."

"Yes, thank you." She gave him a smile. "How is it going?"

"Why, we're going along like a house on fire, ma'am. Taking a few leaves off here and there. Get a bit of sun now, and we'll be well away. And I'll tell you one thing, ye'll not see a dozen crops like this from here to Bordeaux. That ye won't. The only thing is I wonder if we'd better not spray again?"

"What, more mold?" she said in alarm.

"No, no. Not a sign. But you never know. There's enough

437

all around. Then I'm thinking we're too close to harvesttime."

She said, "I think the grapes were safe as soon as they turned color. As far as I know, the oïdium only attacks when they're green. Still, I'm not sure."

"Perhaps we might spray a few rows over by Monsieur de Montferrat's side?"

"No, just keep your eyes open. And if you see anything, come and tell me at once."

Come and tell me! Heavens, if every woman on the American prairie had stuck in bed three weeks after her child was born they'd never have got far. Nor the peasant women here, out in the vines a day or two after. So she was restless all day.

Her mind turned to the afternoon drive on the interminable road from Poitiers when she had first arrived with Francis, the dappling light, the sense of expectancy, the apprehension. And that arrival, with Abel-Cherubin coming out on the porch and then the silver candlesticks on the table and the family all there. She wished she had tried harder to understand Madame Gautier. Oh, what a waste of time their hostility had been. Why had they fought each other so vainly? And she remembered the day, last November, the Day of the Dead, the great family reunion day, when they had all gathered at Abel-Cherubin's and gone to lay chrysanthemums on the family graves and attend the church services. Those yards of crepe and black veiling, brought out as if the dead were just newly in their graves. And she had revolted and would not go. They had excluded her from the family and she would not go. She saw Madame Gautier's rocklike old face again, secretly so hurt. Ah, she wished she could have a chance to repair that now. If she could only take it back. She wished it so much.

It was seven o'clock in the evening when Francis came home. She heard the carriage on the gravel outside and his voice speaking to Joseph. The lovely late August evening was still and soft with a sky like yellow silk streaked with blue, and at an angle through the window she could just glimpse the vines undulating gently away to the west. She sat up in bed, pushed up the pillows behind her, looked in the mirror and arranged her hair. He came in brisk and bright and cheerful, but she could see he was tired out.

"Sue." He bent and kissed her and caressed her cheek. "How are you?"

"I'm all right. And you?"

"Yes, yes. Fine." He turned away and pored over the baby. The child was awake and looked up at him silently. "She's really getting plump, aren't you, little devil?"

"Well, is it over?" Susannah said.

"Yes, thank the Lord." He was still bent over the baby. He wouldn't volunteer anything, she would have to force it all out of him.

"What happened?"

"Oh, nothing."

"Nothing?"

"Oh, they put the blame on me. They . . . they censured me."

"Censured you? What does that mean?"

"Nothing much. It's a sort of administrative thing. Doesn't entail much."

"But exactly what?" she said.

"I . . . I suppose I'd find it a bit hard to set up in shipping again right away. A bit of a commercial handicap." He gave his boyish chuckle, rather rueful, not looking at her but still bent over the baby, crooning at it, putting his finger into the little fist and tugging it out again. It was all defensive playacting and she let him go on with it.

Then he moved away, took off his coat and collar and rolled up his sleeves, and pulling the window wide open stood looking out on the peaceful evening. And she saw, clear as daylight, that something was on his mind—something *else*. Now it must come. She must know. She couldn't live with the uncertainty any longer.

"Tell me about it," she said.

"Nothing to tell, really. It was mostly deliberation today."

Drag it out of him!

"But they said something?"

"Yes. They said—well, one thing they said was the steamer wasn't designed for passenger traffic."

"What did they mean by that?"

"Well, you know, the refit when we had the passenger saloon put on. That sort of thing. All pretty dull."

"What about the refit?"

"Oh, they said it built the superstructure too high. Made her unstable. Topheavy. So when she got into the seaway—"

439

"But you had a certificate. What's it called, the sailing certificate—certificate of seaworthiness?"

"We ought to have got that changed or something, but
they admitted that wasn't our fault." A little wave of the hand.
"They had to say something. Had to find some excuse." He
smiled brightly, looking so boyish. "It's all right, Sue. How have
you been? Wasn't the doctor coming?"

"What about money?" she said with her eyes on him.

"What?" He wet his lips rather nervously. "Oh, it's all
right."

"What is Georges Gaveau's share of the loss?"

"Well, as a matter of fact, it's not much. He turned his
share over to me some time ago."

"Has he got any share at all?"

He looked across at her from the window, lifting his eyebrows with a little shrug. "Not really. I bought him out."

Not really! Not in fact. She raged in herself. "So it was a lie
that it was all his money?"

"Oh, nobody ever said that. No. Georges has been very
good. He's a good fellow."

"What else is there?" she asked in a flat voice.

"Well . . ." his fingers tapped once or twice on the windowsill and he grinned down as the little guinea fowl gave its
squawk below. She knew he would pretend that his whole attention was absorbed down there if she let him.

"Frank!"

"What?"

"What else is there?"

"Oh, well, as a matter of fact, I met Baynes. I . . . it might
be a bit awkward there."

"For God's sake, can't you tell me! What's Baynes got to
do with it?"

He gave a deep sigh. "Well, you see, I raised some money
for the steamer, and the business and so on. I had to. I mean,
you can't run a shipping line on nothing. So I couldn't do anything else. And he's got the notes I signed. I mean, I was going to
redeem them when the steamer was a going concern. That was
the idea. If we'd had a fair chance it would have been easy. And,
of course, I've been paying interest. But . . . er, well, Baynes
has got the notes. He must have bought them up from Fouquet,

because it was Fouquet who advanced me the money. And . . . well, you see, now he's, Baynes is, saying he wants La Guiche."

"He wants La Guiche?" She stared at him.

"That's what he says. I mean, I—"

"You mean you gave La Guiche as security for the loans?"

Nettled, he pulled in his mouth with a patient, slightly long-suffering expression. "Sue, you don't understand. You don't understand how business is done. So why not leave this to me?"

"Please explain!"

"In business you *have* to give some security. You have to. Fouquet is not a philanthropist exactly. It's the normal thing. Absolutely normal. Like a mortgage. You give security. And . . . well, I gave my share of La Guiche. Nothing unusual."

She threw back the covers and got out of bed.

"What are you doing? Get back." He moved toward her.

"Leave me alone! Do you think I can lie in bed now?" She reached for her robe, flung it furiously on and faced him. "How much have you borrowed?"

"Well, we had to have quite a bit. I mean, one way and another. Mother lent me some, enough to keep paying the interest and so on. I told you about that. And I still owe some to the shipyard for the refit. And there are one or two other things."

"How much?"

"I don't know. About twelve thousand francs. But mainly it's Fouquet."

"And how much did you borrow from him?" Her face was grim.

"About . . . I think it's about forty thousand francs."

Forty thousand! She was utterly baffled and her spirits sank; but only for a moment, because it was too mad. More than fifty thousand francs.

"But what did it go on? It's—"

"Damn it, we've had all the expenses here. Damn it, Sue, I mean—" He caught himself, checked himself, his brow furrowed, rueful now. "I mean, it wasn't just the steamer. We've had all the expenses here, the running expenses. If you'd leave things to me . . ."

She wanted to scream at him. Yet really she was too amazed at his self-blindness. She almost hated him at this moment.

". . . and the oïdium," he was saying. "I mean, it's the oïdium's to blame. If we'd had a normal yield here we'd have been perfectly all right. And with the steamer running and everything, it would have been easy."

"And it's all gone?"

"Sue." His voice was appealing. "Sue, it'll be all right, believe me. Just . . . just leave it alone." He turned rather fretfully away from the window, moved across the room and back, straddled a chair but couldn't sit still and got up again.

"And what exactly is Baynes saying?"

"Look, really, I've had a hard day." He sighed desperately.

"Tell me!"

"I've *told* you! He says unless he gets paid he's taking La Guiche."

"There must be a date then, a time limit."

"Yes, it's overdue already. Fouquet let it run on. I paid a bit extra and he let it run on with no new date. But it's due any time."

"But did you authorize Fouquet to dispose of your notes of hand or whatever it was you signed?"

He blinked at her, brow furrowed. "Well, you see, that was when the money was due. He told me he wanted the money repaid."

"Fouquet did?"

"Yes, Fouquet. And when I said I didn't have it, he said he'd either have to take over the property or sell the loan to a third party. It could run on a bit if I paid him extra, which I did. He must have sold it to Baynes."

"But nobody lends on mortgages here. Even I know that. Baynes has been hand in glove with Fouquet all the time, it's obvious. You must have realized there was something behind it."

He blazed up. "I didn't realize anything of the sort! What are you getting at me for? It's not my fault. I didn't wreck the ship. I didn't spread the oïdium. Why get at me? Anybody'd think I'd done it all! Here I've been slaving like a madman, trying to do something better than this, going to Bordeaux three and four times a week, getting the business on its feet. Doing my utmost. And you! What have you been doing? Nothing but scandal! Madame Francis Gautier, with a fine reputation. And

442

what do you think that's done for me? Everywhere I go people saying, 'There's Gautier. You know, his wife.' 'Oh, the one they had a duel over.' A fine thing for my business."

"Stop it!"

"A fine help you've been! All over Bordeaux—Madame Gautier. This is a decent respectable town and you think you can flaunt yourself and behave like a—"

"Stop it! Stop it!" In blind rage she hit him across the face —forehand, backhand. She saw his cheeks quiver with the blows.

Up flew his hand and caught her wrist. Rigid, he glared at her. "That's it! Why don't you get a whip? That's how they do it in America!"

"Stop it!"

He flung her hand away.

"I hate you!" She screamed at him. "You're weak. Weak! It's always somebody else. Never you. You're angelic. Only one angel here and it's you!"

"And you—you can't stand criticism. Nothing wrong with Susannah. Don't dare say so!"

"You daren't face the truth. You think you're a victim," she screamed. "You can't manage. You get into a mess and then you lash out, hit out at anybody. Anybody, it doesn't matter. I hate you!"

"Susannah!"

She pushed back her hair. "And because I won't kowtow to your stinking respectability, I'm shameful. I'm notorious. I'm scandalous. You're like all the rest of the men here. You want me under your thumb. Well, you won't get me there. You've picked up a live American rattler. A creature with some life in her!"

He stalked out of the room.

God, she could hardly contain herself. The baby had begun to cry. She went over, picked her up, soothed her and put her back in the crib. She felt shaky on her feet and strange. She opened the wardrobe, got out her clothes, put them on and sat at the dressing table doing her hair. She flung down the brush, turned away on the seat, still seething, elbow on the dressing-table top.

Fifty thousand francs! Two thousand five hundred gold

443

louis. And to Baynes. All the fight with the oïdium for nothing —for Baynes. It was monstrous. She couldn't bear it. She could not bear it. She blamed herself for letting it go on so long. For not forcing him one way or another to tell her about the finances. She knew his character, knew his weaknesses. She should have foreseen it, at least seen a glimpse of it.

Oh God, it was too much.

She got up, drifted about the room in a fury of frustration. Couldn't take criticism, couldn't she? Maybe she couldn't—not his criticism. In the dressing room his black and gilt papier-mâché box of cheroots was open on the table, and on impulse she took one. She lit it and went back into the bedroom and stood smoking at the window. She felt brooding and furious and frustrated all in one. She couldn't bear it. There it was before her, the vineyard, rich with fat ripe bunches of grapes. All for Simcoe Baynes.

She could not accept it. She *would* not. She must make a fight for it. Fifty thousand francs—and God knew how much more it really was. She would have to get it somehow. And she would have to do it alone, she knew that. If a man like Fouquet lent forty thousand francs on Francis's share of La Guiche, it was worth more than that. Much more.

Something came back to her. What was it she had heard Regis saying not long ago about the Pereires buying up the old Palmer estate, Château Palmer? Yes, they had bought it up last year from the Central Mortgage Office in Paris for—what was it? Over four hundred thousand francs, she remembered that. It was almost exactly twice the size of La Guiche and, of course, the price had been very low. So for forty thousand Baynes would be getting a bargain indeed.

Yet there was something she didn't understand. What about the other shares? Madame Gautier's—temporarily blocked until her estate was legally settled—would be split up among Abel-Cherubin, Francis, James and Raynal. Monsieur Parenteau had told them that, by law, Madame Gautier had been entitled to dispose of a quarter of her share as she wished and she had left this to Raynal. The rest of her share must be divided up evenly among her other three sons, Abel-Cherubin, Francis and James. In that event . . .

She turned restlessly across the room and sat down at the

dressing table again. No good trying to decide what to do until she knew more. Until she knew the whole situation. She sat there, chin in hand, brooding, the smoke of the cheroot curling up. Presently the door opened and Francis came in. He stared in surprise. "Smoking? With the child in the room?"

She took no notice but saw he was chastened. He shut the door behind him and came to her. "Sue, let's not quarrel," he said miserably. He laid his hand on her shoulder but she turned away impatiently. "Please, Sue, I'm sorry."

But she couldn't swing back from anger to softness as he could and she kept her eyes away from him. When he bent down and kissed her cheek she held herself inwardly away from him. Impossible those quick swings for her. Her anger meant something! Her soul had to quiet itself before her mood could change. Maybe it was ungenerous of her—a defect—but she couldn't help it.

He moved away across the room. He looked sheepish now and even more like a boy with his collar open and his curly brown hair. What was he now putting between himself and reality? She had better find out what she could, or God knew what excuse he would find for more concealment.

She said, "You have James's share and your own, that's fifty-six and two-thirds per cent. Isn't that what you told me?"

"I've got my share. Twenty-eight and a third per cent."

She looked at him. "That's what you borrowed the forty thousand francs from Fouquet on?"

He nodded.

"But what about James's share? You've got that too, haven't you? You bought that when he was twenty-one?"

He looked down at the floor. "Well, as a matter of fact, I didn't. It . . . I just didn't think of it."

"You mean you haven't bought it?"

He shook his head.

"Then if Baynes is after La Guiche he'll surely get it."

"I should think so."

"James hasn't said anything?" She eyed him with contained anger.

"Well, as a matter of fact, I did write to him a while back, and he replied that he had sold his share but he wasn't at liberty to say who to."

445

"Then it's surely Baynes. It must mean Baynes. He's got it already."

"I . . . I should think so."

There was a pause. She crossed to the window, threw the cheroot out and turned around to him. "Are the account books written up?"

"Oh, not really. Things I haven't put down."

"I want to see them. You'll just have to remember what's missing. I've got to know where we stand."

"Very well, tomorrow. You shouldn't be out of bed."

"No, now. *Now!*"

Much later, in the night, she heard him turning restlessly in the dressing room and she felt torn for him. She knocked gently on the wall. He opened the door and looked in.

"Something you want? Is it the baby?"

"Come to bed. No good tormenting yourself."

He crept into the bed with her. She took him in her arms and he pressed his face to her shoulder.

At eleven thirty next morning Regis Gautier drew up in a hired carriage outside the porch of La Guiche, climbed down and took off his hat. Susannah, who had spent a maddening morning, was just coming down the stairs from feeding the baby.

"Hello," Regis said. "I didn't know you were up." They exchanged kisses and stood back surveying each other. "How is the baby?"

"Oh, she's very well. She's just going to sleep."

A handsome man in his dark way, she thought, with his strong eyebrows and good forehead, improving as he got older. He always held himself well and had polished his manners very pleasingly.

"I had to come up to Margaux, so I thought I'd look in. Do you mind if I walk around?"

"Of course not. Francis is in Bordeaux, but Balavoine's probably out there." She looked out across the vines. "Yes, there he is. Will you stay to lunch?"

"With pleasure. Thank you."

"In half an hour then. And if you are going back to Bordeaux I might come with you."

"As you will."

The morning had set her on edge. Over her had crept a terrible sense of urgency, the conviction that Baynes would get a court order against them if there were any further delay. He might have it already. And here she was, isolated out here, unable to move because of the child. It would be easy to find a wet-nurse in the village. But the child was so small! And the idea of binding her breasts up and stopping the milk revolted her. She could not do it. Yet she *had* to go to Bordeaux to see Fouquet, see Parenteau, see what the legal situation was, go into the whole thing, try to raise money. And at all speed. The ticking of disaster was loud now.

Francis had gone to Bordeaux to settle various things and she was glad to have him out of the way. As soon as he had left she had walked a short way through the vines to see how they were. Everywhere the grapes hung in heavy ripe bunches on the little stocks. And so many bunches to each! All the worry vanished momentarily as she looked at them, row after row. How beautiful it was! It was worth every moment of care and labor to see this bountiful return from the old stony earth. And if the fine weather held for a few days more, a fine harvest.

But there was the other reality.

"Good morning, ma'am." Balavoine came up and greeted her. "Didn't expect you up so soon. To tell you the truth, I'm glad ye are, for I could do with a bit of money. There's four of the men not had a penny for three months or more, and I'm short myself. Marcilhac's wanting to be paid for his sulphur and I need twenty francs to put up the enclosure and pay the lads to keep guard, or we'll have 'em in here stealing for sure."

"Very well, I'll see to it," she said.

An hour later the advance guard of the vintagers had appeared. Thomas, their usual commandant, and his lieutenant wanted to bargain out the terms and arrangements for the harvest in advance. And she had had to send them away, saying she would decide later. Queer looks they had given her. She had the finest grape crop in the district and had to send them away!

Now she went through to the cook and told her that Regis would be staying for lunch. From the cellar she brought up a magnum of Cantenac Brown 1844, uncorked it carefully herself and laid it in its cradle on the table.

Regis came back from the vines all smiles, and when they sat down to lunch he said, "Really, I congratulate you. It's amazing. The grapes are superb. I've not seen anything nearly as good. You know you've got a better crop than Margaux. Better than Lascombes—I swear it—better than Gruaud-Larose. Extraordinary! Balavoine tells me it was sulphur."

"Yes. The despised Marquis de Talabu recommended it."

"What, the old original?"

During lunch they talked about the oïdium, briefly and rather cautiously about the steamer and the inquiry which neither of them wanted to dwell on and, as usual, about the Bordeaux social doings that Regis had been following.

His pleasure in the Cantenac Brown was evident. Susannah found him more sympathetic than usual . . . and she wondered about him. She wished he would stop wanting to shine in Bordeaux society, be a bit more individual and independent. He obviously had ability and was sharp at business, and this constant straining for social notice spoiled him. Sometimes he seemed lonely to her. Wasn't that it? He lacked some quality to combine with his own abilities. He needed an ambitious woman really, and perhaps this, unconsciously, was what he was looking for. She liked him much more than before and found today to her surprise that there was something rather touching about him.

Toward the end of the meal she said, "I'm sorry it didn't turn out well for you with Aurelie Hagenbach."

He obviously didn't expect it. He colored, hastily picked up his glass and drank some wine. There was a moment of busy silence. Regis looked hard at his plate, then he raised his head and said in a deliberately hard tone, "You know you're the only person who's said a decent thing about that to me?"

"Oh, I'm sure the others are sorry too."

"They're damned well not. They've either laughed or sneered. And not even secretly sneered, some of them."

"Then don't mind them, Regis. Why should you care?"

"Yes." Across the table his eyes rested on her face in a long look as though he was discovering things in her. "*You* don't mind them, do you?"

448

"In the end they can't harm you."

He gave a little reflective nod, then a chuckle. "You know, I don't mind either. Live and learn."

Good! she thought. A spark! And he's not sorry for himself either.

"At all events," he said, "thank you, my dear. I think I understand you a bit better lately."

"Have some more wine," she said. "And give me just two fingers. I really shouldn't drink."

He poured the wine, they smiled at each other and drank. Emilie came in, cleared the plates and served the cheese. Regis waited till she had gone out, then said, "You know, I came here today for a purpose."

"Well, before you say what it was, you'd better know that we may not be able to keep La Guiche."

"What do you mean?"

"Simcoe Baynes has bought up James's share and wants to take over."

"Simcoe Baynes has?" A deep frown. "What makes you think that?"

"What makes me think it? Well, James confirms he has sold it and can't say who to. Baynes has bought up the notes of hand Francis has been signing to finance the steamer and so forth. And he wants to take over."

"*Baynes* has bought them up?" His eyes drifted away, searching the room as he leaned back in his chair in deep reflection. For a moment he sat quite motionless, then looked up at her. "I've bought up James's share."

"What! You're joking."

"Not a bit. I bought it months ago."

"*You* did?"

"Months ago—when I hoped Aurelie and I would be married." He reached forward and gently and reflectively twirled his glass stem. "I'd just made an excellent business coup and it seemed a good opportunity. I've always wanted a nice piece of property. I went to Paris, saw James and concluded it on the spot. But I asked him not to mention it until I said so." He looked up at her. "That, as a matter of fact, was what I came to tell you today."

A weight fell from her. "Regis, I'm . . . I'm enormously

glad. It's still in the family. But Baynes has those notes and I don't have enough money for the running expenses, let alone the harvest, so I—"

"I'm sorry, Susannah," he interrupted. "But it's no good asking me for money. I'd help if I could. But I've just had some *bad* luck on the Bourse—a disastrous loss in fact—and I may have to sell my share."

"Oh."

"That was the other thing I came to tell you today."

"You may have to sell it?" she said thoughtfully. Things could never be simple, could they?

He nodded. "I'm afraid so. I'm pretty hard pushed."

She gazed at him across the table. "Not to Baynes, though. You won't sell to Baynes?"

"Well, I've no intention of actually *assisting* Mawdistly Baynes to install himself here with Aurelie."

"Oh! Is that his idea?"

"So I'm told. But if I *have* to sell, well, I couldn't stop Baynes getting hold of that share later on the open market."

"No. But at least you won't sell before you tell me?"

"Very well, I won't sell before I tell you."

There was a pause. "What are you going to do?" Regis asked.

"I don't know. I thought, as a last resort, of asking John Lovell to lend me money, but . . . well, it's difficult. We've got no guarantee to offer him and it would be embarrassing if he couldn't do it."

"Yes."

"Can you let me have a hundred francs now?" she asked.

He smiled. "I've got three louis with me and I have to pay for the carriage, but you can have two with pleasure."

"Thank you, Regis."

"How much do you need in all?"

"Oh, more than fifty thousand francs. One can hardly think about it."

Simcoe Baynes paced the carpet of his office on the Pavé des Chartrons and swung around on Chabot. His plump round face was pink and his moist protruding eyes full of resentment.

"So this is where we get with your fancy promises, eh? Mr.

Somebody comes in, snaps up the property under your nose, and ye're asleep! What do ye call yourself? You think I've laid out good money to be made a fool of like this?"

Chabot stood bent forward at the waist, dry-washing his hands. "*Part* of the property. Only *part* of the property."

"Part of the property! Twenty-eight per cent. And ye didn't know it. *I* want it, d'ye hear? *I* want it. I told you I wasn't having bits and pieces. Do ye think I'm having my son go into La Guiche and ask, 'By your leave, Mr. Twenty-eight Per Cent' and 'If ye please, Mr. Twenty-eight Per Cent.' Aye, and ye don't even know who's got it."

Chabot shifted his feet uncomfortably. "As I've explained, James won't say. Says he's bound not to."

"But can't ye go to the Land Registry Office, man? The sale's got to be registered."

"First thing I did, my dear Baynes. No new name there. Those postings are very slow. Clerks old. Papers don't come through. Often takes years for a new owner's name to come up."

"Then find out from Parenteau."

Chabot gave a grunt and a cough and muttered, "Parenteau is very close. He won't say either."

"And here's this Raynal who gets a share now."

Chabot waved his hand. "Two per cent of the whole. Not worth sneezing at. We'll buy him off."

"By God!" Baynes's fat chin quivered with anger. "Ye've fair led me up the garden path with this mess, Chabot. I want that property. I've set my mind on it and I'll have it." He swung across the office, a furious strutting figure. Back again, he faced Chabot. "And I'll tell you one more thing. You'll get that woman out of the way. I know a mettlesome young mare when I see one and she's that, I'll give her her due. But she's trouble to me and I wouldn't put it past her to try to trip me. Aye, by God, for that matter I wouldn't put it past her to try to get hold of James's share one way or the other. So get her out of the way. Ye hear me?"

Chabot caressed his chin. "Don't know that I can."

"Eh?" Baynes eyed him. "Ye told me ye knew something against her. Or was it more of your fancy talk?"

"No. No. True enough."

"Then use it. You understand? Use it."

451

"Very well."

Baynes crossed to his desk and stood leaning on it with arms spread wide, the signal that the interview was over. Disconsolately Chabot picked up his hat.

"You promised to deliver me La Guiche, Chabot, and I want it. I want *all* of it. Or I'll make *you* a promise. Ye'll be needing some mighty good friends. And now good day to ye."

18

The carriage rolled through the September afternoon. It was stifling inside and Susannah had drawn the blinds to shield the baby in Emilie's arms. A whole day in Bordeaux—it had tired them all out. She had been obliged to take the child along, leave her with Emilie and Joseph on the Place des Quinconces and feed it between her errands, hurrying from one place to another in the dust and heat.

And for what? Oh, she had been wrong in the first place to try the banks, the Viticultural Credit Office and three loan offices, she saw that now. Those whiskered men, gravely seating her, politely listening to her case, when they knew perfectly well who she was and had already made up their minds. Was she the owner of La Guiche? No. Had she her husband's power of attorney? No. An estate of her own, perhaps? No. Hm. So ponderous in their grave courtesy as they inclined their heads and regretted they could not help. And somehow they also conveyed that even if she had all these things they would not lend her a penny. Where else might she try? That, madame . . . Oh, the deep chagrin in their shrugs! And they had showed her out with bows—a married woman with nothing of her own, a nullity.

But Parenteau—she didn't understand why Parenteau should have been so deaf to her pleading. Yes, a small sum. He could advance Francis a small sum from Madame Gautier's estate. To her? No, madame. Nothing, madame. Always the distinction between her and Francis, between the man and his wife. She, a mere married woman, hardly existed. The only realities were males and property. True, if she had property, even a mere woman acquired a sort of reality—but on strict conditions. It must be *her* property. Fully and solely and jealously separated from her husband's. Not shared with him in any way. Because even if it were *hers* and shared with a husband, it came under *his* thumb, and she existed, as it were, only by his leave. She would need his signature, his agreement, his permission to dispose of what she had contributed to the partnership.

So depressing, listening to all this from old Parenteau. There was a coldness to it which repelled her. It seemed to her like a breach of faith between the man and his wife. Marriage was a true sharing, surely? She still had that feeling with which she had come to marriage—that they must share. It was all for better or for worse, for richer or for poorer. Everything. But this cold separation—touch not my property! To live with a deep reservation, a guardedness, keeping your partner at arm's length about what was nearest to your soul, your property—it was horrible.

Then, what could she do? Old Parenteau had been beady and impassive. Try to delay the Baynes takeover. Fight him with legal procedures—which would merely gain time, of course, not cancel the debt. And it would cost money. Lawyers had to be paid and they would want some of their fee in advance. The grape harvest would be attached, placed under control of the court. Baynes was rich and resourceful. And he relished litigation, reveled in it. She should make no mistake about that. On the other hand, if she found the money in time, Baynes could not refuse payment. Yes, she might raise a little by selling the grapes unpicked. No, it wouldn't bring much.

Strange how hard the old man had been. So detached. That was the law, though. But it depressed her. And so it had come to nothing.

The sun burned against the carriage blind. She leaned over and eased the clothes at the child's neck. The poor little thing was hot. They jogged on. Susannah's discomfort grew, the slow clop-clop of the horse irritated her. All day the idea of asking John Lovell for help had been at the back of her mind, yet for some reason she hadn't been able to bring herself to it. Terribly difficult, simply to go and ask him for money.

The child moved feebly in the heat. The sun burned against the glass. They were only a couple of miles outside Bordeaux, but it was too late to go back. Too late, too late. The hot faces of Emilie and the child accused her. They had waited around all day in the stifling heat and dust. How could she drag them back again? And Lovell might not be there.

Clop-clop, the horse went on. Too late now. So they would lose La Guiche? She could see no escape. Feebly the child began to whimper; the girl rocked it in the crook of her arm, fanning it with the other hand.

"Too hot," Emilie said.

It seemed to Susannah that her life was slowly falling apart with the steady clop-clop, clop-clop of the horse. It was the end of La Guiche, the end of all this. It was fate. She had done all she could. Francis wasn't really to blame, he had tried too. Roadside foliage threw quick-flickering shadows against the blind, dazzling her, then they were rolling down a gentle incline, traveling a little faster. Everything was going. Let it all go. Let it all go. Ah, to relax, to be cool and relax.

But that feeling was gone in a minute. She couldn't let it go! She had *not* done all she could! Not yet. She rapped for Joseph, got up from the seat and put her head out. "Go back," she called out. "Go back. I've got something more to do."

He reined in and looked around. "Back to Bordeaux, ma'am?"

"Yes. Back to Bordeaux. To Mr. Lovell's."

"Yes, ma'am." He turned the horse around, and back they went. She wiped the baby's face, took her bonnet off, tidied her hair.

At Collard and Sons she found to her huge relief that Lovell was in. She felt hot and untidy, far from her best. Lovell came out, greeted her with evident pleasure—surprised she was up and about—and when he had admired the baby and they had found a cool spot for her and Emilie and care for the horse, he led Susannah indoors and up to his parlor.

"Oh, you've had it redone." She looked around the handsome room—the old paneling brought back to life, the parquet flooring repaired, the eighteenth-century furniture obviously chosen with care. "It's lovely. Your Boulle is magnificent."

"I hope you'll do the same at La Guiche," he said.

"Oh, that's not likely." They sat down. She tucked in a

strand of hair. "Not yet, at all events. As a matter of fact, it's about La Guiche that I've come to see you."

"I hear the grapes are superb," he said. "They looked excellent when I saw them. Allow me to congratulate you."

"Thank you."

"I trust, my dear, the harvest will in some measure help you over your other misfortunes. I was sorry indeed to hear about all that."

"Thank you, John." She dropped her eyes, then looked up at him again. "In fact, unless I can raise a good deal of money to pay debts, we're going to lose La Guiche."

"You are?"

"It's been one thing and another, the steamer and so on. Our share of La Guiche was given as security and now the debt's being called in—by Simcoe Baynes as a matter of fact—and we can't meet it. I've been trying to borrow but . . . well, the notorious Madame Gautier can't raise the wind, as you may imagine, and it looks hopeless."

He was listening gravely.

"You've been a good friend, John, and it seems natural on the face of it to go to one's good friends for help, but when things get to the worst, something seems to check one. Pride or something, I don't know. I found it hard to come to you." She looked up and smiled at him. "But I've got past that and . . . well, I want to ask you if you will lend me the money. I realize that my word, as an unpropertied woman, is worth nothing, but I'd see you were paid the proper interest and give you—"

"Susannah." He put a hand on her arm. "You know you can always come to me."

She paused, then said quietly, "Yes, I do, John."

"Where've you been going?"

"Oh, banks and loan offices and places."

"Loan offices!"

"It's a lot of money—fifty-four thousand francs."

"I see." His eyes scanned her face, and she saw instantly that there was some obstacle.

"That's what you need, fifty-four thousand francs?"

"To redeem all the debts, yes. I need forty thousand to redeem the notes Simcoe Baynes holds."

He looked at her steadily facing him, her shoulders erect, her hair a little loose under her bonnet. And you are doing this?

456

his look said. You are coming to me for the money, not your husband? Pride for her flared in him. Pride and love for her spirit. They wouldn't break her. She was flushed and brilliant in the heat, a little perspiration on her upper lip, her eyes shining. And as always he felt the spirituality in her, the responsiveness, the passion which moved him so greatly. Sitting there in the room above the quayside, there was a communion between them, an unspoken intimacy.

His look of love was so visible she lowered her eyes, then she looked up at him again and put her hand on his. "John, if it's a problem, please don't think of it any more."

"No, no." He gave a rueful little chuckle at the circumstances, as if this were something he had longed to do but now was bafflingly prevented from doing. "You may have everything I've got, my dear, you know that. It's just . . . well, it's *the* most damnable tight moment. It's ridiculous. At any other time I could manage it all, but it so happens that I've just laid out all my spare funds—this very week! In fact, I've borrowed from my own bank. I've bought up Gaden and Company—you may have heard they have gone out of business—and since they had a very fine stock it was an opportunity I couldn't afford to miss. As it was, there was heavy competition, so I've run myself out of money. I have to keep some liquid cash on hand at this time of the year with the buying season coming on us. And I need a certain amount for the running costs of the business . . ."

"I understand," she said. She really felt no awkwardness with him; it was a thing that she had had to do.

"Just a minute." He turned away to the desk, where he studied some documents for a moment, took a pencil and made a calculation. Then he turned back. "I can let you have twenty thousand francs. If you'll allow me, Susannah, I'll do so with the greatest pleasure."

"John, will you?" She abruptly wanted to cry and had to bite her lip. "Thank you. Thank you."

"Will it do? It'll help somewhat?"

"Of course, it'll be of the greatest help."

"I'm sorry I can't manage the whole thing."

There were tears in her eyes. "You are a true good friend."

"And it's Baynes who wants La Guiche?"

"Yes. Apparently for his son Mawdistly. He's going to marry Mademoiselle Hagenbach, you know."

"Well, I must say that makes me doubly glad. I can do you a service and put a spoke in Baynes's wheel."

She blew her nose, feeling foolish. "And you see, with a third interest in La Guiche—which is what we'll have when Madame Gautier's estate is shared out—you'll have good cover for the loan."

"And may I have first choice on your wine this year?"

She laughed, still full of emotion. "Of course."

"How are you going to manage the rest?"

"Oh, I'll find some way."

His eyes rested on her as they sat talking about La Guiche and the oïdium, about the baby, a little about the steamer. At length he stood up. "I'll see about the money. Will you excuse me a moment, my dear?"

He left the room and she sat there listening to the rumble of drays and carriages outside, the cries of workmen. Relief after the hot tiring day flowed through her. It wasn't done with yet, but she was halfway there. And she must fight it out. John Lovell gave her confidence; she always drew that from him.

He came back. "After all, I can manage twenty-five thousand francs."

"Oh, thank you, John."

"It'll be partly in banknotes. I imagine you won't mind paying Baynes in notes? He can't refuse them."

"No."

"If you'd like to take it with you now, I'll tell my cashier to put it in a bag."

She considered. "Could I leave it here with you? I have to pay it quickly, but if I could simply know it's here till I need it, and come for it then, it would be easier."

"Of course. When you want to pay him just let me know and I'll send it around to him on your behalf. Don't worry, I'll see he doesn't know it comes from me."

"I must give you a proper acknowledgment for it. Will you draw something up?"

"A simple receipt, that's all."

She was full of love and gratitude to him.

"There is one thing, my dear. It's bound to be known that you've been trying to borrow money. These things get around."

"Oh, no doubt."

"And that you've been refused. Baynes will have heard, so you ought to be careful."

"Careful?"

"Has he formally applied for repayment of the debt? Has he formally asked for the money yet?"

She gazed away across the room, trying to remember if Francis had mentioned this. "I don't know."

"Well, he has to do so before he takes any other action. He has to make a formal application to you for the money, through a bailiff or a lawyer. Until he's done that he can't carry it further."

"You mean get a judgment against us?"

"Yes. Before he can get a court to take action he must show you have failed to pay. And you don't know whether he's done that yet?"

"No."

"Do find out. And if I can help you further, let me know at once."

"Oh, John, my dear John, thank you." She jumped to her feet, put her arms around him and kissed him. And as she stood back from him he took her hand in both his and looked into her eyes, serious, tender and full of love.

The heat had turned to storm by the time they drove back; they could hear it rumbling in the distance to the north, and the air was cooler. And now the drive was changed! Susannah was in good spirits and filled with gratitude. Where she was going to get the rest she didn't know, but it was a beginning. The baby slept peacefully.

At La Guiche they turned into the drive and pulled up at the porch and as Susannah got down she saw Chabot's carriage. At the same moment, Chabot himself came out of the hall wearing a well-cut gray coat. Since he was bareheaded she got the impression he had been waiting.

For the moment she was busy with the child. She took her from Emilie until the girl had got down, then handed her over again to carry indoors. Then she turned around.

Chabot touched her cheek with his lips. "Trust you are well? Didn't know you were up and about." He exposed his teeth.

"Thank you. Is Francis here?"

"No. Haven't seen him. I've been . . . ah . . . hoping to see *you.*"

She looked at him with a touch of surprise. "Come in." She took off her bonnet and led the way into the hall, where she stopped to arrange her hair at the hall mirror.

Chabot looked on coldly. "I'd be obliged if we could be alone. And be quick."

"Oh?" Arms lifted, she glanced at him. "Why's that?"

"Don't want to be interrupted," Chabot said, showing teeth again.

Unhurriedly she finished her hair, then went silently through to the salon. She crossed to the window and turned around to face him. Chabot shut the door behind him and came forward. "I won't beat about the bush, dear lady. Painful to hear you are in deep water. Very painful."

"I'm obliged to you for your sympathy," she said coolly.

"I gather your husband can't meet his liabilities."

She didn't answer, wondering if this meant something new.

"In particular, he can't redeem his debt on La Guiche. Distressing."

"Are you proposing to help him?"

Chabot tilted back on his heels, eying her sharply, as if this were a joke he did not care to follow up. "Best to let things run their natural course, dear lady."

"And what would that be—their natural course?"

Chabot smiled thinly. "Give up La Guiche."

So that was it. "You mean let Baynes take over?"

"Absolutely. Too powerful to fight, Baynes. Too big. The steamer affair was unfortunate, but best cut your losses. Sure you'll agree, madame."

"Not exactly."

"Painful, but you'll only do yourself more harm trying to fight it."

"Really?"

"Pah!" He made a gesture. "You can't prevent it. Best yield with grace. Great mistake to get up against a man like Baynes. Wouldn't care to myself. Great mistake."

"You seem very interested on Mr. Baynes's account. Is this what you wanted to tell me?"

460

"Exactly. There's been enough damage done. Hate to see you worse off."

"Worse off?" She caught his oblique look. "What do you mean by that?"

Chin up, hands grasping the lapels of his coat lawyer-fashion, Chabot took a turn across the room. "Why, madame, your family in Philadelphia is not of the choicest, is it?"

"My family?"

"Think if it got out. Madame Maxine and Madame Ady. Esteemed aunts who raised Madame Francis Gautier. Ladies of the town, to put it, ah, mildly." He lifted his upper lip from his teeth.

She looked at him with cool anger.

"Previously well known in New Orleans. One with a police prostitution record, so they say."

"That's a lie."

"Oh, but unsavory, eh?"

"You heard of this long ago, I believe."

He snapped a sardonic little bow. "I'd hoped it could be hushed up. But we can't keep things quiet forever. Unless of course . . ."

"Unless I give up La Guiche, is that it?"

Smilingly Chabot bowed assent. "So simple, dear lady, eh? Bound to get out otherwise. Baynes can't stand interference. Wants his way. I wouldn't try to raise money for your husband's debts if I were you. Step back. Keep clear." He flipped his hand at her.

"Yes?"

"It's in your best interests. I recommend it. Wisest thing to do. Baynes is set on La Guiche and he intends to get it."

She looked him up and down with scorn. "Well, sir, Baynes will not get La Guiche if I can stop him, and I care nothing for your threats."

"Oh, madame, not you. But there are others, eh? What about your husband? What about your daughter? Will they be able to hold up their heads, eh? Sweet young daughter growing up with every respectable door shut to her. Hearing tales. Marriage prospects blighted. Hm? People have long memories here, very long. Think of it . . . think of it. All for want of a little common sense now. Come, come, madame, you are a sensible woman.

461

You know your own interests."

With difficulty she kept control of herself. "I am not afraid for my daughter, sir. I would be if I bent to your threats. Yes, then I'd have grounds. I'd be a crawler, a coward. And I'm not really afraid for my husband. Yes, my aunts are what you say. I know it. They brought me up and they cared most lovingly for my mother. And do you think for one moment I'd be *ashamed* of them? That I'd deny them? Why, sir, I'd have to be gutless. Send who you like here and I'll tell them myself. My aunts are not perfect, but they're warm, they're alive. They've got strength. They've had to claw their way up from nothing and they're real! They're generous and genuine—not bloodless dummies afraid of life, afraid of feelings, afraid of other people with their mean, narrow, grasping souls! If Baynes sent you here like his dog to threaten me, you can tell him I spit on him. And now get out! Get out of my house, do you hear? Get out!"

She stormed to the door and held it open, standing with her head up and her shoulders straight as he walked out past her. Finally she couldn't help it and screamed, "And don't show your face here again!"

She slammed the door with a crash and crossed the room shaking with anger. All the fatigue was gone in her anger. The insolence! What had he imagined? It disgusted her. She could not stay still she was so angry.

The sound of his carriage leaving came from the drive. A moment later the door opened and Francis looked in with a startled air. "Sue, are you all right?" He came in.

"Yes."

"What's the matter with Chabot? He's just gone out like a—. What's the matter, did you have a row with him?"

"He disgusts me."

"What's the matter?"

"He'd like us to give up here and let Baynes take over."

"But what did you say to him? He looked so sick. No point in getting him against us. Bad enough as it is."

No answer.

"Sue?"

"Oh, Frank, I spit on Chabot and his mean soul! Now I'm dying of thirst and dust, I want a cool glass of Sauternes. There's one magnum of Yquem 1847 left in the cellar and that's the one I want, so go and get it."

19

And now with the weather fine and sun every day, Balavoine began pressing for them to begin the harvest. Every day he came to Susannah and led her out through the vines.

"See here, ma'am, we're getting just right. Look at this. Ought to begin this week. See here? They'll have to wait a bit on the other side, but here we're as good as ready. Have to begin."

Every morning Thomas, the commandant of the vintagers, and two or three of his men would be in the kitchen wanting to know when they were starting. And when Susannah put them off, they argued loudly, saying there was no sense to it, no reason for it, that she would lose by it, that they would be leaving the district. She knew they wanted a commitment from her and an advance on their pay. Laverne, whom she knew had been quietly making preparations, rinsing the vats out, scalding the barrels in readiness and so on, privately confirmed her opinion that they could wait two or three more days without harm. But not longer. The finest vintage demanded that the grapes be *exactly* right. They must not miss the moment.

Susannah was in a restless, tense state. Baynes would be bound to hear as soon as they began to get the grapes in and he might try to attach the wine. At her questioning about a formal application for repayment, Francis had produced a bailiff's summons, already two weeks old, which he had mislaid and forgotten about. She knew that he had wanted to forget it and so had considered it a mere form and attached no importance to it.

"Yes, he had to send this before he goes to court," she said. "To court?"

"Never mind. Leave it with me." She was not even impatient with him now. Indifference to him had come on her again. No doubt it would go in its turn, but she could not struggle against that too. And he seemed content not to be too near her in these days. He was recovering his vitality, but he steered away from her, didn't bother her, sensing she wanted a distance between them.

At moments she felt an icy panic that in spite of John Lovell's help they might not survive. Every day's delay in repaying Baynes counted against them. Perhaps Baynes was waiting for the precise time they began the harvest to step in and entangle them in legal difficulties. What was it Monsieur Parenteau had said? Baynes relished litigation. Yes. And then she would flare up in anger and defy all the Bayneses and Chabots and company and stalk about the house in a passion.

She was waiting for Louise. Louise was her last hope. If Louise failed— But no, she must *not* fail. Louise was away visiting her sister in Angoulême but was expected back daily. Susannah had left a note asking her to come as soon as she could, and at last at ten o'clock on the Wednesday morning the red and black landau with Louise in the back pulled up at the porch. Susannah left Thomas and the vintagers in the kitchen when Emilie announced her and went out. Louise was in gentian violet with little bows and facings of apple-green and a bonnet to match. She carried a gray sunshade.

"I got your note," she said when they had kissed. "I thought I'd better come this morning—I do hope it hasn't put you out—because Jules-Armand is coming for me tomorrow. I've promised to spend a week with his family, so I wouldn't have a chance to see you unless I came now." Jules-Armand was Louise's brother, influential and respected head of the Ducasse family of Barsac.

"Do come indoors," Susannah said. "Too hot out here."

"Have you begun the harvest yet? Regis says you've got a lovely crop."

"Any day now."

It was cool in the salon. Emilie brought fresh lemonade and then the baby to show Louise, and when the two had set-

464

tled themselves and dealt with the general state of the family, the doings of Toby the pug and Louise's Angoulême visit, all of which had to have their proper measure of time and deliberation, Susannah said, "Did Regis mention anything more about us?"

"Er . . . no, my dear." Louise blinked wonderingly.

"Well, we're in very difficult straits, Louise. That is why I asked you to come. Regis knows. I'm almost sure Abel-Cherubin knows. He must, though he probably doesn't know the extent. I need money immediately."

Louise blinked back.

"I think you trust me, Louise, and I want to ask you to help me through it."

"My dear, if I can I'll be glad to."

"I need thirty thousand francs. In the next forty-eight hours I need fifteen or sixteen, since we've got to begin the harvest. Fifteen as a minimum I must have—or we shall lose La Guiche."

"Oh!" Dismay flooded into Louise's face; she pressed the flat of her hand to her chest. "My dear, so much! I had no idea. What has happened?"

Susannah explained in general terms while Louise listened with growing anxiety.

"I've always understood you had some money of your own, Louise. You'd hate La Guiche to go, I'm sure. Will you lend me what we need? I'll be responsible for it. You have the security of Francis's share, which will cover the loan at the proper market value. And we're healthy, as you can see, we're in an excellent situation this year. I promise your money will be safe and I'll see that you are quickly paid back."

Louise, who had been fidgeting uncomfortably, sat up in her chair and straightened her bonnet with an uneasy gesture. "You see, it isn't that, my dear. I . . . I'm sure I do trust you. I trust you with all my heart, but, you see—this *is* in confidence between us, my dear, isn't it?—my money is all in Abel-Cherubin's business, in the refinery." Her voice was muted and her eyes pleaded for understanding. "It's a private arrangement. You see, Abel-Cherubin needed more operating capital some years ago, and so, you see, I . . . I helped him. Of course, the money is really mine still, but it's, well, it's locked up."

465

Susannah gazed at Louise's worried face. She had half guessed it, half anticipated this, but assumed that Louise had kept *some* money, even a good sum, for herself. "You mean it's *all* locked up—all of it?"

Louise nodded dumbly.

Yet the Ducasses were rich, and difficulties like this—the ordinary raising of capital among the Bordeaux bourgeoisie—were invariably settled by family money.

"But couldn't you ask Jules-Armand for a loan?"

"Oh, no. No, my dear." Louise's anxious flutter became alarm. "That would be such a mistake. He would want to know where my money was. What on earth would I say. It worries me terribly sometimes."

Jules-Armand, Susannah knew, was a formidable figure to Louise, indeed to others, Abel-Cherubin included. And Susannah had no doubt that if Jules-Armand bore down on Abel-Cherubin, Abel-Cherubin would be forced to disgorge. What might happen then to his sugar refinery she didn't know—certainly no good. She reflected on this while she looked at Louise, and it came to her that now she had a weapon against Abel-Cherubin.

"You could tell him you needed it for your own use."

"Oh, no. That would *never* do. You don't know Jules-Armand. He'd want to know all about it. It would give everything away and he would be so angry. So terribly angry."

"He doesn't know?"

"No. You see, he doesn't approve of Abel-Cherubin. He is so concerned and kindhearted really, Jules-Armand, but he's so stern with Abel-Cherubin. He says hard and hateful things, thinks Abel-Cherubin was after my money when he married me. That's why he and the family *insisted* on a marriage settlement, you see?"

And right he is, Susannah thought. Poor Louise. She wished she could get her to defend herself with a bit more spirit.

"But it *is* yours, Louise, and you can make your husband give it back to you, after all."

"No. I did ask for a little once, but he wouldn't hear of it. He said it would damage the refinery. It might put him out of business, you see. He wouldn't let me, and if Jules-Armand found out . . ." She was numbed with apprehension at the idea.

"Doesn't he ask you about it, Jules-Armand?"

Louise twisted in an agony of discomfort. "My dear, you won't tell, will you? You see, he thinks I still have it in the Rentes. He does ask. He's *concerned*, you see, and I . . ."

"Yes, I do see, Louise." Quickly Susannah took her hand, ashamed that she had pushed Louise to that confession. "Never mind."

Louise wrung her hands with contrition. "But, my dear, we must think of something. We must."

"I wish we could."

"I . . . I have some jewelry. I could sell that. Some brooches and rings."

"Oh, my dear sweet Louise, no. I wouldn't dream of it." Susannah leaned forward and kissed her on the cheek and Louise clung to her tremblingly. When Susannah sat back again in her chair there were tears in Louise's eyes.

"Was this what I overheard Abel-Cherubin talking about with Chabot?" Louise said.

"What were they saying?"

"I heard them talking about selling Abel-Cherubin's share of La Guiche to Mr. Baynes. I ought to have told you, but I didn't like to, and then it didn't seem to come to anything."

Susannah nodded. "I have an idea it's been mostly Chabot's doing."

"But what will you do?"

"I am going on with the harvest," Susannah said firmly. She must fight through. Now she was desperate but she thought of all the agony with the oïdium, of the vines full and rich with their grapes, of everything she loved here, and she would *not* give up.

When Louise had gone she went through to the kitchen and found Thomas and the two other vintagers still waiting. They were sitting around the table with their glasses of brandy as if content to spend the day there.

Balavoine was just outside the door and came in when he saw her. "Well, ma'am, it's now or nothing. We've got to settle it."

"Aye, that we have," the others chorused.

"Yes, now I'm ready," Susannah said. "We'll begin."

"Ah! You see? You've got to do it sometime." Laughter and brisk movements of anticipation.

467

"If we can settle the right price." Susannah pulled out a chair and sat down. "To begin with, I'm not going to pay more than seventy-five centimes a day."

"Eh, where's the master? Fetch the master, lass," they said over their shoulders to Emilie, who did not budge.

So they began to haggle. Susannah beat them down on every figure, beat them down hard, knowing they hadn't enough work because of the oïdium and needed the money. She would be breaking into the precious 25,000 francs, but that she must do.

"Where's the master? Is he here?" They kept craning around and asking for the master. And it wasn't entirely because they knew Francis would pay them more. It was because they wanted to deal with a man. Dealing with a woman, they somehow felt, lessened their dignity.

As the arguing went on, as they protested and she yielded only a few tactical centimes here and there, they stared at her and shook their heads, as if it were simply female lack of understanding that was holding them up. They became disgruntled. They were offended. They banged the table. They thrust their rough unshaven faces at her. She stuck to her rates and argued back. She knew she had to settle a price for every single task and have no mistake about it.

"Give me a drink, Mr. Thomas, if you please." She held out a glass. Pulled up, they eyed her. Thomas uncorked the bottle of brandy and poured some, then, when she kept the glass there, poured some more, a man's measure, and they all watched in silence as she swallowed it. The liquor burned her throat and went down like a hot bolt. She put the glass down calmly and resumed. "I don't care why you've had this so-called indemnity or gratification or whatever you call it in the past. There's no justification and I won't pay it."

They looked at her with new respect and a sort of bafflement.

And at last they got through all the details and settled all the rates. Thomas made the last laborious calculation and they agreed on it. The table was littered with the remains of the bread and sausage they had eaten. Susannah pushed back her chair and stood up, heading off the request she could see forming. "I'll give you your advance when we begin."

They were caught by the unexpectedness, looked at her, looked at each other. They had not got their way in the haggling by a long shot, they knew it and they were still too disconcerted to react. A curious puzzlement had got hold of them. They did not seem to know yet how it had turned out so. They stood blinking and nonplused. She picked up her glass, Thomas poured them each another short measure and they all touched glasses with her to seal the bargain. She looked around at their faces. She had control of them! It was almost palpable. Thomas stood holding his empty glass, his eyes resting on her. He gave a little twitch of his head, a little twitch of disbelief and a sort of wry acknowledgment. "Eh . . . I'd say Château La Guiche'll be all right now, ma'am."

"So we start at five on Friday morning," she said. "I've got a lot to get organized before then."

The clock struck two. The men began to move out in reluctant fashion, screwing their hats up in their hands, as if tempted to turn back and try to argue it out again.

"Tell Joseph I want him to go to Bordeaux," Susannah said to Emilie. She would send him with a note to John Lovell to collect enough to cover the advance and pay for the harvest.

And so it was done. For some mad reason despair was gone and she felt exultant. She would pay Baynes half and let him try to take La Guiche from her. Let him try. To the devil with all Bayneses!

20

———————

The moon, the great full orange moon, had risen over the land, casting its own strange stillness on everything. Susannah had watched it rising and slowly turning from ocher to honey color and yellow as it glided upward, and now in the soft dark its white light shone in the lake. In the stillness the trees and the lake were unstirring. Yet the ripple of hidden activity ran everywhere, the ripple of preparation and expectancy, the strong unmistakable pulsing of excitement. It was not like other moonlit nights of the year. The hidden human activity, the hidden earth activity throbbed everywhere. Distant voices, a laugh and a snatch of song came over from the price makers' cottages. The pulse of excitement and activity was in everything. Susannah felt it in herself as if her blood were rising to meet it.

She had been busy since early afternoon seeing that all the remaining preparations were taken care of—the baskets and cutters and tubs assembled, fresh straw for the vintagers' sleeping quarters, the long trestle tables, the cutlery and crockery got out, the cooking arrangements made, the usual quantities of meat, lard, oil, salt, cod, beans, flour, candles and so forth prepared or ordered. Already the workpeople had begun to arrive in the afternoon. There were a hundred details to attend to and they would take all day tomorrow.

Now she turned to the drive, hearing the sound of the carriage arriving. She saw that Francis was in the back. Joseph had evidently waited for him in Bordeaux, which explained the late return.

"Hello, my love." Francis jumped out and kissed her, boyish and sparkling as ever. "Are you all right?"

"Yes. We're starting the harvest. We're starting on Friday morning."

"Really? Good, good. I say, I'm ravenous. I had no lunch."

"Dinner's all ready. I'm coming in."

"Good." He hurried into the house.

He did not want to be involved. He would accept her decisions. He had abstracted himself and was preoccupied in not examining things too closely, in preserving his bright, eager optimistic balance. At a later stage, if they ever got through, he would become interested again.

Joseph had got down and was standing by the carriage, and as Susannah turned back to him he reached up to the driving seat and lifted down a small brass-fitted leather grip, obviously the money.

"Thank you, Joseph," she said, taking it from him. "Was everything all right?"

"Yes, ma'am. Everything all right. Mr. Lovell asked me to give you this."

It was an envelope. She carried it to the lighted porch, tore it open and read the note inside.

> My dear Susannah, I have rearranged matters and I trust this will not reach you too late. The extra sum of 20,000 francs, making 45,000 in all, awaits you with my cashier. Please call on it when you will or instruct me when you wish it sent, and accept my deepest respects.
>
> John Lovell

Sheer blankness fell on her, a void, as if she were numb. She stared at the sheet of paper, and joy rushed in. Her heart was bursting with gratitude and love. Oh John, how generous and good. She stood with the letter in her hand on the porch. So it was all right after all. They were safe. It was all right. She was filled with joy.

Joseph was fiddling with the reins and harness, and as she looked up, still under the sweep of emotion, she caught his sweet old glance—hadn't he silently shared her anxiety? Oh, yes, she had felt it. And tears suddenly filled her eyes and she said with a little sob in her voice, "It's all right, Joseph. Thank you. It's good news."

471

"Yes, ma'am." He gave his brusque nod and climbed up into the driving seat. "Good night, ma'am."

"Good night, Joseph."

As she turned back into the house he clicked his tongue to the horse and the carriage rolled away.

Regis Gautier mounted the three steps from the street at the entrance to Léon Chabot's office and paused in the cool shadow. The afternoon was hot and he was still unaccustomed to all this footwork getting about town. He took off his hat, mopped his forehead and wiped the sweatband. He pulled out his watch. Still a few minutes in which to cool off.

Really now, he was feeling much better about his whole personal situation. Much healthier. He had had to pitch a lot overboard to save himself. His losses had been severe, but it had taught him never again to plunge on the Bourse in that way. Yet now he wasn't entirely sorry it had happened. It had pulled him up. Made him see things more clearly. And he thought that in the end he had been wise to make the sacrifice and sell off the other things, liquidate his stocks, shed the bits and pieces, including the interest in the cooperage house that his mother had left him, to get rid of all that in order to keep his share of La Guiche. Hanging on to La Guiche had reduced him to very low water financially, but he accepted that to keep Mawdistly Baynes out, if for no other reason. He hoped he could hold on to it; it was unnerving at times, but he hoped so.

And Sophie Monteiro, she, in her way, had proved loyal. He had imagined that she would tell Chabot of their confidences, had even imagined in his unhappiness their chuckling pillow talk about him. But no, it seemed he had been wrong about that. Devilish she might be, but she was a woman of pride and her own integrity and had kept his affairs to herself. Perhaps most decent women did? And standing there with his hat in his hand, he smiled with gratitude and tenderness, thinking of her offer to lend him money to see him through. Remarkable woman, Sophie.

Well, time for his appointment. He put his hat on and went up the stairs. The bell on the frosted-glass door to Chabot's offices clanged. He had himself announced by the clerk and went through. Chabot greeted him with an amused smile, shook hands, waved to a seat beside his desk.

472

"Dear fellow. How are you? Not more bad news?" His eye glinted with expectant relish.

"No. I wanted to see you about La Guiche."

"La Guiche?"

"Yes. I believe Baynes is after it."

Chabot's lips twitched in the effort to suppress his smile as he tipped back in his chair. "Matter of fact, I was going to mention it to you. Understand you feel cut up, but it can't be helped. Can't fight these things. Best shrug it off, eh?"

"Let him have it, you mean?"

"He's pretty well got it, you know. Francis's share against debts James's share. Abel-Cherubin's selling him his. Francis's wife is trying to bluster, but she can't change it. It's as good as settled."

"No help from you, of course," Regis said.

"Who, Baynes? Help from me? My dear fellow, nothing to do with me. All over my head. I know how you feel, but it can't be helped. Hate to see Mawdistly and Aurelie there, eh? Love-nest, what? Ha-a."

Regis put his fingertips together and looked at Chabot. "Well, for your information, *I* own James's former share. And I'm not selling."

"*You* do?" Chabot's jaw sagged; he came forward in his chair. "But . . . ah . . . this is news. When did you acquire it?"

"Months ago."

"But, but that was a great mistake, dear boy. It'll mean more trouble for you. You can't possibly fight Baynes. I advise you to sell while the going's good."

"It seems to me you have been lending Baynes a hand, haven't you?"

"I don't want to see more trouble. Baynes'll go to court. Cost you a mint of money. Break you. And he'll get the property in the end."

Regis sat back and crossed his legs. "You'll have to disappoint him." Chabot looked at him with suspicion. "I was up there at La Guiche the other day," continued Regis. "Have you seen it lately? The vines, I mean. No? Well, there are not half a dozen vineyards like it in Médoc, Graves, Sauternes or Saint Émilion. And with care they're going to get a very high price for the wine. The vineyard is in better condition than it has been for years. And it's Susannah's doing. All of it. I don't know that Abel-Cherubin is going to be all that eager to sell when he sees that, you know."

"Pooh, of course he will. It's as good as settled."

"Well I've just heard she's paying off the debt."

"Tales. Bunk." Chabot waved it aside.

"I don't think so. She's got a few resources of her own."

"Ah?"

"Mind you, they'll be needing some running expenses for the coming year. And I thought that could be your contribution, say ten thousand francs. Matter of keeping La Guiche in the family, if you know what I mean?"

Chabot gave a hollow chuckle tinged with mistrust. "Aha! Yes. Very funny."

"Don't you think it would be a good idea?"

"Capital. Capital idea!"

"A loan, just as a family matter, you understand?" Regis said.

"Capital idea! Save Mawdistly and Aurelie from moving in too, eh?"

"I mean it."

"Sure you do! Sure you do." Chabot, more confident now, laughed outright.

"Otherwise your business with the *Dorade* might get out."

Chabot's hilarity was cut short. "What did you say?"

"I said your business with Captain Kergo and the *Dorade* might get out. How would it sound: 'Prominent citizen engaged in slave trade. Several voyages by the *Dorade* . . .' Remember those voyages?"

"No."

"I can give you chapter and verse."

"Don't know what you're talking about."

"Well, on the twenty-fifth of April, 1850, the *Dorade*, Captain Kergo, Mate Jean Quennec, sailed from Bordeaux for Senegal with the usual cargo of trading stuffs—cotton goods, tinware, cast-iron utensils, brandy, kegs of gunpowder . . . Let me see if I can remember one or two items of that particular cargo which will remind you— Wait a minute, yes, six mahogany armchairs, a quantity of best silver-plated buttons. Oh, yes, ten red sashes and two cocked hats for 'dashes,' presents, that is, to Chief Bussi at Goree and—"

474

"You couldn't prove anything," Chabot said in a small voice.

"No? Do you remember you bilked Kergo? Well, he suspected you might be going to do just that, since you'd squeezed him before, so on the last voyage he told the people on the other side who his principals were. I got my agent in New Orleans to get a sworn copy of the papers. No reason for them to hide it. None at all. And there is your name with your co-principals Faget de la Saigne and Balu. And you wouldn't like *them* to hear this, would you?"

Chabot was white. He eased his neck in his collar. "Not . . ah . . . necessary."

"I'm just giving you family advice, you understand. All strictly within the family."

"You . . . Regis, my boy, you wouldn't —"

"Just write out a bank order for ten thousand francs, so that we keep it all in the family. The money will be an unsecured loan and naturally will bear no interest."

"Regis, my dear boy, you—"

"And I'll leave it to you to impress on Baynes that you represent the family interests now. That you have La Guiche at heart. He'll be sure to understand." Regis's lips screwed up in a smile as he regarded his uncle.

Chabot's mouth opened and shut wordlessly.

The day had come clear and cool with a thin veil of cloud that would keep the heat down for several hours. The vintagers were assembled—the women and children with their baskets and scissors, the men, carriers and emptiers, the inspectors, the oxcarts and loaders. Thomas, the commandant, was with Susannah. Susannah had made them wait until the dew had evaporated, for this time they were going to bring in the grapes and make the wine with the greatest care. In the vatting room Monsieur Laverne and his men had everything ready.

Susannah had been up since dawn. They were taking the best side of the vineyard first, and only the perfect grapes from there would go for the first wine.

"You've told them all?" Susannah asked Thomas. "We'll do it three times, as it should be done."

"Yes, ma'am. I've told them they're only to take the best grapes, leave the rest and we'll take them with the next lot."

"And hurry them along, keep them moving. Once we start filling vat number one I don't want Laverne hanging around waiting for the next load. Balavoine's got extra carts. We've got to fill that first vat by tonight. Are you ready here? . . . What about you? Have you got enough baskets?"

She walked up the rows with Thomas. The grapes hung in heavy bunches. Row by row they went till they reached the end of the section.

"All right, ma'am?" Thomas said.

"Yes. Let them begin."

He turned around and gave a blast on his whistle and the women and children moved forward bending to the vines. Susannah watched for a while, then walked back to the vatting room. The light came slanting in through the openings, and it all had the fresh smell of washed brick and stone and old vinous wood and wine. Laverne and the men were hanging around waiting for the first load.

Laverne, in good spirits, beaming and red-faced, took her arm affectionately. "We're just right. Couldn't be better."

"Good."

"Better than your first year, eh? Do you remember that?"

"Oh, Lord!" They laughed together.

Presently the cart approached outside, the first tub was hoisted up and swung in and the grapes tipped out onto the press. Susannah looked on as the work began, watching the careful inspection of the grapes, the removal of the stalks, then the men treading them, the fiddler, a thin comic-looking man with a cast in his eye this year, scratching away, and the first liquid running out into the *gargouille*. She waited until the second cart arrived, making sure there was no break, then left them and went outside again.

And so the morning passed. Back and forth went Susannah. She went to the house only to feed and change the baby, to have an egg with a cup of coffee and freshen herself, then she was out again in her rough brown skirt and bodice like any of the women, seeing the work done as it should be.

And then, half an hour before noon, as she came out of the vatting room into the bright sunlight once more and crossed toward the vines, there was Abel-Cherubin's bulky figure in tall hat and gray redingote. He was leaning on his cane and watching the cutters and carriers at work.

It was a disagreeable little jar in the bright morning—and unexpected. Always something disturbing and hostile in him. This was his first visit for weeks. No doubt because he had decided to sell out to Baynes. Then why come now—unless he had already heard that she had paid Baynes off? No question of any change of heart with Abel-Cherubin. If he sold or kept his share it would be pure self-interest, she knew that. Perhaps he had not yet made up his mind and, hearing from Regis of their good crop, had come to see. And anyone wanting to sell *this*, in the present state of the Bordeaux vineyards, would have to have some compelling reason. Abel-Cherubin would not need to have that pointed out.

Yet the old hostility was unchanged, she knew that too. And undoubtedly he could *get* a high price now, never better. Yes, but now things were a little different, now she had the knowledge about Louise's money. That was an arm against him. After all, if it were a question of his refinery business against his share of La Guiche, he would not give one up for the other. Oh, she wouldn't use it, not unless she had to. But a hint at the right moment would be enough, and Abel-Cherubin knew now she was a woman of her word.

So she lifted her chin and walked across to him with her skirt swinging. Abel-Cherubin turned as she came up, tipped his hat and kissed her coldly. His eye ran disapprovingly over her working clothes, then he turned back to watch the people.

"A fine sight, isn't it?" she said with a smile. "Look at them!"

"Hm."

"I'm told we have the best crop in Médoc. Better than Margaux or Lafite."

Another grunt.

"And no oïdium."

They began to stroll past the rows.

"We're only getting in this one piece now. The grapes are exactly right. You see?" She stopped a carrier and the man held his tub for them, piled to overflowing with the black grapes, great ripe bursting bunches with their lovely bloom. As Abel-Cherubin, still pinched, looked down at them, she took two of the most sumptuous bunches and held them up. "Aren't they lovely?" She gave a little laugh of joy. She knew he wouldn't show it for worlds, but if he had seen any of the other oïdium-stricken vine-

477

yards, as he must, he couldn't help being impressed.

He said nothing, however, and they strolled on. A few rows beyond, she stepped forward to examine a tub being filled. Her full skirt swung from her hips. They stopped to watch again farther on. Standing beside him, Susannah put her arms up to adjust the loose hair behind her head. Abel-Cherubin's eyes went sideways to her figure, then as she turned to him he looked quickly away again.

"Won't you come and see the pressing?" she said. "We're doing it very, very carefully and we'll have three separate pressings. It'll take longer and cost more, but of course it's essential."

Slowly they strolled past the rows of men and women working, and then Abel-Cherubin said, "Yet I hear you're trying to borrow money in Bordeaux."

"I *was.*"

"May I ask what for?"

"Yes. Simcoe Baynes wanted La Guiche. He held some notes of Francis's—the steamer ran us into debt, as you must have guessed—and Baynes thought he'd get the property cheap." She spoke coolly, aware of his quick snap of surprise. He looked at her sharply; a true Bordelais, he had never in the world expected such candor.

"He knew a good thing, of course," Susannah said.

"How much? How much did he want it for?" *Surely she wouldn't answer that!* His finger dipped into his waistcoat pocket.

"Forty thousand francs!" Susannah said and turned her eyes on him with a smile, as if to say, Wasn't it ridiculous? And when Abel-Cherubin said nothing, she added, as though he were silent from incredulity, "Really! I'm not joking. He's such a mean, grasping creature, always after something for next to nothing. But, of course, you know that better than any of us."

Abel-Cherubin stopped again and turned his face away, pretending to watch the workpeople, but she saw the reddening of his neck. A moment later he turned back. "You mean you're no longer trying to raise loans to pay these . . . these debts?"

"No. They're paid." She turned a radiant smile on him and brushed her skirt with her hand. "You needn't be afraid, Abel-Cherubin. Baynes won't get La Guiche. He's eliminated. If he had been successful he might have tried to buy your share from

478

you—on the cheap, of course. But there'd be no point now, since he can't get ours. So you see it's all right. I'm sure you're relieved, Abel-Cherubin, knowing your . . . um . . . knowing your sense of moral responsibility about keeping the property in the family."

Abel-Cherubin struck the ground with his cane and became interested in the cart they were passing with its full tubs.

They walked to the vatting room, Abel-Cherubin silent and reflective. Inside, he became intently absorbed in the work, strode round, questioned Laverne, stared sternly at the *égrappage* and the pressing, inspected the barrels next door. He became brisk. He was proprietorial. He gave an order or two. Susannah watched him. She was confident now he hadn't sold his share to Baynes, and she was confident he wasn't going to.

She left him there and slipped outside. In the vines some of the women and children were pausing and squatting down for their simple midday meal while the rest continued the work. Susannah saw the next cartload away, then turned back toward the house. It was hot now in the full noon sun.

She had saved La Guiche! It was going to be a struggle to keep it; there were still the other debts to pay off, besides the debt to John Lovell. But she would do it. No more selling the wine for anybody to mix up with other stuff. *That* was going to be a fight!

Now this was their true beginning, the beginning of many things. She felt exultant and proud, and her soul launched out into the future. Yes, she was going to found a great wine dynasty. She was going to make La Guiche a great and famous château.

She remembered the day she had first seen the long rows of barrels in the cellar. She saw it again now, a famous place, the cool gloom, the rows of barrels faintly gleaming with their glass bungs, the tang of wine in the air. She saw the cobwebby cellar below, the magnums of the great years maturing in their bins. And in herself she felt the earth spirit, brought here to fructify. She felt that it moved in her. La Guiche gave itself so bountifully, and she in return would give and they would be fruitful for each other. What could be more fitting than that she should come from the New World to fructify here? Fructidor, the month of fruitfulness in the old revolutionary calendar, Vendémiaire, this month of vintage—how sweet those names.

There must be more children, sons to learn and take pride, acquire the art and follow on. She would need plenty of sons. Some, at least, would have to be quiet, level-headed young men who would marry a little money and expand the estate, build up the trade, feel the strength of a great tradition. She would teach them to accumulate capital to finance the stock—one of the great secrets—to keep it together and resist temptations to disperse it on other things, to judge the markets, to choose the best men. Oh, there was a hard-headed, realistic touch to her vision seeing. There had to be, or it would come to nothing, she knew that. Not so lost, after all, Aunt Maxine's and Aunt Ady's teaching, she thought with a smile.

And Francis, whom she loved too, he would go brightly on if he were not pressed too hard. She thought she would never separate herself from him. They were apart now but would join together again, she knew, and she did not fret about it.

Across the vines the house rose before her. There was the old dreaming magic of the place as she had first seen it that evening among the trees. She was bound up inescapably with it now and she must open the shut rooms, bring back the old paneling, bring it all back to life. It was all symbolic to her.

And she thought of John Blood, saw him again in the candlelit room as he held out the glass to her and remembered his words that living is being willing to accept the wounds. She knew it was true. She didn't want to shut up her soul to avoid being hurt. Open it, open it to all the joys and all the wounds too. No good withholding oneself, no good keeping away or keeping a space around oneself, because that was death. Shut out nothing, exclude nothing! Nothing—not even the bad, since the bad is a necessary part of the universal system as it has been ordained.

Two slow-stepping oxen with their cart came past. The slow gliding step of the oxen and the weathered old face of the driver were beautiful to her. She loved it all with a deep love. Francis, she saw, had come out onto the porch carrying the child, and she called out as she went toward them.

480